The person borrowing this item is responsible for its
return to the library on or before the **Latest Date**
stamped below.

Overdue charges accrue until the maximum fine is
reached. Consult the library fine schedule for details.

A **minimum** $50.00 replacement bill will be issued
after the **maximum** fine has accumulated.

STOCKWELL-MUDD LIBRARIES, Albion College

EQUINOX

A Novel by

Allan Seager

1943

SIMON AND SCHUSTER, NEW YORK

Second Printing

ABOUT THE APPEARANCE OF BOOKS IN WARTIME

A recent ruling by the War Production Board has cur-tailed the use of paper by book publishers in 1943.

In line with this ruling and in order to conserve mate-rials and manpower, we are co-operating by:

1. Using lighter-weight paper, which reduces the bulk of our books substantially.
2. Printing books with smaller margins and with more words to each page. Result: fewer pages per book.

Slimmer and smaller books will save paper and plate metal and labor. We are sure that readers will understand the publishers' desire to co-operate as fully as possible with the objectives of the War Production Board and our gov-ernment.

TO MAX WILKINSON AND W. R. STURGEON

PART

I

PART

I

SINCE HE embarked at Cherbourg, Miles had been sitting most of the days and a part of the nights with these two men, listening spasmodically. He was grateful for their company because they irritated him. They were the itch that you claw to distract you from a toothache. One was a Hungarian across the table from him now, a baron with a long bald head who was continuing the performance of his personal reminiscences with great energy, talking loudly and glancing at the other passengers the way people do in public places when they have a good thing to tell and wish to invite eavesdropping that they may be admired.

The other man, now absent, was Archibald Loudoun, a Scottish school inspector. Miles shared a stateroom with him. This was Loudoun's first sea voyage—he was going, a month late, to teach English in an American high school under some exchange agreement—and the refugees he found in third class upset him. They were Poles, the fortunate ones who escaped, who had relatives in America. He seemed to feel that they demanded an extravagant sympathy. Twice every day, before the morning broth and before tea, he went down into third class to stare at them. He was down there now at the bottom of the steps looking over the gate. Miles expected him to return any moment red with his sympathy and voluble.

They had left Cherbourg in sunshine, but now a storm was blowing up. The ship had begun to roll and pitch, and in the bar of the tourist class they could hear the screw pound when it came out of water. Smiling vacantly, his temple on his fist in a pose of courteous attention, Miles watched the porthole beyond the Hungarian's shoulder. Punctually the black waves filled it, drained away, and left the sky again. The woodwork creaked, cracked, stopped, and creaked again. "This is the equinox, the change of weather," he thought. With the sea swell, the melting ice chuckled in the glasses, and the Hungarian slapped on the table with his palm and shouted for the waiter.

"I am like a tiger in such matters," Ipolyi said.

Such matters were women. He had described the women in his past with enthusiastic detail, and now he was going on to the young Dianas of New York, so voluptuous yet so innocent, tripping on such pretty feet toward him, Ipolyi. Eventually, give him time, and no beautiful woman of that city could enter a room without finding him in it. He would seep through cracks and keyholes like the wind. No beauty, yellow-haired or dark, could walk in the street without feeling his caress as she felt the warm sunlight. Ipolyi, the winsome tiger.

The handkerchief in his left cuff and perhaps his lapels were drenched with cologne of a sweet and lardy reek that carried to the next table, where three haggard Polish priests sniffed the fragrance and eyed him with reproach. Happy in the midst of his aura of pork sweat and carnation, the Hungarian evoked his future and what he called the years of his youth with an enormous repertoire of hackneyed gesture. When he laughed, he slapped his thigh. For surprise he popped his eyes and made his mouth an O. In his fits of intensity, he scowled, spoke through his clenched teeth, and pointed his finger like an old actor. On a former visit to America he had even picked up the flowing-downward movement of the hands to indicate the outline

4

of a woman's figure. When he had described her hair, eyes, teeth, the grace of her neck, and the opulence of her hips and bosom (they were always opulent), he would make this sculptural descending movement and then throw back his head, close his eyes, and suck loud kisses through his lips, the tokens of ecstasy remembered or ecstasy to come. To the priests who remembered not ecstasy but the flames of Warsaw and to all the decent people on board Ipolyi was, considering the situation, shallow and heartless.

Yet Miles listened to him and to the Scotsman. He bought them drinks and encouraged them, as if what they had to say was important and fascinating. The Hungarian was a fool and the inspector, he was beginning to think, crazy, but he listened or pretended to.

Ipolyi, he noticed, had ended his love list. He stuck out his chest and drew in his chin. Miles watched. It turned out that the new posture was an aid to the recital of his career as a soldier. He, John Ipolyi, had been a member of the Noble Guard. Forty Hungarians, forty Austrians. The Hungarians wore red uniforms with silver frogs and epaulets and rode white horses; the Austrians wore red uniforms with gold frogs and epaulets and rode black horses. It was the duty of these noblemen to perform a ceremonial guard mount whenever the Emperor came in from Schönbrunn. There they would be, all comfortable, playing whist in their shirt sleeves, eating caviar and drinking champagne, when T-I-N-N-G! the telephone, and an equerry would say, "The old boy's on his way in." Eight of them would struggle into their tunics, comb their hair, and shout for the servants to flick their boots. Chic, you see? They would hurry to their places, ready to stand to attention and salute when the Emperor passed, answering with a forefinger.

The ceremony took only eight men, *comprenez*, and there were eighty in the guard. That meant you had to serve only once in ten days, but often a group would remain on duty two or three weeks at a time and when the term agreed upon was finished they would go so joyful *pour faire les vacances* at the French Riviera where the same champagne and caviar awaited them as well as the baccarat and the women, my God, beauties positively international: actresses, highpriced harlots, decayed noblewomen, and eager mothers of good

5

family with their tender daughters. He, Ipolyi, younger then but debauched, hence fat, wore a corset in Vienna so as to look neat on duty. But at Nice, Monte, Cannes, no. No corset. It was too much trouble to be taking it off again all the time. Here, Ipolyi, uncorseted, threw back his head and laughed loudly, "Ho, ho, ho!"

Miles heard the coarse laughter as an echo. At nineteen, reading Oppenheim in the bathtub, the robins crying rain outside, he had yearned toward Monaco, the Côte d'Azur, the Corniche roads. *Faites vos jeux, messieurs.* Slender but with thews of steel (jujitsu privately practiced) he would saunter into the Casino with whom? Marilyn Miller on his arm, the cynosure of all eyes. A little supper, caviar and champagne, the *maître* himself removing his cloak, folding it with reverence. The cloak always had a lining of pink watered silk.

"Ipolyi, did you ever have a cloak?" Miles asked. "A cloak with a silk lining?"

Interrupted, Ipolyi frowned, said no, resumed.

Fourteen years ago, when he had first gone to Europe, his first foreign assignment, he had leaned over the rail, a new pigskin bag beside him, whistling, watching the towers fade into the smoke pall of New York. In Europe beyond the horizon all things were possible. He would become an officer. Coldstream? *Totenkopf?* Something with a fur hat. Take your pick. He would uncover an Irish earldom, the sleeping patents found in the church at Ballyclough—no one would laugh. Money also, an oak chest hidden in the castle? No—he had rejected that. Rents rather, potato money, the black pig sold for the clement master. And then: Lord Miles at Ascot, the Grampians in August, Le Touquet, Monte Carlo.

Here was Ipolyi, the kind of man, even to the barony, he had gone to Europe to become. In his first journey, he had strained after this shameful cliché as a goal and now, returning, it was an irony to have it sit before him as Ipolyi, scented and chattering. But at least he had outgrown it and could ditch this hunky at Pier 58.

"Look, there is the inspector," Ipolyi said. "He has had his afternoon wallow in sentiment and now he takes his tea. He is methodical like a sow."

6

Turning, Miles saw the back of Loudoun's head dipping as he drank his tea with milk.

"Does he tickle the young girls? An inspector would have opportunities. Myself I never saw women during the whole of my education. Except after dark. Did I tell you?"

"No," Miles said.

"I am a baron. I am better than you, a journalist. Just born, steaming yet, the umbilical cord hanging from my little arm, I am better than you will ever be if you are President of Standard Oil. Unpalatable? You can't take it? You bet you can't. But do not resent it. It is a fact you cannot help. Now, as an embellishment, once every two or three generations, my family educates a son. It is useful but really unnecessary like the olive in the Martini. It was I who was so exquisitely educated. Listen to me, I had a tutor, an Englishman, Jesus College, Cambridge. My God, he was cold and aloof—that was why he was hired. The nobility of my country is debased. Why? Because we won't work. We are not stern. Except myself. I am stern and I learn my sternness from that English tutor. My Latin I learn from the monks. Did I tell you?"

"No," Miles said. "Have a drink first."

"*Viele danke*. I will."

Miles beckoned to a waiter.

"I will pay this time. I have money but I am stern with it. I will show you: in Paris I look over the passenger list before I buy my ticket. I ask myself, 'Is there anybody sailing first class who can do me benefit in New York—any Henry Ford, an A. P. Morgan?' There is no one like that, only frightened opera singers and King's Messengers with the rope around the wrist. Why should I waste the money? I come tourist class and I will buy this drink. You will let me, my dear friend? *Bon*."

From his pocket he drew a leather wallet. Miles could see that it was stuffed with money. Ipolyi took out a thousand-franc note, tossed it cleverly into the air so that it floated, tipping gently back and forth on to the waiter's tray.

"Your health, sir," Ipolyi said and drank half his drink. "You know I go to New York to become purchasing agent for my government.

No? It is true. They want someone who knows the country. I do. Who speaks English perfectly. I do, with the slang, O.K. baby. Who is personally impressive. I am not now—*je suis en pantoufles*—but wait. My silly government, my God they are silly—here is war beyond the window and the War Minister he keeps all the ammunition for the army in his where? You will not believe it but it is true. In his kitchen. This *espèce de gouvernement* they buy trucks last year, good American trucks, International Harvester. All this year the trucks haul wheat from the Rumanian border to Germany. They are hauling still but on the rims. Why? Because the government forgets to buy spare tires. In the summer—another instance—they send two cabinet ministers to buy the spare tires, big shots, one related to the Esterházy family, very charming gentlemen but inefficient. What do they do? They spend their time riding up and down, up and down in the elevators in Radio City like children. They buy no tires—only dressing gowns and fountain pens, dozens of fountain pens for their friends in Budapest. They are not stern.

"But now, the government sends me and *I will rent an office, by God*. I will have steel filing cabinets painted green and a paperweight on the desk. I will hire a frightful stenographer with legs like an elephant. The position is a sacred trust, but I will make a lot of money all the same. And I will be efficient or bust—note the slang. I speak good American, yes?"

"Wonderful," Miles said. "You were going to tell me how you learned Latin from the monks."

"I was but I forgot. The monastery was like a jail. Every day was alike. The monks were very dirty men, very lazy, very fat. They wear brown serge, like bathrobes. (Myself, I am *croyant* only when in trouble. The rest of the time, the hell with it.) Before each brother's place at table there are two big silver mugs, one full of wine, the other full of hot grease. I give you my word—they were full of hot grease. They drink the wine, good, O.K., but then they drink the hot grease." Ipolyi seized the remembered silver cup, threw back his head gulping emptily, and, done, sighed roughly. "They loved it. The only Latin they taught me was the epigrams of Martial, very filthy. I am boyish then, pearly with innocence, and I go home and

8

tell my family these filthy *maximes*. Back in the monastery, the monks laugh, ho, ho!"

Miles had learned Latin in a clean brick building full of windows, all with steel sashes. Bells rang every hour. Crouched in a seat warranted not to induce curvature of the spine, Miles had followed Caesar's dreary journey into the French woods. Except for a few bright shreds, he could not remember the campaign, for Miss Sarah Burnham Cooke, in navy-blue shirtwaist with gold watch pinned to it and a net collar stayed up to hide her aging throat, had insisted on the verbs—they were the words of action, perfect and pluperfect. Julius Caesar was a very clever man, he sat in his tent dictating three letters at once. There was also a barbarian who surrendered, Vercingetorix, bearded, tall above the dagos, and when Caesar crossed the Rhine, the class had built a model bridge of twigs and picture wire. The only thing to snicker at was *horum, harum, horum*. And now he was returning. Pearly with innocence?

"The inspector has finished his tea. What a drink! Look at him," Ipolyi said. Loudoun had gotten up from his table and was standing with his legs braced wide, looking out of a porthole. He was working the muscles of his jaw.

"He is trying to discover an excuse to talk to you. He wishes I would go away," Ipolyi said. "Again he is full of tea and outrage."

Loudoun was shy but he was a talker. The first night out from Cherbourg before they had met each other, before Miles, in the confusion of a wartime departure, even knew he was sharing the stateroom, he had come in to go to bed. He found Loudoun sitting on the edge of the bunk in long woolen underwear paring the corns from his bony blue feet with an old-fashioned hollow-ground razor. There was some blood which he had stanched with a hand towel. Loudoun looked up as the door opened, looked back at the foot across his knee with a shrewd mechanic's eye, and began slowly to cut and talk.

"Man plunges through life, leaving little waste things behind him: ravelings, toenail clippings, the grubbed-off mammets of shoe leather, beard ends floating in drains with turds, scabs of small sores—if not eaten, thrown away—deposits of dandruff in combs, bits of snot secret in corners, lint, gray umbilical fur, the summits of corns like these and hardened skin hewn from the soles of toes, specks of eye cheese, decayed meat on old toothpicks, even piss dilute and yellow after the rush of water journeying, red and yellow earwax clotted on the hairpin dropped by the lady visitor." He stood up waving the razor. "Proofs of the tenancy! I have lived."

His wide lids fell and sadness passed through his ugly face. "But hasten, microcosm, put on the coat, walk, comb, shave, shit, pluck at the navel bud, the mother tie, bruise yourself, eat and pick your teeth, clip your nails, keep clean the Eustachian trumpet, sniffle and piss, titivate the eye corners—the organism decays. Hasten! But what also of the other wastes—the wasted glance as she was climbing into the limousine, too thick and pobby they were; useless to give ear to the account of Polish fights when the static came in; and to place the hand in darkness carefully on the hot-water pipe—that was crude, wasn't it? But our losses are graver, brutaler still: what to do with the moment of courage, now, alas, flown, when you would have hit him but for the fear that came too soon; and in the nave at Winchester that hot day, you wanted to kneel down—why didn't you? Because one doesn't believe in God any more? Bickering till the bedstead shook when you really did not want to quarrel any more, but rather to kiss her and be soft and comfortable in the darkness, yet persisting still till it got light and there was no tea in the canister." He jerked up his head and almost whispered: "Man's actions do not correspond to the dignity and intensity of his desires."

This was Miles' introduction to Archibald Loudoun.

Perhaps he was nervous about submarines and wanted to be awake if a torpedo struck. Loudoun talked late every night after Miles came in. He fell asleep talking. Daytimes when he could find Miles alone, he talked in the soft, phlegmy burr of the Lowlands, always with this daft intensity about Man, although sometimes at night, with the candor lent him by the darkness, about himself.

"The identity of Man is a secret," Loudoun said.

Lying in the bunk above him, Miles thought he could play ball that far. True enough.

"A secret that has been revealed, however."

Miles quickly said, "Christ?"

"The Mortiser had better stayed home. I know about Christ. I know fully. My father was a minister of the kirk, no cooking and the shades drawn on Sunday, coughing and sobbing his way through a two-hour sermon twice, spitting blood on the verses in the book, a consumptive, whose faith covered him like a new gamp against the rain of doubt. He died innocent. No, not Christ."

"My wife died of consumption," Miles said.

"My wife is fat," Loudoun answered.

"What about this revelation?" Keep him at it.

"Hae ye never heard of Shakespeare?"

"Oh," Miles said. Not bad, at that.

Loudoun talked as if the plays had been buried or hidden and he, Archibald Loudoun, had alone discovered them, knew them, as if he were their sole owner and proprietor. In the bones, in the silent racing through the veins, with the heartbeat and the squelching of his guts, Man *believed* he was immortal, yet in the front of his head, in the brain, that late-come usurper, he *knew* he must die. In this conflict lay the tragedy, and that cold night along the Danish rampart, the astonished Hamlet, young man, first discovered it and it set him thinking, and Lear, old man, spared in jail with his Cordelia, spared to hope until the button was too tight, found it just before the curtain. Under the vast bald helm, the Bard's gray eye had seen what struggle wasted Man.

"He knew there was a boil on either buttock and we can't sit still, and so to fill the little pause between our birth and our decay, he tore out the dignity that is in us and put it featly in the plays for us to learn from." Loudoun paused. "Do you know why I am going to America?"

"I should like to sit in one of your classes," Miles answered, he thought rather featly himself.

"I am going there to join the Communist Party."

"Do you have to go to America? Wasn't there a branch of the party in Scotland?"

Scotland was tea and scones, tea and scones, tea and scones and an egg, and a walk afterward. The hills were real enough to him, the little tinkling burns, the sheeppens and the cottages with the piles of yellow Swedes in front of them, but his wife, Miles suspected, he valued only as a dumpling of flesh to be chucked daytimes and smoothed and slept with nights, and the people around him in Ayrshire, in Kilmarnock, Loudoun did not recognize at all. The pupils and the schoolmasters he inspected were clots of stupidity, the oatmeal working out of them in warts and wens and knobs and whelks. The laborers? The laboring men, the toiling masses, wore caps and scarves and cheered the Rangers or the Hearts of Midlothian at footer matches, silly buggers.

Scotland was a pocket, a crevice in the surface of the world. The "world" inhabited of Man, the veritable *homo*, was south of Carlisle in England perhaps (though not across the Irish Sea—they were "papes" over there) or beyond the Channel or the Atlantic or in Russia —he conceded that Man might have fulfilled his promise in Muscovy. He did not know; he could afford to read nothing but the Glesca papers, and a journey there was impossible. But he could get to America. It was the least he could do.

"But just what is the connection between Communism and Shakespeare? I don't get it," Miles asked.

Snorting with exasperation, Loudoun said, "You *ought* to be *in stat pup*, a little whey-faced scholar boy. Shakespeare defined the grandeur of Man. Marx showed us how to make it real."

"Thanks."

Marx fought oppression. Oppression was injustice. Any fool could identify it. (It was plain as a dragon breathing blue and crimson flames.) If one fought injustice at Marx's side, it would be banished. Injustice and oppression gone, Man would assume his natural, now potential, stature, frank, free, and honest as Shakespeare saw him. It was simple.

"But about economics . . ." Miles began.

"Bah! Countinghouse ethics. Marx cared nothing for economics. He was merely tainted by the shopfronts of London."

"What about the labor theory of value?"

"Dust in the eye."

"It certainly sounds simple, the way you tell it."

"Save your scorn. You're a mere newsman. You are *post hoc* with knobs on—chasing after the event. But *I* know."

"It must be very warming to have so strong a belief in an ideal," Miles ventured to conciliate.

"I have it. I pursue it. Good night."

Every night when they were alone it was like this. Yet Loudoun was a shy man, ugly, his hair a fading red with streaks of gray in it, and on his face the oatmeal knobs and wens he accused his neighbors of. Miles wondered why he listened to him but as he wondered he knew. Loudoun and Ipolyi kept him from thinking.

As Miles watched him looking out of the porthole, pulsing the muscles of his jaw dramatically, he knew that Loudoun was getting ready to join them, trying to overcome his diffidence, and, that done, to accuse them, to act as if pity were something he had thought up himself, an invention which had not caught on. He would tell them about the refugees and arrogantly demand that oppression be abolished. He would pull at his knuckles, working himself up until his blue eyes stood out and he was shaking with the emotion that the possible fortunate destiny of Man aroused in him. Miles had come to believe that he had read better than he knew—the study of Shakespeare had made him an actor. If humanity were reformed, it would only be to provide suitable companions for Archibald Loudoun.

He approached the table. Ipolyi did not see him until he pulled out a chair. Miles, unwilling to break the flow of Ipolyi's military memoir, nodded pleasantly. Ipolyi was drinking but he bowed as well as he could, without smiling lest the whisky run out of his mouth. He also made a cordial wave with his free hand.

"I've been downstairs to look at the refugees," Loudoun began gloomily.

Ipolyi, refreshed, his mouth newly wiped with his scented handkerchief, began to talk again smiling and ducking his head as if to excuse himself but also to assert his prior right to Miles' attention. Loudoun sat down and looked straight ahead of him. Miles could tell he was ready for a tirade but was balked, still shy, by Ipolyi's impregnable garrulity.

"In the Carpathians it was no fun. The Carpathians are high." Here

Ipolyi indicated the height of the mountains with his hand. "I was captain in a cavalry regiment and it was no place for horses. We walked. We eat bread and turnips, pfui! I have only one amusement. You have been at Coney Island? You know the stalls where you buy three baseballs for a thin dime and throw them at dolls, yes? The dolls have little skirts. When they fall down, the skirts flutter. So. When we shoot the melancholy Russian from his cliff, the long skirts of his coat flutter like the dolls at Coney Island. I have a hunting rifle, telescopic sight, beautiful walnut stock, a very accurate weapon. Every morning I shoot a Russian—flutter, flutter, flutter, bop!"

Loudoun had grown attentive in spite of himself. He said contemptuously: "They could not see you, I suppose?"

In a way Ipolyi was intelligent. His incessant talk was only a sign that he was glad to be on his way to New York, where he would make a lot of money. He also knew something of Loudoun's enthusiasms because Miles, to fill the short gaps in Ipolyi's monologue, had told him. He said, "Slavs have myopia. It is probably a deficiency in diet or a refusal of the eye to follow their vast steppes to the horizon. It gives them a peering look. Many people take them for idealists, dreamers." Ipolyi here looked straight at Loudoun. Then with his former lightness he continued, "No, they did not see me. The Russian was the enemy. I liquidated him. It was very sporty shooting."

Loudoun began to get red, and Miles could see a quarrel coming. He had no affection for either of these men. They were pastimes till he docked, yet more out of habit than anything else, he tried to find an innocuous question, one that would soothe Loudoun and make Ipolyi keep to his tone of warm reminiscence.

"Did you spend the whole war in the Carpathians?" Miles asked.

"No. Only the worst part. At the end I ran a pogrom in Rumania."

"You what?" Loudoun cried.

"I, Ipolyi, captain of hussars, was managing director of a pogrom in Bucovina. I made all plans. I was the boss."

"How do you plan one of those things?" Miles asked quickly. He did not care really; Ipolyi was baiting the Scot deliberately. The fight would come now, he thought. He could not stop it.

"We ride into the village. I sit in the square on my horse. I scowl,

14

you see." Ipolyi scowled, threw out his chest, and put one fist on his hip. "I shout to my leftenants, 'Bring me the Jews.' They bring the Jews squawling like cats, '*Oi, oi, wehz mir, wehz mir.*' I procure a table, good, solid, four legs. The individual Isidore is tied face up on the table, an arm to a leg, a leg to a leg. He makes a nice design." Ipolyi drank thirstily, watching Loudoun over the rim of his glass. "My men run to the thickets and cut sticks. The army regulations concerning these affairs are quite strict—the sticks must be no thicker than my thumb and no Jew can be given more than twenty-five strokes a day. But we get around them. Oh, we evade authority. I put one man at *each* corner of the table and *each* they give twenty-five strokes, beating time like the metronome, and Moischa is hamburg without the onion."

Loudoun looked sullen and intent, and Miles could not tell whether he was trying to pretend that he was mastering his anger or not. "It is quite necessary that the Jews be beaten," Loudoun said sarcastically.

"They were hard campaigns in the Carpathians. They are very tired, the men are. There were many casualties—have you ever seen a man wounded and then preserved by freezing? Natural refrigeration, very interesting but not a sight to cheer you if the man is a neighbor from your village—iced. The men have seen many neighbors thus. They are dispirited. The morale is low. Some amusement must be furnished, so we go to Bucovina for a little party."

"A pogrom," Loudoun repeated.

Ipolyi smiled and lifted his shoulders. "They are only Jews. It gives the soldier the feeling of power—the flesh beneath the stick. As an officer, educated as I have just told Miles, a baron, I am of a different class. I have more resources. More things than one give me the military *esprit* that is essential. Sometimes I stand at one corner of the table— you say 'whaling?'—whaling away with the lowest private in my company. Other times I merely sit on my horse and watch the proceedings. Here comes Mrs. Cohen. She has a shawl around her head. She is wailing, 'Oh, Captain, let Sammy off. Please, Captain. He is sick. He cannot stand it. P-l-e-a-s-e let Sammy off.' I look at Mrs. Cohen—I say 'Cohen,' *comprenez?* The Rumanian names are difficult— I smile and wave the hand. 'O.K. Let Sammy off.' I am merciful, you will note. That also is good. It gives me the necessary feeling of power."

Loudoun jumped up. "You swine! You devil! You bastard . . ."

Ipolyi lay back in his chair, smiling, looking up at Loudoun. "You intend to insult me. The tone has weight, you observe, Miles, but the epithet 'bastard' means nothing. Sixteen quarterings were necessary before one could be received at the Imperial Court, and the Emperor has called me 'John' many times. So—" he paused, narrowed his eyes and looked like a Mongol, "I make allowance for you, Loudoun. Your papa was a preacher, *hein?* One of the sects of the Scottish hills, Miles, a shaggy Presbyterian. He has watched the old man pray and now he imitates those seizures, those shameful ecstasies which are simultaneously an insult to the true Church and a sexual release, maybe the only one he knows. If I would stop talking, you would forget your anger, old boy, I bet you money you would forget your anger and try to convert me to the Communism you lack the intelligence to understand."

People were watching. Miles murmured, "Come on, Ipolyi. Cut it out. Cut it out."

Ipolyi turned to Miles and went on jovially, "He stands there wondering if he should strike me, the recourse of a peasant, a blow. But he is restrained because I am his brother . . . all men are brothers, yes? He has churned the Christian milk into the Marxist cheese, but the curd remains the same. We are equal, pfui!"

Loudoun threw a glass of Scotch and soda in Ipolyi's face. A woman three tables away gave a little yip of surprise and the priests stared. Everyone in the bar stood up, and Ipolyi, smiling, drew his handkerchief from his sleeve and calmly wiped his dripping face.

Ipolyi tucked the handkerchief back into his sleeve, raised his hand to hold off the waiters who had run up when the commotion began, smiling all the time. As if he were merely about to leave the table, his smile covering a defeat, he moved past his chair toward Loudoun. Suddenly Ipolyi tripped him. He fell down, and Ipolyi kicked him three times in the face.

With a gracious wave of the hand to include all the astonished passengers, Ipolyi said, "*Entschuldigen sie.*" Then he bowed and walked

16

slowly out of the saloon. Loudoun was sitting up and the blood ran down his face. Miles gave him a handkerchief to wipe it with.

As the waiters lifted him from the floor and everyone began talking at once, Miles turned away from the crowd and went out on deck. On the lee side he found an empty deck chair in a corner sheltered from the wind. A green plaid rug lay over the arm. He sat down, pulled the rug over him and began to smoke.

The entertainment was over and it would be three days before he reached New York. He had seen refugees before in the Ohio floods, in Barcelona, and lately at the destruction of Warsaw, all pitiful weary and uncomprehending, all lugging the inevitable mattress. These below in third class, the successful ones who had escaped, living, if wounded at all, slightly, some even with suitcases, they did not interest him. He could not talk to the priests or the other passengers and it would be silly to get drunk and stay drunk. He was beginning to see that he would have to sit alone someplace and figure out why he had quit a good job as European correspondent for a newspaper syndicate at the beginning of the war to come home and take on a responsibility he had never acknowledged, a daughter.

He did not want to think about it and so far he had avoided most of it by listening to Loudoun and Ipolyi. He was like a plant in a clay pot being carried from one soil to another, the roots and tendrils of his last bed broken and those of his destination yet to form. A month ago a cable had come to him telling him his wife had died. He had been divorced from her ten years and the cable was from her mother, perhaps to wound him with whatever memories the death would start.

It did not hurt him to remember his wife. She was a girl he had married because his friends had praised her and who then had worn out what tenderness he had summoned by trying to shame him away from newspapers into advertising and the bond business. It did not hurt him to think of her dead as she now was, wasted by tuberculosis and heaped with barbaric piles of flowers rotting in the darkness. Surprised at his callousness, he had tried to resurrect their happy moments, but they had all been tainted by what followed them and he regretted nothing that had passed with her, not even when her

17

mother's letter arrived a few days after the cable and the old woman, bitter and self-righteous, had thrust his daughter back on him, Mary, now in a convent school, nearly seventeen years old.

As he read the letter the girl did not seem his. She was like her mother, and her mother, and her aunts. The last time he had been in America, seven years before, Constance had brought her to see him. They had met in a hotel room. He had ordered cocktails and a lemonade and tried to be jolly about everything. But the child, primed by her grandmother, had stared at him as if he were a crocodile, curtsied solemnly, and said, "How do you do, Father?" Constance had left this little figure as a reproach, a daughter taught to disapprove of him. He did not want a daughter.

In Paris, in the turmoil of packing and breaking in the man who was to take his place and saying good-by to his friends, he had put off thinking about it. There would be time enough on the boat. In a week in a deck chair he could devise a code or plan or something that would fix their relationship and prepare him to be a father. After his farewells he regretted leaving and he hoped the dislocation of the journey would give the regret a chance to crystallize into what would then be the fact that he was no longer a citizen of Europe. But he had neglected these things to listen to Ipolyi and the Scotsman.

He did not really want a daughter. He had lived too long alone, made his own echoes in the house, eating with the newspaper propped against the carafe, reading and chewing, and at night if there were no woman with him, giving the big sigh as he lay down without thinking of anyone else. He was a newspaperman and had seen considerable of what, when he was old and people asked him, he would call the pageantry of history: the searchlights in the sky at Nuremberg, the crowd shouting at Beneš on Hradčany Hill, the unruly army of the Catalans. His memory was stuffed with crowds and it was hard for him to consider events merely personal.

One of the priests on board spoke English, and in a weak turn of shame at his own laziness, he had thought of asking the priest's advice. Through the lattice of the confession box a priest absorbed the secrets of the heart. Perhaps this one could tell him how to make friends with a hostile daughter almost grown. But the priests talked all day about what was happening in Poland. They had been sent by Cardinal Hlond to get help in America, and it would be impolite to intrude. He remembered out of many the gentlemanly-looking man he had seen in Warsaw just after the surrender. The man wore a double-breasted blue overcoat and a bowler hat. With five other men he was cutting up a dead horse that lay in the street of apartment houses almost untouched by the bombardment. When the carcass had been awkwardly divided, he had received a piece of the neck, unskinned. All the men shook hands; they were strangers. And this man had gone off down the street carrying the chunk on his shoulder with the horse's mane hanging down blowing in the wind. Such a man, he thought, could face the priest boldly, having the right to be helped.

Suddenly Ipolyi came around the corner, strolling, his hands in the pockets of his overcoat. He wore no hat and the stiff breeze had disheveled the hair that fringed his bald spot. Miles said nothing, hoping he would pass by, but Ipolyi saw him and stopped.

"I am pooped with apology. I shook hands with the purser. I begged the barman's pardon. All around I am sorry. Any man, you see, can call me bastard. It is a joke because it is not true. But to throw whisky in my face, that is rude. It also makes the clothes stink."

Without asking, Ipolyi sat down on the footrest of the deck chair. "You recall the administration of Béla Kun in Hungary after the war? Cohn his name was. You remember?"

"Yes."

"Against the wall of the carriage house my uncle was shot. My aunt they clubbed to death with a chair in her boudoir—they poured out the perfume and stole the bottles. I myself slept twenty-six nights in different beds because the Communists were looking for me. I should have killed that inspector."

Miles looked away from the sea at Ipolyi. He saw that he was speaking quite seriously.

"As it was I felt his jawbone break."

"Has the doctor looked him over? I think I'd better go see him."

"That Communist?"

"He's not a real Communist."

Ipolyi shrugged, stood up, and walked away.

Miles went down to his stateroom. Loudoun was sitting on the edge of the lower bunk with his head wrapped in a towel. He was rocking back and forth like an old woman, and there were large red patches on the towel where the blood had soaked through.

"Have you seen the doctor yet?" Miles asked.

Loudoun shook his head.

"Don't you think you'd better see him?"

Loudoun's mouth and chin were swathed in the towel. He pulled it away to speak. One side of his mouth was turned nearly inside out.

"I'll lose my post now," he said thickly.

"Your post? Where? In the States, you mean?"

Loudoun nodded glumly.

"Why should you?"

Loudoun pointed to his face.

"A motorbike. I was going to buy a motorbike with the money I saved." He pulled the towel up over his chin again as if it were a comfort and began to rock back and forth again with the pain.

"They won't fire you because of a shiner and a busted tooth. Why don't you go see the doctor?"

Loudoun shook his head and looked at the floor.

Miles went out. Going up the steps to the bar, he discovered with surprise that he had made his last farewell to Europe. He found that he had counted on stringing it out, a sentimental slow withdrawal to be ended only when he saw the first gulls from America. He had intended to go over in his mind tenderly, wistfully, the places he had been happy in, but these two knockabout comedians had cut him off. They were Europe.

Now there was nothing behind him. All the memories he fumbled to recall had the quality of cheap postcards. Too late he was learning what the Continent had meant to him. It was elaborate costume play, and the props were Chartres and *La Gioconda*, quaint Bavarian villages and the beaches at Antibes and Santander and first-class carriages on trains (*défense de se pencher en dehors*). The actors were always some distance away, smiling or weeping across the footlights at you, and you grieved or applauded in a loose theatric way but you left the play untouched. This melee between Loudoun and Ipolyi was the epilogue.

"Maybe it's astigmatism," he thought. "Maybe it's working for a paper—you look to see only how one thing connects with another." He watched the priests who were still sitting around a table talking gravely, and he tried to feel what they must be feeling, from Poland as they were, but he could not do it. He was disgusted with himself. For fourteen years he had written the news as honestly as he could and he had seen nothing. The truth came late and to see it or tell it was not a matter of intention—it was a gift. And if he had been lucky and had written the truth, it was only because he had a gift for it and knew nothing about it really.

2

To a man afflicted with carious teeth, seated in a dentist's office fighting time with this issue of this magazine, this photograph, if he noticed it, would show a beautiful young girl (the editors hoped) leaning dreamily (they intended) against a house wall near a garden in a tropic night. To all members of the Junior League everywhere, to ambitious wives of foundry owners in small industrial towns, to women of the settled rich, it would be another photo of a famous movie star (No. 7, box-office ranking) in a perfectly darling Augustabernard gown. To the publishers it was one more exercise of a strategem worn so familiar that it was unrecognizable: they knew without thinking about it that chlorotic little girls with the braces just off their teeth, begirdled younger married women now plumping too far out and anxious, and the women of unadmitted age, straining and dieting, blowsy when uncorseted, bitten by reminiscence, would all, bare ribs or *embonpoint*, fat haunch or skinny, want to buy a copy of the gown because with the trust once given to fairy tales they would believe that some metathesis would take place, some strange change would work in them, and they would somehow look like the actress in the gown. Then if all these women bought gowns, the publishers would raise the advertising rate on the dress shop that sold them and profits, profits. To the editors themselves, the confecting of the picture took a boring afternoon.

There was a geniune hedge of privet growing in a box and behind it a night sky was standing, made of dark blue board quaintly spangled with stars of silver paper. The white clapboard side of a house had been wheeled up on rollers at a right angle to the hedge and between them some false rock flagstones lay in a lawn of paper grass. Between the edge of the grass and the camera was a tangle of rubber-sheathed wires leading to the various lights and flood lamps parked tentatively around the scene. The camera was a battered Graflex with a black hood hanging down.

The photographer's helper, everything done, was picking his teeth with a sharp match. The photographer moved a light an inch, a reflector back a little. Against the wall of the studio behind the camera, Mrs. Raynes, the editor, an old woman with blue hair, talked with her associate, Margery Elliot. The actress who was to pose was still in the dressing room having her gown fitted by a woman from the shop that lent it, having her face made up by her Swedish maid.

"Look how long she takes. She's been in there an hour," the photographer said.

"Gregor," the editor said reproachfully. Then to Miss Elliot, she said, "She's gained. They had to take the seam out and change the zipper. Right across here—pounds, my dear."

"She looked a little heavier when she came in," Miss Elliot said.

"An hour, and I got to take those clasps and those handbags when I get done with her," Gregor persisted.

"Oh can't they wait until tomorrow, Gregor?"

"They got to go to the printer tomorrow so she takes an hour because she can't cut out the whisky getting her a big stomach." The photographer turned away in disgust. He wheeled, throwing out his hand. "A press agent! When she was a chorus girl . . ."

"Carolyn Buckmaster. First *Little Show*," the helper said.

"Yeah, the first *Little Show*. She was a chorus girl. She has a press agent, a *press* agent and he sends me pictures, cheesecake, till I'm blind trying to get her picture in the magazine. So now she's in Hollywood she can take an hour. Watch her when she comes out: 'Move the camera. Turn the spot off. Tear up the grass.' Watch her, that's all I ask. Buckbuster, hah!"

"She had a nice shape then," the helper said.

"She has a beautiful figure now," Mrs. Raynes said coldly.

"Fat," the photographer said.

"She is taking a long time," Miss Elliot said. "I think I'll go in and see if I can do anything."

But the door opened and the star came out.

The photographer's helper loyally looked at her stomach. Mrs. Raynes began to chatter with the accent and stress she kept for people whose names were in the headlines. The photographer stood tense waiting for her criticism of the lights and properties.

"Where do you want me?" she asked.

The photographer placed her on the flagstones by the wall of the house. She looked around quickly, professionally. Could the sky be moved a little? There was a star that would stick in her hair. The photographer nodded to the helper and the sky was moved. Put that spot over there, she said, it would cut the shadow. The photographer nodded and the shadow was curtailed.

"Is everything like you want it now?" the photographer asked in a threatening voice.

"Oh, I think so." She glanced around once more. "Now, how do you want me?"

"Full face."

The star turned full face. Her face was blank and ready.

"O.K. It's night. You're dreamy."

Mrs. Raynes was eager. "It's after dinner. The men are having their brandy and cigars and you've crept out into the garden alone."

The photographer caught Miss Elliot's eye and raised his eyebrows and pursed his lips. He stooped, picked up his black hood, and threw it over his head. The helper stood beside him with more film holders.

The star, her feet together, folded her hands in front of her at arm's length against her dress and lifted her head, staring upward.

"Back a little," the photographer said under the hood.

"He says back a little, please," the helper repeated. The star moved back.

"O.K. Hold it."

"O.K. Hold it, please," the helper said.

The camera clicked. They took two shots, changed the carriage of her head, shot the new pose once, moved her hands, and shot again.

"Are you nearly finished? I'm giving a cocktail party at the Waldorf for three hundred people," the star said.

"Oh, I know, my dear," Mrs. Raynes twittered. "But just one more. Gregor, we have time, haven't we? What shall it be? Oh, I know. . . . Gregor darling, why not put her against the side of the house in profile and . . ."

"O.K., profile, please," Gregor said, lifting the hood. "Get the lights," he said to the helper.

"How you want 'em?"

"So she can look at the moon, dope. Put the moonlight in front of her."

"How are my feet?" the star asked in profile. She had small feet.

"They show. The feet are nice," the photographer said. "Like that."

"Just like that, please," the helper said.

The shutter clicked three times.

"Couldn't you turn her head this way, Gregor? Gregor!"

Under the black hood, Gregor muttered, "Turn her head off from her neck." He emerged. "Now how you want it, Mrs. Raynes? Tell me how you want it."

"Why, I just thought we could have her looking at the camera."

"O.K. Now I will make a wonderful photograph. Really wonderful," Gregor said. He began to jerk the lights around, talking under his breath. "I should work for women. I will look her at the camera. Now, you dope, that one goes there, so. And the other—see what I'm trying to do? You see it?"

"I got you, boss," the helper said.

"And now if you please, miss. Bring the right shoulder down a little. Good, that's fine. You like it, Mrs. Raynes? That's fine. That's swell. That's good. Just keep that."

By the change of the pose and the lighting, the lady's bosom had become a huge smooth hillock, brilliantly illuminated. Mrs. Raynes and the star did not notice it. Miss Elliot and the helper did.

"Art study, hey, boss?" the helper whispered.

Gregor ignored him. "Now please, the face. Look like at a man."

The star licked her lips and turned her face toward the camera. Her mouth was open a little, her back was arched, one shoulder down, and her chin was almost resting on the other. She winked her eyes to freshen them and then half open they gazed at the camera. It was her famous expression.

"My God, not that," thought Miss Elliot. "We can't print that. They've seen it everywhere." Everywhere. Even in Damascus. She had heard there was a movie there, the performance sometimes interrupted by sandstorms. Lascivious Arabs hot from their camels had scanned in the darkness that eight-foot face; herring fishermen at the North Cape; sandhogs, miners, insurance men, pimply little college boys had sinned in thought while looking at this set of her features, alluring, beautiful, and stale. The look was as plain as a green golight. "Gregor," she whispered, "you can't take that."

"No," he said softly. "You're damn right we can't take it. Look at her chin."

The star had finished a picture three weeks before. She had arrived by airplane in Newark the next morning and, since then, had been resting. Every day she had slept till the afternoon. She had eaten things covered with Sauce Mornay. She had drunk too much every night. She had been happy, but it showed. Beneath her chin barely visible resting on her shoulder was a tiny roll of fat.

"I'm sorry, miss. Raise the chin."

If she raised her chin her mouth would close and the juicy acquiescence would go out of her face. The star knew how she looked. She always knew how her face looked no matter what they told her to do with it. Exhibitors loved it when she looked that way because it packed them in at the box office.

"I don't think it's so good with the chin raised," she said.

"It is better, I assure you," Gregor said.

"Why must she raise her chin, Gregor?" Mrs. Raynes complained.

"You want a nice picture, huh, Mrs. Raynes?"

"Why, of course, but . . ."

"Then ask her please to raise the chin."

"You look perfectly beautiful the way you are, my dear. Keep your chin where it is," Mrs. Raynes said to the star.

Gregor slammed a plate into the camera. "O.K. You want fat stuff—you gonna get fat stuff."

"Who's fat stuff?" the star hustled toward them.

"What you think is all over your face, marmalade? Can I make you beautiful with two, three chins? We want fat in the magazine, you think? You got too much face, Buckbuster."

"Gregor!" Mrs. Raynes shrieked.

"I was not aware that I . . . oh, God damn you." The star turned and walked into the dressing room, swinging her arms. The door slammed. Mrs. Raynes followed, bent-kneed.

When the door closed a second time, Gregor and the helper began to leap softly about like clowns, thumbing their noses, making faces and obscener gestures at the dressing room. Miss Elliot watched them, giggling a little. Then she sat down on a stool to wait for Mrs. Raynes. She stuck out her foot and looked at her pump.

"So we ain't got no art study this month," the helper said.

"She better not come next month. Next month she's drinking her usual case of whisky and she's big as a young mother coming up." Gregor staggered around holding his hands in front of him as if he were carrying a pumpkin.

"Yeah, worse," the helper said. "For a swell form, I'll take you, Miss Elliot."

"Why, thank you, Charlie. How long do you give my chin?"

"Aw, yizz and yizz, Miss Elliot."

"Look, Elliot, a chin, for one chin extra, listen at 'em," Gregor said.

Through the door came the low whooping of Mrs. Raynes' apology. As Miss Elliot yawned and waited, she considered how funny it was to work for a fashion magazine.

Mrs. Raynes came out of the dressing room, the stretched skin of her face flushed. She began immediately to Miss Elliot in a low voice, "Oh, my dear, it was awful. She was beside herself with rage, absolutely beside herself but furious. I thought she was never going to . . . oh, Gregor, how could you?"

"Mrs. Raynes, she's got a double chin. In the picture, finished, it would look like a Parker House roll. Better I should tell her myself than waste a negative."

"Do you want me to wait around until she comes out?" Miss Elliot asked.

"No. I don't think so. I got her softened up all right. More apologies would only irritate her. You run along," Mrs. Raynes said wearily.

Miss Elliot left for the day. The receptionist, hired because she lived on Park Avenue and spoke a supercilious bogus English, said, "Good night, Miss Elliot." The elevator boy said, "Good night, Miss Elliot," and leaned out of the car at the ground floor to watch her ankles. She was tired but pleased and expectant. The comedy of the afternoon had amused her and, although she knew it was stupid to be, she was flattered by the compliment of Gregor's helper. She walked easily through the crowded lobby of the building, holding herself straight and swinging one arm a little because it was one of the crimes of the city to show fatigue and you never knew whom you might see. At the newsstand she bought an evening paper, folded it, and stuck it under her arm. In the subway she sat erect on the woven straw with her ankles crossed, knowing that the men swinging from hooks above her were looking down at her. She folded the newspaper lengthwise and read the headlines. Richard would expect her to know what was going on. *Hitler Speaks to Reichstag Tomorrow. Polish Peace Terms Forecast.*

At Fourteenth Street she got off. She found a flower seller in the Square and bought some marigolds. She bought a bottle of good gin, a yellow color, at a liquor store on University Place. From there she hurried to her flat on Tenth Street because she did not like to be seen carrying parcels. Her grandmother had once said, dozing under the catalpa tree where she read Mother Goose aloud on sunny summer mornings, that ladies and gentlemen did not carry parcels. She did not remember this. It was only that she did not walk well with the bottle in one hand and the paper cone of flowers in the other.

In the flat she went at once to the bathroom and turned the tub taps half on. She shook some bath salts, scented and effervescent, into the splashing water, then, turning, she looked in the long mirror set in the door to see if her eyebrows were straight. There were two stray hairs. She took a pair of tweezers from the medicine cabinet and plucked them out. There was only a small spot of redness on her brow and it would go away before she finished her bath.

She slipped out of her dress and put on a quilted house coat of black satin. She hung the dress carefully in her bedroom closet. It would, she noted automatically, need cleaning after another wearing.

She went into a kitchenette four feet square. She took a small squat vase of blue Mexican glass, ran some water into it, and thrust the flowers in, touching them once or twice to arrange them. They were not the right color for the room and they could not sit near her eyes, but the flower seller had nothing else but garish wilted roses. She could put them on the side table across from the divan.

In the icebox lay an onion with the top sliced off, beginning to shrivel. She peeled it and chopped it fine in a wooden bowl. She picked the foil from a lump of Roquefort cheese and mashed it in the bowl, moistening the mixture with a spoonful of rye whisky. When it was smooth, she spread it on little crackers filled with celery seed.

She took from the icebox a half-empty jar of Beluga caviar, a gift. She spooned it into a dish and looked around on her shelves for a different kind of cracker. Then she remembered—he always ate his plain with a spoon. She put two spoons on a tray and beside them she set the crackers on a platter. She unwrapped the gin, took off the top, and set it on the tray with a decanter of Scotch, a bottle of vermouth half gone, a soda siphon, and a tall thin jug to mix a cocktail in. From the table drawer she took a hammer and a screw driver and pounded the ice trays loose in the refrigerator. She ran warm water on them to loosen them and put the ice cubes in a dish. As he did not like napkins, everything was ready. She took up the tray and carried it into her living room and set it on a low table in front of the divan. She opened a small smooth silver casket. It was nearly full of cigarettes and there

29

were fresh books of matches initialed ME on the ash trays. If he came before she was fully dressed, she could let him in and talk to him from the bathroom.

Her bath was ready, a tub of thick foam. She stripped and took some bobby pins from the medicine cabinet to fasten the waves in her hair tightly against her head and pulled a black rubber cap down over them. Then she stepped carefully into the tub and sat down. Out of the wall across the tub she let down a tray full of lotion bottles, jars of cream, and a folding mirror. She did not notice how she looked in the mirror, for she was busy covering her face thickly with cream, rubbing it in with an upward motion, careful not to get any under the cap into her hair. Done, she lay back among the bubbles. It felt good. She was tired. Ten years ago, she would have washed her face with soap and water and she would not have cared how she felt.

Civet, castor, musk, or ambergris. Which? One of these, he had said, the *émigré*, the prince, against the lemon-yellow hangings of his shop, craned over her hand as if he would kiss her elbow. He had given her the bath salts, the cologne, and the *flacon* of perfume. "For you, a gift. It is a pleasure I allow myself. Flowers, no. You would kill the perfume of flowers. It would be a discord." She stirred the warm water with her foot and the breaking foam released a stronger reek of civet, castor, musk, or ambergris. (Which?) This was it. This removed the daylong pressure of the leather against the instep; this weakened the cicatrices of the garters so they would not show; the light galls of the ribbons on the shoulders disappeared; it cleaned and scented her. This was the pickle that had kept her fresh ten years and with luck would keep her ten years more. She stretched, relaxed, and limp, expectant, sighed.

Richard was back. She swirled the water in play and clucked cooing to herself. She knew. She knew what he wanted. My love from over the sea. Out of the black telephone his voice had come asking to see her. "It has been five years, hasn't it?" It was so long ago, and with a twinge of alarm she remembered their meetings like old, cracked and faded snapshots, it was that long ago, like a childhood. The garden party at the Embassy, the day it rained all morning and they had hurriedly erected a marquee and then the sun had emerged boiling hot, and everyone sweated under the striped canvas. A tall bony face with a mustache, and she could see the long, straight cylinders of his fingers holding a drink. "And you, *mignonne*" (which was a lie), he said. "What do you do here?"

"I'm one of the help. I translate things."

The day of their first meeting he had been very happy because he had wormed his way into a fifteen-minute parley behind a hedge with Alexis Léger, who seldom went to garden parties but lived alone with his mother and the secrets of Europe. Ah, Richard was lovely. Everything returned, uncracked, unfaded now.

What was this Richard? A foreign correspondent employed by the North American Newspaper Alliance? No. Sex: male; race: white; height: 6′1″; weight: 184; eyes: blue; hair: brown; married: yes? Certainly not. Hat so carefully from Locke, suit from Hall Brothers, Prince's Street, Hanover Square, shod by Peal, ties from Sulka on the rue de Rivoli? No. Richard was always without his clothes, lank, a light fell of black hair across his chest, the muscles full and no pooched-out belly. Definitely he was not his clothes. And he was not the time they had awakened that May morning in the *Rose Revived* and looked out over Berkshire through a latticed window and after breakfast played that simple game with coins, shove ha'p'ny and gone swimming under the willows in the Thames, nor the time they had taken a night train third class from the Quai d'Orsay to Perpignan and the train was full of soldiers, Sudanese, magnificent tall black bucks with white officers, and they had sat up all night long, Richard trading Lucky Strikes for wine for them both and she had learned to sing *Un beau jour, Villarette* and that other funny one, *Dans une tour de Londres*, from a Gascon *sous-officier* and there had been fog in the southern mountains in the morning. He was none of these times, well lit and sunny, accompanied by people. They were the green leaves of memory but not the flower, the sun on the feathers before the bird sang.

Richard like every man she knew identified himself in darkness. He somehow was music. There was one, a stockbroker by trade, and how she laughed about this, who was the sea; another was the mountains she had seen. There was a Negro on One Hundred and Twenty-

31

sixth Street with a long ellipsoidal head and a scar on his face whom she sometimes visited who was fire, all flames, yellow, blue, and green. She did not know why this was. In strangers there were hints in the eyes and in the movements of the hands, and sometimes if she saw them in the face of a cab driver pale above the dashlight and if it were late at night, her street empty, she would ask him in. He would get out of the cab mystified, reluctant, mumbling, "But jeeze, lady," and later he would come down and drive away, saying, "Boy, oh boy." She had heard them, listening above, naked at the window.

She could never tell. She knew she could never tell anyone. At Princeton coming in cold from a football game, warmed four times beforehand with a swig of scalding second-rate whisky out of the bottle in the darkness behind the locked door of a back room in a dining club, there, pressed down on a frayed leather sofa among the coats and hats, she had discovered her endowment. And when they were through, the boy had led her blinking through the lights, the smoke, and the people out under a tree. Standing before her, his vest buttoned wrong in haste, he had put his hands on her shoulders and whined, "Margery, say you'll forgive me."

In fourteen years she had made herself, discreetly, a woman who could be had without any consequences, and with extravagant courtesy she gave her friends the pleasures of a long chase, the tricks and sleights, poutings and withdrawals, performed with great neatness because they were calculated, the compliments of the management. It was very amusing—she always had to show herself as a prey. What would it do to the character of a hound who was run to earth by a fox? This was why, lest Richard presume on his homecoming, she had asked Henry Verplanck to come in for a cocktail also at six-thirty. Henry was an amateur psychiatrist of some sort. When he looked at you, you felt that he was always suspecting something, blandly but shrewdly. Yet he was solid and at forty imposing, and Richard could not think she was impressed by his return, salted as it was by the appearance of a rival.

She sat up in the tub suddenly and began to remove the cream from her face quickly with tissues. As soon as it was gone she soaked bits of cotton in an astringent lotion and patted it over her face. She moistened the cotton again with the lotion and leaning back lay still a moment with the cotton over her eyes. Then she sat up in the tub winking and opening and shutting her mouth rapidly. She dried her face a last time with tissues, applied powder with a lamb's-wool puff, touched her cheeks with rouge, and with wide-open eyes, looking sideways in the glass, she drew the narrow line of her eyebrows with a pencil. Last she designed the shape of her mouth again with lip salve on her little finger.

She pulled the plug of the bathtub with her toes, fitted the tray back into the wall, and stood up in the sinking water. Dried with a rough towel, she painted her armpits with a deodorant, blew a steam of cologne over herself with an atomizer, and dusted herself with powder from a puff on a stick, not thinking coherently, nothing she could put into words, no pictures, because what she was trying to remember and anticipate happened in darkness, the eye was nothing and for the sound, the music inside herself, the ear was a useless curlicue. The true center where it all took place was equipped only with the present tense, yet the effort to recall her pleasure pleased her.

While she waited for the deodorant to dry, she looked at herself in the long mirror. She did it after every bath. She lifted her chin and turned her face first one side, then the other—there was no roll of flesh there. Leaning forward, she scanned her neck for lines on the throat beneath the ears and hollows along the clavicle. She lifted her arms. They were firm and round. Her breasts were heavy but did not sag. She turned in profile—she would never need a girdle if she stayed this way. She only glanced at her legs. They had always been good and they would be the last to go. She was lucky with her feet. They were small—she wore a size five shoe—and they were uncramped, straight, and shapely. It is, she thought looking upward over her body, it has been a beautiful instrument, a tool that fits men's hands very easily, and a weapon if I have to have it.

When Miles came, he sat in an armchair facing her. She reclined on the divan with her feet up. If you curled up with your calves pressed against your thigh, the muscles were mashed flat. She stretched one leg out accurately at the angle that would best take his eye. He would want time to appraise her, and all she was doing was waiting

33

until her display could take effect. Although she did not believe that talk meant anything in an affair of this kind, she talked, asking what she thought he wanted her to, each answer a fair counterpoise to his question, bright, pleasant, and welcoming but only waiting really.

"You were in Warsaw, weren't you?"

"Yes."

"Somebody told me about your stories. I didn't run across any. How was it there?"

"It was an excursion, a conducted tour. I was with the Germans."

"How was it really?"

"They were showing off. They let you see nearly everything. You've seen the pictures they took, haven't you?"

"Some."

"Well, the pictures are bad enough but they leave out a lot. The smell, for instance."

"Was the smell bad enough to send you home? I thought you liked wars."

"I never liked them. I was sent to them. Once in a while you saw something that—oh, I don't know—take Madrid."

"You were all through that too, weren't you?"

"Yes. There was a lot of war there, but it was the way it might have been with Lee in Virginia before they sent Grant east. There was a chance for a long time. One man, an individual, could do something. There were exploits, you might say. In Poland, no."

"So you came home."

"You get so sick of it, and it doesn't help to know you are watching history unravel. Five hundred years from now, you see, the historians will say that this was one of the wars that destroyed nationalism as an idea. Before this show is over, they'll be fighting everywhere and whoever wins will have to take responsibility for the whole world. If Germany wins, it's rule by force. If it's the Allies, some sort of equity will be established, I hope. But either way, it's the whole round globe."

"You're more serious than you used to be."

Miles looked at her a moment, knowing that she did not understand or care. "Oh, this beautiful detachment is easy here. But I have seen dead people in the streets. And their houses sheared right through the

34

middle with the dust still coming up. The clock still ticks and maybe dinner is on the table, and history seems a hell of a long way off." He continued more lightly. "I didn't feel like hanging around to watch the new internationalism flower in the corpses and the dust heaps, and then too— Constance died. . . ."

"Oh, I'm sorry. That's too bad. Or—is it?"

"No, it's not too bad."

"You've never talked to me about Constance before. What was the matter with her?"

"Tuberculosis. Her mother implied that I infected her deliberately."

"But you've never had it."

"No. I hadn't seen Constance in seven years. Her mother doesn't like me, that's all."

"You're too late for the funeral. What did you do—come back to weep at her grave?"

"I came back to ask you to marry me." It sounded well. It came out pat and it had enough truth in it to make it stand up. And he felt that once he had said it, enthusiasm would follow.

"*Marry* you?"

"Yes. Why not?"

"It's terribly flattering, Dick, but . . . You took the vows literally, didn't you? 'Until death do us part.' Didn't the divorce take?"

"Don't tie into me because I'm late. I know I should have asked you before. I should have spoken up in Paris, but you wouldn't have had me then. You wouldn't even have considered it. You know you wouldn't."

"And I won't now," she said, softly, smiling.

"Because I'm the ten-o'clock scholar?"

"Don't be a fool. I haven't changed. I won't marry you now for the same reasons I wouldn't then."

"Why not?"

She thrust out her hands, bare of rings, palm down for him to look at. "I'm not bespoke. That's the first thing that came into your head, isn't it?"

"Why won't you marry me?"

"Please don't get grim and dogged with me, Richard," she said

35

facetiously. Then she went on in a natural, everyday voice, "Ask me what's wrong with you. That's the next step."

"Well?"

"There's nothing wrong with you. I like you as well as any man I know. Better, I guess." She stood up, bent over suddenly, and offered him the crackers with the cheese. "Here, have a cracker." She began to walk up and down. "Be realistic. Be practical. What would it get me, Dick? Do you like this apartment? Would we live in a better one?"

It was bright, sparsely furnished with conservatively modern furniture. There were some colored Van Gogh prints on the walls and an original drawing by Vertès. It was clean and comfortable, and her marigolds gave it a touch of freshness.

"Do you want me to show you my bankbook, Margery?" he said, putting on a stupid look.

"Well, what would it get me? Look, I make a hundred dollars a week. . . ."

"Are you on the radio?"

"You never write letters, do you? If you did, I might have written you. I work on a fashion magazine. Oh, I know. It's a joke, but they think I have taste and I write little blurbs about Mona Williams and Liz Whitney."

"And a hundred dollars a week is all you want."

"Translated it nearly is. I can get clothes cheap because of my job. They give me second-night tickets to all the plays. The rent isn't very much, and I know a lot of people."

"And you're f-r-e-e," he sang. "You talk like a man."

"I'm not, though."

He got up and made himself another drink. "You know, I'd forgotten New York was like this."

"Like what?"

"Everybody talks just the way you do. Flippant, sassy. Now that I'm back I do it, too. Why? What's funny about asking a woman to marry you?"

He knew this kind of talk. All New Yorkers picked it up when they came here along with the conviction that something wonderful

36

must happen tomorrow. It was the conviction that kept them here, hurrying anxiously to and fro, some adopting rubber heels to soften the day's eight thousand shocks, some learning sometime, some never, that it is only the conviction that is wonderful. The clever ones, the successful, the naïve—like Margery—acquired this manner to hide their disappointment. It was beauty's false bosom, the sun-lamp tan of the old beau. They had to show they had not been deceived. Perhaps if he kept talking this way long enough, they might arrive at a point—how far away?—when they would run out of situations she had attitudes to cover, and then he might talk sincerely and mention his daughter.

"Seriously, Dick, then. Why do you want me to?"

"Why don't you want to?"

"I don't want to get married. It's not you—it's the institution. You spent some years in it. You ought to know. I like it the way I am."

"A spinster."

"All right. A spinster."

"You're thirty-one years old."

"So you'd stoop to threats."

"Thirty-one."

"Do I look it?"

"No, you don't, but—this gets rather hackneyed here—but have you ever thought of children?"

"Yes, I have, and from time to time I have taken precautions not to have any."

The buzzer sounded.

"That must be Henry," she said and got up to press the button.

"Who's Henry?"

"Henry Verplanck. He's very nice. He's a psychologist, a psychiatrist, I think, only he doesn't practice. He's an amateur."

Henry Verplanck was six feet tall, with sandy hair, light, mild eyes behind gold-rimmed spectacles, and a plump well-battened face. He came into the room, awkward, polite, carrying a long box of flowers and a new book for Margery. Irritated by this arrival, because he himself had forgotten gifts, because he had not thought they were necessary, Miles merely nodded his head at the introduction and sat down again.

"Richard's just back from Warsaw, Henry. You've heard me speak of him."

On the divan Verplanck moved his head forward out of the carapace of his brown suit. "Is that so?" he said in a voice that combined interest and surprise. He seemed to expect Miles to answer.

"Yes," Miles said. "Just got back."

"Those poor people. I am very sorry for them but you more than I, since you saw it directly. But your dispatches allowed me to respond somewhat. As a correspondent, you aroused my sympathy."

"What I wrote was only an account, not a plea."

"You yourself did not pity them?" Verplanck asked in a shocked voice.

"Oh, sure, but you have to write facts for a news service."

"Richard has seen a lot of war," Miss Elliot put in.

"And naturally the antennae become blunted. You would not respond as—as fervently to the second or the fifth as to the first. Yet the facts themselves were very moving. I found myself imagining the effect of a prolonged bombing—as a human being, of course—the terror while unharmed, and the gradual inuring oneself to the terror. Is that true, Mr. Miles, does one became inured to terror, careless of it because it is familiar?"

"It's better if you are with people. If you are alone, in a house or an apartment, I suppose it depends on the individual."

"Yes. It must. Your experience there must have been very illuminating, to be able to observe the results of mass physical trauma on that scale. It is hard enough to keep oneself steady and recognizable under the strains of peace, but war . . ." Verplanck clucked. "It must have been absorbing."

"Quite," Miles said rudely.

"You are now employed in New York, Mr. Miles?"

"Not yet. I probably will be."

"What are you going to do, Dick?"

"I don't know. Colston Leigh is after me to lecture."

"In a cutaway. Are you going to?"

38

"No. I'm still footloose."

"I hope you will have dinner with me sometime soon. I should like extremely to talk about the war." Verplanck brought out a wallet of black leather and with niggling care opened a compartment in it and slid out a card. "Here is my card." He held it in his hand and fished in his inside coat pocket.

Miles stood up. "I must run along."

"Just a second, Mr. Miles. I'll put my phone number down." Verplanck had found his pen. Holding the card on his knees, toeing in, he wrote the number. "If you'll call me first, please." He gave a very pleasant smile that broke the smooth fatness of his face.

"Thanks," Miles said.

Miss Elliot went to the door with him. She was annoyed. Miles had changed. After her efforts to keep herself the same, it made her feel that time was passing, had past, and it was abhorrent. "I'm sorry Henry came in just when he did."

"Oh, it's all right. I was finished."

"Now don't go off and sulk just because I won't marry you, Dick. Call me tomorrow, will you?"

"Yes. I'll call you."

"We might have dinner."

"Well, I'll see you then," he said. He went out into the darkening street.

He was not really disappointed that Margery would not marry him. His proposal was jetsam he had thrown overboard to test the current that was carrying him. After years of acting quickly, brusquely, with what may have been an illusory freedom (yet the illusion was perfect) he was mystified that he should have left Europe without a sound reason, and now confused, he became wary and looked for signs and omens as he had done when he was a boy. He once had carried papers, the local daily, in the town where he was born. It took him from four o'clock in the afternoon to six to cover his route. At six, he would often walk over the whole route again with his empty bag in the growing darkness because he was sure that a girl named Ernestine, two years older, the cook's daughter at the hotel, would love him if he did. He had done many childish tricks to compel the future. Now grown older

39

he was thrown back upon this augury. His work had been to interpret and foretell for a million readers the sleights of parliaments and the frights of little kings, and now he could not even trust his hindsight for himself, one man. Bitterly, he said he ought to have a caldron, a mess of shoulder bones of sheep, and a flight of pigeons to read the guts of.

"And there is another sign also," he told himself sarcastically. "I am being warned by the passive voice."

She had lain on the divan against the pillows and across her a stripe of light from the door that opened into her courtyard. All through the bright smart twitter that led to his proposal he had been looking at her, the curve of her hip repeated in her calf, her breast lifting as she lifted her arm. The talk had been a meaningless obbligato. He wanted to go to bed with her and with a rake's caution he had wanted to see her first to gauge if she were still worth a night. That was all his visit had meant, he surmised, not marriage, no care for his daughter, merely a weather flag.

Margery was thirty-one years old, that was right. She certainly looked good. Well, she took care of herself.

"I am thirty-eight years old and I look good and I take care of myself," he thought.

He had taken care of himself and only himself too well. He had been able to live for fourteen years on a talent he had never examined on a Continent he had never understood, seeing it as a goose sees the country it flies over going south, honking. Whatever adolescence was, it had congealed in him and now he must slough it off.

What about the daughter, this Mary? Why couldn't he take an apartment and the job the syndicate had offered him, bring her to New York, and, well, just live? To say it keenly and boldly to himself like this made him wince. It was simple; it was obvious; it was what a friend would advise. He saw all that but murkily felt that it was not the solution, and he allowed objections to float into his mind. Better to have the flat ready before she came. It might throw the schedule of her education out of gear to remove her hastily from school. Then a more solid reason: which in this little architecture was his bone, which from Constance? She had been taught to hate him.

Would she like him now? Would it be wise, even a kindness, to uproot her? He began to walk faster through the emptying streets, to look about him sideways and upward toward the windows high above him shining in the late sunlight. He would go to his hotel and write her a long letter telling her to stay where she was for a while.

3

A<small>T SEVEN O'CLOCK</small> Henry Verplanck left Miss Elliot's and walked toward University Place. At a lamppost he bought the evening papers. He crossed the street and went into the Hotel Lafayette to eat his dinner. He asked for a small table at the side of the dining room and ordered a *carbonnade de boeuf à la flamande*, *rissolé* potatoes, a salad, and coffee. Waiting, he read the papers.

It was early and the dining room was nearly empty. Behind him two waiters spoke in French. Stimulated by the war, one had written to his brother at Lyons for the first time in eighteen years. The letter had been returned only today: *Adresse Inconnue—Mobilisée*. The brother was twenty-eight years old, *il s'y connaît en machines*. He worked in a factory at Lyons. The other waiter said there was nothing to worry about. The Boche would not attack this winter, and the brother meanwhile would live with all the comforts in the casemates of the Maginot Line. The first waiter wished to point out with clarity that he did not worry about his brother; he had never liked him. He was thinking rather of France. . . .

As Verplanck sat listening, he decided that nothing could be learned about war by a single observer. War was a mass phenomenon. There were too many individuals in a nation at war to come within the scope of one man. Then, too, in any mass action there was a pitch of emotion? Perhaps; anyhow a moment of psychic tension when the individual reaction ceased to have definition as such and began to lose itself in the action of the mass as a whole. The pitch, the timing of the moment, would probably vary with the intensity of the stimulus. If the stimulus were great enough, would all people behave alike? Take the bombardment of Warsaw. Was it severe enough to make all people take cover, and if it was, would they think and feel alike, crouched in cellars and areaways? Would adrenalin be secreted at the same rate in all and would the resulting conscious emotion be terror? Terror as fear of death, cessation of the self, or terror as fear of pain? It might be possible, he thought, buttering a hard roll, to ascertain these things, to watch the population of a whole city acting and feeling in absolute concert, given the simultaneous explosion of enough thousand-pound bombs. But, of course, there would be the difficulty of getting around the city fast enough oneself to note them all. Probably few taxis would be available. Still it would be very interesting. This Richard Miles, he was stupid but he had seen it. He would ask him.

The waiter brought his dinner.

"Oh, thank you," he said. "It looks very good. No. No wine."

He propped his paper against the oil and vinegar cruets and read the news while he sliced the tender beef and the potatoes and forked them into him, flecked with brown crumbs of onion. He was well into the editorial pages with the salad, and as he sipped his coffee and smoked a cigarette he read about the early college football games. When he had finished, he paid the bill and left the waiter a fifty-cent tip. It was the waiter with the mobilized brother.

"I hope you find your brother," Verplanck said.

"You understand French, sir?" The waiter was old and courteous.

"A little. Your next letter ought to reach him."

"It is nothing if it does not. He is, he's—*c'est un maquereau.*"

43

"Oh, I'm sorry to hear that."

Verplanck passed out of the restaurant and took a cab in front of the hotel. He gave an address on Hudson Street and slid back on the slippery cushions. He was proud of his manners, his politeness. They made people trust you. The waiter had looked pleased when he said he was sorry his brother was a pimp. Pleasure at the benign attentions of strangers was always curious. Did it mean that low expectations were happily mistaken or was it a glow that came after being further identified and singled out of the crowd? All city people wanted that regardless of how it was achieved. I don't care what you call me, only spell my name right. Pleased and serenely full of beef, Verplanck watched the crowded sidewalks of the Village.

Hudson Street was not well lighted. The cab drove slowly along by the curb and stopped in front of a store that had ANTIQUES lettered on the window.

"This where you want it, mac?" the cab driver asked, looking back.

"This is fine," Verplanck said. He got out and paid him.

Beside the door was an old-fashioned bellpull. He pulled it and opened the door. The bell went on tinkling back and forth. He edged his way past tables and bedsteads in the dark shop until he came to a door at the back. He knocked once or twice and opened it.

In the room beyond, a woman looked around and a man with a red beard stood up.

"Oh, hello, Henry. We're just at dinner. Sit down. You'll have a liqueur with us, won't you?"

"Thanks, I will, Seward. Where do you want me to sit?"

"Oh, put it anywhere. Over there'll do."

Verplanck sat down on the large unmade wooden bed, a moil of pillows, quilts, and sheets with a gray nap of dirt. "How are you, Helen?" he asked.

"Eating, thank God," she said through food.

An electric stove with a single burner stood on an upturned wooden box. An aluminum pot heated on the stove. It seemed to be filled with a stew of some kind. The woman fed herself from the pot with a large spoon. The man picked out potatoes and pieces of meat with his

44

fingers, eating with gusto and licking off the gravy. He saw Verplanck watching him.

"Only spoons in the house, Henry, damn it. I won't have forks; the tines are sharp. Weapons breed dissension lying around and we scrap enough as it is." He seized the pot and offered it. "Here, have some. It's all beef, prime and juicy, what there is."

"It's shinbone, Henry, and I wanted steaks," the woman said.

"Steaks? What the hell would we do with steaks and no skillet? Sit on 'em to warm 'em? It has been done but only by Attila."

"We should have gone to Spain last year. You could have got a book out of Spain, poems or anything," the woman said. She was about thirty and plump, rum-bloat-plump.

"I know you for a woman," the man said. He continued to Verplanck. "This complaining tone is not unnatural. She eats like a horse. I went out today to look for work. No. I was sent for to be given work, that was it."

"Did you get it?" Verplanck asked.

"We'd have steaks if he got it," the woman said.

"I went up to this place. I was admitted, and there they all were crouched around the huddle desk . . ."

"The huddle desk?"

"That's what he called it. It was a big semicircular table with scallops cut in it like a pie crust. In every scallop sat an ad writer on a little chair. They all leaned forward—in a huddle, see? It was a conference." He lit a cigarette. "The Chief looked up when I came in, wiggling his head and blinking, *you* know, striving to shake off this fierce concentration. He recognized me. 'Stephenson,' he shouted, 'what is it everybody wants? What is it they want more than anything else in the world?' The other slaveys looked up too. Did I hold the key? I, the messenger from the outer chaos?"

"Well, did you?" Verplanck asked.

"He kept it up. 'What is it everybody wants more than anything?' I stood and studied making like I was lost in thought. At last I said, 'Everybody wants to be dead.' They all turned and looked at each other astounded, their glimmering, shimmering miniature minds arrested—was this the answer? Was it right or wrong? Was this the

45

slogan that would sell the product? I could have counted five while this electric silence lasted, before their brains meshed. The Chief recovered first. 'Hell,' he shouted. 'That won't do.' "

"What was the product?"

With forced meekness, sighing as if with regret, Stephenson said, "A breakfast food. *Eat Cream of Corn—it'll just kill you.*"

He reached down beside him and brought up a square tin gallon can. Out of it he poured three fingers of a clear liquid into a small glass. Without rising he took a lemon from the mantel behind him and with his fingers tore off a tatter of lemon skin. He dropped this into the glass and offered it to Verplanck.

"Ever since the closing of the monasteries," he said soberly.

Verplanck tasted it, bracing his throat. It was grain alcohol.

"This man didn't want you to write ads, did he?"

"Ads, pah! It was radio. I was to fill the mouth of that great voice."

"But you didn't. Something went wrong, I daresay."

"You're a bold man, Henry, to dare greatly. He was a very strange guy. He began by saying that the radio business was one long cliché, him, an advertising man."

"He said cliché?"

"Yes. He might even have been to college. Some little secret academy probably. He was well dressed too. His necktie was practically what Charvet calls a scarf. I thought maybe he was intelligent."

"But he wasn't, I take it?"

"Huh. You listen. He said he had a client who was eager to put on a daytime serial. 'A soap opera?' I ask. 'That's just it,' he said. 'My client doesn't want anything like a soap opera. He's sick of them. He wants to revolutionize daytime serials.' I said it was time that radio had its Lenin and be damned if he didn't say, 'Exactly.' You see? A fooler. He had a rind of right answers."

"Well, what went wrong?"

"Oh, everything eventually."

"How?"

"It was quite gradual. He wore a seal ring in a green stone. You know the kind, heavy, ornate. It was a false note . . . his clothes were right and his talk was right, so far, that is. I kept watching that ring. We

46

went on sparring. I let fly a few times about what I thought was wrong with radio, how it was, as a medium, thin and ever shall be because it provides the listener with only an aural image—my God, that's beautiful, 'only an aural image.' Listen to it. I'll just fix that while it's fresh."

Stephenson bustled eagerly from his chair before the cold fireplace to a desk in the corner. It was piled with books, and a shelf of books, old ones in leather bindings, was nailed to the wall over the desk. From a pile of manuscripts, bills, and letters, Stephenson pulled an envelope and stuck it into an old portable typewriter. With his two middle fingers, he typed out "only an aural image" and repeated it aloud with satisfaction. "I listen to myself to catch the beautiful rhythms of our common speech. I, πώητης."

"It really isn't very good poetry, do you think, Seward?" Verplanck asked mildly.

"Shut up, you bloody psychologist. There's no poetry in schizophrenia."

"By the way, Seward. That friend of mine bought your long poem."

Stephenson got up from the desk and walked over to Verplanck. "How much?"

"A hundred." Verplanck took out the bills and offered them, limp across his palm.

"My God," the woman said. "Why didn't you tell us when you came in?"

Stephenson did not take the money. "When does the first issue of this magazine come out?"

"Any day now, he said."

"Just who is this guy?"

"A silent partner. He doesn't want his name attached to the enterprise in case the magazine doesn't succeed."

"Come on now, Henry. Don't gimme that stuff."

"I'm not giving you any stuff, Seward. You wouldn't know this man. He's from Ohio. The magazine's going to be published out there. He's in New York just to get material."

"Why don't you bring him around then? Introduce him as Mr. X. Hell," he said, flinging his hand toward the desk, "I've got a hundred items he might buy."

"I'll bring him. He's up in Westchester right now."

"You don't have to work in mysterious ways your wonders to perform. *Is* there a magazine?"

"Seward, shut up," the woman said crossly.

"There is a magazine," Verplanck said.

"And this guy bought my piece for a hundred bucks?"

"You see it."

Stephenson sat down slowly. "Thanks a lot, Henry." He looked at the woman. "I guess we'll be all right now for a while."

"He might want some more poetry," Verplanck said. "I'll give you his address when he leaves town."

"I'd feel a hell of a lot better about it if you gave me his address before he left town. If this is some more of your skulking charity . . ."

"I don't believe in charity," Verplanck said.

"Let me see the money, Seward," the woman said.

Stephenson gave her the money folded haphazardly, damp from his hand, and watched her count it, smooth it, and lay it out neatly across her palm like sliced bacon. He stared without knowing it, leaning forward, mimicking the movements of her hands with his own empty ones. He ticked off the five bills with his forefinger as she counted them over, nodding his head in time, happy. Then awaking to this dumb show, he sat up, pulled his beard, and smiling said to Verplanck, "She likes money."

"Tell me more about this radio job," Verplanck said courteously.

"Oh, forget it, Seward. Please forget it and let's have a party. You don't have to go anywhere, do you, Henry?" the woman said eagerly.

"One moment, wench. You keep the brooms and pots." Stephenson sprawled at ease in his chair, pulling his red beard, clever again. "As I say, the Chief deceived me. He spoke grammar, an advertising man. He flushed a covey of poetical references. He gave me, in short, a seasoned imitation of a literary man. I thought it was going to be a real job. What he wanted was to put the American small town on the air. *Ah, Wilderness* was the note and I could do better if I liked. It all sounded very good. We went on talking. He bought me a rich, indigestible lunch with wine and see-gars."

"Well, how did it all end?"

"Henry, it is not wickedness we fight. It's innocence."

"You can make a sound observation occasionally. What did he want?"

"He wanted a show about a middle-aged fat man in a 1910 town who was always doing kind deeds."

"That's all right, isn't it?"

"Nothing but kind deeds? You're fat. You're past your first youth. Do you do kind deeds?"

"He brought us the money," the woman said.

"Only the Red Cross is monotonously benign. There are people Henry hates—we happen to be his friends. Given the right situation, Henry would be a stinker. I am merely defending your humanity, you understand."

"You are very kind," Verplanck said.

"What this innocent adman wanted was a benevolent Nosey Parker, seamy with charity, pocked with kindness, and when I suggested that nobody was like that, he was astounded. I pointed out that there were about forty people on the air who gave perpetual care to their neighbors—the age, sex, and poundage varies, of course, but they are all the same. I argued about it, but he really wanted an imitation of all the rest. As for plot: something simple, credible, he said. You could have gangsters come to the town and the fat man run them out, and this lively action could be paralleled by a clean love affair between a youth and a maiden. Simplicity, that was what he wanted. His front—that 'cliché'—and his clothes were just tricks he had learned and remembered the way you remember addresses and telephone numbers."

"How did you escape from this wicked man?" Verplanck asked.

"Simplicity, he kept saying, that's the keynote. Like a loaf of bread. 'What I want in this show is a loaf of bread.' I told him I would think it over and left, and at the first delicatessen I saw I bought a loaf of French bread about three feet long and had it sent up to him by a Western Union messenger. . . . Feh! let's get drunk."

"That's what I've been trying to say, but you wouldn't let me get a word in edgewise," the woman said.

Stephenson seized the gallon can and shook it. It sloshed and tinkled a little.

"I'll get brandy. Give me some gelt."

The woman handed over one of the twenty-dollar bills.

"Put the others in the dictionary. I'm just going up to the corner. I'll be back in a minute," Stephenson said and went out. They could hear him whistling and banging against chairs and tables in the dark shop outside the room.

The woman got up and put the rest of the hundred dollars in the big dictionary as Stephenson had commanded. Verplanck noticed that she wore broken huarachos and no stockings. The huarachos slapped on the floor when she walked.

"That's our bank. We always put money in the *M* section." She sat down again and poured out the last of the alcohol and seasoned it with lemon juice.

"How has he been lately?" Verplanck asked.

"The same as ever," she answered with some defiance.

"Is he drinking much?"

"We drink when we have the money. It's not often. This alcohol is on the cuff at the drugstore."

"What is he working on?"

The woman did not answer. Verplanck could not tell what she was thinking.

"He works all the time. You know that. Why do you always ask these questions?" She was very angry and trying not to show it.

"Don't be so jealous of him, Helen. I'm interested in Seward. You know that."

"And you give him money."

"No. I just sold a poem for him, that's all."

"I don't believe it. You're rich and you think you can . . ." She stopped. For something to do, she bent over, picked up the empty gallon can, shook it, and set it down again. She straightened up, smiled, and said in a friendly voice, "Look, Henry, go get him, will you? He's at Joe's Place—to your right as you go out the front door at the end of the block. He ought not to spend this money on bar drinks."

Joe's Place catered to men only. There was no place to sit down. Verplanck saw Stephenson standing with one foot on the bar rail, half facing another man whose back was to the door. Stephenson was talking with great earnestness.

"Hello, Henry. You've heard me speak of Preston Maury. He's from Virginia," Stephenson said, as if Virginia were heaven or Cathay.

A tall, well-dressed young man sagged, straightened, and mumbled something that ended with a loud, "Suh." Then he held out, formally, a groping hand.

"I don't like to intrude, Seward, but Helen sent me after you."

"Lilies," Stephenson said and pointed. On the bar in front of him lay three wilting calla lilies wrapped in a newspaper. "I bought lilies for her. Lilies and brandy. Home long ago but here was Pres looking for me."

"I know you live near here," Maury said slowly.

"We'll just have another quick one. Joe!"

The barkeep filled their glasses adroitly and waited near them behind the bar. Stephenson took his.

"We'll have a toast. You like a toast, don't you, Pres?" To Verplanck, Stephenson said, "Pres likes a toast. He lives on an estate. Tidewater. Niggers. Terrapin. All formal. Where's your wife, Pres?"

"Home." He looked at Stephenson a long time blankly. Then he smiled. "You ole drunk devil you, how come you so drunk? Ole Steve."

Still seriously, Stephenson said, "Pres hunts foxes. He has a pack of hounds, English foxhounds, Peterborough standard, by God." He reached out and began to finger Maury's lapel. "Feel of that, Henry. English clothes. He has 'em sent over. A gentleman. He lives on an estate. Us Yankees burned it once." The glass was still full in his hand. "He married a beautiful girl. Most beautiful girl in Richmond." The glass spilled on his thumb. "Propose a toast, I will . . ."

"Most beautiful girl in Richmond. Go on, Steve, tell some more about me," Maury said.

"Come on, Pres, drink a toast."

"O.K.," Maury said, and tossed the whisky off.

"Whoa!" Stephenson cried. "Now we gotta have another for the toast." He drank his drink. "Joe!"

"Seward," Verplanck said. "Helen's going to be sore if you don't . . ."

"Helen? Pres, I give you Helen." He lifted his glass to touch Maury's.

"Here's to General *Lee* and his di*vis*ional com*man*ders, *Long*street, *Jack*son, *And*erson, Mc*Laws* . . ."

"Hey, Pres, cut it out. We're drinking to Helen."

"O.K." He drank. "Who's Helen?"

"Who is she?"

"Helen."

"Have you ever seen marshland in the spring with the wind on it? The wind's grace among the rushes is her grace."

"Go on, Steve. Say some more." Maury saw Verplanck watching him. "Ole Steve. Sure is one slick little ole talker."

Stephenson had struck a pose, one hand on his chest, the other with its empty glass stretched out.

"When tears of dew break and run so lightly down the petals of a flower—that is her fragility. More beautiful than heartbreak, God damn it. Tender as a kind touch on the head of a hound. This is Helen."

Maury cheered, then said, "Where's she at?"

"Safe in our little mews, working, probably. Faithful and kind. She loves me, Maury."

"Just lemme meet her. Just lemme shake her hand."

Without speaking, Stephenson paid the bill. He picked up the lilies and turned to Maury. "Come. You too, Henry. We will surprise her with our gifts. Wait . . . where's the brandy?" He slapped his pockets, searching. "Joe, a bottle of Hennessey."

When they reached the antique shop, Stephenson put his finger to his lips, "Shh—we must not startle her."

He and Maury tiptoed carefully through the aisle of furniture. Stephenson kept whispering, "Delicate—fragile—a lily."

And Maury would answer, "Come awn, lily."

At the door of his room, Stephenson paused. "Gently. This is her shrine." He straightened the stale lilies.

He threw open the door proudly.

The woman lay on the bed, naked for the night, fat, her stomach shadowed by her heavy breasts, and hanging over her shoulders two braids of hair. She threw down a magazine and shouted, "You God-damn drunken bastard! Where have you been?"

She was drunk. They were all drunk, except Verplanck, who walked quietly out of the shop.

Henry Verplanck was well pleased with the evening. He let himself into his apartment on East Thirty-eighth Street quietly so as not to wake Charles, his servant. Charles was a Negro seventy-one years old. He read his Bible every night and went to bed at ten o'clock unless Mist' Hinry was entertaining. As he had been chef in a club in Balti-more, Verplanck treated him with great kindness.

He walked carefully upstairs, avoiding the fifth and seventh treads of the flight because they were squeaky. He tiptoed softly into his library and closed the door. It was a long, high room facing uptown, and there were bookshelves to the ceiling on three of its walls. They were chiefly on philosophical, biographical, psychological, and medi-cal subjects. A file cabinet stood beside his desk.

Verplanck threw his hat and topcoat on a chair. He went to a liquor cabinet and took out of it a bottle of brandy and a siphon. In a tall glass holding about a pint he made a drink. He drank it warm, for if he went to the kitchen to get ice, Charles would hear him and try to get him to accept a cold lunch.

He took the bottle, the siphon, and the drink to his desk and sat down. He found a fountain pen in the center drawer and anxiously tried its point on a scratch pad. It wrote freely and he was pleased. It was late, quiet except for the faint roar of the city that never quiets, and he worked best then, calmly, easily, if he were not annoyed. From a side drawer of the desk, he drew a large mottled notebook like those used by college students. The edges were frayed and in the label on the front it said in his precise handwriting *Notes on Seward Stephen-son*.

To fix his mind on the subject, to give it a certain perspective for his work, Verplanck opened the notebook and commenced to read. Only a rare taxi horn disturbed him lightly. He read slowly, occasionally sipping his warm drink and sometimes looking out of the window at the lights of the towers and buildings always burning like jewels.

On the first page, after an index, there was a neat diagram of Seward Stephenson's family tree: father, Charles Stephenson, Jr., 1872-1925; mother, Caroline Seward, 1880-1907. The branches ascended the page only as far as a paternal great-grandfather, Eleazar. On the page following there were notes on the looks and characteristics of his ancestry as far as Stephenson had ever mentioned them: Charles Stephenson had been a minister, as had Charles, Sr., and Eleazar. He had had red hair, a fierce temper, and he had been close with his money. The grandfather of the female line had died of cancer but it had not turned up afterward in his children. Stephenson's mother had been sickly and had died bearing her only son. There was a phrase about her evidently quoted from Stephenson: "hammered on the anvil of the Lord." She had kept a spaniel. The family, it was easy to see, had been respectable, hard-working, and poor as the Protestant clergy are poor. All the males noted had been to college.

Further on there were the scattered details of Stephenson's childhood: he had been fond of animals and his father had allowed him to keep a pet goat with one horn. At seven he believed that the world ended mysteriously at his heels and wherever he was he was always whirling quickly to look over his shoulder or sneaking up to mirrors to see if he could catch a glimpse of infinity, a dark blue place full of stars. His first sexual experience, extensively described in Verplanck's neat hand, was at the age of five, when a little girl begged him to come under the front porch of the Presbyterian manse, his home, and "there they mutually exposed themselves." Charles, Jr., in accordance with a tradition of the family had taught his son Greek at home, and young Seward had entered Yale at sixteen.

Here Verplanck's entry was, "It was at this time that I met the subject personally." For a hundred pages or more, Stephenson's life at New Haven was described. He began to drink—it was then 1922—and to write poetry. With calm and precision, as if no one had or would ever write again about the period, Verplanck had given its political, moral, and psychological background, ". . . resentment against this unpopular law enacted as it was, when a large portion of the voting population was absent, manifested itself almost abruptly . . . felt to be an invasion of the personal liberties . . . the tenor of the law, strict, old-fashioned, and containing more than a tinge of hatred, was an exact projection of the latent Puritan mores of a large mass of citizens . . . the government had become too strongly paternal and each individual displayed in his violation of the law the natural but unconscious hatred of a son against a father."

With the background once elaborated, Verplanck discussed the "subject's" relations to it and his personal motives for drinking, "the childhood imitativeness . . . group conditioning . . . one of a multiplication of channels of ego extension concomitant with adolescence . . . impelled by purely social motivations, the subject endured, although with repugnance, his first harsh experience with liquor, until a personal motivation established itself, an appetite for the relaxation of the inhibitory processes resulting in a feeling of freedom and power."

A list followed of what Stephenson drank. He made gin in a crock out of alcohol, distilled water, juniper extract, and glycerin. He bought occasionally from his friends, the bootleggers, Canadian whisky in imperial quarts. Some speakeasies sold him applejack hastily distilled in New Jersey. Southern friends like Preston Maury returned from their summer vacations with corn liquor in charred oak kegs. There was a dark-red wine, almost black, that his friend Luigi's mother made in Westchester. On week-end trips to New York, he came to know the sailor joints near the North River piers, where, from Danes and Norwegians, he bought genuine Scotch whisky at twelve dollars a bottle, Ross' Irish whisky, sherries, clarets, and sauternes that he did not value because they were too weak, and he drank, gulping out of a teacup, aquavit, slivovitz, moustika, and more rarely liqueurs like Benedictine, Grand Marnier, and Goldwasser from Danzig. In Armenian restaurants where he ate boiled wheat and lamb wrapped in grape leaves he drank Greek wine, bitter and full of tannin. Sometimes, uptown, he would wander into conventions or parties given by frantically prosperous stockbrokers and there he filched champagne real and false. Once in one of the aimless automobile trips he made with his friends, he had stopped at a hobo jungle in Pennsylvania and Stephenson had drunk the liquid strained off canned heat with the bums. By his senior year he drank merely alcohol with a lemon squeezed into it if he had remembered to buy lemons. "No psychic or organic degeneration was noticeable in the subject at this time."

The next section contained only one page filled with newspaper clippings pasted on. They were reviews of: *Poems:* by Seward Stephenson, Knopf, $2.00. The reviews were favorable, "richness of imagery" . . . "a promising young man" . . . "a lost Elizabethan." The clippings were faded and beneath them was a blank space. Verplanck had made no comment.

March, 1933

The first evidence of organic involvement beyond changes extending the alcoholic tolerance was observed at this time. The subject made the rounds of the editorial offices with a sheaf of manuscripts. He had grown a coarse red beard. He was wearing a slouch hat, a penwiper greatcoat like an eighteenth-century highwayman's, and he leaned heavily as he walked with mincing steps on a heavy olivewood cane. It was his illusion that his feet, certainly small and delicate, were too frail to support his weight. With him he had three small mongrel dogs on leads. He did not notice their scrambles and barking and he treated them with great affection. He was entirely oblivious of the incongruity of his dress, of the stench of sweat and alcohol that surrounded him, and he was extremely courteous.

Upon investigation it was discovered that he had moved away from New York into Jersey City, where he had engaged a room above a public automobile garage. There was little furniture beyond a cot, a table, a chair, a washbowl, and a few books that he had been able to salvage after his discharge from his position as editor. Every morning on rising, he said, he was sick in the washbowl "and without expectation of childer, due to my mechanics, male as they are." It was evident from his tone and the offhand manner he used that it did not distress him. He regarded it only as a nuisance. He refused to submit to medical attention.

He supported himself during this period by writing verse for children, a "routine" that disgusted him since he could find no one to buy his more serious efforts. He accepted a loan of fifty dollars gratefully, and during several interviews he seemed to be cheerful and confident.

There was no sign of any permanent psychic disruption. He consumed, he said, about a quart of ethyl alcohol a day, mixed with a little water.

June, 1934

On Saturday, June 9, 1934, the subject made his first marriage, to Weir Halliday. She was twenty-six years old. The wedding took place at a justice's office in Waterbury, Connecticut, after a long motor drive during which he drank an entire bottle of Scotch whisky. He made the responses in a loud voice and when the justice asked him to speak lower, he offered to fight him. After the ceremony, the wedding party, including the investigator, ate a meal in a Greek restaurant. Dissatisfied with the food, the subject threw his dishes at the counterman and ripped the booth in which he sat away from the wall. He was arrested on a charge of disorderly conduct and spent his wedding night in jail.

Paid twenty-dollar fine. Loaned subject fifty dollars.

December 3, 1938

The regular visit to the subject disclosed that he had taken a mistress. He gave loneliness as his reason. The woman is three or four years younger than himself, a plump and disappointed writer. Whatever beauty she may have had now lies in a few nearly obliterated traces. The relations between them were tender and marked on the subject's part by what may be called his customary chivalrous affection.

As it was the anniversary of the first week with his new mistress, the subject demanded a "party." This consisted only in his drinking more rapidly than usual. His tolerance for alcohol has risen steadily to so high a point that a physical breakdown is probably imminent. An estimation of his consumption on this occasion would be three ounces of ethyl alcohol every half-hour for at least three hours. At the end of this time, his speech was unimpeded but somewhat louder than normal. The language became tart and florid. There was increased manual gesture. A slight dyspnea was evident. An opportunity to record pulse and blood pressure would have been welcome but obviously none was given.

Loaned Stephenson twenty-five dollars.

The entries in the notebook continued through the year 1938 and into the year 1939. Verplanck read slowly, drinking the brandy and soda in little sips, smoking one cigarette after another in a sanitary holder. When his glass was dry he filled it from the tray beside him.

He read all that he had written about Seward Stephenson. He picked up the pen, tried the point again, and began a new entry. In his dry, detached manner, he described the events of the evening: what he had found them eating; how Stephenson had refused the job; and the drunken comedy of its end. Before writing his conclusions, to get them clear in his head, to make sure they were honest, he paused and looked out of the window.

The subject refused to accept a job in radio out of pride. If Jung is correct in holding that personality is a kind of conscious principle of individuation, a deliberate selection from the ragbag of our lives of the events we will remember and of the "qualities" of which we wish to construct the Ego, then pride is at once the result of these selections in the past and the judge of future ones. When a man shows pride, the observer can induce from the act of pride not what the man is but what he thinks he is. There are two kinds of pride: the elation following the performance of something that will reinforce his conscious notion of himself, in the sense of being "proud of" something, and there is also, as in the case of this subject, the refusal to perform something he knows is alien to himself, something that if performed would change or contribute to the attrition of the "I" that he has counted on so far.

The subject needs money. He has accepted money for work repugnant to his "poetic talents" before this. If this repugnance were a constant element in his personality he would have refused to write the children's poems in the same spirit of pride he exhibits now. Since it is not constant, it is probable that his present show of pride is caused by factors immediately operating but unconscious. Thus, by the familiar process of substitution, his pride is a manifestation of an anxiety deeply rooted and unknown to him. At a signal from the Unconscious, he protects himself, his "I," in the only pattern of behavior he knows. It can hardly be doubted, then, that the real basis of his "pride" is a fear of physical disintegration caused by his drinking.

However, there is no overt evidence of great physical decline. The conditions of this study make a complete medical examination of the subject impossible. A slight vascular ecchymosis, acne rosacea, and distortion of the pupils of the eyes cannot be considered symptomatic, nor can the ataxia which was obvious toward the end of the evening—these are the stigmata of all drunkards. He is fat, but his father, a minister and a total abstainer, was fat also, and little can be drawn from this fact. Yet, granting his extremely high tolerance for alcohol, it is hard to believe that years of steady indulgence in massive amounts has not gravely impaired the internal organs. Some organic failure may be confidently expected. That this failure will be preceded by a commensurate disintegration of personality is probable but, considering the subject's tenacious hold on his basic identity, it is still a matter of fascinating conjecture.

Loaned Stephenson one hundred dollars.

Verplanck finished. He blotted the page, wiped the pen point on a bit of scratch paper, and read his latest entry over. It seemed to be accurate and sufficiently objective. He had taken pains and he was satisfied. He was a scholar.

4

T HE NUNS had come into town to buy a station wagon, and the two of them stood sorrowfully by the red gasoline pump, turning their shoulders to turn their heads, and the light flashing on their spectacles hiding their eyes when they nodded. They were not really sorrowful; they looked sorrowful because of the black of their habits and it was October and the leaves from the trees across the street had blown down hard and stuck yellow and scarlet on the wet sidewalk, and the nuns were nuns, and they taught and cooked and sewed their lives away and when they played tennis, they still wore their habits and looked funny. The brides of Christ, Sister Anastasia and Sister Anne Bibiana, nodding and stiffly turning, talking with Mr. Schaefer about wheel base and horsepower while she and the postulants stood in a clump and watched, waiting for the deal to get done.

Sister Anastasia did the buying for the school. They said she was old and shrewd, and she had brought Sister Anne Bibiana along to show her how to be shrewd also. Sister Anne was young and being old would come in time, but the shrewdness must be learned. Neither of the sisters looked old or young. The habits held their chins out plump and no hair showed and you could not tell. All nuns looked the same age and they stayed that way because the Church was eternal and they were each a part of the Church. She herself was young, however, and because it was October, the dying year, with all the leaves blown down and the nuns standing as sorrowful and eternal by the gas pump as they would stand so many nights at vespers in the chapel, she felt young and felt that she had too little time.

On Thursday nights the boiled beef was gray. It looked like a tired meat; and her father could teach her French better than the nuns, who were always asking her to save the French stamps on the letters from Paris. On the daily health walk Sister Mary Angeline pointed at the maples; "*Acer campestre*, remember," she said. She had said it twenty-nine times this term, always speaking of the maples, never of the elms. But the worst times were when Mother Crescentia met her in a corridor or called her into her office for a talk. Although she was a boarding student, the talks were to "search" her to discover if she had a vocation to the Church. The vocation was never mentioned but that was what the talks were for, and she was always embarrassed, ducking her head so as not to have to look at the holy light on the old woman's face and saying, "Yes, Mother," although it should have been "no," but it was better to be venial than mortal and if she had told Mother Crescentia that she could not understand the eternal glory of the Blessed Virgin or the Christ who sitteth at the right hand of God the Father, Mother Crescentia would have caught her breath and said that she had a pain in her side as she always did when someone had offended her. "Eternal" she could understand. It was eternal when the priest chanted *in saecula saeculorum*, the echoes throbbing through the nave. Eternal was the sound of the wind at night but not in the daytime, although that was foolish because the wind was always blowing somewhere, the trade winds up the Atlantic, the siroccos, the typhoons, and the hurricanes. Eternal was the blue glass knob on the drawer of the bureau at Grandmother's house when she was little. The bureau had been thrown away when the house was remodeled but it was really always there and she had put her eyes to the glass and looked down, down, down forever. And, of course, her soul was immortal. But the Blessed Virgin was always the bald woman holding the old-looking baby in the Fouquet picture in art class, she could not help it, and the Christ in the stained glass, the Christ in the Daily Missal, and the Christ in the statuary did not look like anyone she ever saw. She might have told Mother Crescentia about eternal but never in the world about Christ or the Virgin with the smooth dead face and the round, bare breast. None of this was what she wanted. She wanted to see her father.

But she was not supposed to. Her grandmother would prevent it if she could. On the last day, when Mother was dying, raising herself on her elbow, weak and tense until you could see the cords in her arm, to cough blood into the paper cup, looking over the rim of the cup with such wide eyes that she did not see her or Grandmother standing there or Father O'Connor with the vessel of oil, the coughing went on and on, a hopeless thing to do. When it stopped, Grandmother said, "I hope this satisfies you. You see now what he brought you to." And Father O'Connor had forgotten himself and shouted, "Get out. You're a terrible woman." It was then that she knew for the first time how much her grandmother hated her father. They had kept it from her before.

Probably the reason was that Grandmother's marriage had been so happy. No one had ever made happiness so nasty. On Christmas and New Year's, Grandfather's fraternity brothers would come to the house for eggnogs, all tanned old men with white hair; sometimes they wore tail coats, and Grandmother had her hair marcelled and wore all her diamonds. They would sing fraternity songs, *The Owl Song* and *Dear Old Shrine*, and Grandmother stood braced against the sideboard because she always drank too many eggnogs, weeping and singing and waving her silver cup in time. And when the singing was finished, the weeping would go on because Grandfather had been such a fine fellow and they all weren't getting any younger. The next day Grandmother was never ashamed because it was in honor of Austin. It was a rite. No man had ever been such fun, no man kinder or more considerate all his life. Which was more than Mother could say, of course. Married and divorced.

A year ago in the vacation when Mother was first taken sick, she heard the two women talking in the bedroom. It was not the scandal. The family had lived in the town long enough to stand that. It was not the scandal, she heard her grandmother's baritone say. It was her stupidity in ever letting it reach the point of a suit. Petulant as if she were annoyed with a woman her own age, Grandmother had scolded her mother for not having quite enough beauty, "When I think of the money we spent on your teeth and on that riding instruction to make your legs straight," for not having simulated more of an interest in his work, "What difference did it make? You could have pretended you liked newspaper work," and finally because she had not employed a whole catalogue of tricks and ruses as a glue to keep the two of them together. Her mother had coughed three or four times but she had said nothing in reply. And now that she was dead and no longer there to be scolded, Grandmother driving home without tears from the cemetery, clutching her hands in their black gloves, exclaimed, "Think of the disgrace. Think of it. Oh, how I hate that man." It was clear as she remembered these things that her grandmother would never turn her over to her father unless she thought it would annoy him.

She could not ask her grandmother to let her go, leave school and go away, because her grandmother would say things to her that she could not answer. She knew the answers, but her grandmother was old and because she was old she was right and asking would make the back of her throat ache and she would probably cry like a fool from merely excitement when the angry old woman would tell her that her father was a rotten drunken reporter who had wrecked her mother's life. She was not yet old enough to say right out, "He didn't wreck your life. All he wrecked was your schedule." She had figured that out by looking at the old electric coupé that was preserved on stilts of heavy wood in the garage, and by hearing her grandmother in gloves and a wide straw hat damning the zinnias because they flowered too late for the Garden Club show. She had learned it when she watched her clean her diamonds before a party with tiny, twisted spills of tissue paper, and she had sensed it most of all when her mother was sick and her grandmother had not feared it as a disease that might kill her daughter; she had resented it as an intrusion, like cockroaches in the drains. Everything was timed and planned and so it was safe, and if it was safe it was right, and the worst thing that could happen to you was to be surprised. She knew all this and in a year or two, sometime, she would say it, and that would be the time her grandmother would know she was an old woman and go change her will.

Yet she could not wait here in the wet street among the nuns and postulants, and she could not walk every day another year under the maples, *Acer campestre*, nor study and take sewing instruction and pray—this was the month of the Blessed Virgin—until she was old enough to face her grandmother, and she could not go to her father now, even though he was in New York and not Paris. The letter in her pocket had come this morning; ". . . and so I think you had better finish this term and maybe the whole year," he had written.

"Will there be a jack?" said Sister Anastasia.

"Oh, if a tire blows on you, Sister, you can always telephone us and we'll come right out," said Mr. Schaefer.

"Perhaps the house near by will have no telephone," Sister Anastasia said. "Will there be a jack included?"

"Yes, Sister."

"At the same price you quoted?" said Sister Anne Bibiana. The old nun smiled fondly at her pupil.

"At the very same price," Mr. Schaefer said.

Her father had blown a tire near Cerebère, coming from Barcelona in a stream of refugees, a baby born near him by the roadside, and because he had not thought to bring a spare and had no jack, he had been forced to leave the car, the whole car, he had written, and had hoofed on into Narbonne, a long way even on the map. For the lack of a nail the shoe was lost, for the lack of a shoe the horse was lost, and what did she lack that she had lost her father? It was her mother who had died, and in the church and on the mat of false grass by the grave, she had stood among the perfumed old women and she had felt nothing and she had searched herself to find it. "Poor child, now that you have lost your mother," the old woman began. Her mother was not lost—it was too easy when she shut her eyes to see her mother's pale, accusing

64

face and to recall her bitter voice. Once she had shaken a worn glove at him. There was a hole in the finger, worn through. There was, it seemed, no money for new gloves but there was always money found for gin. Her father had merely smiled. There were other times throughout her childhood, the same look, the same tone, and they always spoke in front of her because she was a child and would not remember. And at the end, when Father had not settled down, when he had gone away to Europe again "to bag Winston Churchill coming out of the House" and to eat "*homard*—it's a kind of crab—at La Pérouse" (such beautiful names, a jeweled beast of rubies, *homard*), the old accusing look on her mother's face had softened into bafflement, and, dying, into wonder. She was not lost; prayers were being said daily. It was her father she was losing somehow. It was not until after the funeral that any cable had been sent to him and he had written her from Paris, "Now that your mother is gone, I am coming home and we'll get an apartment and live together. We never have and it's time." And now this morning, the second letter had come, putting her off. "Wait another winter."

Didn't he ever want any calm? When the Bishop visited the school and she had knelt among others to kiss the rich episcopal ring, although she had determined not to, she trembled weakly and her mouth had filled with bile, and bending for the kiss she had nearly missed his hand through fear and nervousness because the Bishop was a famous man. What about her father, then among the lords and ministers? She had seen the photographs in the newspapers: the charming Blum who looked like a badger; the austere, genteel, one-armed and pious Halifax, a lord; Göring, cruel and tubby, whom her father called "Herr Marshmallow" in his letters. He had seen all these, the rulers of nations, and he must have trembled also or at least been jumpy. This was his work, to clack with echoing footsteps through the long halls of the great to interview them, a nerve-racking business. And when he was finished he could go to a hotel past the endless pairs of shoes in the corridors to open the door of a room that was always dark, with no one ever waiting there for him. It must be terrible, she thought, never to let yourself into a lighted room or be welcomed. And eating in restaurants ruined your stomach—even if it was Grandmother who said it, it still counted, except, of course, the *homard*, scarlet and splendid, at La Pérouse. Faintly—she did not dare come right out and wish for it—thrust back timidly to the edge of her thoughts, there was the dim hope that he was tired of the richness of his life, the strain and all the palaces and wars, and perhaps he would expect her, his daughter, to make a quiet place for him, it had never been quiet with Mother around, a place like the houses she passed sometimes on winter nights here in the town, with the yellow light streaming from the windows over the snow and inside were people, calm and happy.

The Sister said in sewing class, stitching away with gold thread on an altar cloth, "The home is the foundation of happiness." In baking a cake, it was the creaming of the sugar and butter together that was the important thing—you always stirred in one direction. He had put the recipe for salad in one of his letters, "Your mother always wanted canned peaches and mayonnaise, but this is a real salad." It was, roughly, three of oil and one of vinegar, although the waiters who made it for him never measured, and you must rub the bowl first five minutes with clove of garlic. She had practiced by permission with leaf lettuce and a wooden chopping bowl in the kitchen of the school while the cook nuns watched her, laughing. He liked corned beef—you boiled it all day with peppercorns. In roasting meats and broiling them, all directions were wrong—you could not estimate so many minutes to the pound, you must tell by the look of it, and a roaster, he said, was born, not made. She could darn socks. The nuns had let her learn instead of making herself a nightgown. And for the windows you could have drapes made of toile in bright colors very cheaply.

There must be something he wanted from her. After seven years alone in Europe, among the embassies and restaurants, there was no one essential to him unless, as she was beginning to hope, he was tired somehow. When she looked at his pictures, the one taken at Antibes in bathing trunks, and the formal one from Budapest, she could see how easily he could have got another wife if he had wanted another wife. He was thin and young-looking and from his face you knew he would never misjudge people or expect too much from them. He was not like the fathers of her friends whom she saw during vacations, men with glasses and bald spots and pussy little stomachs growing on them like gourds, who talked too loudly. Often when she touched her hair at the back of her neck she would catch them looking at her breasts and always when she crossed her knees, their glances would automatically dip and they would stare and she would have a flash of terror. They played golf and talked about business, and in his letters her father wrote only about people and places. And now, it was just possible that he was tired of them. Europe was no bigger than the state of Texas, and he had seen it all. He had interviewed all the great men of those tiny countries. It might be fatigue, she thought. He had come home for some reason certainly. He said it was to live with her. She was ready to make him comfortable, to love him and serve him—she was embarrassed to think of these words, so vague and so demanding, the sort of words nobody ever spoke right out seriously, but she meant them. They were the only ones that would do. He could trust her better than a wife, and to trust someone signified that she would never talk him over as if he were a stranger as she had heard her mother and her grandmother do. But she couldn't wait another winter. Three gray days in a row made her angry, and in the terrible nervous fragrance of spring she knew she would run away.

From a list made out in pencil, Sister Anastasia asked questions of Mr. Schaefer. How long was the wheel base? Was the windshield and the window glass shatterproof? But if it did shatter, what then? How many miles would the station wagon run on a gallon of gasoline? How often would the motor need oil? Was it true the battery required fresh water every thirty days? It seemed strange to her that air should weigh anything, but she supposed that thirty pounds of air was the right pressure for the tires? Sister Anastasia had examined the speedometer, the oil-pump gauge, and she had tapped the dashboard with her fingernail and asked if it were made of soybeans. She had heard the motor run quietly and smelled its burnt-paint odor. Over the fender she had peered, ignorant, beneath the hood at the tangle of wires and pipe, at the jagged stalactitic mass of the motor. She was a shrewd buyer, they said, and she had heard them say it. She enjoyed herself.

"How many passengers will it hold?" she asked.

"Seven not counting the driver. This one is roomier than last year's," Mr. Schaefer said.

"It should hold more. We do not want to make any more trips than we have to."

"It might hold more than eight if they were not too big."

Mr. Schaefer had married a Catholic and to avoid any argument he stood meekly once a week in the church, his dull eyes rejecting the mystery and the holy punctilio of the celebrant. He passed the hour sneaking glances at the congregation to see if he could discover a sales prospect, and if he did, soothed by the chant, he computed the prospect's bank balance. Mr. Schaefer was not pious. For him, nuns only prayed; they sang; they walked the streets silently in pairs, sliding the beads of the rosary between their fingers. They did not, they should not, buy station wagons and ask about the horsepower and the batteries and the tires and every other God-damned thing.

"The students are not big. The postulants are not big. We might try and see how many can get in comfortably," Sister Anastasia said.

"About nine, I think, Sister," Mr. Schaefer said.

"We will try," the nun said. "Sisters!" she called to the postulants. "You see there are seven postulants and one of our students, Mr. Schaefer. We'll just see. Sisters!"

Three of the postulants said, "Yes, Sister," and all of them moved forward a little toward the station wagon.

"Just climb in and sit down. All of you. Don't crowd yourselves, but don't sit too far apart either. Climb in."

They opened the doors of the station wagon and climbed in.

"Mary! Mary Miles!" Sister Anastasia called.

"Yes, Sister."

"Come over here and get into the station wagon. We want to see how many it will hold."

"Yes, Sister."

The girl left the wall of the building and, helped by Mr. Schaefer, climbed in and sat down in fifteen inches of space between a postulant and the door.

She could hear Sister Anastasia cry, "Shut the doors!" The doors slammed. "Roll up the windows, Sisters. I want to see if they work." Obediently the postulants rolled up the windows. Sister Anastasia stood with Mr. Schaefer outside, asking more questions, stroking and tapping the station wagon here and there as if she doubted its solidity. A murmur of talk rose from the postulants.

Inside the wagon it smelled of varnish and new leather and after a moment this mingled with the special odor of the postulants, an almost ammoniac reek of sweated cotton. The girl knew they were allowed to bathe once a week. It was the odor of sanctity, more than the frankincense at Mass or the cold smell of stone in the chapel.

Suddenly she decided to run away at once. The bank was open until three o'clock on Saturdays. If she could get away from Sister Anastasia she could go and draw her money out and she could slip out of the dormitory at night somehow.

She began to rap on the windows of the station wagon. "Sister, let me out! Sister!"

Her father would have to take her now. With Grandmother angry and with Mother Crescentia shocked and hurt and gasping about the pain in her side, there would be nowhere else for her to go.

"Sister!" she called.

5

H E HAD a drum on his back which he beat with a drumstick strapped rearward from his elbow. A brass cymbal was hitched to a thong around his waist, and he struck it with another in one hand. Leathers studded with little bells ran around his ankles, and, jigging and shuffling, stopping and stamping, he made them ring. In the midst of the jingle, the drumbeats and the clash ran a weak tune from a harmonica he fingered with his other hand. He turned in circles to look for an open door or window, nodding upwards a lunatic bearded face, smiling.

Naked, Miles watched him sleepily from the window. The fading clamor had wakened him. It was bright day and the line of brick houses opposite cast no shadow. He saw it was already afternoon.

Softly he turned from the window to see if she, feeling him gone, had wakened also. She lay on her side half covered with a sheet, her head on one outstretched arm. He saw the taut skin on her ribs gleam as she breathed. A mole was shining on one shoulder. The air was stale with perfume and the bed smell. He tiptoed out, teetering but unseen.

In the bathroom he washed himself quietly. It seemed appropriate. And stared at the bevel of his jaw in the glass—he could not shave here. Staring he saw Richard Miles up from his lechering, older now and home again, fagged and bearded. He had been too cautious to drink much and he had no hangover, but his head ached dully from the bad air in her chamber and the cold water on his face did not refresh him.

He had never seen anything in a mirror that pleased him. Like another touch or eyesight, when he was little, he had felt a link of friendliness with familiar things. He could almost remember what it was like to have it, years gone now, of course, its expiry unnoticed. But at ten years old, his bicycle, a Dayton "copper-frame"; or the brilliant pageantry of *Custer's Last Stand* flyblown in the window of Schwartz & Emmer's saloon; the willows lithely shielding the brown water of the hole where he swam, diving from the wet roots; and such simple things as the leather wrist guard worn because it made his forearm veins stand out like an iceman's or a brewery teamster's, and the baluster in his house that looked like a Chinese soldier—all were bound to him as real as rope until he looked in a mirror, a glance a proof this web was nothing really. He was alone.

On Sundays he faced the looking glass while his mother jerked and panted to get the knot of his necktie to slip inside his starched collar—it was the only time he ever heard her swear. In high school he larded his hair with some kind of patent spittle from a jar until it laid away from the part as set and final as a coat of paint. Later there were the crude grimaces of shaving and the faces he made, expressions tried to see if he looked like the man he imagined himself to be, a catalogue of callow scowls and pursings. He had stroked and even rubbed with oil the first sprouts of his mustache—he would seem older to the British, suaver to the French. Now, older, suaver, he seemed to have a dirty face; his breath was foul; his hair uncombed. The line between his eyebrows, a heritage from his mother, was deeper. Only the mustache and eyeballs were all right. He did not like to look in mirrors. They always gave you this unwelcome message from outside.

He opened the door of the medicine cabinet and found a liquid in a bottle to gargle. He took a mouthful and squirted it through his teeth into the washbowl. From a comb he plucked some long brown hairs, wet it, and combed his own. Then alert for a squeaking hinge, he opened the door carefully and went out into the living room. His clothes lay on the divan.

He put on his socks and shoes, and as he drew up his shorts, he heard the twang of bedsprings in the other room. He pulled his shirt on over his head. There was a scrape as her mules were dragged by a toe across the floor. Because he had things to say, he did not want to be caught bare-shanked in his shirttails. He heard the wire hangers clash in the closet and he buttoned his shirt. Beyond the door she paused. Nimbly he tied his tie, sliding the knot quickly himself on this Sabbath, and slipped into his coat. There was silence still. "Titivating," he thought. "Redding up for the entrance." There was a slopping clack of heels, and the bedroom door opened.

"Hello," he said cheerily.

"But, darling, you're up and dressed." Unwashed, balked from the bathroom, sullen as he knew she must be to be forced from the antics of a dream to show her daytime face, she looked good. She had laid on a bogus freshness and she was smiling. Wrapped tightly around her was a black-satin dressing gown (for the high lights, he thought automatically). Her wavy hair lay loosely on her shoulders.

"That one-man band. He woke me up."

"Oh, he's always around here Sundays, but you don't have to get up and dress, do you? It can't be noon yet."

"It's twenty minutes to three."

"What of it? It's Sunday."

"I've got to be getting along, Margery. Your friend Verplanck's asked me to dinner at four."

"Nonsense. You haven't anything to do. You told me last night you haven't. Henry will wait—he's patient." She started toward the bathroom rapidly. "Just let me wash my face and . . . how do you want your eggs?" she called back over her shoulder as she shut the door. Faucets spouted, and he did not answer.

What he had to do was to tell her before she could defeat him merely by being busy or defeat him by feeding him or distract him by her perfume and the accurately tossed glimpses of taut satin and the graces of her forearm and the arches of her feet. He was going to tell her that he was not going to see her any more. Why he had to tell her, to say it all out like a fool, he could not say except that it was a special situation. Once he would have broken it off quite easily. It was a method, a technique: gradually to make a longer interval between one telephone call and the next, one visit and the next, until the woman began to understand, regretfully, he supposed, perhaps not, until finally he did not ring her up at all and made her no more visits and when he met her on the street he would tip his hat.

He had often laughed at a ship's captain he once heard of. Christ, what a thimblehead! He was a good officer but he was lonely, and once in harborage at Yokohama, at the Yokohama Sex Store, he had bought and brought aboard in secret a "rubber Diana," a doll, life-sized, nude and beautiful, made of soft sponge rubber with a smooth surface adroitly tinted. The doll had shared his cabin on the long voyages, and the captain had come to love it dearly. It had been very funny to think of the captain alone in the salt darkness kissing with terrible solemnity the resilient passive lips—what a commentary on women, he had laughed, ha, ha! Now, pulling his thumbs on the divan, waiting, he saw that all he had ever asked of his own dolls, beyond resilience and softness, was intelligence enough to elude him deliberately for a time, to hinder but not prevent his little triumph. Women who had attracted him, his wife even, at first, had been at the time and to his memory only tissues of curves and pressures, and if they were modest, well read, or proud for any reason, they had offered him but more to be beaten and overcome. He had been silly for twenty years and he did not relish this matin clarity that made him feel it. Well, now he was going to explain, too blind to scorn them as a penance, the reasons for his departure, although he sensed that she would find them tedious and incomprehensible.

She came out of the bathroom, washed, self-scanned, and confident. "I've got some ham and some lemon juice. We can have them Benedict the way you always liked them," she said.

"I'm not going to eat your eggs, Margery. Come here. Sit down."

"It won't take a minute. I can make them before the coffee's done."

"I don't want any breakfast."

"But why not?"

"Because I'm so hungry."

"And you drink because you're not thirsty."

"Most of the time I drink because I'm not thirsty, you're right."

"Now don't be silly, Dick. You're hungry and . . ."

"Yes, I'm hungry, and if I eat I'll eat a lot, and then I'll relax and I won't say anything I intend to say. Come here. Sit down over there."

She sat, with mock patience. "Yes?"

"I don't think we'd better begin all this again, Margery."

"It was only last Tuesday or so you asked me to marry you. You're not flinging off in a huff, are you?"

"Do you know why I wanted you to marry me?"

She lit a cigarette and slumped down in her chair with her shoulders high and her arms propped on the chair arms, the cigarette with its rising ribbon of smoke stuck in her folded hands. She crossed her knees and the satin fell away. He could see her top thigh white above her stocking. He admired her assurance. "Go on, tell me," she said. "I've been expecting another session of this."

"Don't be funny."

"You wouldn't want me to be anything else right now, would you? Honestly, Dick, you do the damnedest things."

"I have. But I'm not doing one now. Do you know why I wanted you to marry me?"

She held her cigarette up and looked down her nose at it. "Oh, it's just a phase, I guess. About eleven people have asked me, younger than you or a lot older. With the old ones it's the last flare-up before they bank the fires for the night. It's different with the young ones—they're thirty or just turning. Some of them are rich and blooded. They are dull but they think I would look well at Nassau or peeking out of some old brick cave with a porte-cochere in Maine. I would be an asset but prettier than a bond. Then there are the poor ones—they like my shape and the way I can cook. But actually I think fear's behind all their talk. What's behind all your talk, by the way? Few men have the stamina for immorality they can recognize—they

74

want to marry you and fix things up. I don't marry them and so I remain in their memories ulcerous but beautiful."

"You're a candid devil," he said.

"Ulcerous but beautiful. I talk well, don't I? Don't I talk well, Richard? That's because I've known so many men. They taught me. And now you want to coop me up where I can't talk to anyone but you, my master's voice. You puzzle me, frankly. At your age you ought to be just about immune."

She raised her arms and folded her hands on top of her head. The loose satin slid down to her shoulders. He did not want to be diverted by looking at her and by this wispy talk.

"Why don't you take that thing off? You've tried your conversation, your eggs, and your legs. Take off the peignoir. Do a few bumps. Then I might stop talking."

"Don't be so damned nasty, Dick."

"It was just to get your attention. I am going to try to talk honestly with you." He paused.

She leaned her head on her hand. "I thought better of you, Dick. I thought you had the stamina. Well, wake me up when you get to *Let your lights so shine before men.*"

"I know it sounds foolish, but you're going to listen to it. I wanted to marry you because I want to start or found or make a home for my daughter."

She sat up. "That's so. I'd forgotten. How old is she?"

"Just about seventeen."

"Is she nice?"

"I don't know. I haven't seen her. She's at school."

"What are you going to do, take an apartment and bring her on here?"

"I don't know yet."

"Don't you think she ought to finish? Do you think it's best to take her out now?"

"She wants to come now, but I wrote her to wait awhile. Until spring maybe. I want to get settled."

"Why, I think that's marvelous, Dick. It'll be such an adventure for you. But I just can't see you as a father, nor I a ma*ma*. I hope you

75

planned to have us both clothed in the Misses Department at Best's, didn't you? People would say, 'You know, you can hardly tell them apart.' We could dress alike and this winter we could skate together at Rockefeller Center like Sonja Henie and her mother—I don't know if her mother skates or not. A little, probably; all Scandinavians do. They have to keep up with the reindeer and the *smörgåsbord*, don't they? But it's all off, you've decided, isn't it? We aren't going on with this, are we? It's unkind, Richard, to hold this vision in front of me and then snatch it away."

"I wanted to tell you, that was all. The other day when I saw you I thought it would be a wonderful arrangement. She needs a woman around her about now, and you and I could have had what we've always had."

"Don't go on in this dull, plodding way, Dick, please."

"But when I talked to you, I saw that you didn't want to get married and I thought what the hell, we can go on as we always have. The kid needn't interfere with us."

"And now we can't," she said sarcastically and slowly, nodding her head to stress each word.

"No," he said. He had got this far on words of one syllable without accepting any of her lures. She did not believe anything he had said and because of her unbelief she was not really angry yet. She was only petulant because they were out of bed and the night was over.

"Why?"

"I don't know as I can tell you exactly."

"Because of last night?"

"Yes, in a way."

"And what did I do last night or fail to do?"

"Nothing. It was just as it always was. That's the point; it seemed repetitious."

"*Oh*, my God. 'Repetitious.' "

"I'm trying to talk with the words that I know. I'm not trying to be tactful. I know I sound funny to you, but if I try to make this a conversation, I won't say anything. It'll all evaporate in wisecracks."

She leaned forward. "Look, Dick, if you want to insult me, out with it. If you want to go, get out—your hat's behind you. But don't sit here and give me this self-righteous whine. I don't know what's the matter with you . . ."

"Neither do I."

"Well, then," she said, cooing, smiling, "if you're going to leave me, let's have a drink, a stirrup cup, and then you kiss me nicely on the brow and tell me I'm a good girl and go. Don't sit there and nag at me."

"No. It wouldn't be fair."

"How old do you think I am? I don't expect justice any more."

"I'm not thinking of you. It wouldn't be fair to me."

Now, angry, she stood up, turned suddenly, and walked to the window.

He went on, "I'm leaving you for the same reasons I left Europe. You know how the river looks in Paris down toward Notre Dame with the barges and the trees coming out in the spring? You know those damned Nicolas wineshops? Remember Les Halles at five in the morning? You're as much Paris to me as all that, and I don't like Paris any more. You see, I've always done what I wanted to do and I got everything I wanted pretty close to the time I wanted it, not twenty years later. I think of myself as a lucky man, maybe because I've forgotten my bad luck. Until now. All of this until now or a month ago when I decided to come home and take care of my daughter. Now I want to forget Europe and I want to forget you and all the bright, smart, twittery things I've learned. A clean surface, I guess. I don't know." He stopped. He still did not know why he had left Europe or why he was breaking a lease on the best figure he ever saw.

She turned from the window. "Are you finished, Dick? Please go." It was quietly, intensely dramatic. Her face was grave; she looked him in the eye; and her simple words were spoken softly.

"Oh, I know," he said in disgust. "I've hurt you he-ah." He pounded his chest with the tips of his gathered fingers like a cheap actor. "You don't know if the Brevoort barbershop is open on Sundays, do you?"

From the window she watched him go. Her own house cast a shadow now, and two or three streets away she heard the thumping clash of the one-man band. Leaves from the chartered tree across the

77

street whirled crazily in eddies of dust. It struck her, she thought without sadness, that the dead leaves made a damned conventional setting for his farewell. "It was the October of their romance." Yet he was the first one to go like this, talking.

They all went. They got married—that was all right. They had one last big night and told her in the morning (just like this), pleading, sometimes holding her by the shoulders, begging as if they were off to Antarctica, "Don't ever forget me, will you?" leaving this with her, something more she had to carry, the image of themselves BEFORE. The AFTER and the girl who was going to create it, they never described. Or the firm was sending them to Kansas City or Chicago, São Paulo or Bombay. Some, the older ones, had died, sliding quietly to the floor in the bathroom, the wife blubbering anxiously in curlpapers and a wrapper with creamed, shocked face and the doctor injecting nitroglycerin.

The ones she had chosen, those who had been permitted a beginning and so—it was inevitable—a farewell, had all been gallant gentlemen. When they went away, they made their departures with tact. They did not descend to accusations or to the vulgarity of gifts and keepsakes. Oh, she knew what drew them from her—she was the flower they peeped over the edge of the rut to see. She knew their women; they made the rut and kept it comfortable. To oppose, however bravely, their corseted firmness, one had to relinquish something to win anything, and so she had never expected a permanent relationship with any man. (Men weren't built that way.) They came and went, accepting from her what she liked best to give, and when they wanted to return, she was always there. She was, she thought, like a harbor, like Rio in the darkness as she had seen it two summers ago, beautiful, her arms outstretched supinely soft, and, well, eternal.

Unnoticed, the one-man band had come back. He capered diligently in the empty street, jerking glances upward right and left, seeking those whom he had annoyed or pleased to toss him dimes or nickels. He saw her. He stopped and shook the spit from his mouth organ and bent to ease the weight of his drum. Then he began to play to her, a fresh tune. He stomped and nodded, tossing his head and winking at her. She did not move. He quickened the tempo and added an awkward soft-hoofed kick with his broken shoes. At last he stopped and bowed, wrinkling his forehead above his blue vacant eyes beseechingly. No coin came down. As if he had found just the thing, he shook his finger at her coyly, hitched up his belt, and struck a pose—his chin high, his buttocks thrust out, beginning a slow tune, clumping a double-step in a circle, beating out the time with the drum, the offbeat with the cymbal.

Suddenly she left the window and ran to the bathroom and opened the door that had the mirror in the back. She slipped off the dressing gown and let it lie. As she began to look at herself, the drumbeats went on. "My God," she said to herself fretfully, "doesn't he ever get tired?"

6

CLEAN, PLUMP, and ready, Verplanck began to eat his soup, a consommé, using his spoon like a little shovel, tipping it silently, shoveling briskly. The Melba toast crackled under his thumb as he broke it on his plate left-handed. When the soup was gone, he found the electric button under the carpet without groping, looking toward the door from the kitchen, and at once, almost coincidentally, old Charles, the Negro, entered with a respectful kidney-foot, step-and-a-half walk, carrying the fish on a platter. He slid the platter deftly onto the table where Verplanck could watch it, pleased and eager, while he carried off the soup plates. Verplanck had not spoken. He drew a knife through the sole, divided the sauce, and dished it all up neatly. He had begun to eat again before Charles had time to bring in a bottle of Meursault chilled. After a remark, a compliment, and a question answered all with nods, Miles thought, watching him, *"Er isst nicht. Er frisst. He does not eat. He feeds."* After the fish Charles brought two plump little roasted ducks, *sauce bigarade, pommes soufflées* beautifully done, and fresh asparagus. Only then did he hustle for the wine and return with two bottles of Château Lafite to set them gently on the table one at each place, evidently Verplanck's habit. The only sounds were the clicks, little gratings, and the tinkle of silver, crockery, and glass, and Miles, himself eating and drinking quickly to keep up, had begun to marvel at this silent voracity when Verplanck, bowed over a thighbone in his hand, tearing the succulent moist meat from it, champing and swallowing smoothly, looked up suddenly across the table, narrowed his blue eyes in a childlike smile, and winked.

A salad followed the little skeletons of the ducks, and as Charles with his exquisite promptness was bringing in a whole Roquefort cheese with its base wrapped in a napkin, Verplanck sucked in the last limp leaf of lettuce hard, so that it snapped up on his upper lip, and as he picked up a water cracker a tear of oil glistened on his cheek. With a blob of cheese on each cracker, Verplanck stuffed four, one after the other, into his mouth with two fingers and then reached for an apple from the centerpiece. A graceful ribbon of apple skin dangled from his knife, and he leaned back, paring, and exhaled, sorry that it was nearly over. Charles brought coffee and a bottle of armagnac, and while Verplanck buttered slices of apple with cheese and ate them, Charles warmed his brandy in a *ballon* with his old pink palms. At last, Verplanck took the huge glass, a sip of brandy, sniffing enjoyably, and began to ask Miles about the war. All the force and elation of his eating vanished and he became timidly polite. Charles, silently and touched obediently with mournful regret, removed all the food, leaving the coffee and the brandy on the bare, spotted whiteness. After two rounds of brandy, Verplanck, evidently remembering the table full of shiny, smoking, rich, luscious dishes, now clean, and saddened that he could eat no more, such a tiny organ the stomach really, no bigger than a Bull Durham sack, stood up and suggested to Miles that they ascend to the library.

Miles would find this the most comfortable chair. Charles would bring up a bowl of ice in a moment and they could have a drink. Meanwhile, he found Miles' remarks on the German staff work very interesting. It was actually the cause of the Polish defeat? The Poles were unable to foresee, to plan as well as the Germans? With Pilsudski dead, it was to be expected, Teutonic orderliness, method, quite. But if the Poles had been, not that he would intimate that they were not brave, braver perhaps? Did the bravery of the individual soldier have nothing to do with it? (He will talk now, fed and drinking, and drinking, later, more. It was a look he had that afternoon in Margery's parlor, a most interesting look of confusion, almost despair—he has it now and I will find out what it means. Something has sent him home here now. Cowardice? Shot and shell? Perhaps. Or he may have only quarreled with the woman. The mild stupidity will disarm him. Mute the voice. Blink the eyes. Qualify the statement with finical caution, as if you feared his scorn of your ignorance. Compliment him. Wait.)

"An ignorant man has to use his bravery sooner than a trained one," Miles said. The chair he sat so deeply in was plump and soft, covered with red leather.

"Exactly. And the Poles were relatively untrained."

"Yes. I would have to be very brave to go into a burning building. A fireman wouldn't think twice."

"Oh, I quite see your point, Miles, perfectly. And you say these plans were all matured before the invasion commenced? In the midst of peace, so to speak?"

"Yes. Years before."

"Who devised them?"

"Why, the staff," Miles said irritably. (Was this why I came home, to be skewered with crass questions from a glutton? "You came home to do your duty." I was a dutiful member of the Raven patrol, a tenderfoot after three years because I could not tie the knots. On Decoration Days, I haltingly recited martial poetry on a dais in the rooms of the Aldermen at the City Hall, requisitioned for the occasion, wearing, like Grampa and the veterans, a small bouquet of violets and pansies wrapped in foil in my lapel—the fresh dirt scent of these flowers is the smell of old people for me still—and, later, listened to them speak of duty and the flag in high nostalgic voices, sour-breathed, but even so of battles. Duty has wilted in my mind. Behind his glasses, opaque in the glare from the window, he watches me, still questioning.)

"Who is the brains of this staff?"

"Oh. Well, ask them and they say *der Führer*—it's the ritual. But Keitel, Franz Halder, Jodl, all of them probably had a hand in it. And there was certainly a Polish invasion problem given to the younger staff officers, the promising majors and colonels, back about 1934 or '5. Two or three of them may have done most of it."

"But not one individual?"

"I doubt it. Not in the German army."

"General Keitel is chief of staff?"

"Yes." (It should be easy to write a mere letter to your daughter. You have only to sit down and say "Come" with a pen. It should be easy to decide. Think of the dozens of your friends, fathers of children, some small, whom you, Uncle Richard, could not bring yourself to visit in an apartment on a Sunday afternoon. These fathers are not plagued with their fatherhood. [No?] What worries them lies elsewhere. [Yes?] What worries me lies elsewhere too. Not knowing the ropes, I cannot tie the knots. What have I come to the end of? Europe has decayed for me, like sugar in whisky. And I have cast off from the woman. Something at least has been done.)

"But the basic conception, the belief in the necessity of a Polish invasion at this time, must have come from the mind of one . . . oh, thank you, Charles." (It will go better now. This dullness of his will vanish with a drink in him.)

The old Negro put a dish of ice on the desk. "Yassuh, Mist' Hinry. You want the curtains pulled to or leave 'em open way they is?"

"Leave them open, Charles. That's all, I think."

"Yassuh. Want me to take the cat out?"

"Why, yes, you might. I have a Persian, Miles. Let him up here when you come in with him."

"Yassuh," Charles sighed and limped his kidney-foot walk away downstairs.

Verplanck opened the liquor cabinet. "Scotch?"

"Yes, thanks."

"You know The Glenlivet? It's a straight Scotch," he explained fussily. "Very mild. I hope you'll like it." He had taken the bottle, two of his large glasses, and a siphon out of the cabinet. "This has been extremely interesting, to get this information from one who has seen it firsthand. I don't see how you do it. In fact—I hope you won't think me too inquisitive—but I've often wondered just how a foreign correspondent gets a story, what are his sources, how does he handle it? My own work deals with the fringe of things just now especially, I think. I'm afraid I've never been at the center of anything that shook the world." He plopped the ice into the glasses. (Now he will have to talk about himself.)

"Oh, neither have I."

"But . . ."

"Oh, I can give you an example . . . thank you." He took the glass and drank. "You remember Danzig? Last summer? When it was overrun with those hundreds of German tourists?"

"Yes. It is a lovely old Hansa town, or was when I saw it. Were you there?"

"I was in Paris. We had a man in Danzig. He telephoned the story to me—the international phone service has improved a lot in the last few years. The Danzig man gave me the essential facts: several hundred German tourists had suddenly come into the town, all with luggage. The situation, you remember, was already tight and their arrival was bound to have political repercussions all over Europe. It was up to me to do the whole story, repercussions and all. Remember, I was not in Danzig. I had seen nothing."

"You were not what is called the leg man," Verplanck said as if bashfully.

"No. The first thing I did was call my friend at the Quai d'Orsay. He is an undersecretary. We played tennis together very often in Rome a few years ago. He is quite trustworthy and in my phone conversation I am careful to *give* him the information. I don't ask him anything. I do him a favor, you see. 'I have just had word about tourists in Danzig.' The chances are that his diplomatic sources have already told him about it, but maybe not. In that case it *is* a favor. I ask him what the government is going to do about it as far as he knows. He tells me perhaps that Daladier has or has not foreseen this and that he will or will not address the *Chambre* this afternoon on the subject. Nothing will come of it, say. France is determined to ignore the whole thing. There I have the official French angle on the story."

"This is fascinating, perfectly fascinating." Verplanck was sitting, bent forward attentively.

"Then I call the American Embassy and ask for the military attaché."

"You know him?"

"He knows who I am. There are two kinds of military attachés, smart and stupid. Suppose this one is intelligent. I give him the tourist information and ask him just what the military importance of several hundred tourists could be. He replies that, if they are trained men, they could very easily seize or destroy power stations, docks, arsenals, civic buildings, and so on. There I have the potential military importance of the situation."

"And if the attaché were stupid?"

"I should have gone to the Embassy and taken him out to lunch. After a few drinks he would have told me all he knew and I could pick out what I needed."

"I see," said Verplanck blandly.

"Next thing I call our syndicate man in London. He will have heard about it direct from Danzig. 'What is Chamberlain going to do?' His sources have told him that the government . . ."

"His source would be an undersecretary like yours?"

"Someone in the government, not an undersecretary necessarily."

"I suppose he would be lucky if it were Chamberlain himself."

"No. The two best sources in Europe would be Vansittart in London and Alexis Léger in Paris. They are the permanent heads of their respective Foreign Offices—but you can't get them. You don't want a Prime Minister ever. He doesn't know anything."

"How do you mean?"

"All the facts of national policy reach him every morning in a small memorandum, neatly typed and predigested. How can he know anything?"

"I see. I'm sorry to interrupt you."

"My London man has said that the government will open it up in the Commons that afternoon and recommend a strong protest, backed

85

up, say, by a couple of cruisers that will leave Scapa Flow for the Baltic at sundown. In the same way I pick up the German attitude from our Berlin man, who will probably say—he *did* say, as a matter of fact—that the Wilhelmstrasse is surprised and shocked at the imputations and has denied that these happy tourists have any military intentions whatever—they are merely good German workers on a *Kraft durch Freude* vacation tour. All the telephoning has taken me two hours and a half or three hours with luck. In another hour I can get the cables off. Assuming that my first information reached me at nine in the morning, the complete story will get to America in time for the early afternoon editions."

"Why, it's amazing. I'm afraid you'll think me very ignorant but I really didn't have the foggiest idea how it was done. Did you stay in Paris permanently? Let me get you another drink."

"Thanks. No, I got around. Sometimes I was the man in Danzig."

"It must have been a marvelous opportunity to travel."

"The Fuller Brush people offer the same."

Verplanck laughed politely. "Yes, I suppose they do. But at least it's not a sedentary life." (Now give a sighing glance upward and around at the books. *My* little life, unmuscular, sitting down.) "When do you go abroad again?"

"I don't. I've quit."

"Really?"

"It's becoming realer all the time."

"But how can you . . . why, you've met, you've interviewed, the heads of states."

"Even Prime Ministers. Hitler, Mussolini, Chamberlain, Daladier, Horthy, and once I was nearly allowed to enter the Kremlin, but I was not Roy Howard and the deal fell through."

"You see what I mean, don't you?"

"Oh, sure. You can't see why I gave it up."

"Well, you are taking a rather disparaging line toward your work, work that I would call extremely absorbing . . ."

"It was." (Am I romantic to him, the city mouse?)

"And I gather, excuse me, I gather the pay was adequate?"

"Adequate and a little over."

"Yet at Margery's the other day I heard you say . . ."

"Look, Verplanck, if I can arrange it, I'll never go near a newspaper office again. It's going to be hard because I like to work in a place where you can throw paper on the floor . . ."

"Oh, that's good. That's very good," Verplanck giggled. "That strikes that reckless note exactly."

"But I'm tired of being a vicar." (Ho! Look what comes out if you talk long enough.)

"I beg your pardon. I didn't . . ."

"Any newspaperman is a vicar. I don't mean with a dog collar and a black dickey. I mean . . ." He drank. (Now I know, having said the word. Four days out in the Atlantic, I discover why I left that little landscaped continent, and at noon with the sun up high after a night spent thumbing my way over my little floating island, Margery, such a beautiful, titillating, palpitating journey. I learn when I tell her about it that last night was the last night. And now I seem to be about to inform myself why I have left my trade. Say another word and maybe the reason will follow. This fat sponge here is growing dry. Speak and find out what you think.) ". . . a vicar for the average reader, paid to have the experience publishable."

"If you mean in the sense that . . ."

"I am the eyewitness, hired and ignorant . . ."

"Why ignorant?"

"Who goes and sees instead of the reader himself."

"But why are you ignorant?"

"Anyone sees only what he has been taught to see, what his education, upbringing, and travels permit him to see. That is why you run a nail in your foot. You can understand that, can't you?"

"Oh, yes."

"When I went to Europe as a correspondent fourteen years ago, I went for purely romantic reasons. I wanted to see Chartres and drink Johannisberger. I remained there for the same reasons, supporting myself on a talent I merely happened to have. Now just how much, considering this bias, do you think I saw really of Stresa and Geneva and all this inching up to war?"

"You think it will be a big war?"

"Colossal."

"Why, I should say you saw quite a lot. Enough to satisfy the readers. They kept you there fourteen years. That is, I mean, their employers . . ."

"That's only because of the talent. A facility, a slickness. I got tired of being a cockeyed licensed spectator yawning around the chancelleries. . . . I'll just freshen this drink if you don't mind." Miles poured two inches of whisky into the huge glass.

"Go right ahead, please." (This is going to turn out to be a very near thing. Will he be drunk before he is candid? I should have set out the smaller glasses.)

"And then there's another thing, Verplanck. It's the myth."

"What myth?"

"Basis of our religion. I helped to make it. Maybe you didn't—I don't know what an amateur psychologist does."

"You didn't quit journalism for religious reasons, did you?" (One of these fanatics perhaps? A member of the Oxford Group, a Buchmanite? It would be very interesting to deprive a fanatic of his crutch.)

"N-a-a-h," Miles said coarsely. "Or maybe I did, come to think of it."

"Lonely people are finding two sorts of religion very consoling just now—Catholicism and this Oxford Group movement." (The "lonely" will give him a key to open himself with. See if he picks it up.)

"Oh, hell, I'm not talking about God. Look—do you read the health columns of the daily papers?"

"I've seen them, of course."

"You know how they say 'You' need so many thousand calories a day?"

"Yes."

"Who does? Who is the 'You'? Henry Verplanck? The dieticians don't know you, Verplanck. I should think not. 'You' is the name of the unknown god—the average man, with average hair that needs a sixty-second workout, with an average face that breeds a five-o'clock shadow, with average teeth that need soaps and powders, with the average stinking breath so you have to gargle. What I mean is, we have all, except you maybe, all of us have been pushing a conspiracy to obliterate ourselves." He stopped. (It had been a mouthful. Keep going. This is sufficiently true.) "We have been trying to make ourselves the same size, the same size shoulders, chest, and bottoms and feet, the same length life, the same weight minds."

"All right. Why?"

"Do you believe what I'm telling you? Do you see what the myth is?"

"If I follow you correctly, you mean that we are all alike or ought to be."

"Did you ever see an assembly line? It has been devised so that any-one can work on it, anyone as long as he keeps a certain low sanity."

"But it is more convenient to have standardized products."

"And it is still more convenient to have a standardized consumer. Take an office. Have you ever worked in an office? Do you know the procedure?"

"A little."

"What do you think of the memorandum in triplicate?"

"I never thought about it, to be perfectly frank."

"It is an insult to everybody. An adding machine implies that no one can add. A carbon sheet implies that every employee is either dishonest or has no memory."

(He has been drinking. He will not keep to the point if you nudge him off it. Talk about him.) "But it seems to me that you have been able to work alone. You are not merely a cog in a machine," Verplanck said with deliberate triteness.

"Pooh. My focus was determined when I was a lousy little foot-in-the-door police reporter. I learned then that there were things I was not allowed to say. And after I learned them for what they were, I never even saw them. The taboos were blinkers. Average news for the average man. That's me or was. You were talking about religion. When I was a kid, we had a hired girl. It was a small town and hired girls came from farms. Once I went out to stay on the farm that Lizzie came from, and every night before supper they had family prayers. Everybody knelt down and put their elbows on the seat of their chairs. That's in my lifetime. Now, as you say, only Catholics have a ritual they can believe in, but give us time, give us time—the priesthood is ripening, altars will be erected, and all the faith we once offered Yahweh is being laid before the Average and Heaven will be the land of Norm. I'm drunk."

"Oh, nonsense, Miles. You're talking very well."

"Much obliged," Miles said sarcastically. "I haven't talked this way in years. All I need is a PBX system and a stump to stand on, don't you think?" He moved his glass in little circles and watched the whisky circle in it. "No. What I mean is: the machine is the central fact of our lives, the most useful, the most fascinating. How it got that way, I don't know, but it is. And everyone singly and in the mass tries to adapt himself to it. Would you say I'm right?"

"Oh, obviously."

"It's not so damned obvious." He looked up at Verplanck, smiling. "I'm sorry. I guess I've been away too long. Maybe it's just not obvious to me. You see, I think that one way of looking at Communism and Fascism shows you that at bottom both systems are trying to arrange, curtail, improve—whatever you want to call it—their populations to suit the machine. Politically it will be very convenient when you have a standard man. He will behave consistently all the time, won't surprise you ever, you see. You can use radio to educate him—propaganda was never really possible until radio came in—and he will act in any way that he is taught. If he is taught peace, we will have it; war, we will have that. The resemblance ends there. The ideologies enter now, but the point is: the manner, the way men will handle themselves politically, will conform to an average, no matter what the ideals are." Miles stopped. "I don't know why the hell I keep going on about these things. What I really want to do is talk about myself."

"Do you believe you are a standard man or in danger of becoming one?"

"I'm one of the entrepreneurs. I help level everybody off. In a small way, of course. The machine has made the world little. It is important to know about the whole world now, where once your orbit was only your home town or even your street. But everybody can't be everywhere at once. Physics forbids it. So journalism and radio are everywhere at once and they disseminate this knowledge of the world. What happens in Cape Town or Warsaw is available to the citizens of Dubuque almost immediately. Not what really happens, merely a defective view of it, but it is the standard view, the machine view. If our civilization has a style, it is mechanical, even our wars. Look at the Polish campaign. I'm still not talking about myself, am I?"

Verplanck smiled. "Then we have got to be all alike to exist at all, you say?"

"No, not forever, but you and I will be dead before it is better not to be. The pressure to be similar, more like each other, will increase in our lifetimes."

"And, am I wrong, you do not intend to submit personally? You are going to keep your identity?"

"Whatever it is. Somehow." (I have been stupid. This is all true enough, but what I wanted to say was only that I am disgusted with my work. That is the secret message that grew true as I said too much. By swinging the dumbbells of religion and politics I have at last proved merely that I was tired before I began. Better go home now.)

"Have you decided just how you are going to accomplish this withdrawal?"

"It's not a withdrawal."

"I mean—have you picked a new vocation?"

"Yes. Next spring, I think, I'll be a father."

Downstairs old Charles could be heard shutting a door and in his high wheeze uttering cute commands. A Persian cat as large and silent as a cat in a dream bounded into the library. Verplanck snapped his fingers, and the cat leaped onto his lap, a huge muff of grayish fur with calm, hard, yellow eyes.

"Why, congratulations. That's splendid," Verplanck said heartily. (I have wasted an afternoon. One of these late-marrying men full of this bland self-gratulation, surprised and pleased that the orgasm worked, saying farewell the other day to Margery, once his girl, now sturdily forsaken. Get rid of him.)

"Oh, it's not that. My daughter is seventeen. I haven't seen her for seven years."

"It will be very pleasant for you and your wife to set up a home again after your long stay abroad."

"My wife's home is already set up—stone and copper, eight hundred dollars. I omitted flowers."

"Oh, I'm very sorry."

"Not at all. You see, I have quit Europe and, you may as well know, Margery Elliot and now my trade, so that I can assume these parental responsibilities." (Or is it the other way around? But it is what you have been trying to say since Cherbourg. It suffices. Now go before you fall out of your chair.)

"Is your daughter here in New York?"

"She's in school. I'm going to bring her on when she finishes in June."

(A confused and lonely man, worth keeping track of now that I shall soon be finished with Stephenson. He has too fond a notion of his daughter and what she will mean to him. A wife dead and her successor cast off to make room for this girl. Ask him more.) "And you have not seen her for seven years?"

"No. I know very little about her. The other side of the family has had her in tow." He stood up suddenly. "I must go, Verplanck. It's been very pleasant."

"Oh, please don't rush off. It's early yet."

"I'm sorry. Thanks very much. It was a fine dinner."

"Well, if you really must go . . . You'll excuse my not rising. He expects this after his walk," Verplanck said, stroking the silent cat. "His name is Brigham."

"Brigham Young?"

"The all-father," Verplanck tittered. "Coochy-coochy-coochy!" Verplanck whined a falsetto. "I enjoyed our meeting very much. It has been a most interesting afternoon. You'll come again, won't you?"

"Thanks." (Will I? The duck. Yes.)

"If you'll just telephone me first."

"I will. Good night," Miles said and walked toward the doorway.

"Good night." And then Miles heard him to the cat, "Coochy-coochy-coochy! Brigham bad?"

Miles took a cab to his hotel, watching vapidly through the window the flow of lights, red, blue, and yellow, on the stores they passed. He was glad he had said what he had but he was heavy with the whisky and ready to sleep. In the lobby, he stopped at the desk to pick up his room key. The clerk threw the key down and handed him a yellow envelope.

"Telegram for you, Mr. Miles. It came late yesterday afternoon but you were out and . . ."

"Thanks," Miles said. He tore it open.

HAVE LEFT SCHOOL ARRIVING NEW YORK EIGHT-TWENTY MONDAY MORNING

MARY

7

AND SO NOW he was calm. It was only a little after seven-thirty, a clear, sunny day outside, and he was in no hurry. He was dressed, and before him on a portable table covered with a cloth of the peculiar glazed hotel stiffness lay the debris of his breakfast, the plates streaked with jam and the yellow of his eggs, a coffeepot still warm, a demolished pat of butter, the crusts of toast, and, overturned, sweating warm beads of steam, the silver lids that had protected his dishes through the sleeping corridors. Under the rim of the serving plate, though Miles was still drinking coffee and reading a newspaper, already protruded a dollar bill for the waiter. It was a gift he had made in gratitude for the calm he felt, to bribe somehow or to cajole the good will of this impassive Scandinavian as if, because he was neat, had spilled nothing and so was at home with his work, had a certain power over his duties, he might also in some vague way be able to preserve the welling elation Miles was enjoying, even at a distance from the kitchens and the pantries, this calm.

Sitting sideways to the table with his legs crossed, he drank his coffee and read for the first time in a month the way a reporter would read a newspaper, quickly and professionally. He noticed where the story was placed on the page, the headline, the aptness of the lead, and the way the event was handled more than the event itself. The *Herald Tribune* lay scattered on the floor and he was scanning the *Times*. "Lochner—he has been with the Germans too long," he thought. And at the head of the Rome dispatch he saw the name Matthews, who had replaced Cortesi, and he remembered how the elder Cortesi had wangled the story of the Pope's death, but he could not remember which Pope.

Since he left France he had read the papers timidly, like a banker, fidgeting at distant calamity, wondering what was going to happen, but now that he had something to do, something necessary to do, to meet the eight-twenty train at Grand Central, he had resumed his old habit unconsciously—it was important to begin the day with the early editions, and they had always been his last relaxation before he went to work.

Dimly he kept the time in mind. It was nearly eight o'clock. Before he left his room he intended to ransack the top drawer of his trunk to find some photographs of his daughter, although there might—he did not concentrate his mind on it—be a need for haste. The train might pull in and she might get off, unknown, unmet. Yet still he read on, reluctant to break his tranquil elation, a new thing, never had it before, turning his critical glance to all the stories in the *Times*. At last he finished his coffee and threw the paper down.

He had unpacked the trunk except for the top drawer. From it he took two dirty dress ties, an engagement book, a pair of Bausch & Lomb binoculars in a leather case, some maps, folded and dingy, and an empty dressing case. He laid them all on the top of the trunk. He doubted that the photographs would help him if he found them. None of them were less than seven years old, yet he wanted to look at them. Beneath a new Lüger pistol he had never carried he found a packet of letters from his wife. Briskly tearing the already opened envelopes, tearing the letters as he hunted, he opened them all. He did not know why he kept them, unless he had counted on a belated flood of senti-

95

ment, a desire that had not come even with her death to regard her affectionately. A torn fragment of note paper caught his eye. In her correct college backhand, once so chic, the sentence lay: "Why must you always . . ." and it continued on the back of the leaf which he did not turn. "Why must I always what?" he thought. "It was everything 'that I always.'" As he tore or turned each letter inside out in a businesslike way and chucked these last memorials of his wife into the wastebasket, he was glad she was gone, leaving his daughter for him. He began to whistle *My Hero* softly.

Then he stopped. "Always." Every single thing. For the first time since her death it struck him that he was being hard on her. Laughing at her this way was cheap. She had not "understood" him, and for the first time in his life he recalled with wonder that he had never "understood" her because he had not thought it necessary. After his wedding he had believed the old wives, corseted, stupid, and malign, who inferred that the marriage lines properly witnessed guaranteed felicity.

The year before he had legally deserted her, she had been frantically and continuously irritable, and it now occurred to him, lugubriously and too late, that it might have been his fault. His scorn of her was wrong and wrong because it was what? Unauthorized. "It's no way to behave"—an echo from his mother. Most people learn what they ever learn about conduct from their parents, and when they go away or their parents die, they go on acting from Daddy's rules their whole lives, very conveniently, too, if they are never excited and find the right rut, but if they leave their childhood orbit, they have to make up their own minds how to behave. My mother never told me not to laugh at a dead wife. I have always, always behindhand to be sure, but nevertheless always done as I pleased. Why now, what has happened suddenly, to what am I referring when I think that I lack the authority so to laugh? He looked at the crumpled letters all on gray initialed stationery as if he intended to stoop and pick them up, perhaps to keep again. But he did not. He sensed that it was nearly eight o'clock.

He found two photographs. He had taken them both. One showed Constance with short bobbed hair, holding up baby Mary, smiling at

96

her fondly, a mother's pride, Pudding and Pie, and the baby's dumpling face stared curiously at the camera. The other photograph he had
taken of Mary at a girls' camp. Visitors' Day, a fleet of canoes riding
the lake, group dancing in cheesecloth chitons, bird-calling and bed-
making, all healthy, and there was the child, ten years old, in shorts, her
loose dark hair hanging well combed to her shoulders, a face, but not
his face, grave for the occasion. Here was the matrix of the face that
she had now: what had Constance done to it? What petulance or
slyness had her grandmother put there, and had the nuns made it
bored or meek? It would have been nice to recognize his daughter
from the snapshot, to pick her out of the crowd before she spoke to
him, but it was no help. He laid it carefully on top of the trunk beside
the Lüger. As a child she had had large gray eyes, that was all that
would remain.

The Scandinavian waiter came in to remove the table and the breakfast dishes. "You are quite finished, sir?"

"Yes, I'm through. You can take the table."

"Yes, sir. It's a fine day, isn't it?"

Miles looked at the thin face and the smooth, lusterless fair hair.
The statement, though perfunctory, was not necessarily recom-
mended by the management and Miles felt his first elation return.
He looked out of the window, squinting past the sun. The sky was a
light, clear blue that would deepen in the afternoon, and if there had
been trees to see, maples, they would be yellow and crimson, burning
like flames. The maples in the woods near the town where he was
born, where, himself ten years old, he had tugged his coaster wagon
to fill the box full of walnuts, faded burning into a blue haze like
smoke. At night, at home, after she had spread the walnuts out to dry
on newspapers in the attic, the smell of burning leaves drifted in
through the grillwork under the eaves and he heard the shouts of
children in the darkness jumping through bonfires, and before he
went to bed tired, his mother gave him apple cider. It was a fine day
and Miles was pleased that he had left a dollar beneath the plate.

He went to get his topcoat and hat from the closet and as he
shut the door and turned with his coat over his arm and his hat in his

hand, he saw a half dollar lying on the writing table. The waiter, bent, carrying the load of dishes, was just going out the door.

"Didn't you want the dollar?" Miles asked.

The waiter smiled. "Thank you, sir. A dollar is too much."

Miles got out of his taxi and entered Grand Central from the Lexington Avenue side. Office cashiers, receptionists, and bookkeepers on their way to Forty-second Street and Vanderbilt Avenue overtook and passed him in the long hall of buff stone, their voices and their heel clops bouncing from the vaulting above. Secretaries to 8:30 small executives, clerks, and messengers approached and passed him to debouch in Lexington Avenue or the Graybar Building. Miles, his check stubs in his breast pocket showing $12,432 on deposit, saw their haste and sensed their coffee breaths.

In the great hall of the station the sound of hurry changed, grew steady, lowly roared. Walking slowly, he was passed, brushed, and buffeted from every side. The sun was not yet high enough to cast its famous pattern of mote and beam through the huge arched window behind him. He saw that he had four minutes still and walked past the row of doorways leading to the secret trains, glancing upward at the signboards. He found one headed THE WOLVERINE and stood back away from the doorway beneath it, trying to make an island in the stream of hurriers.

He stood still, one knee bent. He walked a few steps one way, returned, and stood again. He lit a cigarette and found his mouth was dry. He threw it down and set his heel on it meticulously, as if the stone beneath it might catch fire. Once he looked over his shoulder. Europe was not there behind him, shining maplike through the broken clouds of his desire, that toy continent, the rampant sea beast of Britain, really fixed but always gliding northeast, its open mouth, the Firth of Moray, swallowing the North Sea, with a flying mane of the Outer Hebrides; Italy's perpetual jackboot swung to kick Sicily; and that other serpent, Scandinavia, limber-necked with its jaws open, Skagerrak, Kattegat, jawlike names, ready to engulf pert Denmark, and eastward, hanging down, the shrunken claws of the Greek peninsulas; none of the ancient cities, the vineyards and the plains, its soft little Rhone-Rhine rivers or its corrupted mountains. And there was no typewriter behind him jerkily spewing out the tale of the Old Country's catastrophes, with statesmen and soldiers dancing on the keys. And there were none of the women, naked, gowned, dishabille as he remembered them, no fragment of night—it was a fine day—there behind him for them to move in, swelling or diminishing, all thronged on the edge of a grove of trees in full leaf, green, each making politely her gesture of farewell. Behind him were only the crisscross streams of people and the ticket windows of the New York Central Railroad.

Now that it had come to the point, his last moment as a man somehow free, he was surprised as usual by the unforeseen intensity of his emotion. He had two minutes yet to wait before the train arrived and he was endeavoring to quench a feeling, it was damned silly, not of a proper love and affection for his daughter, but of immolation. He could argue that while his calm had fled he was willing, even happy, to assume this burden, yet there were still two minutes—he could run, he could hurry away like these other people, but to what? He thought that when he looked over his shoulder, if he had actually seen Europe, all the women, and his fourteen years of work rolling out of a black, gigantic, dreamlike typewriter, and then if he had turned at once and looked as he was looking now at the gateway to the train, the impossible scheme of time would have been perfect: the past, that elaborate vision behind him all jammed up against the ticket windows like a traveling circus; here himself in the middle, alone, stopped, but surrounded by the flow of people, awaiting meekly what was approaching him, coming into the light, the future, his daughter. He wished that his only thoughts could be of welcome, but she was the springtime of a country he had not visited. He did not know her and he doubted and shifted, waiting.

Suddenly the train was in. Travelers were emerging from the doorway he faced: the stout old gentleman blinking at the light, hustling the red cap with his bags, his belly shaking with the splat of his spatted oxfords. Two voluble young men with brief cases, and eyes redrimmed from last night's club-car whisky, talking of the deal. Three plump women in silly hats stilting by on choked feet. Where? The mother with the two well-brought-up little boys in cricket caps who stared upward at the great window (now performing). Had she somehow missed . . . ? A girl in a *tailleur*, too old, his automatic eye receiving the image of her ankles. The long, shaking face of a parson wilting down over his cleric's starch, seamed with the runnels of piety. A woman with tweeds flung on her and spectacles on a brick-red disk. He was looking for his daughter, a little girl with dark, well-combed hair hanging to her shoulders. A man in a derby hat. Two men. A woman, old. Where?

"I beg your pardon . . . are you my father?"

He turned. It was the girl (too old?) in the *tailleur*. "Are you . . . ?" (Those are the large gray eyes.) She was found and he could afford composure now. "Hello, Mary. You've grown up on me." He stooped and kissed her. "Had your breakfast?"

"Yes. I had it on the train."

She was carrying a small overnight bag. He took it from her. "We'll get a cab," he said. If they were going to talk, they would have to talk loudly here, so he walked along toward the Lexington Avenue doorway, swinging the light bag, smiling but perplexed.

"You sent me the money, don't you remember, and I bought it and didn't tell Grandmother," she said, leaning toward him to make him hear.

"What did you buy?"

"The suit. You said I've grown up. I didn't tell Grandmother because it makes me look older."

As they came out into the sunlit trough of the avenue, a cab with an open top pulled up from the rank. The driver took her bag, opened the door, and set it inside.

"Where to, boss?"

"Drive through the Park."

The driver winked and grinned. "It's eight-thirty in the *morning*, boss."

"Drive through the Park anyway."

"O.K. Through the Park slow."

Miles got in beside his daughter and they both stretched out their legs.

He could tell that she did not know what to say, how to begin the acquaintance, and he could not help her. He had expected a young girl.

"I ran away from school." She had thrust her hand through the strap of her purse and was looking at it, narrow and delicate.

"So I gather." It was a hell of a grim thing to say, and he smiled, but she was still looking down.

"I couldn't stand it any longer. They're always talking about graduating with your class and Mother Crescentia gets you into her office, especially the seniors, and tries to wheedle you, she doesn't exactly wheedle, but you always know she wants you to be a nun."

"She's the Mother Superior?"

"Yes."

"You just slipped out? How did you do it?"

"While they were in chapel. It wasn't hard. I drew my money out of the bank Saturday afternoon and bought my ticket and then I called the taxicab company and told them to have a taxi waiting outside the gates Sunday evening. Last night when everybody went to chapel, I just walked out."

The cab was turning out of Fifty-seventh Street into Fifth Avenue, and ahead, past the hacker's shoulder, he could see the trees of the Park.

"Are you going to make me go back there, Father?"

"Look, do you like flowers?" He called to the driver. "Hold it just a minute." The driver swung his wheel and edged in to the curb. Miles got out and ran into a flower shop.

"What have you got for a small corsage?" he asked.

"A small corsage? Would these little chrysanthemums do?"

"No. Everyone is wearing those little chrysanthemums. Violets. Have you got any English violets that smell?"

"Yes. Just a moment, please."

From the cool fresh scent of flowers he looked out into the bright street. Her head was framed in the taxi window. The sunlight lancing downward softened her face in shadow. She was still fearing that he might send her away. She looked like neither one of them except that Constance's eyes were gray, and the cheekbones and her forehead were molded a little as his own were. Mother's windows, Father's sashes.

"Oh, thanks very much. Yes, these are fine." He paid and hurried out of the shop to the clang of the cash register.

"Here," he said, thrusting out the little fountain of violets. She looked up. "I think you're beautiful and you can do anything you want to do. And here's a pin."

"Oh, Father, they're lovely." She held them out, turning them.

"You need a spot of color with your suit, and they'll smell sweet all day."

She was fastening them to her lapel, her chin drawn in. As if she did not want to say it looking at him, she said, "I can do anything I want, you said?"

"Name it and you can have it."

"Can I stay here?"

"Go to school here, you mean?"

"No. Stay with you."

"Why, I . . ."

"Couldn't we get an apartment and let me keep house for you? I can cook, honestly I can. The nuns let me learn, and I know about herbs and salads the way you told me. And . . . we could go places together, and it would be like I always wanted it."

"You think you would like that, taking care of the old man?"

"You're not old."

They passed a girl in jodhpurs riding a beautiful chestnut horse. Cantering after her, a young man, a young executive surely, the commercial sternness set in his face which was propped by the blue folds of a turtle-neck sweater. What was it Mary wanted? Had she been enchanted, there at school in the Middle West, by the legends of the city: the Rich Men (*the Racquet and the Union League, not the Brook*), the Poor Men (*Pig Snouts with French-fry Pots & Coffee, T, or Buttermilk* 10¢), Beggar Men ("*A finif until Tuesday, Benny?*"), Thieves ("*And I'm taking a short heave in Arnold the Furrier's doorway and I hear the shots so I run like hell. It seems these two greaseballs are sticking up a fourth-floor cloak-and-suit payroll, a sucker job, and we take 'em in the alley. These are the guys. See, it says, 'Deliver* two males.' Sure, Riker's Island"), Doctors (*Alexis Carrel, a photo of, in black laboratory cap, peering at that chicken's heart*), Lawyers (*Cravath, de Gersdorff, Swayne & Wood*), Merchant Chiefs (*Second floor, the College Shop, lonjeray, shoes, formal dresses, sports attire, everything for the young girl. Second floor, coming out, please*)? Was it the theaters, the night clubs, the museums? Did she want a beautiful chestnut horse to ride on fair October mornings in the Park? Or did she want him?

And if she did not want him, if it were only the romantic excitement of coming to the city to see if all that she had heard about it were true, would he send her away? The Mississippi makes a valley and she had always lived on the rim of it. All valley people want to go over the hill. All Middle Westerners must make their journey. The world is always yonder somehow. It is curious but true. Maybe the journey has to be no farther than Detroit, Kansas City, or Louisville, and the people with the short hopes can go there, stare and possess them, proving with their eyes that there are, as they have heard, wonderful things beyond the edges of the home towns, and, having seen them, go home soothed, the itch for movement larded over, healed. Others like himself, perhaps like Mary here, must rope in more to feed their memories. He had Europe (for what it was worth), and if she wanted New York, he could not say no, not any longer, having seen her, sitting beside him and still afraid of him, even after the violets, a stranger.

"Have you had a telegram from school?" she asked.

"Not yet."

"They'll probably notify you."

"That you've escaped?"

She looked up and smiled. "Cute" was a big word with kids that age. Did she think he was "cute"?

"I suppose the nuns think that all they have to do is notify me that you've run away and I'll see that you're brought back immediately."

"Yes, that's what they think a father would do." Then, with anxious haste, "But you're not going to, are you?"

"No, I'll wire them when we get back to the hotel. I'll tell you, I'll get a room for you and you can stay there for two or three days while we look for a flat."

"I'm going to stay, then? I don't have to go back at all?"

"Sure. Didn't you hear me tell you?"

"But now look, Father, I've run away from school. It's a serious thing. The nuns will be jumping up and down, and Grandmother will be crazy by now."

"You don't have to be so fair about it."

"But you don't seem to realize. You take it so lightly."

"Now don't treat me as if I were a featherweight, giddy and irresponsible. I know you've run away from school, deliberately in the dead of night. I know you're wrong, and it's all right."

"Grandmother thinks you are," she said, looking at him out of the corner of her eye, smiling again.

"Thinks I'm what?"

"Giddy and irresponsible. Worse than that, even."

"Did she say that to you?"

"Not to me. I used to hear her talking to Mother."

"When she was sick?"

"Yes. She used to go into the bedroom. You know Grandmother's voice."

"And I'm no good?"

"Grandmother used to admit it. She would grant that you were lazy and you drank too much, and you and Mother didn't live in the right places. She would concede all that. Then she would say, 'But.'"

"But what?"

"But that didn't excuse Mother. She ought to have kept the home together in spite of everything you did. There had never been such a scandal in our family. I felt sorry for Mother, lying up there in bed, having to listen to that all the time."

Listening to that. Maybe she had had fever, unable to think clearly, eyes hot, listening to the scandal, terror-struck because the neat grammar of her life was about to be stopped. He pitied her.

"What did Constance ever say about me?"

"She never said much. I was to remember that I was a child of divorce. It seemed to me, I don't know, I think she resented you because you always got what you wanted. She was always nice to me, but I couldn't cry. I cried at the cemetery, but that was because everyone was looking at me, expecting me to."

"Yes, I know."

"They were always watching me. They wanted to see whether I was a Miles or a Harrison."

"And any of the Miles had to be stamped out."

"Yes, but Mother never hated you. It was envy."

Funny he had never seen that. Of course, that was what it was, envy.

"Oh, look! What's he doing?"

Ahead in the road, a boxer in a sweat suit was skipping rope, a neat two-step, bobbing his head as the rope came over. As they approached, he dropped the rope and began shadowboxing. He jab-jab-jabbed with his left, threw a right across, and finished the pattern with a left uppercut, dancing away on tiptoe. He snorted through his nose and stroked it rhythmically with his thumb, and as he crouched and straightened, shuffling warily, he picked up his hind foot, smartly bending his leg at the knee. His face was solemn as they passed.

"He's a pug, a prize fighter. He's training."

"Like Joe Louis?"

"Not very much like him, but it's the same trade."

"I'm going to like New York."

This was her first coin found, the little treasure she would stow away—a St. Nicholas prelim boy working out in the Park, stranger than a nun to her. She was like him, a magpie, picking up little bright things to keep. Was that why Constance envied him, the richness of his petty hoard? Mary was like him, a Miles all right.

"What you think your grandmother will do?"

"Well, she'll know where I am . . ."

"Why? Have you been talking about running away from school?"

"No, but she'll know the only place I'd go is where you are, and she'll probably take the first train."

"Why should she?"

"To put me back in school. 'Finish my education.'"

"If she comes on here to New York and wants to take you away,

I will give her blue hell. Now let's go back to my hotel and you can unpack and after lunch we can go out and look for a place to live."

"I haven't anything to unpack. My trunk's still at school."

"We can write them a letter and tell them to send it on. There may be some telegrams there, too."

"So I'm really going to stay?"

"Yes."

"I'm glad."

When Miles stopped at the desk of his hotel to take a room for his daughter, there were two telegrams as they had expected. The Mother Superior was agitated. Miles calmed her with ten words, straight message paid. The other telegram was from the grandmother, "Arriving New York tomorrow to take Mary back to school." Miles showed it to his daughter, grinning, and stuffed it into his pocket.

He looked forward to her grandmother's coming. The old girl would be a dragon he could kill for her. And as he learned how much he wanted his daughter's admiration, he regretted that people never say what they mean. This morning, riding through the Park in the sunshine with the leaves coming down and the chestnut horse and the air-slugging preliminary boy, he should have told her all this straight out. He had tried to when he gave her the flowers, but she was not used to it, no one was used to it, and seeing her frightened or uneasy, he had stopped. There would be time, however.

8

NEVER IN my life. No one has ever talked to me that way. No one ever even raised their voice. I never allowed it in *my* home and to have my own son-in-law . . . *do* you know what he said? Do I look like some old totty you can say such things to? He just shouted it with his own daughter sitting right there listening, right to my face! The door was open and you could hear him way down the corridor. And all I was doing there in the first place was trying to help him. I was just trying to see that his daughter finished her education and that's all the thanks I get. *Yes*, sir, with the door wide open so anybody passing by could hear him.

Well, you know Mary ran away. She just picked right up and ran away to New York without telling a soul. It was the last thing I expected, she was always such a quiet sort of girl, you never know what's going on in her head, but if I'd have thought she was mean and stealthy like her father, I'd have . . . She hadn't been gone an hour before they called me from the school, long distance.

It was a terrible shock after all I've been through with Constance, the funeral and all, and as I say I never suspected for one minute that . . . She was so quiet, she never took any interest in boys, not that I cared—girls that age are a nuisance when they go boy-crazy—but she seemed so sweet, de*mure*, you might say, and then when they told me she had run away, well, she's just a little sneak. What I went through with her in that hotel room! How a girl her age—she's just seventeen, you know—how in heaven's name she could even *think* such things!

You see, I was at Bill and Ginny McWhorter's when the call came in. We always play bridge on Sunday nights, Bill and Ginny and Amby Fowler and I. Now that I'm alone, I always eat just a light supper Sunday evenings and Amby picked me up about seven and we stopped by the Greek's for a bottle of Scotch and some soda water and we went straight over to Bill and Ginny's. When Austin was alive, the four of us used to play every Sunday night of the world—Bill was in Austin's class, you know. They roomed together their junior year, and after Austin passed on, Bill asked me if it would be all right to get Amby Fowler to make a fourth so we could keep the game going. He said to me, it was just a week after the funeral, "Emmy, I'm not even pretending that a lousy Alpha Delt is worthy to sit in Austin's chair, but Amby's a nice fellow and he plays bridge for keeps," he said. Well, I don't believe in letting sorrow wreck your life, do you, and I thought it was sweet of Bill to be so cute about it.

We used to play a tenth of a cent. You know Austin—he liked to talk about everything in the world, just ramble on, while we were playing, but now that Amby and I are partners, we play half a cent and you may not believe it but you know my mink coat? Austin paid three thousand dollars for it at Jaeckel's in New York, but it was too long, you know how short they're wearing them now, and I had to have it fixed, and actually I made enough playing with Amby to have it shortened and not only that, I paid the insurance on the house, too. We win a good deal oftener than we lose, even against Bill and Ginny, and Ginny keeps saying things like we ought to be incorporated and hinting that there's something between Amby and I.

Now obviously there's nothing between us any more than a rabbit, but I like Amby. They say he took ten, fifteen thousand a year out of Primex Paper right through the depression, but you know how kind of prissy he is, he always has his nails manicured and they say he has his clothes made in London—I don't think it's London. New York. But they say London and maybe it is. And he certainly is polite enough, he never takes his coat off when we're playing even on hot nights in the summer, he has beautiful manners. But I don't know— last year, for instance, when they had the paper- and box-makers' convention in Kansas City and Harry Loud said there were some girls, the usual convention sort of thing, and one of them made up to Amby. She tried to sit on his lap and he got mad. Now Amby's a bachelor and Lord knows there was nothing for him to get mad at, but she tried to sit on his lap and he stood up and it dumped her on the floor and Harry said it made a couple of fellows sore at Amby— they were paying the girls twenty dollars apiece for the evening and who the hell did he think he was, Primex Paper or no Primex Paper, pushing the entertainers around, that's what they said. You see what I mean. He's cold, aus*tere*, kind of, and he reads a lot. Austin called him a God-damned pansy, not to his face, of course. Isn't that awful? But I believe marriage is a permanent thing—Austin was good enough for me and he'll always be good enough for me even up there in Elm- wood Cemetery, but Amby *is* a marvelous bridge player and I like to play with him.

Well, we got there a little early, and Bill and Ginny were having coffee in the living room. You know Ginny keeps a nigger maid, Irma—she likes to pretend that nigger help is more exclusive or some- thing, but I know for a fact that she gets Irma for three dollars less a week than I pay Louise. I don't think Bill McWhorter's practice is what it used to be. I know Amby doesn't think so either or he wouldn't bring a bottle of Scotch every time we play. Well, anyhow, Bill said something about the early bird getting the worm and asked us to have some coffee and Amby gave Irma the Scotch and the soda water and we all sat down, except Bill—he went to get the card table out of the closet.

Speaking of Bill's practice, Ginny serves the vilest coffee, that three-pounds-for-thirty-nine-cents stuff you get at the Super. I saw

Irma in there buying it one time when I stopped in to get a head of lettuce, those large stores always carry a fresher stock. We hadn't any more than sat down when Bill and Amby started in on Roosevelt and I had to say something to keep from drinking that awful coffee and I noticed Ginny had on that black satin-back crepe that Miss Carey remodeled for her from two years ago and that reminded me—you see, I didn't expect a phone call. I was just sitting there. I didn't think anyone knew where I was, but they called the house and Louise told them—but, as I say, that old dress of Ginny's reminded me that I had spent all of Saturday afternoon looking for a dress myself. Of course, there's no place to look in this town but Benson's and Berg & Rosenbaum's and those Jew stores cheat you anyway. I just wanted something, I remember telling Ginny—it's curious how things work out, isn't it? I told Ginny I didn't think I could afford to go East this fall to get anything and anyhow I just wanted something to wear afternoons or, well, to play bridge in like that night and I said, "You'd think somebody in Benson's would at least *hear* of *Vogue* or *Harper's Bazaar* instead of that dreadful old stuff they keep in stock." As a matter of fact, I *told* Claude Benson that right to his face. We were coming down in the elevator and I said, "You're going to run your trade out of town," I said, never thinking that I was practically on my way to New York when I said it.

Oh, and another thing that was prophetic. Ginny asked me how Mary was doing at St. Hilda's. I can see how she wanted to change the subject, sitting there in that old satin-back crepe, and I told her "Fine," and then she said, "What do you hear from Richard? He's in New York now, somebody said." And I told her I hadn't heard anything from him since the funeral and she asked me if he was coming out here and I said, "I'm sure *I* don't know." You see, I once told Ginny that it was my firm belief that Richard was in love with Constance when she divorced him and it's still my firm belief, for that matter, and I suppose Ginny expected him to come out and weep at Constance's grave because she said, "Feeling the way he did about Connie, I should have thought he would have come to the funeral as long as he was coming back to this country anyway." And I told her that his return was totally unexpected and had nothing to do with

Constance's death—I think he was fired, myself, but all Ginny was trying to do was pump me, I could tell, and that's one thing I won't stand for, people prying into your personal affairs.

Well, we played five rubbers and Amby and I won most of them. The second was a scratch and Bill and Ginny took the last one but we were in them, oh, I guess maybe twenty dollars on the three we won, but when they won the last one, Bill got all excited and put his handkerchief on his head and said his luck had changed and he wanted to make it a cent a point. Amby said all right, but I kept still because Bill can't afford a cent a point but if they want to be such fools as to . . . and Bill said, "We'll make it two cents. I'll show you, my fine-feathered friends." Ginny didn't want to play that high, I could tell, but Bill kept heckling Amby about the licking they were going to give us and Amby said to me, "Do you want to make it two cents, Emmy?" and I said it was all right with me, and while Irma was making some fresh drinks, Bill started telling stories—it makes him feel good to win, even one rubber.

Have you heard this one? The one about the plasterer? Oh, you needn't worry—the humor exceeds the smut. Well, there was a woman who was having her house done over, painting and redecorating, and there was fresh plaster in the upstairs hall. And the woman's husband came in late that night? Have you heard it? He came in late and there was this plaster and when he got to the top of the stairs he slipped a little and stuck out his hand to save himself, you know how you do, and he left a big handprint in the plaster. So the next morning when the plasterer gets there to go to work, the woman says to him, "Before you start, I wish you'd come upstairs. I want to show you where my husband put his hand last night." *Wait*, now wait. I know it's a scream. And the plasterer, the plasterer said, "Nah, lady. I'm too old for that sort of thing but I'll split a bottle of beer with you."

Well, I nearly died and everybody was simply rocking with laughter except Amby. He sat there with his face longer than the moral law, going tisk! tisk! pretending he was shocked, to cover up the fact that he really does disapprove of stories like that in mixed company. That's the way he is.

I didn't want Bill to get started on his repertoire because I wanted to start another rubber. You see, whenever Bill has won a little and he's had a couple of drinks, he always overbids. It only takes two drinks and he can hardly see the cards.

Well, Ginny dealt and I nearly dropped dead when I picked up the cards. I really did. I had a seven and a half honor count, a hundred honors in three suits with an outside king. Julia Satterlee had a hand something like that two years ago out at the Country Club and she played it all wrong, but, well, as I say, you could have knocked me down with a feather. You *hear* about such things but the odds must be practically astronomical.

Ginny passed and I bid two spades. Bill passed and Amby bid three spades and when it came to me again I said, "Six spades," and Bill doubled and I redoubled. I was perfectly sure somehow that Amby and I could make it, and I remember starting to talk because I hate to gloat especially when people are such poor sports as Bill and Ginny. Seeing that awful old crepe dress of Ginny's reminded me and so I began talking about the dress I was trying to find and I said I would like to get something in a green—green's so becoming, don't you think? —and Ginny asked, "What color green?" and I said, "You remember that Cadillac Ernie Robertson had five or six years ago?" and she said, "No," and I said, "Oh, you must. Don't you remember that big open car he always drove with the top down? With the wire wheels?" I said. *You* remember it, don't you? "Well," I said, "that's the color." And Ginny said Ernie Robertson hadn't even had a car since 1933 and I said, "Well, maybe it was longer ago than that."

Then Bill McWhorter said, "They haven't had wire wheels on Cadillacs in fifteen years. It's anyway fifteen years."

And I said, "I'm not *talking* about how long ago they had wire wheels on Cadillacs. I'm talking about the color of Ernie Robertson's car. It was a sort of bottle green, you know, dark? Well, I think that would be just the color." And it would be. If there's one color I like, it's that rich dark bottle green.

And Amby Fowler chimed in, "The color for what?"

And just as Amby said that, the phone rang.

Irma answered it. "Iss for you, Miz Harrison. Long distance."

And I said, "Long distance!" because you don't expect people to call you long distance when you're out playing bridge.

Well, it was Mother Crescentia at St. Hilda's, and the first thing she said was that Mary had run away. She hadn't come to chapel and they thought at first she was sick so they sent a nun, it was Sister Anne Bibiana, and Sister Anne hunted high and low and said she couldn't find her, and Mother Crescentia had the night watchman search the grounds and *he* couldn't find her, and she asked if she was with me and I told her she wasn't. "I haven't seen her," I said. Well, did I have any idea where she might be, and then she asked me if she should notify the police and I said, "My God, no," right in her ear— I didn't stop to think who I was talking to, probably shocked the old woman to death, but notify the p*olice*. Nobody in my family has ever had the police after them and they're not going to start now.

Of course, all this time I had to whisper and talk low because I knew Ginny was listening and I said, "I think I know where she is," and she said, "Where?" and I said, "In New York. With her father. I'll wire him."

She asked would I do that and let her know immediately. And then she went on about the reputation of St. Hilda's and what an unusual occurrence this was and on and on until I thought I'd scream. I wanted to get back to my hand because while I was talking I had already decided to go to New York on Monday and get Mary and buy a dress while I was there and I could tell that if Bill and Ginny lost as much as I thought they would, I could help out a lot on my trip with my winnings.

Well, finally Mother Crescentia said she would pray for Mary's safety and I said, "All right, I'll let you know as soon as I can." I said it very loudly so they could hear me in the other room and I hung up.

It's not that I would mind telling Amby Fowler but I absolutely refuse to reveal my personal affairs to Bill and Ginny McWhorter. You might just as well broadcast it into one of those radio microphones. Ginny's bridge club meets on Wednesday and then there's the D.A.R. meeting on Thursday and I don't care to have every woman in town pawing over my private business, would you? There is such a thing as dignity.

When I came back into the living room—it was dark in the hall—I rubbed my eyes and I said, "My, I should have put the light on."

And Bill—now whatever you say about him, Bill McWhorter's nobody's fool—Bill stood up and said, "Anything important, Emmy?"

Now he knows perfectly well that the only people who would call me long distance are my sister in Cedar Rapids and my brother in San Francisco but Bill knew Fred is too close with his money to do that unless they had another earthquake *or* he knew it was something about Richard, so I quick said, "Oh, it was Olive Warren." You know Olive Warren.

"Olive Warren?" Ginny said. "What's she doing calling you way here?"

And I said she was getting a group of girls together over there to knit socks for the British and she wanted to know if I'd start doing it here in town. I wasn't lying. I had had a letter from Olive just the day before, asking if I'd start a group here. And Ginny wanted to know why Olive Warren was taking it on herself to help the British Empire and she said the British had stumbled along several thousand years without any help from Olive Warren and Bill swelled all up like a poisoned pup and just burst out, "Knitting socks for the British. By God, that's the limit. You watch what I say—that God-damned Roosevelt is going to shove us into this war as sure as you're a foot high. Knitting socks for the British."

And Amby said in that mild way of his, "Why, I don't suppose Roosevelt told Olive Warren to start knitting personally."

And, oh, they got into a terrible argument. Bill got just rabid, you know the way he does. He said that Roosevelt had to get us into war to cover up the mess he's made. He said he had to get us into war before election so he could get out gracefully into private life with his charm and that big cigarette holder, and Bill said that was all this scare was —the Germans don't want war. He said when he was in Chicago last month he was talking to a man in the dyeing business, makes dyes for rugs and clothes and things, and this man had just been talking to a German, a representative of the big German dye trust—he called it some name, the I. G. Farm Industry or something. Anyhow it's German for dye works, and this man said positively that Hitler wanted peace and that all Roosevelt was doing was trying to get us into war to hide the mess he's made in this country. Well, there I was with this marvelous hand to play and they *arg*ued and they *arg*ued until I thought I'd go out of my mind.

First Amby would say, "Oh, come on, Bill, I don't think we're in such a mess."

And Bill would say, "Not in a mess? You don't think we're in a mess? Why, good God Almighty, you had a *strike*. Primex was shut down eleven days. Your factory. The factory your father started. A bunch of God-damned Red agitators coming in and telling you how to run your business. I suppose you *like* to have Roosevelt shove the C.I.O. into your plant. I suppose you *like* to pay strawboard cutters ninety cents an hour. I suppose you *like* to shut down on Saturdays so your employees can lay around on their God-damn ass drinking beer." That's what he said. Imagine!

Well, of course, Ginny just screamed at him and Bill subsided and begged our pardon and I thought before they got to fighting I'd just remind them that we were playing a hand of bridge so I said, "Are we going to play bridge or are we just going to cuss Roosevelt?" and everybody laughed and we started to play.

Bill had an ace of hearts and the king singleton and it fell. And after his next lead, I drew trump and it was a lay-down. I could tell Ginny was furious. She hates to lose anyway and when you can't afford it . . . Well, I made about twenty-seven dollars the whole evening, and with what I won the week before I could nearly pay the fare to New York the way fares are now.

Well, I got to New York and I went to Richard's hotel and the desk clerk gave me the room number and I went up. They were on the twelfth floor and I wish you could have *seen* those rooms. He'd gotten her a *suite*, living room, bath, and, just imagine, a suite for a child of seventeen. Well, I knocked at the door and immediately before she even knew who it was, Mary said, "Come in, Grandmother." The door was unlocked and I walked in and there Mary was.

I said, "Well, young lady."

And she said back, just as saucy, "*Well*, Grandmother." She was mocking me. And then she said, "Sit down." It was just as if she were in her own house and I was a guest or something. And I tell you the place looked just like a greenhouse—there were flowers everywhere, roses, chrysanthemums, violets, just bunches of them, and I guess she was just starting to unpack because the wardrobe trunk Richard got her when she went away to school was standing open in one corner of the living room.

Then she said to me, "Did you have a nice trip?"

And I said, "Now see here, Mary, *you're* going back to school. You can just start packing right up again. The idea, running away like this." And I said, I spoke very pleasantly, "Now come along. I'll help you pack." You see, I thought as long as Richard wasn't there if I could just get her out of the hotel and leave a note . . . so I told her, "I've got a return ticket for you and . . ."

She interrupted me, "But you can turn it in if it's not used, can't you? Can't you turn it in and get your money back?"

Well, by that time I was standing over by the closet with my arms full of her clothes. I was going to help her pack and I turned around and said, "What did you say?"

"I'm not using the ticket, Grandmother," she said.

I was so surprised I just stood there. "What do you mean you're not using the ticket?"

And she said, "I'm staying here."

"Staying *here*?" I said. "Well, you certainly aren't."

And she said, "Now, Grandmother, put my dresses back and sit down a minute. Please."

I didn't pay any attention to her. I folded the dresses and laid them over the racks in the trunk.

"Grandma, please listen," she said.

And I told her, "Mary, there's nothing to listen to. You're coming back to school with me. Do you think I want *my* granddaughter sneaking away like a thief in the night? How do you think it makes me feel after all I've been through with your mother—and your father too, for that matter—to have the Mother Superior call me up long distance, she was nearly beside herself. It was all I could do to keep her from breaking down right there on the phone. I was over at the McWhorters' playing bridge and she called the house first and Louise told her to call the McWhorters' and their hall is right off the living room and . . . what will people think?"

And she said, "I don't care what people think."

"You'll care when you're older," I said, and I had just started to say something else when she jerked my arm, why, she was just like a tiger, she nearly tore my dress, and she *looked* at me—I've never *seen* such hatred in a girl's face—and she said, "But I'm not older. I don't have to care. Now is not the time to care what people think. You have to do things. Don't you see? You have to do things you want to do and there isn't any time." And all the time she was talking she kept pulling at my sleeve.

Well, I could see she was overwrought and she was nearly crying, so excited and all, so I said very quietly and soothing, "Now, Mary, sit down. Right there. Come on. Sit down. There's a good girl." I thought I could reason with her but she just flung herself into the chair —she was just as sullen as she could be—and I said, "Now tell Grand-mother just what it is you want to do so much." Personally I don't think she was doing very well at school. Her grades were all right but she had probably made some enemies—Lord knows I wouldn't be sur-prised, if she acted the way she did with me. It certainly surprised me—or one of the nuns had corrected her or something—so I told her to tell me what it was.

And she said, "Why should I?" Just like that, why should I? "You're only trying to do your best for me, an old woman's best," she said.

Now one thing I pride myself on is: I can keep my temper, so I said, "But Grandmother can't help being old."

And then she said the strangest thing. I'll tell you what it means in a minute. She said, "Now the other paw." Can you imagine? "Now the other paw," she said.

"What other paw?" I said, naturally.

"Sympathy," she said.

Well, of course I couldn't make head or tail of what she was talk-ing about but I said, "Well, it might not be a bad idea for you to have some sympathy for older people."

And she said, "Oh, stop referring to yourself in the third person. You're not a good fairy." Imagine!

And I said very calmly, "I'm not pretending that I'm a good fairy. I am merely trying to help you and if you'll stop throwing yourself around and acting like a two-year-old and tell me what it is you want to do . . ."

"Oh, don't be bland," she said. "Don't hold yourself in. Gossard does that wherever it's possible."

"*Mary!*" I said.

"And don't be shocked."

And I said to her, "Mary, I forbid you to talk like this to me."

And she said, "I never could at home. There was something about the chairs—the way they looked at you—and the sideboard falling forward on you and the way the light came in the windows. I was tied to it and I was tied to you. But I can talk to you now," and she said, "You're just a mean old woman who has to command someone."

And I said very quietly, "Whenever you're through with this tirade, kindly let me know."

But she went right on, "First it was your Austin—you tossed him from one paw to the other, first you cringed and then you bossed him and then you killed him. Then it was Mother. Loving you or duty, love and duty, love and duty until she didn't want to live any more. And now you want it to be me—somebody you can grind, somebody you can wreak yourself on like a vengeance." Well, did you ever in your life hear a girl talk that way, a young girl?

So I just said, "If you're quite finished, you can assist me packing."

Well, she just screamed, "*I'm not going with you!*"

Of course, Richard *would* have to come in just then and he looked right past me and said to her, "You go on in the other room, Mary. Take a bath or something."

Then he looked at me and he said, "Hello, Emmy."

I just said, "Humph."

And he said, "What do you want?"

And I said, "You know very well what I want. I came to put Mary back in school."

"She's not in school," he said.

"Not in *school!* Why, I just talked to the Mother Superior . . ."

He cut me right off. "You talked Sunday," he said. "I withdrew Mary yesterday. By telephone."

"I don't suppose you thought it worth your while to consult me," I said.

"Why should I consult you, Emma?" he said. "Is there any reason?" Any *rea*son.

"Only that Mary has been in my care. It would have been courteous to let me know," I said.

"Now we have Mrs. Austin Harrison of the D.A.R. and the Huguenot Society. The riposte genteel to put me in my place, eh?" And then he said, "Why, Emmy, you old fraud, you know you come to New York every fall." And he said he bet me that I had bought a dress or something that day and he said that when I said I had come to New York to get Mary, it was just a self-righteous pretense for a shopping trip. Why, I just told you a minute ago that the only reason in the world I went to New York was to get Mary. Oh, he talked perfectly vile to me.

And I said, "I am only trying to do what I conceive to be my duty to my grandchild."

He talked as if he were bored to death, "Oh, go on, Emmy. Get out. Go on back home."

"I think I have a right to know what is going to happen to Mary," I said.

"Well, I'll tell you," he said. "She's going to support me. She's going to make paper flowers here in the room. And on Saturdays and Sundays when it's snowing, I'm going to buy her a little tray and she's going to sell them in the streets. And when she gets home, I'll beat her if she hasn't made enough money."

"If you can't be serious at a time like this . . ."

"All right, I'll be serious," he said. "I have removed Mary from under your supervision. She will stay here with me from now on. I am not grateful for what you have done," he said.

Well, he made me just furious and I said, "You can't have her."

And he just grinned and said, "I've got her."

And I told him I was not going to allow him to corrupt Mary the way he had Constance, and I said I could think of better companions for a young girl than a drunkard and an adulterer, and I said, "If she stays here, you'll kill her just as you killed your wife."

And he came right over to the chair where I was sitting and grabbed my wrists and pulled me up standing.

"Get out of here, you old bitch," he said and he pushed me right out of the room into the corridor and slammed the door.

9

H E PASSED the arch. It looked like a ruin in the fog. Across the Square he could see, laced over by the bare branches of the trees in front of him, the three lighted windows of his apartment. His topcoat glistened in the aura of the lamps and his hat was wet. On a litter of damp moss in a box under his arm lay coiled the stems and buds of three water lilies and their green pads, wilting perhaps. Yet he did not hurry.

When he passed a man in the Square walking a spaniel, he nearly spoke to him. He was very glad and it made him feel neighborly to be walking home through the fog carrying flowers for his daughter, but he could not quite acknowledge it to himself and he would not have confessed it to a friend, for he was one of the generation to whom anger was the sole emotion that could be displayed openly.

The day after Mrs. Harrison had gone, he had asked his daughter where she wanted to live. If she had answered, "The Waldorf," he would have been willing. If she had said, "Flatbush," or "Red Hook," he would have telephoned a rental agent with properties to lease in those regions. For she, after her arrival, had filled him with surprise and wonder. She was so tall. She had such a lovely face. He was charmed by the movements of her thin hands, to be, soon, so graceful. She answered his questions shyly at first but intelligently. And although still a stranger, she was alive—he understood now that he had counted on a little girl, ungrown, silent and motionless as in the photographs, a care and a responsibility. And in the relief and, he believed, the growing delight in discovering what she liked and what she knew, he would ask her questions so that he could watch her lift her head to reply, attentive only to the movement of her lips, the light on her hair, and the sound of her laughter if the questions were silly.

"And the dog? Do you like dogs? How about the dog, as a beast?"

"The dog is man's best friend—I'm a girl." And then, "No, I like them all except Bedlingtons, I think. I'd rather have a real lamb than a Bedlington."

And, as if she might leave him suddenly, with a vague half-hidden fear that he might be unsatisfactory, not kind enough or sprightly enough—what did a young girl want, a daughter?—he gave her flowers every day, anxiously, almost as a propitiation, the violets, roses with strange names, the cheap street gardenias, and now these lilies.

In his first few days with her, as he watched her stare into the shop-windows on Madison Avenue or bend her head to examine a menu, and especially in the elevators in tall buildings, both of them curiously silent as most people are in elevators, he was able to discover what he expected from her. At first it seemed to him selfish that he wanted to give her a place to live in, furnished as she liked, the clothes and enter-tainment a young girl wanted, and his companionship, say love, such as it was, and in return for these things, which after all it was his duty to supply, he could have this innocent, foreign happiness in looking at her and listening to her. It was, he thought, a possessive pleasure which he could not share, that no one else would enjoy. It was fresh because it was accidental, almost astonishing, and the only state it resembled at all was the hypnotic fascination he remembered watching his grandmother knit when he was a boy, or in a man digging ditches, and once in Czechoslovakia he had found it in a Sokol—the soothing enchantment of following a repeated physical movement.

Yet, as he thought about it more, he could see that he did not value her merely as an aesthetic spectacle (*Performance Continuous—Show Now Going On*). It was more as if her loveliness in movement or repose could exist only in an atmosphere which itself created. She carried her island with her, and he, as a father privileged, could bask at its periphery not as a father but as a man at once devoted to beauty and modestly hopeful of forgetting an unhappy journey. He wanted to be with her because he could reject himself and the stupidities of his past that, committed once, had now misshapen him, and with her he could overlook the emblems he had seen of an inevitable future: he was graying and with little dewlaps beneath his jaws, puffs of fat beneath his navel, and little twinges here and there; he would grow older and so would she—to marry. And, worse, like a man who knows he has a cancer in him, tumid and incurable, heavy beneath his skin to his secret, exploring fingers yet somehow (since there is death in it) not admissible, ignored, and not admitted, he could neglect the signals of war as long as he was with his daughter, the war Verplanck had asked about, the war that had begun. He had seen the samples. Passing the Gestapo headquarters in the Alexanderplatz, once he heard a scream and a *Schupo* had hustled him on. At Croydon he had been dismayed by the vulturine smile of Chamberlain, who did not even know he was a bird. And in the barbaric, thick, complacent necks—where he could place no foot—of von Bock's army in Poland. At first he had taken sides. In 1933 Paris was plastered with *affiches* headed LA GUERRE PRÉPARÉ OUVERTEMENT PAR HITLER, and he would condemn the Germans to anyone. After Munich, awake three nights, he had been sick in a *Luftkranke* sack on his way to London, "from cynicism," he said later. Now, at this distance, he was sad and afraid and his daughter could shield him from the sadness and the fear for a while.

"Where would you like to live?" he had asked her. "Do you want to stay here?"

"I don't know. I haven't thought."

"A hotel's a nice place. You can have breakfast in bed."

"Yes, that's true, but I'd get tired of it."

"Convenient to the midtown shopping centers, the theater district, and many other points of cultural and historic interest."

"Could we get an apartment, do you think?"

"Yes. What kind? Do you want a man with gold braid standing in front of it? The best ones have old men with white mustaches. They wash the mustaches in water with bluing in it. It makes the hair seem whiter."

"You always joke about everything."

That was true. He was facetious because he did not want to startle her. There had been few opportunities for him to express naturally the kind of tenderness he felt. "I'm sorry. What kind of apartment?"

"Something that doesn't cost too much, where I can do the work."

"Do the work?"

"Yes. Cook. Keep the place clean. A home, sort of."

It would be indelicate to notice her sincerity. As she said the word "home," he almost protested that for him, born an outlander, a foreigner by profession until now, a home for him in New York City would be impossible. The city was a place where you did your work and then, as the colored boy said, you et a few peas and laid down. The shaded streets of his birthplace, the brick house where still, if he should ever visit it, he could place his hand accurately on the wooden ball of the newel post of the banister in the dark, the line of the roof next door against the sky, all these were linked together by a time, his childhood, when all familiar things lie in your heart then and afterward. The city had been a workshop or a stopover. He knew he could not find himself a home in it, in this thick air, along these treeless streets, but maybe she could find him one.

"You mean a bed-sitter and a bath and . . ."

"No. About five rooms."

"That'll be a lot of work to take care of."

"I'd like it. I've never had a place like that."

"Sure?"

"Yes."

"All right. We'll find something. But where? What part of town do you want to live in?"

"I don't know New York. You pick it out."

"Do you like to ride on trains?"

"Long train rides, yes."

"Short train rides, no?"

"Yes. No." She giggled.

"That lets out Ossining, Harmon, Croton, Poughkeepsie, and points north. Also Connecticut. Are you social?"

"How do you mean?"

"High-toned. If you had a daughter, would you send her to school in France, let her hunt a season with the Quorn or the Bicester . . ."

"Fox hunting?"

"In a pink coat. And then have her presented at court in London . . ."

"Fox hunting's silly."

"Well, you might say kings are silly too. They used to call this one Dirty Bertie when he was young. And then come home and have a big debutante party at the Waldorf?"

"I'm not social."

"Then we won't live on Park Avenue."

"That's where it goes through the tunnel?"

"About Forty-second Street, yes. Just give me a sketch then. What have you got in mind? You must have had some notion, didn't you, when you were escaping?"

"When I was escaping I was thinking all the time about Grandmother. I knew when she caught up with me, she would say, 'Well.' . . ."

"Out of the reveries of the menopause."

"What?"

"Nothing. Go on."

"She would say this 'Well,' and that would mean she knew I knew I was in the wrong. You see? As if she were going to say, 'Well, this is a fine way to act,' only she never finished."

"She said it, didn't she?"

"Oh, yes. Grandmother never surprises you."

"Well, this isn't finding us a place. Now that you're free, what kind

125

of . . . you really know you're free, don't you? I mean, Grandma's a dead pigeon?"

"Yes. As soon as I defied her, I felt older. I'd been waiting for that for a long time. I could almost feel my face changing."

"You can do as you please now."

"I don't please to do very much right now. It's nice just being here with you."

"Please to select a place to live, will you? Come on now, think, weigh, select, and we'll go look."

"There's a lot to see here. I don't want to be in the middle of it. Do you think we could find some place fairly quiet, without too much traffic and people going by, and a tree maybe?"

"We might look around Washington Square."

"I remember that. Mother took me there once—for the history. I remember the arch."

A pale-yellow glow shone through the fanlight above the white door. He pressed the button under the slot with his card in it, engraved *Richard Miles* in script, and underneath in ink, *Miss Mary Miles*. There was a buzz. The lock clicked, and he went in and began to climb the two flights of stairs, flipping the lapels of his topcoat back and forth and striking his dripping hat on his thigh. It was an old house, remodeled, and while the handrail on the stair was made of walnut, a deep brown, shiny and fatigued, a beautiful mirror for any light, there was a musty smell in the hallway like a cellar's. As he climbed, he heard the door upstairs open and he looked up.

He saw her leaning over the rail, looking down at him, smiling. "Hello," she said. "Did you get it?"

"Yes."

"What's that under your arm?"

"You wait and see."

"Did you bring the steaks for dinner?"

"I forgot. I'll go get them in a minute."

As he reached the hallway before his door, she kissed him on the cheek. "Oh, you're wet."

"Fog out and I walked from Sheridan Square."

"You got a job?"

They went into the apartment. The thought crossed his mind while he was speaking of something else: this is what I want. Home enough, even with the wilderness outside.

"*Auf befehl, Herr Hauptmann.*" He clicked his heels and bowed.

"Father, I have only the French *politesse*. That's all I was taught. Don't speak German."

"You know it's German?"

"Yes. I can tell that. What does it mean?"

"At your command, Herr Captain. You said you thought it was time I got a job—so I got a job."

"I didn't mean you had to rush right out and . . ."

"You were perfectly right. No man, I don't care who he is, looks well in a dressing gown for three days running. Even if there are pajamas underneath, there's that décolleté, sometimes fluffy, that looks queer. You were right. It was time I got something to do."

"But I didn't mind. I liked hearing about Hitler and Chamberlain and Daladier."

"But it was time I went to work just the same, wasn't it?"

"No. It was just that I didn't think it was a lot of fun for you to sit around talking to me. What is the job?"

"Translating French cables for Havas."

"Can we live on it?"

"How do you like potatoes?"

"Oh."

"I've got some money. Later on I can get something else."

"Why later on?"

"Oh, when we get really settled. I don't intend to make a career translating military communiqués—*Nuit calme. Activité des avions.*"

"But I don't think we ought to live . . ."

"Beyond our means. Neither do I." As soon as he had said it, he saw that it had always been a conviction that he took some pleasure in violating. He had never paid much attention to finances. He had been lucky selling feature stories and magazine articles. "Look, do you want me to make a lot of money? I can lecture. There's a man uptown who wants me to. He suggested, mornings, *The Menace of*

Hitlerism, and *Why I Fear Russia* evenings. I can buy a shad-belly coat and we can travel and see the women's clubs. Do you want to do that? Money in it. Choke a horse."

"What's in that package?"

"Here, you open it." He gave her the flowers and went to hang up his coat and hat in the closet.

When he returned to the couch where she was sitting, she had undone the package and sat looking at the water lilies.

All she did was to look up and smile.

"I'll put them in water. The buds will open then."

She came back in a moment with the flowers in a bowl of glazed red clay and set them down on a side table at the end of the couch. She sat down with her chin in her hand, looking at them as if she expected them to bloom at once. There was a little fireplace opposite her, and a flame hovered above the coal, lighting her face. She did not know that she was sitting with her feet toeing in. She touched the buds with her finger lightly. Miles sat across from her in a chair, in warmth and leisure, an ankle on one knee. He knew now that this was what he had not known he had been searching for, and he hesitated to say or suggest anything because he wanted to keep her just as she was, absorbed.

She looked up. "They always said I'd drown if I went to look for these. I never had many before."

"They're hard to find this time of year, but I thought you'd like them."

"They look nice there on the table, don't they?"

"Wonderful. The whole place is wonderful."

"I meant to ask you. Would you like a party? A housewarming? I mean, you must have people you'd like to see or come in for a drink. Just because I'm here, don't . . ."

"A housewarming? I don't know."

A party? With Gilbey, Sports, of the *News*, with a gaunt nervous wife, hiding in a powder pallor the wrinkles of an age she tried to deny in an iron vivacity? With Felsch and Brewster of the *Herald Tribune*, Felsch single, an incipient military expert with whom he had covered the war in Spain, and Brewster, married with two children, fathering his way through the evening (with photos), no longer a drinker but drinking? With Abernathy of the *Eagle*, with his country wife, down on a murder story in Delaware and returned with this beautiful, black-haired girl, like a Eurasian, Shanghai, Bubbling Well Road, a skin like white bond paper and lips of a natural purple, slow in speech and movement, silent, and, honest to God, her name was Schultz before she was married at seventeen to Abernathy and she played the saxophone in the high-school band?

Were these the people he wanted? The professional friends of a widower?

GILBEY: I and Whitey Bimstein have got a piece of a tiger who scuffles under the name of Fighting Babe McNulty, the Texas Cyclone. Our tiger is a mean party and he's tough and he can take a punch but he's a splasher. For an extra two bucks fifty he'll cross us up. When he ankles down the aisle he looks like a wild stallion. He spits and swears and tugs the ropes like Dempsey used to do, and he won't shake hands with his opponent for hell. When the bell rings for Round 1, he pops out and slams his man smackdab on the beard. And bingo! just like that, the Cyclone is down from a whiff that went by him and he won't get up. He's a mighty man and unafraid but he's a blood cheater—the level hurts his feet. We toss him in with Mohammed Fahay, the Turkish middleweight from the Bronx, and the Cyclone belts him out. This is a surprise to the management, so we ast our man what happens and he says he don't like no Turks.

BREWSTER: And this is a picture of Junior when . . .

FELSCH: . . . before my money gave out, I lived in a little joint on the Calle Santa María de la Cabeza, reading von der Goltz and Jomini. It's not far from the Prado. I lived on fish. Then I joined the Brigade just before Brunete. That's where Jimmy Hollingsworth got it. We were lost, sneaking along all bent over, and a bullet sails up from behind and plugs him in the kidney, it was about there, I guess. He fell down and he looked at me and said, "Jesus, this hurts." And I opened his shirt and pants and his guts were all outdoors. It was an explosive bullet and it blew everything to hell, purple, green—you ever see guts?—blood all over. And Jimmy had read books and he was going to be brave, keeping his face stiff, sucking in his breath, and trying not to look at himself. I threw a couple of shots where the bullet came from and nothing happened, so I tried to patch him up. I couldn't move him, the way he was, and I knew he shouldn't have anything to drink. About all I could do was fold his shirttails over the wound. He was brave for about two hours and then he started to holler and after a while he died. I didn't believe it. I'd seen them shot and fall but I had never had a guy die slow right in front of me. When he was dead I started to paw out a hole to put him in, but it was hardpan and getting dark, and what the hell, he didn't need a hole, so I left him. When the fighting was over, coming back in the truck, the grapes were ripe and people were picking them in the vineyards and if you held out your hat, they would toss you a bunch of ripe grapes and yell "*Salud!*" Fish and those grapes were all I remember eating much in Spain.

BREWSTER: And here's Emmelyn down at Jones Beach the first time she swam without anyone holding her up.

ABERNATHY: . . . amiable enough, capable enough, but I'm positive he's a Commie. He called this meeting after the Russo-German pact and insisted that it was very urgent that the League get out some literature praising Russia's continual effort for peace. All of us thought Russia had betrayed the Popular Front and we all said so, nearly all of us anyhow. Thomson made a speech and Rothstein made a speech against Russia, and everyone applauded except him, of course. He got up and said the matter would come to a vote. We thought, "Let it come." We voted and it was "No literature." We voted again. Still "No." He tried it a third time and there was not a single change in the balloting. He turned a light green, with fear, it was, I'm sure, and said, "I'm afraid I can't accept the vote." Rothstein asked if this were parliamentary procedure. "I can't accept the vote," he kept saying. That was when we resigned from the League. You see I'm positive he was under orders to get out a brochure and he was willing to do it after a vote if the vote was favorable. If it wasn't, the brochure would be published anyway. I'm certain he's a Commie.

BREWSTER: (*Drunk by this time*) Gahdammit looka these pictures. You talk romance. These kids—reality, future of the race, anastigmat lens.

And if they came to warm his house, how he would play the sporting gent with Gilbey; finger Brewster's photographs; hoist up the memories of war with Felsch; grieve and attack the men of bad will with Abernathy out of politeness; and all the while, in an attitude depending from the mantel, actually touching his mustache from time to time, how he would play the sahib with Mrs. A.!

"I don't think you would like my friends, Mary," he said to her quite seriously. "Would you really like a party?"

"No. Not particularly. I just asked."

"We can have one if you like. I know enough people, God knows, but it would just be drinking and . . ."

"Oh, that doesn't bother me. I've watched people drinking often enough."

"No, I don't think we'll have one. It would be dull for you and I'd like to keep my anonymity for a while." He stood up quickly. "I'll go get the steaks."

"How long will you be? I can take the potatoes out of the oven in about ten minutes."

"Oh, there's a place around the corner somewhere. I won't be long." He took his hat and coat out of the closet again.

As he turned toward the door, she said, "Do you want to be anonymous, Father?"

He was embarrassed. He had thought he might get away without explaining. Now he would have to combat the old instinctive fear of telling anyone too much and fumble to be honest.

"I don't like who I was. Do you see?"

"Not exactly."

"That was the reason I came home—I was tired of what I was looking at and reporting and I was tired of what I was looking with. It wasn't interesting any more. Europe changed while I watched it, and I changed too."

He noticed her flush a bright red. She said, looking down, "I can understand that."

He went on boldly, "And as soon as I understood it, then I knew you could help me and maybe I could fix things up a little for you."

Before he had finished she was looking up at him, smiling.

"So you see, these friends, well, they're worn out. One or two not, maybe, but most of them. I don't like them much any more."

"It's all right, Father. Anonymous just seemed a funny word."

He put on his hat, "You don't think I came home because there was a war in Europe, do you?"

"No. It never occurred to me."

Sliding his arm into his right, then his left sleeve, hunching his shoulders until the collar was set, he said, "What I really came home for was to be your pap."

"Get out of here. Get out of here," she said.

It would be time to take the potatoes out in a minute, she thought. Potatoes were friends and you, anonymous to them and all vegetables, wore them out. It didn't take long, not so long as the bedroom at Grandmother's with the windows shaded by the soft maples and the baritone complaining down the corridor and the answer of the soprano, soft, husky, and flawed with disease. And when the voices stopped, they echoed, fretful and insistent, inside you. The dormitory at school where she and the students lay in rows at night, dark, with no firelight, was like a bureau, and God and Saint Hilda on their rounds, gigantic sheeted figures, each lighted with his nimbus, could pull out the top drawer and look at the Upper School, neatly sleeping, and say, "They're all right." And then they could pull out the bottom drawer and if Dodie Burchett and Ellen Cheever were scrapping as usual, God and Saint Hilda could fill their hearts with automatic peace. Presumably they never grew tired of protecting the school. The school never wore out for them the way it had for her.

She was like her father. The people and the places had decayed for them both. For him the fountains in the courtyards of the palaces of Austria had ceased to play. The cathedral at Chartres, which he knew as she knew the photographs, had toppled and the Alps gone flat, a rubble of stones and dirty ice. His friends, unknown, whom she conceived to be geniuses, prime ministers, and kings, had melted crazily like wax dolls, crowns and top hats wilting in the flame of time, and, like him, she bore the stains of echoes and the scars of her passages through the house, upstairs and down, unliked, grown too familiar, and the voices of the nuns a tether she had broken now. She was like her father all right, an inheritance now proved but never explained in biology class. All they had said there was that a planted seed grew into a flower.

But she had escaped and he had withdrawn. He had gone haphazardly to a doorway IN and she had run to a doorway OUT and here they had met. What was shelter for him was freedom for her, here in this room with the glowing fire and the lilies on the table. She would buy books tomorrow, her own books. He would bring her flowers again. They could ride up the Avenue on the bus in the wind and he would take her to the theaters, the galleries, and the bridges, leading her outward through the city, and she could bring him home again secure to this mysterious safety. "To love is to serve," said the nuns.

This was love then.

In serving she would receive. To scrub potatoes and put them to bake and broil the steaks and make a salad and a shelter for her father, would this be happiness before the pictures had been seen in the galleries, the wind felt burning her cheeks on the bus top, and the danger of the bridges? Would she have to wait until the tickets were stubs, the music heard, and the ballet remembered, until she knew that in the kindness of her father's eyes were all the beautiful things she had foreseen, promised herself, and prayed for? Was she waiting for this now? There must be no trickery about this, no swap, no barter. "I am not commercial," she thought. "But this is not complete. Yet. Somehow."

She had come here for something else. She could not feel it or say what it was. Like a name you know but cannot remember. It was not a presence. Her father was all she wanted. Certainly not Grandmother, nor her friends at school whom now, older (she had felt the change in her face), she could disdain. And her mother did not appear in dreams and visions, white, haggard, pleading from the bed with her eyes or as she had been earlier, healthy in the Glen Urquhart skirt she wore to play golf in, nagging briskly. Her mother was dead with a stone on her head.

To Europe there was no admittance because of the war which, ignoring her father's tale of the saurian tanks and the pterodactylic bombers, she still saw, from Tennyson, as a cavalry charge with bugles, a frieze of young men *morituri* in white litevkas and lacquered boots, each waving a sword, and the lovely curve of the horses' rumps catching the light as they galloped. South America was jungle and in jungles you ate quinine. China would come later, and India. No, New York was the place she would have chosen even if she had wanted to travel alone. It was not that she wished to be anywhere else. Like a name or a phone number, it just escaped her. If you waited a minute and thought of something else, it would come to you.

In the warmth of the room, one of the water-lily buds had opened, the green foil split showing white. In the cove of the lake she had gone with Grandmother's chauffeur rowing, never alone so that it might be beautiful and secret, but always with Rex, who complained of the blisters on his hands from the oars. On the shore of the cove were dark trees whose shadows made the water black, and there she was allowed to lean over the side of the flat-bottomed boat (since there was no danger), seeing first the reflection of her face, then moving the lily into the reflection, breaking it, the bland, sweet fragrance rising from the water that you sniffed and sniffed as if in the heart of the flower, even in the root trailing deep below, there were a final sweetness never yet reached, piercing and complete. "*Castalia odorata.* Grows in ponds and still water," Sister Mary Urban said. Like *castitas*, the motto of Saint Hilda. *Sancta Hilda castitas.* "Tomorrow, if I wait," she thought, "it will have blossomed, white and yellow. If I wait."

She bent over the opening flower and sniffed, but the scent was just as it had always been, mild and inconclusive. She encircled the bud with her thumb and forefinger and, pushing back the green of the pod, blew into the petals. "Open, damn you," she whispered. "I can't wait any more. Open up."

PART

II

I

WHEN THE TAXI drew up into the fan of light from the marquee, they both got in. Miles knocked the crown of his opera hat on the low ceiling of the cab. He took it off and snapped it shut. Expecting his daughter's laughter, he turned to her, falsely meek and ready to be mocked at, but she was bent forward, looking out of the window at her right and then at the back to watch the leisurely flow of people going from the theater. He kept still, envying her excitement. As she looked over her shoulder, he could see the tendon of her throat drawn tight. There with her husband was the plump old woman with the jewels and the wide black velvet ribbon around her neck. She saw the man come out who had spoken to her father. He stopped, lit a cigarette, and waggled his hand to put out the match. She could still hear faintly the horns of the orchestra. And as they pulled away, a town car glided softly into the curb behind them. The footman and the chauffeur wore plum-colored livery and the footman jumped out like a monkey.

"Where to?" the driver called back.

"Where is this place?" Miles asked her.

"Do you really want to go there?"

"Sure. This is your party," he said, smiling.

"No, but if you . . ."

"No. I'd like to go. Where is it?"

"It's on Fifty-second Street somewhere."

"Fifty-second Street," Miles called, leaning forward. "We can find it when we get there. They'll have a sign out."

The cab turned into Broadway. It was not night there unless you looked upward, and there the sky was pink. The sidewalks were choked with people inching along, their blank faces pale or green or tinged with yellow in the light from the electric signs. She watched peddlers with their backs to her, shouting neckties voicelessly from trays, and at the street corners stood pushcarts stacked with huge blue grapes, apples, and Japanese persimmons. An old man tended a brazier with hot chestnuts smoking on the lid. Once she looked through the rear window to see the brilliant, stately fish on the Wrigley sign.

"It's wonderful," she said. "Who are all these people?"

"God knows. Citizens."

"Is it always like this?"

"It has to get a lot later and colder before the crowd falls off."

"But what are they doing?"

"Just what you're doing—looking. They're not going anywhere. Or only a few of them."

"I never saw so many people in a place that was free."

"More than you expected?"

"Yes and it's brighter. I didn't know there were so many lights."

They went up Seventh Avenue and turned into Fifty-second Street.

"Do you see the place?" Miles asked.

"All I know is the name of the piano player."

"Y'ain't lookin' for the Stork Club, are you, lady?" the driver turned and asked.

"No. It's a place with a band. Wait. There it is."

As he paid the cab driver, Miles could hear the band. They were playing *Shine*.

Inside it was dark. The platform at the far end where th[e]
played was brightly lighted, but in the rest of the place there
only a few lamps along the walls, covered with blue paper. W[hile]
Miles was checking his hat and coat, a plump headwaiter came up.

"Table for two?" Miles asked.

The waiter ducked his head apologetically toward one shoulder,
"I'm sorry, sir. How about a table for four? It's all we got left."

The tables were set close together, and as Miles followed his
daughter and the waiter through the narrow aisle, he noticed one or
two vacant tables with tops no bigger than a bushel basket. He touched
his daughter's sleeve.

"Look," he said above the music, "he thinks we're rich. He's seen
your new dress."

It was a large table against the wall. The waiter drew it out with
elaborate courtesy and turned at once, clapping his hands for an
underling.

From a slow, suave, rocking-horse trombone solo, the band swept
into an intricate coda and finished *Shine* on a clarinet run upward.
There was great applause and shouting. The band got up for an inter-
mission, crescents of sweat showing black under their arms.

"Do you like it?" Miles asked.

She nodded. "A lot."

It was a good band. There were six Negroes, five of them fresh from
Kansas City, and they kept five pints of gin hidden with the porter in
the dirty-towel hamper in the washroom. The brass was not shiny
and the trombone had a dent in it and they carried no drummer, only
a nervous little brown man who swept and patted an old suitcase with
a pair of brush brooms. It was the piano that had the class, painted
white and set with rhinestones by the management, and the leader,
the well-known one, the Harlem boy with the greased straight hair,
held his wrists high and lolled at the keyboard, plucking out the
chords with his long, limber hands as softly as if he were playing a
spinet.

They did not want a singer and they played all the time the kind of
pieces that every band will test themselves on once in a while, knowing
they must play them well before they can be a good band: *Twelfth*

Kansas City they got three dollars a night apiece in a garage for these tunes or they got gin at weddings on the side or a chicken breakfast or nothing. Now they were making more than scale for playing them in Fifty-second Street, and if waltzes came in and the white kids didn't want to listen any more, they would go back to Kansas City on the bus as dazed as they had come, but without regret, to play in the converted garage again. It was not that they tried to be popular: they did not know any other way to play. All they were doing with the brush brooms and the horns was blowing and beating out the rhythms that made their Grampaw's back lame or trying to echo the ball bat on the biscuit dough on the marble slab in the kitchen of the Big House they had never seen. They knew that if you have to shine shoes to eat, you have to shine the shoes but you can flip the rag—tickety-tickety-tickety—they let you do that. Sometimes in Kansas City they sang:

> *Did y'ever chopa cotton? . . . Huh-huh.*
> *Did y'ever sweepa floor? . . . Huh-huh.*
> *Did y'ever drive a mule till the hame-strap brokenha-ho,*
> *ha-ho, ha-ho, ha-ho.*

It was very sad music really, but the jitterbugs who swarmed around the bandstand called them a "solid combo" and gave them compliments they grinned at but failed to understand because they were only drunken Negroes.

"They'll be back pretty soon," Miles said.

"Have they gone out to smoke reefers?" she asked.

"Just to cool off, I should think. It's stuffy in here."

It was hot and the haze of cigarette smoke was cut off neatly about a foot below the ceiling by the draft from the ventilators.

"Would you like a drink?" Miles asked.

"I don't think so. A lemonade would be swell."

"No Scotch?"

"I tasted of it once."

"You're right. It does taste like old fence posts soaked in creosote. I thought perhaps at your Grandmother's . . ."

cornet's turn. A lot of people stopped dancing to listen. He made the whole thing important. I think Mozart would have liked it maybe. When he stopped I pushed through the crowd, stepping over the shoats and the prize poultry—they got loose, you see—and I asked who he was. Goldkette said, 'Kid named Bix Beiderbecke.' Name mean anything to you?" Miles asked, smiling.

"You've heard him," she said reproachfully. "Was he as good as they say?"

"Better. I went every night after that. Then I lost track of him until one time I was here in town talking to a man, a reporter, and he told me he was dead. He died of pneumonia someplace on Long Island. It was August, very hot weather, and he had lain naked for two days with an electric fan blowing on him, trying to get cool. He probably had a cold and a fever then. He died a day or two later."

"That's tragic, isn't it?"

"I think so. It's tragic because he asked for it."

"He wasn't very old, was he?"

"You mean the young never ask for it?"

"Well, why should he?"

Miles lifted his glass a little off the table. "It was this stuff really, I suppose."

"Whisky?"

"Liquor. They say he drank gin mostly. You know, ordinary people if they drink enough just turn into stew-bums, male if they are male and lady stew-bums if they're women. But the cornettist, I don't think so."

"I've never seen a stew-bum."

"Oh, yes, you have."

"Who?"

"Your grandfather Austin. Don't you remember?"

"I was too small."

"That soft, gentle manner. That little cackle he used to give—it was like a tic, and he had tantrums just like a little child. When anything went wrong, if he sold out fifty shares too soon or if he couldn't get a shirt stud in, I've seen him cry, the tears run right down his face—that was toward the end, of course."

"Why, I didn't know that."

"He kept a bottle in the pantry and a bottle in his desk at the factory . . ."

"Oh, I remember. I found a shoebox full of old corks down cellar one time, and I asked Grandmother if I could have them . . ."

"And she slapped your jaws and took them away from you."

"Just about. She sent me to my room and made me stay there all day. I was five years old, I think."

"Those corks are your grandfather's monument. Emmy never admitted it. As a matter of fact, I don't think she realized how much he drank. She never recognized the condition. You have to have seen a lot of them."

"I never saw one. She never said."

"Maybe I shouldn't have told you."

"I'd have found out sometime, wouldn't I?"

"Yes. I guess you would."

"Well?"

"Well, you take Beiderbecke—always a lot of people around, always with a band. Clubs, hotels, driving around summers to play in those little pineboard dance pavilions, never by himself for a minute. I think the gin gave him quiet so he could listen. Do you see what I mean?"

"In a way. Go on."

"It blotted everything else out, the way you can tune out a radio show. Then he could hear what was running through his head. A bum drinks to make everything easy, and while he's drinking, everything is easy. Austin was very charming when he'd had a few. That's what he wanted to be—charming—and the liquor gave him confidence. It became finally the only climate he could live in. But for Beiderbecke, gin was only a technical device that helped him play his cornet better. I suppose he knew in a vague sort of way that it would break him down or kill him. The wonderful thing was—he didn't care."

"Why is it so wonderful?"

"The willingness to die to make a little horn music?"

"I should think anyone who wanted something would go after it that way."

144

He smiled, pleased at her naïveté and indulging it. "It's not so simple. It's hard not to be turned aside. He was like a saint—no home, no wife, no children. Just the cornet and what he could blow out of it."

She was stirring the cherry in her glass round and round with a straw. "Would you like to be like that, Father?"

"I don't know. . . . Yes, I think so."

"I could have stayed at school. You didn't have to come home."

He saw that he was talking about one thing and she another. "Did you think I was talking about us? I wasn't. I wasn't making a comparison. There's nothing I want to do more than what I'm doing now."

"I haven't . . . trapped you then?"

"My God, no. What makes you think that?"

"I don't know. Tonight when that *Fortune* man was asking you all those questions, I guess I had the feeling that you would rather be back there in the war."

"No. This is what I want to do."

"You're sure?"

"I'm sure."

"Because I'd run away."

"Don't even think about it."

"Well, I wanted to know. You can see how I would." She looked up toward the band platform. "They're coming back."

"You're not going to worry about this, now, are you?" he asked.

"I believe you, Father. Honestly."

Led by the pianist, grinning and combing his shiny black hair with a pocket comb, the band was sauntering in from the washroom at the back. The audience clapped and whistled. A young master of ceremonies dragging a microphone strode out into the middle of the little polished floor where no one danced. He was immediately illumined by a spotlight. He bowed and turned a professionally earnest gaze one way and another as if he could hardly contain the gravity of his message. Suddenly he clutched the stalk of the microphone in both hands, drew up his shoulders, and began, "Now, friends . . ." He wanted to tell them that the old club had struck pay dirt this time and he didn't mean hay. He meant the money the club would derive from the liquor that was sold here tonight, sure, why not? But he also meant that the audience here tonight would be paid for their presence and their kind attention by some of the dirtiest gutbucket driving, jiving heat that he had ever heard in all his experience with high-class entertainment, and moreover, "friends," he said, the old club was able through the kind patronage of the audience here tonight to bring to them for their delectation that genius of the black keys, the one they had all been waiting for, the one and only . . . Here the M.C. was interrupted by cheers, shouts, handclaps, and the tinkling of knives on glasses. He begged them not to forget that next week the old club would bring them for one week only that peerless tosser of the licorice stick, Pee Wee Russell, and his orchestra for one week only. "And now, friends, we will hear the old master giving out with his rendition of Cole Porter's famous melody, *Begin the Beguine*. I thank you." The M.C. led the applause, holding his hands far out away from him as bait. The spotlight was shifted to the pianist, and the M.C. dragged his microphone off into the shadow. Talk stopped.

The pianist blandly rubbed his moist palms with a silk handkerchief and stuffed it with a flourish into his breast pocket. Then he laid his fingers on the keyboard and let the heels of his hands hang down, pretending to wait for quiet. His head fell forward and he began, with his left hand, a sleave of chords. The place was quiet.

At the doorway of the joint there was a sudden commotion. Miles heard a loud foreign voice. "No, no. It's all right. Every bit all right. With friends. Plenty of room. We're with friends." Turning among the hisses of displeasure, Miles saw Ipolyi squirming down the aisle between the tables, bowing, patting men on the shoulder, and leading by the hand a tall, beautiful blonde girl who seemed nearly naked in the dim light.

"Miles!" Ipolyi called above the music. "Miles, old chap. Sorry we're late."

Ipolyi, moving with the agility of a waiter, shoved the girl gracefully into one of the empty chairs at Miles' table and sat down in the other. With one hand at his mouth, he said in a loud whisper, "We're with you, *entendu?* You've been waiting for us. The manager may come." In a normal voice he went on, "This is *not* my secretary. I

146

pinched her one day as she was getting off a bus at Fifty-ninth Street. It is irresistible, *la pince. Je lui ai pincé une fesse,* I tip my hat, *et puis voilà,* a lovely friendship is established."

As he spoke he gazed with cupidity at the girl's bosom, occasionally cocking his head as if to get a better light and murmuring, "*Incroyable.*" She moved restlessly and put her elbows on the table. Ipolyi laughed, winking at Miles, and stroked her arm. "I am all for the U. S. A."

The pianist in the middle of the *Beguine* raised his head, scowling. People at the tables near by *shhed* and looked at them angrily. Ipolyi paid no attention until the plump headwaiter came to the tables and said reluctantly, "I'm afraid I gotta ask you to be more quiet here."

As if he were utterly astonished, Ipolyi rose. "For Negroes?" he said. His face relaxed. He smiled, and Miles saw him poke a folded twenty-dollar bill into the waiter's hand. "Surely not," he said as if the manager had made some gaucherie he was being generous enough to overlook. "A mistake, old boy, all a mistake." The waiter bowed and edged away.

"It's like a circus, going out with him," the blonde girl said.

Ipolyi sat down again. "She spoke? What did you say?" he asked, turning to the blonde girl.

"I said a date with you was like going to a circus."

Ipolyi ignored her. He drew his chair to the corner of the table and leaned over to talk to Miles. "I am delighted to find you, Miles. How many times have I called all newspapers, all magazines, asking for you and never once did your voice answer. It is very good to see you."

"We were just leaving, Ipolyi. Sorry," Miles said, bending forward, beginning to rise.

"Leave? *Now?*" Ipolyi asked.

"I'm awfully sorry. Maybe we can get together again. You can call me at Havas."

"Oh, but you cannot leave me. N-o-o. You must not vanish. I have looked for you too long. Permit me." He placed his hands on Miles' shoulders and forced him gently, half risen, back into his chair.

"Damn it, Ipolyi, I . . ."

"Oh, let's stay. Please let's stay," his daughter said.

Miles sank back, resigned.

Ipolyi winked at Mary and began to call out loudly, snapping his fingers and kissing the air. "Bring champagne."

The blonde girl said, "He'll have you jumping through hoops yet."

"You really want to stay, Mary?" Miles asked.

She nodded, amused.

The waiter paused at the table with a wine list. "What kind of champagne would you like, sir?"

"Pommery, Heidsieck, Mumm's—it's all nine dollars a bottle. Bring me four bottles. I will draw the corks myself."

"Mumm's, sir?"

"*Allez, allez.* Bring me quickness and four bottles of Mumm's."

"Yes, sir."

"I am happy, Miles. I am rich; you see *la bella bionda;* and I serve my government." He ran his hand elatedly down her bare spine and evidently pinched her on the buttock. Miles saw her jump. "Darling," he said and thrust his long, pale face against hers and rubbed her nose with his. "She is beautiful and soft as cream and I esteem her, my God, how I esteem her in the nighttime."

"Well, you don't have to advertise it even if you are a baron." She looked at Miles. "He says he's a baron. You know him. Is he a baron?"

"*Chut!* You would love me if I were that fat waiter. You would love me because I got what it takes. *Le bon dieu* gave it to me." He nudged Miles and winked. "Give her the old slang, *hein?*" He became serious. "And you, Miles, are you well? You are corresponding with some newspaper. Of course you are. You must be happy. Like me. We must all be happy in the Oo-Ess-Ay."

"Miles," the blonde girl said. "Is he really a baron?"

"He's a baron all right," Miles said. Did his daughter think this was one of his friends? He glanced at her. She was staring at them fascinated.

"Well, I been to Europe and I never saw anybody like him and I met lords, too."

"*You* have been in Europe?" This surprised Ipolyi.

"Sure. My girl friend and my girl friend's boy friend and me."

"And where did you go?"

148

"Paris, London, Monte Carlo. I was with Felix Ferry's show. I got a hat I bought on that street in Paris, you know, the rue dee la Pakes?"

"Son-of-a-gun!" Ipolyi said. Then he saw the waiter and a bus boy approaching the table, each with two champagne buckets. "The champagne! I shall drink your health, *bionda*. *Give* me the bottle." He jerked a bottle away from the waiter, twisted the wire free, let the cork pop and the wine foam out into the glasses. "For you and you, Miles, and you and me. Now I give a toast. To *la bionda* . . . a . . . broad." He drank thirstily, glancing at Miles over the rim of his glass to enforce the pun.

"Say, just what the hell does '*bionda*' mean?" the blonde girl asked Miles. "He's always calling me '*bionda*.'"

"It means 'blonde.'"

"Oh," she said, mollified. "I thought it was something like that crack you just pulled."

"Dar-ling, you are thirsty, no? I have amused you all evening. Drink your champagne and let me have a long important talk with my friend Miles," Ipolyi said, and his left hand disappeared under the table.

"He's always trying to grope me in public places," the blonde girl said to Mary.

"We go soon, baby," Ipolyi said. He pulled his chair closer to Miles and talked loudly to drown out the music of the band, which had started briskly into *Tiger Rag*. "Miles, I must tell you. I am a great success. It has restored my confidence. I am once more youthful— you notice it? Don't look at the bald spot. That is dead like the moon. I mean my face. I am no longer *fatigué*. I am fresh, *vif*. Because of this success with the tires. You see it? You notice it? Look." Ipolyi turned his face in profile to Miles. Then he turned it the other way. "It looks good, yes?" He set his face in what he must have conceived to be a romantic mold, his eyes half closed, his lips in a *moue*, and presented this expression to the blonde girl. "Soon we go, baby."

"Have you made a lot of money?" Miles asked.

"Ritz-Carlton, five rooms. Come up and see me sometime," Ipolyi shouted with laughter. "Seriously, Miles, it is a wonderful proposition. You know the Ritz stationery? It is stiff like tin. When I have arrived, I sit down and look up the names of all the rubber companies in the telephone book. Then by hand I write them notes. You know the kind of thing: 'The Hungarian government requires . . .' It is the snob appeal, that stiff paper with 'Ritz-Carlton' printed thick like a scab on a sore leg, the writing by actual hand and I sign myself 'Ipolyi,' nothing else. Champagne?" Ipolyi filled the glasses. "Champagne, ladies?" He filled their glasses. "You are having a beautiful female conversation full of secrets, ha?"

"What did the rubber companies do?"

"They send me young go-getting men in bowler hats who call me *Mr*. Ipolyi and I do not enlighten them. Here I am sans-culotte. I am democratic and republican and I spit through my teeth. I say, 'Seddown, boys,' and have whisky sent up to the room. They tremble with eagerness."

"You're giving them business. What do you expect?"

"I expect the tremble. I want it. I encourage it. Because." Ipolyi pursed his lips, leaning forward, and held up one finger. "I know where lies the stumblingblock. I know all right. I give them each an order and nineteen drinks—Goodrich, Goodyear, U. S. Rubber, all of them. What pals we are! I have *la bionda* serve the drinks in a peignoir. You see the hair? You see *la belle poitrine*—don't slap me, baby, I am talking business. Now fix your imagination on this thin peignoir, thin like the spiderweb, and the bosom—*ces font les culbutes*—and those long white legs. You cannot see—she is sitting down—but the effect, *wunderbar*, I assure you. Do you think I am the white-haired boy of the American rubber business or not?"

"I guess you are. Usually you don't work to give away orders," Miles said.

"Pfui! I give away nothing. It is my express hope that once they love me, they will get me the navicert from the British. You know the British—they are great gentlemen but they are slow. Their minds work with the rapidity of the lower bowel, no faster. They exist under the mortmain of a few simple ideas and one of them is: Hungarians are not gentlemen. It would be difficult for me to approach the British consul personally."

"The fact that Hungary is at least friendly to the Axis would have nothing to do with it," Miles said.

"You are shrewd, Miles. It would have a great deal to do with it. Champagne? Ladies, champagne? I will not keep your Miles much longer, ma'mselle."

"Oh, that's all right. I'm enjoying it."

"It is a very serious conversation. About me. You are very kind to spare him. Your health." Ipolyi bowed and drank all his champagne. He poured himself more. "You are very shrewd, Miles. To the British consul, I am politically suspect and socially I stink."

"So you get the rubber companies drunk . . ."

"You know what a navicert is?"

"Vaguely."

"It is a ticket to the Mediterranean and the box office is the British Consulate. Without the ticket, no tires in Hungary."

"But by your finesse, you persuaded the rubber companies to get you the navicerts."

"No. Not at all. The scheme failed completely. The whisky is gone but she still has the peignoir however. The rubber companies co-operate like the devils, but the consul says no."

"So what did you do?"

"I remain desolate for three days, living on sherry flips. Three days in bed—nothing but sherry flips. I investigate the possibility of Vigo as a port of entry—my embassy does not recommend it. They also say that it would be unwise to sail the tires to Vladivostok and put them on the Trans-Siberian. They must go through Gibraltar to Taranto."

"Why? I should think Vigo . . ."

"I ask myself why also and immediately I give myself the answer. It is as if electric. It is graft. Somebody is getting paid off. I know this because I know my government, but the knowledge does not help. The tires are on the pier at Hoboken."

"So you're hooked."

"So I grow a mustache."

"Why, for God's sakes?"

"Hair is dignity. I put on a dark suit and one of those low, hard collars with the rounded points that you see in photographs of English statesmen. I have my shoes shined dully. I go to see the consul and *I speak English*—it hurts the throat but I speak it as I was taught. I do not stay long. I just contact him. That goes on three weeks. I woo him with my glottis."

"And finally he thaws?"

"He convinces himself that I was up at Cambridge."

"He convinces himself?"

"*Ja.* I merely throw out the hints and he picks them up. We are great friends. One day he gives me a bundle of documents—they are the navicerts. I run like hell to Hoboken and give them to the ship captains. The whistle blows—they are off to Taranto."

"Oh, hell, Ipolyi. It's not as simple as that."

"It is not. You are right. I have given you only the high lights. However, the tires have gone. More go every day. I have made fifty thousand dollars already and I will make more." Ipolyi poured himself some champagne. "It is my chef-d'œuvre," he said with a coy modesty.

"What are you going to do with the money besides . . ." Miles glanced toward the girl.

"Oh, she is cheap. She demands nothing but kindness and the room rent. She thinks I am royalty and it purifies her. No. I am investing the money in Ecuador."

"Why Ecuador?"

"Would you like to live in Budapest for the next ten years, or Berlin or Paris or London?"

"No."

"You are shrewd. You can see what is coming."

"It's not hard to see."

"I am not young. Sometimes at night, with her, I know I am not. In ten years I shall be seriously old. A war is no place for the old. And in Ecuador they pay ten per cent on money invested. I shall live in a pink house with a speaking parrot and drink rum."

Miles' daughter got up from the table. "Excuse me a minute," she said and went away up the aisle between the tables. Ipolyi stopped talking. He watched her go. He was leaning toward Miles with his elbows on the table. He began to strike his teeth with his thumb-nails.

"You know? I am a fool," he said.

"In just what way?" Miles asked.

"I would be happier with intelligence."

"Aren't you intelligent?"

"I? Of course. But watch me. Listen to me and listen to the answers." He turned so that he was no longer facing Miles and began to speak to the blonde girl. "*Bionda*, you are happy here? Feeling a little bit tiddly from the champagne, no? You like the place?"

"Oh, sure. I like a hot piano," she said.

"Good. I am glad the piano is hot the way you like it because I must talk to Miles."

"It's O.K."

"Good. We go soon." Ipolyi turned again to Miles. "You see? 'Sure. O.K. I like a hot piano.' Feh! How would you like an ice-cold cello? I always betray myself this way."

"She is very beautiful."

"A beautiful stupidity is good for one night as long as it is silent. You can admire it, kiss it, tickle it, beat it, and *roulez sur le lit*, but in the morning, it talks." He looked toward the blonde girl. "He says you are very beautiful, *bionda*."

"Nuts."

Ipolyi shrugged. He said to Miles, "You see?" He drank some champagne. "You are the shrewd one, Miles."

"*I* am? How?"

"I have been watching her all the evening, watching her watch you. I am very jealous. She adores you, and supporting the adoration is intelligence—it is in the bone. She is lovely; the ears do not wilt when she speaks; and she loves you. You are extremely adroit, my dear Miles. You work quick."

"What the hell are you talking about?"

"Your girl. Who else?"

"She's my daughter."

"*La bionda* is my sister."

"Stop it, Ipolyi. She's my daughter."

153

"I am not that jealous, Miles. You need not protect her that way."

Miles stood up abruptly and left the table. He walked toward the front of the place and stopped near the door of the ladies' room. Ipolyi followed him.

"Miles, I am desolate. I did not know. The way she looked at you, it was not like a daughter. How could I tell? Pardon me, Miles. I beg you, pardon me."

"Pardon you, hell."

Miles did not look at him.

"You refuse?" Ipolyi said.

"Beat it," Miles said.

Ipolyi bowed, started for the table, stopped and looked back at Miles, raised his open hands and bent his head on one side, and went on to the table.

When Miles' daughter came out, she found him waiting. He had his coat over one arm and his hat in his hand.

"Are we going?" she asked.

"It's getting late. I think we'd better," Miles said. He tried a smile.

"Should I go say good-by to the Baron and . . ."

"I wouldn't bother. They're pretty drunk. They won't miss us."

"All right."

They went out onto the sidewalk. The doorman whistled for a taxi.

"Who is he?" she asked.

"Ipolyi? Oh, he's just a guy I met on the boat."

"He's funny."

"Did you hear everything he said?"

"Not all of it. He was talking to you most of the time."

Miles looked up the street. "He's funny all right."

"You didn't have any trouble with him, did you? I mean, why we left so quickly. There wasn't a quarrel?"

"No. There wasn't any quarrel," Miles said.

2

SOMETHING to wither, tickle, or assassinate," Stephenson shouted, plunging his hand, daggerless, at his plump chest.

The woman did not turn. "What about?" she asked. She sat with her chin on one hand, waiting for the water to boil on the electric plate. Beside her on the floor lay dirty plates and two tin coffee cups with a beach of sugar in them where she saw three flies tilt and rub, tilt and rub, tilt and rub and sip. It was noon.

Stephenson was naked except for a clotted bathrobe of brown wool and a pair of Dorsay slippers, creased and slick. His chair scraped and he faced her. She glanced at his chest and sagging belly as the robe fell away. "A poem is not *about* anything," he said severely.

"I just asked," she said.

"It is not a message."

"All right."

"It is not a mirror. It is not an object of and by itself. A poem is a child."

She lifted the top off the kettle, looked in, and put it back again. "You going to write it this afternoon?"

"I am hermaphroditic, the fother and the mather. Simultaneously tumid and receptive. Gestation will begin at one o'clock sharp and in the dusk time I shall be delivered swiftly and easily like the old nigger woman, 'Ah has one ever time Ah sneezes.' Even now I have an anticipatory pain in my gut. A drink would help," he finished briskly.

"There's that Scotch Henry brought. There's some left."

Stephenson pinched the wings of his nose together with a thumb and forefinger, and began to hum and strike his Adam's apple with the edge of his other hand. The noise somewhat resembled the whine of a bagpipe.

There was an inch of Scotch in the bottle. She poured it into a glass and handed it to him.

He drank it off and sighed. "There. That'll start the little bastard. You get out."

"All right. I'll go see Miriam. Do you want to eat here tonight?"

"You get out and come back about five."

"Well." She rose. "Have you got everything you want?"

"Hell, no. Nobody's got everything he wants."

"I only meant . . ."

"I know what you only meant. Get out."

"Oh, don't rush me. I've got to dress and wash the dishes."

"Leave the dishes. I'll use the hot water for toddies."

She stepped out of her pajamas and reached to the bed for her underclothing. He stared gravely at her hips—comfy, plumpy, dear, and roundy, wide enough, and inside, snug in the cradle of bone, lay the hatchery where his child could kick if he would put it there.

"Some Saturday night I'll give you a kid," he said.

"You'll have to stay sober," she said with her head in her skirt. Her face emerged. "And, besides, Henry says . . ."

"Damn Henry. He thinks books and babies come from the same fount. It's a lie. Who says osmosis says treason. I will not believe that semen trickles up my spine to poach the medulla. Anyhow, it's not Henry talking—it's some of those warlocks he reads all the time. Bring some salami when you come back."

She combed the top of her hair, missing the tats, braided the ends into two braids, and wrapped them around her head. She thrust the pins in. Holding her skirt, she wiggled her hips and pulled down her sweater. "I'll get some rye bread too."

"And mustard. Farewell," Stephenson said. He turned back to his littered desk, waiting for her to go.

He almost heard the sliding rustle of one hand in the right sleeve, the left hand in the left sleeve. He knew the rolling of her shoulders as she settled the collar. Now she was picking up the purse, now the last look with her hand on the latch. She was gone and outside in the shop he heard her footfall. The bell on the street door tinkled faintly.

The kettle steamed and rattled. Stephenson glanced at the empty whisky bottle and lifted a tin gallon can out of the fireplace. He made himself a toddy of hot water, alcohol, and sugar. He sat down again at the desk, sipping and touching the piles of manuscript gingerly with his finger.

Something would undoubtedly occur to him this afternoon. He was alone; nothing moved in the courtyard outside the window but sparrows and old flopping newspapers; there was clean paper in the typewriter—the *e* needed cleaning (he cleaned it); and there was no noise. With an annoyance that was familiar, he recognized that conditions were favorable.

Conscientiously he could not excuse himself. He had only to wait, perhaps filing his nails, to wait somnolently a little while, and it was reasonably certain that a word, a bright suggestive word, or one of the effigies of memory would float by him and he could seize it and begin, perhaps, a little lyric.

Looking at his notes did not stimulate him at the moment. He sipped the toddy, waiting, and with one hand unraveled the thick red hair on his chest.

He was a poet. He could tell himself that. He straightened up and reached to the shelf on the wall above his desk and took from a short row of unsold copies the little book of his poems, a slim volume. He held it out from him, squinting at the cover: *Poems* and underneath, *by*, and beneath that, *Seward Stephenson*. He squeezed the book to feel it resist his fingers.

"That is my name," he said aloud. Then he shouted suddenly, "And poet is my station. A rathole is my dwelling place. Decay, my destination." The shout abashed him. There was no audience. He opened the book.

Some of the pages were turned down, some torn, others smudged with thumbprints, and a few bore raised circular blots where a glass had stood. On one page he noticed a line.

And goat hooves echoed in the grove beside.

The stream had widened into a little basin where the water was clear and quiet, and it looked black because the bottom was a dark silt. Little hummocks of crisp dead grass hung over the far side, and near and in the distance were sumacs with crimson leaves. At his feet in the pathway where the animals came down to drink, he had discovered the deer tracks in the mold. They were wild.

That was all he had wanted to say: the deer tracks were wild. But he had perverted his intention somehow to write about a satyr that he had never seen and could not believe in. Obviously goat hooves, stamping on earth, could not echo in a grove, and the inept alliteration disgusted him. Yet it was poetry. It was printed in a book he could hold in his hand, but this sample did not encourage him to read any more of it. Seven, eight, nine years, he had used the book as a handsel, but it did not work today. He would have to think of something, cold.

He looked briefly out of the window and saw nothing. His focus shortened and he recognized a clump of flyspecks on the sill. He scraped them off carefully, using the point of a stub pen.

He cocked his feet up on the desk and, composed to think, began playing with his fingers. *There is the church. There is the steeple. Open the doors and you see all the people.* How the aunts had cooed, echoing, cooed and chuckled. *That's our fat little red-haired man YES sir. Our little, fat little red little boy YES sir.*

Idly he tangled his fingers again. *There is the church*—my father's house. Only one mansion, however, allowed by the vestry, where the drains were bad and the bedroom wallpaper (five cents a roll, good enough for God weekdays), a pattern of green fronds, had swayed and tossed like a jungle in a storm, on nights when he had fever, and he had waited, sweating with terror, for the tigers to come, burning bright, a luminous slaver dripping from their saber teeth and eyes like flashlights.

And there is the steeple. Stephenson removed one hand to scratch his stomach, stared downward at the weals he left, and laced his hands together again. Why did the enticements never take with me? They socked it to me hard enough. As a child in cotta and spotted cassock, with chewing gun pressed behind his ear to save until the sermon, he, a choirboy, had squeaked the hymns out on Sundays, prayed for in church, prayed over at home, and himself prayed dutifully. And no holiness had clung to him. His father with a shawl around his knees, waiting for the thrombus to enter his heart again, sternly making his professional meekness ready to meet the pain of death, had told him, "You are a godless man." And Daddy was right, by Jesus.

His feet, propped higher than his head, were growing numb. He let them down, sat up, got up, and made himself another toddy. He posed erect with his fingers clutched around the glass on the desk in front of him. Why could he not poise and balance his mind and make it work? No one did nowadays. Had they ever? Immediately he saw the sunlit Greeks, loitering in classical attitudes on the steps of the Parthenon (already ruined). Each Greek had half a head, split longitudinally down the middle like the man in the almanac, and there, visible, was the docile brain smoothly shuddering with great thoughts which were piped directly to the larynx and issued from the Greek's half mouth, divine philosophy.

"No, but seriously . . ." he said aloud.

The city? "In this vast work, Stephenson has expressed as none before the myriad complexities of New York." He must tell Helen to get the laundry. The woman who did it regularly had been taken to the hospital, the little man had said, peering up at him with bright, beseeching eyes. She was swollen, "but no child, no child—a sore inside, a big sore." And Stephenson's linen was now with the woman's sister, who lived with another family on Third Street. The sister's name was de Sylva but the family's name was Grant. Here was complexity but where was scope? Where was nobility?

Consider the littoral, the distant beach, coming in from Ambrose Light with the towers far. Consider the rivers and the oily harbor, the clumps of piling in the slips and docks, dived from, fished from, the liners, the ferryboats, and the Statue (now in these troubled times surely worth an ode . . . "O Liberty" . . .). Ponder the Aquarium, where once he had watched a flounder hang motionless in the tank for five minutes. He had accused the guard of fooling the public. "That is a stuffed fish." How about the Fulton Market and its shouts and bids and fishy fume, the sea hues dying on their flat sides, lemon sole, blind robins, lobster Thermidor, clam chowder Manhattan, menhaden, haddock, hake, halibut, hell, he had never been to the Fulton Fish Market. He did not get out much.

Beneath, behind, at least away—wherever it was—from this sloppy wash of memory, Stephenson wanted to write a good poem, a calm, serious work in which he could identify himself. He wanted to write it and to finish it, safe here in his room, without the taint of his facetiousness, without jokes or the intrusion of the gaudy images that were now habitual to his thought, expecting, as he always did, a listener. He had talked too much. And this morning, before noon, he had spied two gray hairs in his beard. It was time, not that he hadn't known it. Yet he feared to begin, afraid that after the tension and discipline of the effort he would not have said very much.

He got up, poured some alcohol into his glass from the can, filled it with warm water, and looked at it. Then, like a man holding to the amenities, he flipped in a lump of sugar. It lay in the bottom of the glass, sending up a little stream of bubbles.

It should be a long, serious work—blank verse in quatrains? It was good enough for Crane: "How many dawns chill from his rippling rest . . ." He could do that also. What he needed was an idea, a vantage point that he could look from where beneath him—it seemed "beneath"—the city would appear rich as a fruit cake and noble.

"Well, why not noble?" he asked, looking gracefully over his shoulder at the empty bed. The bubbles had stopped rising from the sugar. He drank the lukewarm drink and felt nobility purl within him.

He sat erect in his chair, laid one skirt of his robe carefully over one bare knee, the other over the other. He pulled the robe over his middle and tied a new knot in the cord that went around him. He folded his arms. With his red beard, and the robe and slippers giving him a monastic look, he seemed quite noble and he knew it, a prior or an almoner on Fridays before the poor, God save the foundation, sir. Yet doing it he felt silly, and he knew that too.

A Pullman porter in street clothes with a small bag, boarding the subway uptown for his flat on Lenox Avenue; a checker with a flash-light searching for a lost L.C.L. shipment in the yards, the flimsy bills of lading fluttering in his hand; a chorus girl from a unit show pulling her lip down before the mirror—the tooth hurt; a news photographer in a Third Avenue bar with his personal photos of the murdered girl, unpublished, naked, with her mouth taped, smirking to the onlooker's gasp; safe under the laprobe the calm executive sucks the tablet of milk of magnesia and gazes at the ruck of people crossing before him at the stoplights; a fourteen-year-old boy in a cloud of fur dust turns unceasingly the cylindrical drum containing the kolinsky coat being cleaned; Herbert Bayard Swope pauses in the doorway of the Crillon, pulling on a yellow glove. . . .

Stephenson had relaxed from his monkish pose. He was slouched in his chair, with his feet apart, supporting his elbow with one hand and pulling his beard with a thumb and forefinger. "One of my working habits," he had once told a visitor. "The pain stimulates me."

The pain did not stimulate him now. Neither did the spectacle of Swope half gloved. This was not the poem he intended. He did not want his child to be a painted list of architecture and street fauna.

Yet it was not a bad idea and helplessly he foresaw with what labor he could vary the meter cleverly, splitting the old iambic twang with trochees and anapaests. By looking through his notes again, he knew he could infect it with some brilliance. From his chance records on match folders and the white paper linings of cigarette packages, he would find the solemnities, the nobleness, that would make the poem seem to mean more than it did, a few verbal passes with his sleeves rolled up, the "honesties" of the magician. Old Steve could do it, and as he thought about this, he could see himself marching into Joe's, in slouch hat with heavy stick, hurling the new little book down on the bar and chuckling, "Deathless stuff, Joe. A signed copy.

How about a Martini very dry?" And Joe, flattered, would set up drinks for a month and point him out to sailors and truckmen.

Having only to begin now, confident, he got up automatically and made another toddy. "To Old Steve," he said aloud, and almost unintentionally, with the suddenness of a blow, he said, "My familiar."

With a jerky haste, as if to forestall an intrusion, he unrolled the bent clean sheet of bond paper from his typewriter, picked up a straight clean sheet, and put it into the machine. Right away quick he had a title, *Terror Urbis*. "True and classical," he thought. Everybody is afraid of the city and Old Steve, my familiar, the *Doppelgänger*, the poet, will show them the manner of their fear piecemeal. The poet? Old Steve is not the poet. I am the poet.

He sat back in his chair, looking at the title printed on the paper, and ran a pencil thoughtfully into his ear as an aid to concentration. The first scene or stanza, the first fit, will portray the calm of the old Van Cortlandt house, staring out across the frayed lawn over what is now the cattail marsh at Croton, where once before the river died, they tied their produce barges, full of apples, lard tubs, fiddle brown hams and chains of sausages, cheeses, pears, salt beef and sacks of wheat, while Kiliaen van Rensselaer from across the Hudson watched and old Van Cortlandt tallied. He saw it clearly. This would be history, the age when there was no fear, ah, none, no fear except of the redskin visible. Men in full-bottomed breeches, buckled stout shoes, Van Rensselaer with a beard. Stephenson touched his own and, shifting irritably in his chair, admitted, "Old Steve has a beard, too."

To allay the interruption, he stared deliberately at the row of books above his desk until he could sincerely feel the elation, the somewhat flyblown hope that this might be the real work, that out of the flippancy of its beginning, somehow he might expand, enrich, and vivify his concept until he had said something, extracted the noble kernel he had always relied on to be there. At last he felt the hope and it moved him to begin again.

Down the Parkway, past one suburb and the next, street by street, decade after decade, he would sweep in sections two, three, and four down the length of the island in its mesh of smoke and misty air until, in 1939, at Times Square, he would descry the city dweller racing frightened among the towers where he worked and the warrens where he slept and there, at the poem's climax, anatomize him.

Him? Himself. He looked out of the window into the shallow courtyard. It would be himself, of course. He was afraid, of course. Everybody was afraid nowadays, of course. One assumed that.

But he, he was cute, he was cagey. He had made Old Steve as a buckler to the shocks, a simulacrum to hold in front of him. Oh, he knew Old Steve, yes, sir. It would be a cinch to anatomize him. He drew one bare foot from his slipper and stuck it out and looked at it. It was small, high-arched, the toes shined by the leather and pink. But was it so small, as Steve had always said, that he had to carry a stick to support himself on, a prop for tiny tootsies?

He recalled Old Steve: the night in Joe's when Minnie, the purlieu's learning whore, passed out and lay pale on the floor of the bar, a great amusement. And Old Steve had waddled delicately in, wearing a hat with a bunch of cock feathers on it, dark-green iridescent feathers, a Bersaglieri hat stolen from a costumer. Minnie spoiled his entrance and he, masking his ill-humor, had poked at her with his cane, walking round her, bent, gaping through a monocle bought in a hockshop. While the customers shrieked with laughter, he had even rolled her over with his toe and lifted her skirt with the point of his stick, the poor drunken girl.

Stephenson stood up suddenly, threw off his bathrobe, and, yawning, stretched. He got dressed, whistling because he had done a good day's work. In the corner leaned his thick cane with a large slouch hat stuck over the handle. As he drew on his overcoat, he looked toward the corner. He left his room bareheaded, with his hands in his pockets.

The street was empty and it was raining. He held the coat together in front of him and ran toward the corner to Joe's. He trotted into the bar, panting, and shaking the water from his coat.

"Jesus, take it easy," Joe said.

"A drink for the proud father. Bourbon and water."

"Your wife ain't had no baby. She was in here yesterday."

"I'll pay. I'll pay."

"Then what you a father about?"

"I have just given birth to a great poem," Stephenson said.

Joe nodded his head toward Stephenson and spoke to a policeman in a rubber coat, gorget, and cap protector who was sitting at the bar. "This guy's a poet."

He said to Stephenson, "Got it with you?"

"What do you think I am, a lightning calculator? It's not done yet but it's good."

The proprietor slid a shot glass and a shell of water curling across the bar. He set a bottle of bourbon down beside them. He said, "You want to listen to something good, you listen to the officer."

"Certainly," Stephenson said courteously. "Learn a trade."

The policeman looked him in the eyes a second and resumed as if there had been no interruption, "So in the Fifteenth Precinct you get Bellevue, these thieves, and all the bars on Second and Third Avenue, see?

"One night me and my partner are in the radio car and we get a call from the Telegraph Bureau. Says a lady had called up and told them three guys had murdered another guy and thrown him over a fence at Twenty-ninth and Third Avenue, go investigate. So we park at Twenty-ninth and Third. Three of the corners are blank. They got buildings on them. On the other corner is a building going up and they got a high board fence with an arcade over the sidewalk. We go in behind the board fence and we don't find anything but a lot of building materials piled around.

"But just as we give it up, I see something move, off in a corner. I go over there and it's a vat full of lime and something's moving around in there, I can touch it with my stick. So I roll up my sleeve and dive in with my hand to feel and see and, sure enough, I grab something, a human. I pull it out and it's a lady and she's naked. We hose her down a bit, and she turns out to be about fifty-five with this gray bobbed hair and she's drunk. I try to talk to her, but every time I say something she gives me the big smile.

"I go over to a bar on the corner to put in a call for an ambulance. There is a booth at the back, and coming back from the booth to the door a couple of citizens want to get tough with a cop and I have to take them out on the sidewalk and bounce them around. My partner sees the trouble and comes over. Well, there isn't any trouble, but when we get back to our lady, she's gone.

"Now, the Telegraph Bureau is very tough. If you call an ambulance and you haven't got anything to put in it, they file reports on you and you may wind up cutting the grass at Fort Totten. I think maybe I better go back to the bar and render one of the citizens a stretcher case instead of merely a mouse under the left eye, but we decide to look around. We walk down the block, poking in doorways, and finally we found her. She has climbed into the back of a taxi parked in a garage, still naked like a survivor but drunk.

"There is one of these kid interns on the ambulance, not on the service long. We load her in. She's murmuring and smiling, and the intern says, 'What do you do in a case like this?' And I say back, 'Well, mac, I don't know. I never picked up a naked lady in the middle life out of a lime vat at three o'clock in the morning.'

"So he puts her in Psycho at Bellevue and gets a doctor, a psychiatrist. It's late at night and he comes in yawning. A nice fellow, very polite when he questions her, but not getting anywhere. She just nods her head on one side and gives the smile.

"So I grab her and say, 'Look, lady, we think you been raped.' Just the big smile, that's all. I grab her above the elbows and say, 'You been raped, see?' And like a dream, she smiles and says, 'Well, it never hurt anybody, did it?' "

The bartender laughed. "We get 'em in here all the time like that."

Stephenson began to laugh, but suddenly he shoved at his stomach with both hands and fell clumsily off the bar stool to the floor.

"What's this?" the bartender said and ran around the corner of the bar. He began to slap Stephenson's face. "Steve, hey, Steve!"

Kneeling, the policeman looked. He pulled down the lid of Stephenson's right eye with his thumb. "Take it easy, Joe. He's out. I better call the ambulance."

He stood up and, reaching under his rubber coat, pulled up his belt. "He's all right where he is." He walked back to the telephone booth and put in a call.

When he came back, he said, "You know this guy?"

"Yes. I've known him for years. What's wrong with him?"

"I don't know. Heart, maybe. It won't do any good to move him till they get here."

"Not exactly an ad for the joint, though, him lying there."

"I'm here, ain't I?" the policeman asked. "Besides, it's raining. Gimme one of them Dr. Pepper's."

The bartender opened a bottle. "Glass?"

"No," the policeman said and wiped the lip of the bottle with the palm of his hand.

"What happened with that lady?" Joe asked.

The policeman tipped up the bottle, swallowed, and set it down. "Why, she was setting at a bar in one of those joints. Not bad-looking, see, old but neat, paint on her face, and there's three gentlemen rummies down the rail from her watching her and they get an idea.

"So they ease up to her. She's easy to talk to and she'll take a drink and so after a while they suggest they all take a short walk. So they walk as far as the arcade over the sidewalk and there the three gentlemen rummies jump her and strip her down and enjoy her and when they all get done they toss her over the fence into the lime vat."

3

HENRY VERPLANCK dipped into the bowl of caviar with a knife, loosened a clump of the rich, greenish spheres, and spread them painstakingly on a round cracker. He put the whole cracker into his mouth, and as his jaws worked he admired the drawing by Vertès on the opposite wall. He had brought the caviar to Margery Elliot as a particular gift—he intended that afternoon to ask her to marry him—and he knew she would expect him to eat a lot of it. He had, once or twice before, brought her a jar of caviar and he estimated that she was shrewd enough to count on a jar or two later on whether she accepted him or not. Caviar was good. He was covering a second cracker as she came in with a dish of ice from the kitchen.

She was wearing a suit of a severe gray herringbone pattern, a white blouse with a jabot, stockings of some kind of beige color, and oxfords with short vamps and high heels. He liked the way she dressed, not that dress was truly important, yet if he liked it, he could praise her sincerely for it and the praise would give her pleasure. There would be many such little fillips necessary in their association. (He assumed that she would accept him, if not this afternoon, later. He had a bottle of brandy, Café Anglais, Réserve Spéciale, 1830, he had got off a refugee he could bring her along with, perhaps, more of the caviar.) He was quite aware that, married, it would be a question of discovering many of her traits and habits that suited him in order that he might commend her with a judicious air that warranted its truth. He disliked the attrition of false approval.

She was making him a drink and speaking regretfully of the rainy weather—it had been so fine until now, a beautiful fall. As he watched the graceful movements of her hands, the fingers curl and straighten, and the delicate oval nails, unpainted yet polished, twinkling as they caught the light, he reflected that once this grace had been deliberate and had now become habitual, not a special compliment to him. He could applaud the original effort and himself for discerning that its aim was, in a limited female way, predatory. He praised the drink she had made with a warmth emitted by his thoughts. She sat in the chair opposite him and toasted him and he responded.

It had been such a wearing day, she said, and as he clucked in sympathy and asked the expected question, it seemed to him he could scarcely do better. By supporting herself she had become a good domestic manager, a minor point certainly, but one that insured the continuance of his comfort. And this job of which she was now complaining had given her an independence of spirit that promised splendid quarrels and wrangles that would be unusually fruitful, seen as they would be at close range. Since she had been flattered for years by a number of men, her whims catered to and even encouraged, she would be petulant, and as a lady editor used to office broils and politics, he was sure she would maintain her petulance subtly, without tears or any of the other loathsome obvious gambits. She was an extremely interesting woman, clever, witty, sensual, yet not of a penetrating intellect since she assumed that the male would always approach her by one path, in his brightest plumage. It would be impossible, therefore, that she ever find him out.

Did he not think the Finnish resistance magnificent? He made the proper replies, pursing his lips thoughtfully, looking at the ceiling, letting out phrases containing the words, "Suomi," "Ural-Altaic," "Sibelius," and ". . . very beneficial. They flog themselves with green twigs." It was a conversational effort he was used to.

As he talked, he looked at her, examining her. She was not pretty. The word implied a beauty that was miniature, petite. She was too tall. He would judge her to be five feet six, and her face was not beautiful; better, it was striking. That was because of the high cheekbones and her look of acquiescence which, although one might say it was a supine quality, yet its candor gave it the effect of boldness. Undoubtedly she had been the mistress of several men, that fellow Miles among them, and this was gratifying since it would mean that she would bring a varied experience with her. Undoubtedly she would continue to be the mistress of someone, and her efforts at concealment would be amusing and instructive.

Once, he remembered, he would have feared this accomplished woman, but since he had been analyzed, he had made his own definition of sex and its curious penumbra. (He recalled the antiquated couch upholstered in a shabby velvet where he had lain talking freely and the aroma of stale cigar smoke borne through the gloom from Stekel in the chair beside him.) For him, now, sex was precisely fornication, the initiation at periodic intervals of a pleasant friction briefly maintained to a point of crisis, and on alternate Saturday evenings he had welcomed the hour he was accustomed to set aside for this indulgence. None knew better than he the complexity of the motives, yet in his own case, the act, performed now without hesitancy, was one he regarded as a prophylactic catharsis, a delightful preventive of psychic imbalance, healthful, and now no longer any more trouble, really, than his daily shave. Although milk was cheap, he was going to buy the cow.

He gauged that she was thirty-five or thirty-six inches around the bust and perhaps—it was very narrow actually—twenty-four inches around the waist. Very likely the areoles of her breasts were the large sort. She had a good figure, and Verplanck looked forward to his wedding night with eagerness. Out of his own past and his reading, he could show her a trick or two, seasoned as she was.

Yes, in his geography at school he had learned to call it "Helsing-fors" but now it was "Helsinki," and he admitted that the pronuncia-tion of Viipuri stumped him. She seemed quite perturbed about the Finns. He answered and confirmed and made petty disagreements while he eyed her hips, computing the intercrestal and interspinous measurements with satisfaction. He wanted her to have a child—no study of a woman could pretend to be complete unless it described the psychic changes of her most typical activity. She seemed to be healthy. During the two years he had known her, he had jotted down in a notebook the few little illnesses she had had, the head colds, how long and how severely they had afflicted her, that slight trouble with the frontal sinus. Except for these few, she was apparently as strong as a horse, capable of motherhood and surely unwilling.

He planned to set aside a year of travel, a protracted honeymoon, in which he believed he could persuade her. He was in no hurry. In Bahia, with shy tact, he would reveal his yearning for a son. At Cura-çao, in his cousin's house, he could point to the murky family por-traits on the wall and remind her of the ancient line of Hollanders her refusal would interrupt. This appeal to her snobbery would give her an opportunity to laugh at him, to say that she had not had the least idea he was so bourgeois. And with luck when they reached Taxco on their way back, he could buy her silverware to celebrate her preg-nancy, rings, any bracelets she fancied, or a dish. For a year he would have to be tender and clumsy, her great big bear.

He agreed with her that Russia was vast; its resources which he enumerated fatuously were enormous; resistance was useless. He sympathized when she said it was all a great pity. Verplanck knew he was at the threshold of his life's work and he could see no reason to wait before he tried, at least, to begin it, yet he cautiously made one last survey. If a friend should ask him why he wanted to marry her, he could say stupidly, "She is handsome. She dresses well enough to make other women look at her on the street. She has a voluptuous figure"—and if a friend did ask him, here he would wink jovially. "She has been well educated. She has traveled in Europe and South America.

By earning her own living, she has kept her mind alert. She has a certain wit. She knows how to run a home and handle money, again an effect of her employment. She is not old—our ages agree well—and she is young enough to have children. I believe she is affectionate." And, as a last touch, to convince a friend, he would say, "I am a lonely man." All this was true. No one could deny it.

At the outset, even during the honeymoon, he could weigh and measure her, pretending, foolish scientist that she knew him to be, that it was an excess of love that led him to bring out the scales, the tape, and the calipers for her, and with little hugs and fond twittering to find her size to the teeniest inch—from memory, of course, so he could record it later after the scene was played. He looked forward to the fascinating tedium of his questionings, at dusk perhaps, as old Charles was bringing up the coffee, or perhaps taking her by surprise as he met her coming out of the hairdresser's, "What color were your father's eyes?" and "You said your grandmother died of cancer?" or "It was a smokestack you dreamed of last night, a tall one pouring smoke?" With this pismire energy he would describe the organism, probe the psyche.

He was certain he could arrange finally to discover the right strains and traumata to induce a neurosis in her. Think of that! Heretofore investigations and treatments had fumbled to explore the effects made by causes of little or unknown strength. He would be the first to know exactly the torsion of the strain, to weigh beforehand the impact of the shock. Before he tried that, however, there would be dozens of notebooks to be filled, neat stacks of them locked in his steel cabinet. After the physical measurements he would have to ascertain the psychic disturbances made by routine physical causes: what did menstruation do to her? An illness—was she resigned or surly? And, further, her pregnancy, what form would the anticipation take?

As he savored this foretaste of his happiness, he had an impulse toward a dangerous frankness. He almost wanted to tell her of his intricate plans, as if somehow she might enthuse over them, but he did not, realizing in time that her interest in them would be grounded in an affection he had not yet inspired. He was moved by the rich gloom of her apartment brightened only by the shine of the glasses, the ice, and the beads of the remaining caviar in the light from the single lamp over his shoulder; by the winter rain outside beating the panes furiously (and yet before him the smoke from his cigarette rose in calm, like a flower bending on its stalk); by her face across from him, seen dimly even through his spectacles, beautiful, moving, a smile, a frown, as she spoke with perfunctory anxiety of the battle in Karelia, where men whom she did not know were dying stark in the forest. He could imagine many afternoons like this to come when they would be sitting in soft chairs, wrapped in this dusklight, with drinks and trays of crisp or creamy tidbits (even caviar) at hand. They would talk on some interesting topic. He would kindly feign to be slow-witted to make her sallies and retorts seem clever. They would eat and drink and chat and he could watch her. It would be delightful.

He did not tell her of his schemes because he had not yet proposed, because it would be silly to give the show away, and still more because he recognized in himself a symptom he thought he had outworn of a childhood agoraphobia. The sharp contrast of light and dark, of storm and calm, and especially of this lithe woman, soon to be his, soon fruitful, complaining of these deaths—it was really quite poetic but it was still a symptom because it all happened in a room with four walls around it. It made him feel snug. He did not want snugness and protection, to find himself in places where hunching and crouching he could draw safety around his shoulders like a hood. That is, Stekel had told him he would not want to any more. Yet here it was again all got up very attractively, a reminder that it did not behoove him to count on his future happiness in terms of a weakness he thought he had got rid of. Perhaps he ought to wait. In a month or two he would know whether he would suffer the old twinge of fear when he put on his hat to walk outdoors, the silly terror of the streets and sidewalks, blank and dangerous. This might be only a false alarm. He might wait until 1940. If he did not shy away from Times Square on New Year's Eve, he could be certain that now he was fooling himself. He wanted to bring to his work, this great study of his bride, a fully integrated personality, poised and acute, not flawed as he might now be. It was irritating.

The telephone rang. Margery answered it.

"It's for you," she said, handing him the receiver.

Surprised, he listened. It was Helen, Stephenson's wife. She was speaking from Bellevue—they had taken Seward there. She had called Verplanck's flat first and the servant had told her he was at Miss Elliot's. Seward had collapsed in a bar. They had taken him to Bellevue and put him in a ward and now they wanted money or the promise of some, the credit department, and she didn't know what to say. He had just collapsed at Joe's Place. He had been writing alone that afternoon and he must have gone out to get a drink and he had fallen down while leaning on the bar and she wanted to move him into a private room but the credit department wanted to see some money first and they didn't have any money. She couldn't tell how Seward was. They wouldn't let her see him. The doctors wouldn't say. Could he come right over?

"I'm awfully glad you're in town. I'll come over and take you out to dinner," Verplanck said heartily and laid the receiver in its cradle. He had listened with a growing feeling of self-gratulation. It had all turned out as he had planned: Seward had finally cracked up from alcoholism, and the case, except for the little financial details, was finished as far as he was concerned. Now he could collect his notes and publish a monograph. It would be a prelude.

"I'm afraid Charles is too presumptuous. Telling where I've gone," he said.

"But how did he know if you didn't tell him?" Margery asked.

"He knows when I'm coming here." He tried not to make it sound too coy.

She smiled. "Was it anything important?"

"Oh, friends. They've just come to town and I'll have to take them out to dinner. I'm sorry because I wanted to ask you."

"It's raining too hard to go out. I think I'll eat in."

"You're very self-reliant, aren't you?"

"It comes natural. I used to be a campfire girl."

"Don't you ever tire of it?" The tone he needed now was a sough of muted tenderness.

"Oh, it's not hard to make a sandwich."

"I don't mean that." He paused as if confused. "I mean the loneliness."

"Why, Hen-ry, what are you saying?" she asked facetiously.

He lurched forward off the soft divan and stood up, the open fronts of his double-breasted coat dangling awkwardly. He knew it looked naïve, the gesture of a sincere and clumsy man. "Margery, let me marry you."

She exhaled two jets of smoke from her nostrils and looked up at him. "I honestly think you mean it," she said.

"I mean it." He felt in one side pocket, then in the other, and drew out a small leather jeweler's box. He bent his head and held it close to his eyes, fiddled with the snap, and opened it. "I have a ring." He offered the box to her.

"My God! It must be three carats."

It was a large, square-cut diamond almost untouched by the light.

"It's pretty, I think," he said.

"Pretty?" She took it out and tipped it flashing from side to side under the light. "It's stunning."

"I bought it as our engagement ring." He smiled anxiously. Looking up at him, she could hardly see his eyes—his cheeks were so plump. He stood there polishing his glasses with a handkerchief, rubbing, rubbing.

"So you're going to stone me into submission then? Sit down, Henry. You make me nervous. Don't hover over me that way. I don't want to be rushed."

"Do you like it?"

"The ring? Of course I like it. It's marvelous."

He sat down abruptly and began to explain his love. It was long, halting, and embarrassing, really. The palms of his hands were probably wet and sitting bent over on the soft divan cramped his stomach and he began each sentence with a long breath.

She listened, hoping that she looked impressed and sympathetic. She had never expected this. Someday, in return for the flowers, the bonbons and the books, the caviar and liqueurs, she knew he would have tried to lay these moist fat hands on her somewhere and she had never considered whether she would let him or not—the day had seemed so far ahead. Yet here it was, changed and formal, but familiar.

She wanted to laugh. He looked up to see her smiling at him, looked down bashfully, and occasionally during one of his long sentences, over her shoulder, panting heavily all the while. And since he was a type, the lonely educated bachelor of early middle age, she knew how the plea would go. They all said the same thing and he was saying it. His loneliness needed her beauty, ho, ho!

Smiling, she listened, nodding and murmuring.

It was like talking to someone in a movie. In an undertone you recounted the trials and pinches of the day while heeding those white and giant faces. She listened and answered and watched all at once. On the silver screen of her thoughts, she could see herself: a close-up of her hand, the proffered ring making her gloved finger bulge, then a pan shot of the reception room at the office, the long gloomy room, an imitation of a library in a private home, with book backs nailed, for culture, into the shelves, and fake Ming vases on the Chippendale sideboards, and the desk with the floor lamp beside it, and behind the desk the snooty receptionist. A montage of the whirring leaves of the *Social Register*, fetching up at the receptionist's address to show, admit it, envy. Then a clear medium shot of herself and the receptionist. Carefully she drew off the glove, and on the sound track, "Yes, over the week end. Of course I'm thrilled. Yes. Three carats, just." Cut.

She felt, because she could imagine it, that her acceptance had been decided. As she prompted faltering Henry, she resented the casual promptness of the imagery. It was like a betrayal. (Maybe there was something in this astrology, after all.) How she would have laughed, not the social tinkle but a coarse haw-haw, if anyone had accused her of even thinking of him. It was ominous. It was a suspicious readiness rather urgent and frightening to foresee herself already with his ring on her hand.

"Of course, Henry. I understand," she said.

It was a quandary. Did she want to accept him? The ring, yes. But mild, plump, awkward Henry, courteously shy, so abrasively tender? In a hard noon sunlight, a black shadow apiece tied to their reclining bodies, she could see the two of them on a beach, palm-fringed. It might be Castle Harbor. Because she did not need to smother the outline in a dressmaker outfit, she was wearing a black silk bathing suit, sitting propped on the white sand with stiff arms behind her, wiggling her bare toes to make a play of muscle in her legs that she might admire. Beside her, Henry, a valance of mottled flesh hanging down his front like a bib or apron, to whom, bespectacled, the drift of steamer smoke on the horizon was a problem in optics, and undoubtedly the sand an exasperating sample of geometrical progression. And before them was the sea bearing its eternal rhythm like a shudder, blue and strange.

Henry could give her the sea and all strange things (a thousand dollars a look) because he had scads of money. He could provide a setting, a kind of boudoir, all white, full of feathers and scented furs, where she with her brown body—for she would always be tanned—could lie like a jewel, like the stone in this ring, longing to welcome God knows what brutal, fascinating men with thick, cruel muscles and voices to command her, but would these men come? No. Only Henry, knocking timidly or even scratching with his fingernails as they did at the court of Louis XIV because he thought it was cute. He would be the only one to enter because he had the key, and she thought he was sly enough to see that it was the only key and always in his pocket.

She interrupted him brusquely, "Henry, are you sly? Would you always be surprising me to see if I had a lover?"

Hurt, he said he was not sly. He would never peep at her. And as for a lover, he was sure she was too honorable, that is to say, he was certain she would have too much respect for the vows she would utter to entertain even the notion, much less a fancy man. And besides, he lowered his head with elephantine modesty, perhaps she would not want a lover.

"Let's not brag, Henry. Neither of us is young enough to," she said.

Knowing that her words meant nothing, she kept the little argument alive. Solid, stolid, pallid, fervid, he slouched before her like a parcel coming undone. He was appealing gently now.

It is hard in sunlight to recall the moves and lumber of a dream, what was clear, what was veiled, or what was overlaid with gilt or wood dust. When she thought of it a minute ago, she thought of it as ready, but not for Henry, for whom? It eluded her still. She lay upon this white divan, brown as a gunstock, writhing delicately to see how she looked in the ceiling mirror. The sun would never seep through these drapes, shut to the street throb (and no clock to tick). Would she go on lying there, buffed and bathed, tinted and powdered, twisting to look at herself in a climate of scent and warmth, in this bland light from her shrouded lamps, with a tear of sweat gliding down over her ribs waiting for whose entry like a clock strike? Whose? He was there all the time, muffled and secret, and she could not think of him. Well, Henry could give her this place where she would remain. He could keep her. She supposed he would be tender. After all this talk of honor, it would be the least he could vouchsafe her. Dark in his heavy shadow, she felt him permanent, a flabby mono-lith, cold and moist as a stone trickles sometimes, but soft. He was permanent and rich. Permanent because rich.

Oh, it was Richard, of course. Wasn't she a fool not to have thought of it before? Now she could have this lovely secret place, all white, where he could visit her, and in this room, the beautiful, permanent, scented, secret room, she could show Richard how young she was.

"Henry darling, I'll marry you."

"I had hoped . . ."

"But on one condition."

"You weren't offended by . . ."

"I'm not a child, Henry. We won't mention cheating again. All I want is this—I don't want to be married too soon."

"How soon is too soon?"

"Not under six months."

"Oh, Margery, please. Six months is a hell of a long time."

"Not under three at the least."

"Well," he assented. He stood up again, stamping his foot as if it were asleep. He took the ring out of the little box. It slipped to the floor and he picked it up and put it on her finger. Then she gave him her number-two kiss.

4

IT WAS a quarter past four. She stood in the doorway, the light wind of the side street whirring in the potted bushes ranged at the edge of the sidewalk. There had been two Richard Miles in the telephone book and she selected the one living on Washington Square. It seemed the likeliest place for him to settle. The Square was only a few blocks away and, if she turned out to be wrong, she could try the other one and still be in time for a cocktail. She did not want to telephone him first because he might say they were going out, he and this daughter. And even if he were alone, he might say he was engaged. It was possible.

As she stood in the doorway, pulling on her gloves, she saw a delivery boy for a florist go by on a motorcycle with a sidecar. He wore no overcoat to muffle the neatness of his plum-colored whipcord and he looked cold, bent over the handle bars. The street was growing dark although she could see the sun bright on the taller buildings opposite and farther away. She decided to walk over to Fifth and take a taxi because she did not want her hair to be blown out of place in the wind. She left the shelter of the house wall, walking gracefully, with long steps, swinging one arm a little. She had the holiday feeling of the week end and also, because of the diamond on her finger, a glow of triumph. Before this threat, he would forget their quarrel.

When she turned into Fifth Avenue, a blast of wind struck her and she bent to hold her skirt down with one spread hand, running with little steps toward a cab stand and smiling frankly at the driver who had been gazing steadily at the play of taut silk calf and thigh, her swell gams. In the taxi she scanned the set of her hair in a mirror she took from her purse and touched it here and there about her face with a comb. In the Square there was the usual old man feeding pigeons from a paper bag, corn, very likely. They cooed and fluttered and the wind tossed them when they fluttered too high. A pretty sight. A kind old man.

"Right here, driver. This is the place," she called. She gave him a dollar. "It's all right," she said.

"Thanks, lady. Thanks a lot. It was just a short haul," he said.

She was pleased with her ring, the driver's admiring scrutiny, the pigeons' grace, and the late-afternoon sunlight touching the bare trees of the Square. She went up the steps and in the doorway looked at the row of cards beneath the push buttons. In the center of the row she found one that said *Richard Miles* engraved in script in the English manner and written in ink beneath it was *Miss Mary Miles*. The daughter had not waited for spring, then, and thrifty Richard had not bought her any calling cards. She pressed the button beneath Miles' name.

Almost at once the buzzer sounded and the lock in the door clicked open. She went in.

From above she heard a girl's voice call, "Father?"

Margery climbed several steps until she was sure the girl looking down the stairwell could see her from above. She looked upward smiling and saw the girl leaning far over the banister. Her loose hair parted, hanging down, and almost hid her face.

"No," Margery said. "I'm a friend of his."

At once the girl straightened as if to become more circumspect. "Oh," she said, and then apparently sorry to have sounded rude or indecisive, she called down, "I hope you don't mind the climb."

"Oh, not a bit," Margery said. As she came to the last landing of the last flight, she looked up quickly with what she knew to be a kindly face to see this girl, this child Richard valued so much.

"I'm Mary Miles," she said.

A glance could tell that she was pretty, but Margery's face remained kindly and grew fond.

"I'm so glad to see you. My name is Margery Elliot. I knew your father in Paris." To expunge the old, cold sound of "your father," she continued lightly, with the girl's hand in her two, "Yes, I've known Richard for just years."

"He's not here." The girl paused. "But you can wait. He's buying a new suit and Saturday afternoon's the only time he could get it fitted. He ought to be home any time now." With a sudden cordiality she said, "Please come in and wait."

"You're sure you won't mind?"

"No. If you'd like to see it, I'll show you our apartment."

"That will be lovely. I'd like to see it." Margery pushed the half-open door and went in. The girl took her coat and while she was hanging it carefully in a closet by the door, Margery stood with a minor insolence of pose slowly drawing off her gloves and exclaiming, "Why, this is lovely. Did you do it all yourself?"

"Only a little of it. The curtains, and I made that chair cover. We rented the place furnished because we didn't have anything."

"Oh, I like that chair. Chintz is so gay, isn't it? I think you're very smart to have done it. I know I couldn't."

"Would you really like to look around? My room is over here."

Margery followed and peered in. One window let in gray light from an air shaft. There was a single bed with a blue tufted spread; a side table with a lamp; a tall, banal, mahogany bureau and one stiff, cheap, never-sat-on chair.

"It's nice to have your own room after school, isn't it? I used to hate dormitories so," Margery said.

"So did I."

"It's very neat. You do your own work, don't you?"

"Oh, it's not hard. Cleaning and making the beds. I don't cook very well yet."

"Why, I think you've done wonders. How many daughters are so capable? Richard's lucky to have a girl like you."

She saw the girl blush red, her face and throat, and feeling the warmth of the blood, she turned away and opened another door. She said in a low voice, "This is his room."

It was in the corner of the building, with windows looking out on two sides. A shaft of light from the low sun came through one of them. There was a large four-poster bed and on a table beside it in front of a row of books was a small vase full of flowers, pinks and bachelor buttons. Before one of the windows stood a broad table with a line of books at the back and a large red blotter and a set of pens. Beyond it in the light from the window stood a large winged easy chair with a chintz cover and a footstool in front of it. A reading lamp with a parchment shade stood behind it. Margery remained in the doorway.

"You gave him the best room, didn't you?"

"He needs it. He works and . . ."

"Oh, is he working?"

"Yes. At Havas. You know, the French news agency?"

"Yes. When I saw him last, he was thinking of lecturing maybe."

"He gave that up. He thinks lecturing is silly, and besides, it would take him away from home too much. I'm sorry there isn't a fire in the fireplace. I could build one—it's nicer."

The girl sat down, and Margery composed herself in the chintz chair facing her. "Please don't bother," she said. "We don't really need a fire."

"Would you like some tea, or a cocktail? Can't I make you a Martini?"

"But you don't drink, do you, just coming from school?"

"No, but I can make a good Martini. Father taught me. We used up nearly a bottle of gin before I made a good one, dry enough, but now I know how."

181

"If Richard is coming in soon, why don't I wait? We can have one then."

"All right. I guess I was just showing off, that's all."

"What do you do with yourself—I'm going to call you Mary, may I? Do you study art or paint or sculpt or write things or what? Richard said you were in school. Why did he want to bring you to this awful town?"

"But I don't think it's awful. I like New York a lot."

"But did he just drag you out of school to come and mind his comforts?"

"No. I ran away. Grandmother was furious. I used to live with her vacations, and so did Mother until she died. She used to treat me as if I belonged to her like one of her cats. I'd like to have seen her when she found out I'd gone."

"What did you do—climb down a drainpipe?"

"I walked out when everyone was in chapel."

"You didn't like school."

"Not any more. Not after Father came home. I don't study art or paint or anything. I just wanted to keep house for him."

"And that's enough?"

"Oh, yes."

"You're very domestic. You sound almost like his wife."

The blood ran to the girl's face and neck again but she did not look down or away. "That's all I want to do." She paused. "Miss Elliot?"

"Yes?"

"What was it like to be with Father in Paris?"

"Oh, I was a translator at the American Embassy and . . ."

"No. I mean, I've never traveled with him. I've never lived with him before. There's so much I don't know about him. He said you could take a taxi there, in the spring, in May, in the evening—they have roofs that slide back?"

"Yes. Just like the ones here."

"But you could lie back in the seat and look up and there, there were tree branches and then the sky, and he said after you went far enough it was like looking down into a stream. It was the Boulevard du Montparnasse and then the Boulevard Saint Michel, he said, and you could ride as long as you liked for seven francs."

"Yes. You could do that."

"And at the Jardin des Plantes, he said, there was a gorilla all black like an old Negro and he sat there all day making himself a nest of straw, very slowly, reaching out for a little wisp at a time."

"I don't remember the Jardin des Plantes."

"And in the dark you could stand on the bridges, the Pont Royal, the Pont du Carrousel, the Pont des Arts, the Pont Neuf. Were you with him then? Leaning over, watching the lights flicker on the water and the cathedral there like a shadow. Was that the way it was?"

Margery spread her hands, a gesture of impatience. "I never did those things with him. It wasn't just sight-seeing. I was there too long. You get to know a city. You must remember that I'm older than you are."

"What do you mean?"

"You asked me what it was like to be with him in Paris. Well, being with a man isn't just looking at things."

"No. I know."

"And I knew Richard very well."

"Were you in love with him?"

"I was his mistress."

"But you are not his mistress now," the girl said quickly. She looked Margery in the eyes with confidence. Then she lowered her head and continued in a pleasant, almost shy tone. She played with a charm bracelet as she talked, a light chain around her wrist of golden lucky symbols. "I guess I hate you. I didn't when you came in. You were beautiful and chic and you treated me—not young. You were every-thing I wanted him to have had. I knew he had mistresses. He didn't say so, but I knew. And when you said that about Paris, every time I thought about Paris, I didn't know it but I was with him, in the taxicab, at night on the bridges looking at the water. But you were actually with him there and three's a crowd, don't you see?"

"I told you I never went sight-seeing with him."

"It doesn't matter. You were with him in Paris and the things he did with a mistress he did with you and your name is Margery Elliot. It was all right as long as I didn't know your name."

"But why should you be jealous of me? That all happened long ago."

"Not long ago. I think about him every day and wherever he is, I am with him and wherever he was, in Spain, in France or Germany, I am with him. I didn't know it until you said that. I don't know anything firsthand about Europe but I think about it because he was there while I was growing up before I knew him and all I know is what he tells me about it and I imagined, I can see now I always imagined even from the letters, that I was along, too. But now you are there intruding on us and it spoils it now and it will spoil it from now on. It didn't happen long ago. It happens every day."

"But, my dear child, what's past is past."

"Is it? You came here to see him, didn't you? It's past with him. If he came to see you since he's been in New York . . ."

"He did."

". . . he did it only to tell you good-by."

"He did it to ask me to marry him."

"That is not his ring on your finger."

"No. All I came over here for this afternoon was merely to tell him I am going to marry another man."

"I don't believe you. That's not all you came for."

"Why shouldn't you believe me?"

"Because you're here. Why should you come here to tell him if everything is past and you're going to marry another man? You could have written a letter. Ladies don't come to men's apartments alone."

"Oh, nonsense. You're talking like a child. You are a child. How old did Richard say—seventeen?"

"I may be young but I know why you have come. You want to pull him back into the way he used to live."

"Are you jealous of every single thing that happens to your father?"

"Yes. Especially you. He is through with all of you."

Margery stood up and walked over to the fireplace. There was an open package of cigarettes on the mantel and she took one. It was better to stand; it gave a certain advantage. She did not want to be overborne by this girl, this child really, as she had said.

Leaning on the mantel with one elbow, she put the cigarette between her lips and lit it. She exhaled and said archly, "Doesn't it occur o you that you're being rather hard on me? I stop in here quite innocently to show your father my ring and receive his congratulations and here you are, treating me as if I were a burglar come to steal the silver." She threw the smoking match into the empty fireplace. "Aren't you?" She was standing with most of her weight on one foot. She turned the toe of the other inward and tapped on the floor. She was nonchalant.

The girl got up out of the chair. "I love him."

"Oh, I'm sure you do. Daughters ought to love their fathers. It's marvelous to be so filial."

"You don't intend to go until he comes, do you?"

"No. I don't think so. You can be as rude as you like."

The girl's feet were close together and she looked down at her hands where she was rubbing one thumb with a forefinger. Her hair fell forward and she was breathing hard. "I'm not trying to be rude to you. It isn't important. I would not hate you very hard. It is only like pepper in a thimble. I don't know. I don't know anything really. I am saying this so you will go away or even if you stay you will see that it is useless and that it would have been better to have gone now before he comes. I can't explain how it is except that it is in darkness somehow and I am with him. The heart and lungs beat in darkness safely, don't they?"

"Darkness? What do you mean?"

"I suppose darkness to you is merely when the lights go on. This is different. I think about it all the time but I still don't know. This is like a town in a fairy tale in a valley at night with no moon, where you can smell strawberries. The wind brings you the smell and rustles in the grass at your feet. Maybe you are the witch, but I have drawn a circle around you. Or have you ever gone to bed in the country in a feather bed and it is raining—you know how safe you feel? And it is like a seed, too. There is sun all around and above you and you can feel it and you know it is lovely and correct but where you are it is dark and rich and nourishing and nothing false is there. This is silly but this is how it is and this is how you have lost him. It's not really much of an explanation, is it?"

"But I don't want him, you little fool."

185

"Then why don't you go? There is nothing you can give him any more no matter how you urge him to take it. He is with me now." She raised her head. Her face was pale, and she said proudly, "And the hands he touched you with are mine now to smooth and hold and the face you used to watch to see how he was feeling looks at me and I can love him more than any other woman, more than you, more than Mother, more than anyone, because his blood is inside me and he would no more leave me than he would cut his arm with a knife. Because he would bleed."

Margery straightened, shocked. "Do you know what you're saying? Have you any idea?"

"Yes. I am telling you how much I love my father so that you will be ashamed and go away."

Margery looked at her for perhaps three seconds. "Yes, you are. I actually believe you are." She turned and walked over to the window. There was a heavy, dense, dark sky and up Fifth Avenue across the Square she could see the towers with the sun no longer lighting their windows. Over them like a dull silver egg the Goodyear blimp soared clumsily. Below her, a bus stopped and plain simple people got out and spread, hurrying home to dinner. It was like an admission to observe that the afternoon was over and it was growing dark. Suddenly it seemed to her that all her life she had been playing with toys in a sand pile. She left the window.

"How long had it been since you'd seen your father? Before he came home this time?" she asked the girl.

"Seven years."

"You were ten years old . . ."

The buzzer sounded and the girl jumped up and pressed a button beside the door. "You may as well stay now," she said. "You would only meet him on the stairs."

"Thank you." Margery sat down again in the chintz chair, and when Miles came in he did not see her because the chair faced away from the door. He took off his overcoat and hung it in the closet and laid his hat on the shelf.

"Where were you? You didn't meet me on the landing," he said.

"We have a caller. She's been waiting to see you."

186

Miles walked around the chair. "Oh. Hello, Margery."

"How are you, Dick?"

"I'll go make some cocktails," the girl said. "And some canapés."

Margery watched her as she left the room, to see if any exultation shone in her face, but there was none.

Miles sat down in the chair opposite Margery. "Well, what do *you* want?"

"Can't you be polite, Richard? The last time I saw you . . ."

"It was a perfectly simple question. I know—you want to remind me of everything, don't you?"

"You went away that afternoon and you didn't tell me where you were going. I didn't know where you lived and . . ."

"How strong a hint does it take? If I didn't tell you it was because I didn't want you to know."

"Do you see this?" She held out her left hand, turning it with conscious grace, to let the diamond have the light.

"Who are you going around with now . . . De Beers?"

"I thought you might conceivably be interested to learn that I am going to marry Henry."

"That's Verplanck, isn't it? I hope you'll be very happy," he said perfunctorily. "He's not a Harvard man, is he? You might get him to take up squash."

"That's what I came for, to tell you that. But . . ."

"Well, now I know it . . ." Miles laid his palms on the arms of the chair and pushed himself up standing.

"You can't insult me, Richard."

"Oh, I haven't tried yet. Stick around."

"I know you well enough not to pay any attention to you when you're like this."

"Margery, I hate to say it, but you're getting old. You keep making these references to our dear dead past. After nightfall you're always witty—why can't these quick perceptions tell you that you and I are *kaput*? We're through."

"All right, we're through. Now tell me something."

"Well?"

"How much do you know about your daughter?"

As she said "daughter," Miles heard the faint chuckle of ice as Mary stirred the cocktail shaker in the kitchen. "I don't get you," he said.

"I've been talking to her, waiting for you to come home. She's very strange."

"Strange how?"

"She treated me as if I were a rival for your affections."

"Oh." He seemed relieved. "Perhaps that's not unnatural. Don't children always like their fathers best? And anyone who looks as if he might come between them . . ."

"She's madly, terribly in love with you."

"Why, all right. That's fine. I'm glad."

"I mean, sexually."

Miles had been sitting slumped down in his chair with one leg crossed over the other, swinging his foot. He did not move. He was silent for a moment, looking at her. "How do you know?"

"She told me—not in so many words, of course. She doesn't know it but she revealed it. It showed through what she said."

"Get out of here, Margery."

She stood up, smiling. The visit had been a success after all. "I brought you the tidings and I'm cursed, is that it?"

Miles did not rise. "Get out of here, I said."

Margery took her coat out of the closet and put it on. From the pocket she took her gloves and drew them on with exaggerated care, smoothing them as if they were tight.

"Very well, Richard, my sweet. I shall leave you with it."

She went out of the apartment, closing the door quietly, and Miles could hear the old stairs creak under her tread.

There was a slight clinking noise and Miles jumped up as if he were startled. The girl, walking with small, careful steps, was bringing in the tray of cocktails, watching the glasses to see that they did not spill. She glanced up brightly smiling once and back at the tray. "Oh, she's gone," she said. "I thought you would make her go."

5

STEPHENSON WAS DEAD. Verplanck had waited long enough, he thought, to miss the funeral and now he was going to pay a call on the widow to console her, to give her money for the undertaker and perhaps something extra for herself so she could take a little trip.

He expected a quarrel. She had never liked him, and now that Seward was no longer there to restrain her and laugh and pull his beard and smooth her hackles down, he was fairly certain that she would accuse him in a muddled and bitter way. For this reason he had put on a black tie that she might see he mourned, and an expensive double-breasted, dark-blue flannel suit, and this, he hoped, with his seal ring and his forty-dollar shoes, would overpower and silence her, the brutal force of his wealth. He had even selected a derby that he might seem richer and more sorrowful but after a moment's thought had laid it carefully back in the tissue paper of the hatbox. A derby was too effete for the neighborhood. He was wearing instead an old, ratty hail-fellow snap-brim with grease on the ribbon and a hole in the peak of the crown. As he sat in his taxi bumping up the shallow trough of Hudson Street, already there were wrinkles in the suit and gray smudges on the lapels from the unregarded ashes of his cigarette.

Waiting for his change from the taxi driver, he looked up and saw for the first time that it was snowing. Here the wind had a chance and it blew a storm of hard white pellets down. He tipped the taxi driver a dime, saluted him absently with his first finger, and went into the antique shop. The bell tinkled and the proprietress came forward out of the gloom at the rear, silent, bent like a cat out stalking, with a commercial smile, and an oily rag in her hand.

"I was just going back to see Mrs. Stephenson," Verplanck said.

The woman relaxed, no sale, and began to rub the dust from the top of an old cherrywood table. "She's leaving tomorrow," she said.

"So soon after the funeral?"

"Yeah, so soon after the funeral. I'll never rent to a slut like that again."

As if he were still wearing the derby, he inquired with formal reproach, "Why do you call Mrs. Stephenson a slut?"

The woman blew a cloud of dust from a chair back. "It's been like a God-damn circus in there for two days. Stephenson ain't an Irish name."

There seemed to be nothing to say. Verplanck said, "Oh," and walked on back through the aisle between the rows of dirty furniture, keeping the skirts of his coat from the table edges and the chair seats.

Nailed to the door of the Stephensons' room was a gigantic floral piece, dozens of reddish chrysanthemums pinned to a backing of mimosa and royal ferns and tied at the top with a long, outrageous, drooping bow of purple satin ribbon. The piece was four feet long at least.

The proprietress was watching him. She called, "They wanted to put that on my front door, friends of his, and I told 'em, hell, no, there ain't anybody dead in here. Stick it on their door, I said."

Verplanck could hear voices inside, a low, conversational burble.

He knocked politely. No one admitted him. He turned the knob, opened the door a little, and slid in unobtrusively.

In a glow of light dimmed by moving coils of gray cigarette smoke he saw the widow lying on the bed motionless. She was wearing Seward's old brown bathrobe. Her soiled feet were bare and her hair hung down with a braid over each shoulder. Her face was swollen, and in the light of a shaded electric lamp fixed to the head of the bed above her, the curve of her forehead cast a dark shadow on her cheeks as if she were weeping tears of ink. She was staring at the doorway, at him, bolstered up with pillows under her head and shoulders. Her hands were posed—they seemed posed—one above the other on her stomach and her legs lay straight, covered with the bathrobe to her ankles. A woman sat on the edge of the bed with her back to the door, talking. Occasionally Helen listened to what was being said to her. The focus of her gaze shortened and she turned her head languidly. She did not see him at all.

There were many people in the room. Unwelcomed, Verplanck glanced about for a place to sit. The room had always been sparsely furnished, and there was no chair empty. He recognized Joe, the bar-keep from up at the corner. He was sitting delicately upright in the chair before Seward's desk, preserving with care the long ash of a cigar. He was wearing a gleaming celluloid collar and a tapestried ready-tied cravat encircled below the knot with a diamond ring in a claw setting. He was an old-timer. As he raised a glass to drink, he saw Verplanck. He swallowed and said soberly with a nod, "How's it?" and resumed listening to a policeman who was seated leaning on the desk. The policeman's drink stood on the mantel by his shoulder, the last receptacle in a line of jugs, vases, and tin cans holding flowers, and once he had noticed the row of bouquets across the mantel, Ver-planck could smell the heavy fragrance mingled with the tobacco smoke.

On a kitchen chair with its back to the dead fireplace sat a small, decent woman in pince-nez glasses. The black wolf fur of her coat collar was worn away and the collar was shiny at the back of her neck. Even in the heat and smoke of the room she kept the coat on. She leaned continually forward to yearn toward the bed, clutching at her purse to keep it from falling off her lap and making a sympathetic clucking sound with her lips. A worn suitcase, paper, stamped and enameled to resemble alligator, stood beside her chair.

Beside her and near him, a fat young woman rocked back and forth on the wooden box that had often served as Seward's dinner table. A *mädel* not long ago, she had been lovely but had eaten too much too many years and fat had muffled it all up except her eyes, which were large, staring vaguely, moist, and sad. Patient and lackadaisical, she nudged her enormous bosom with a loosely closed fist and, without looking at the bed, made the orthodox lament in a contralto voice of incredible beauty, ". . . *v'yeesnahsah v'yeeshaddar, v'yeesaleh v'yeeshalal, shmay d'kudishaw bree-choo.*" Verplanck could not imagine why she was there unless she was a mistress of Seward's who had a long and grateful memory for the pleasures he had given her while she was *saftig* yet. Seward had always liked Jewish girls.

No one had recognized him except the barkeep, and Verplanck wanted to sit down. He peeked over a faded cloth screen that staggered across the corner of the room to hide the sink and cupboard. In front of the sink stood a new shiny art-metal stool with a circular red-leather cushion. As he tiptoed behind the screen to get it, he saw that the mirror over the sink was covered by a dishrag and the hands of the alarm clock showed a quarter past twelve, about five hours off, and he could see that the young Jewish woman was a stickler for the amenities, the proper sequelae to death. He took the stool, brought it out, and sat on it between the policeman and the gray-haired leaning woman with the pince-nez.

She whispered to him at once, "She is my daughter. She was his wife."

Verplanck murmured in reply. They both looked toward the bed where the daughter, once the wife, lay staring at the door.

With her eyes still on the bed, the woman bent toward him. "She lies like that," she whispered.

"Yes," Verplanck said softly.

"Ever since the funeral. They keep her under a sedative."

The woman sitting on the bed, a young woman with a lean, what

Verplanck called an *arty* face and a string of wooden jewelry around her neck was giving Helen Stephenson something in a spotted water glass. She drank it eagerly, raising herself and falling back when the glass was empty. On the floor beside the bed stood a white pitcher and a square tin can. What Helen was drinking was clearly alcohol and water, the old family standby. Verplanck smiled. The old ewe beside him was naïve. These were the funeral games in Seward's honor. Helen was drunk.

The little woman leaned over to him again. "She screams sometimes. They have to hold her. It's frightful."

She looked at him and looked away, plaintive, and stiff in posture, dressed in her best clothes. Her anxious gabble was a catharsis. A small-town woman, she seemed. Verplanck said nothing.

The lament continued, and a little behind him from the corner came, in a decent mutter, the conversation of the policeman and the barkeep.

"She hasn't recognized me. I got here this morning and she hasn't even looked at me," the little woman whispered from the edge of her chair.

"Perhaps she will soon," Verplanck whispered back courteously.

Without looking, he recognized the policeman's voice, ". . . and so I'm over by the Morgan Library, my feet dead up to the calf of my leg, and there comes this maid screaming that the boss is dead. Foul play, suicide, or what the hell, I can't make it out. She's Litvak or Russian, one of the peoples of the Baltic rim, and crazy from excitement, so I grab her by the arm and she leads me to the scene of the crime."

Verplanck saw that he would have to wait for some time if he wanted to see Helen alone. With timid, apologetic movements he lit a cigarette, nodding sympathetically to Helen's mother. He shifted his weight to the less numb ham on the stool top and, settled, began to listen to the policeman.

". . . a musician. A grand piano with the top up and one of those busts of the composer Beethoven on the bookcase, made out of plaster of Paris. So in the bathroom laying beside the tub is the boss, the musician, weltering in a pool of blood like in the *Mirror*. Sure. Knocked himself off with a straight-edge razor. It's in his hand. Undoubtedly severed the carotid artery. A guy about fifty but with short hair.

"So I call the medical examiner and meantime I look around the apartment. The maid is out in the kitchen going *Eli, Eli* in Litvak. I can see from the bedroom the guy is married and evidently he ain't a performer—he's a composer, because on the music rack on the piano is a new piece he's made up, in pencil. The notes are put in with pencil. The paper has the lines printed already and you put in whatever notes you like with the pencil.

"I am working on a hangnail when a dame lets herself in with a key. She has evidently been out taking two dachshunds for a walk. The dogs run right on through the room and I don't see where they go because I'm saying hoddayado and acquainting her with the details of the tragedy. She's a nice-looking young dame with a swell form. She doesn't faint or nothing. She just wants to take a look at the body. So I go into the bathroom and son-of-a-bitch if the dachshunds ain't in there licking up the blood from Papa like it was spilt milk.

"Well, by the time I bring her to, the medical examiner is there. You must have seen the type even this far downtown. A lot of guys can't go far in the city employ because their brains are to the bone already. When they get to be medical examiner, it's the last stop and they lay back and get spots on their vest. Then there's the others that have got a bead on the City Hall and the examiner's job is only a steppingstone. This one that comes here has been to Fordham and knows people that know Ed Flynn, see what I mean? He asks some questions, looks at the body, writes in his notebook, O.K. But then the bastard has to turn it into a social call. He tells her two or three times it's tough her old man is dead. He's tender. He's cultural. He's a gentleman, like she sent for him to condole with her maybe. Music is a good thing. He calls it 'frozen architecture.' He just can't wind up the call and get out. He's got to show the dame what nice fellows work for the city. It's a frenzy with him.

"Finally he takes a gander at the music on the piano. He looks at it close up and then he sits down and plays the piano. The medical examiner knows how to play piano and he plays the dead man's music.

He even looks back over his shoulder to see how the widow likes it. Fine stuff, hey? Makes her feel good. I nearly clipped the bastard with the stick."

"Some guys are nuts," Verplanck heard the barkeep say.

Verplanck thought it was a strange gathering. It could hardly be called a wake, because Seward was buried. The air was rank with the smoke, the smell of all the people, and the faint sweet odor of the flowers. The Hebrew phrases were repeated softly. The widow's mother leaned first at one angle, then another, trying to see around the woman sitting on the bed. The policeman and the barkeep had begun to talk about the war. Verplanck began to think that he should go and come back another time. Then he remembered that the landlady intended to evict Helen the next day. Helen was not clever; she was drinking heavily; she would be thrown out and she would escape him. Somnolent, lulled by the talk and the bad air, he was thinking precisely—"escape" was the word that came to him. He was about to ask himself why he was pursuing Helen when she screamed.

She jerked herself upright from the pillows. Her lips stood out as if they were seamed with thread. A vein swelled taut and gray on her throat. Her breasts had fallen dumpily out of the front of her bathrobe and a loud high scream came out of her mouth as long as her breath lasted. She fell back in a silence flawed only by the beautiful Hebrew chant. The woman with the wooden jewelry handed her a glass of alcohol and water, which she took and drank in a tired, matter-of-fact way as if she had only coughed.

Uneasy, the barkeep and the policeman stood up, mumbling to each other, finishing their drinks, glancing at the bed, and making ready to clear out. The barkeep stood at the head of the bed plainly trying to think of something topical to serve as a farewell. He looked down at her. She ignored him. He was holding his hat in his hand. He snapped a fleck from it with his middle finger, sighed, and went quietly out without speaking. The policeman, young, red-faced, neat, and muscular, stepped up unabashed. He said gravely, "Mrs. Stephenson, I thank you for your hospitality. I regret the death of your husband and I'm sorry I couldn't attend the funeral." He took small, prompt steps sideways past the bed. As he reached the door and was settling and tilting his cap on his head, the widow looked up.

"Copper," she said without intonation.

At this, the first intelligible word she had spoken, her mother became agitated. She sprang up and bent eagerly over the bed like a bird tipping down to drink. "Helen," she pleaded, "it's Mamma. It's Mamma. Don't you know me?"

The widow lay inert, her gaze steadfast on the door beyond the foot of the bed.

"I've been here all day and she hasn't even looked at me." The little woman even looked around at Verplanck as if she would ask his intercession with her daughter. "I left last night and got into Grand Central this morning. I haven't eaten or anything and she won't recognize me." She leaned over her daughter again. The woman in the wooden jewelry caught Verplanck's eye, lifted her shoulders, and cocked her head on one side. "Helen! It's Mamma. Don't you know me? It's Mamma." She was not answered or looked at.

"What is this sedative you keep giving her?" she asked the other woman.

"It's not a sedative. You made that up. You keep saying it's a sedative."

"You've been giving it to her like medicine. What is it?"

"Alcohol and water."

"Alcohol and water? What do you give her that for? There's no sense in that. Alcohol and water, why . . ."

"Yes. She's drunk."

The shock dazed her. Her jaw actually fell open and the soft, old, velvety white skin of her cheeks shook.

The other woman said, "That's the way she wanted to be. She said at the funeral she was going to get drunk and she is."

"But she never did that before."

"You must not have seen her in a long, long time."

The little old woman grew tense. "I'm going to get a doctor." She started for the door, angry.

"Wait! There isn't any doctor near here." The other woman followed her out of the door. Verplanck could hear their sharp footsteps and their talk in the shop outside. Suddenly the door opened and Helen's friend stuck her head in. She looked first at the mourner, who did not stop or notice her, and then at Verplanck.

"Are you going to be here awhile?" she asked him.

"I think so. Yes," he said, rising.

"Keep an eye on her, will you? She ought not to be left alone. If she screams again, give her a drink."

"I will."

The woman picked her coat off a hook on the back of the door, and the door closed.

Helen lay on the bed looking toward the door. She had not stirred or broken her gaze for a quarter of an hour. Verplanck marveled at the Jewish girl's detachment. She seemed neither to see nor hear anything that went on in the room. It was a kind of pious rapture, he supposed. Seward should be here to witness it—he would be flattered. Verplanck moved around to the foot of the bed so that Helen was looking directly at him.

"Helen," he said.

Her eyes did not change. She did not identify him. He only blotted out the panels of the door.

He felt rather silly. The place was still now in the pauses of the lament and he could hear the hard snow pelting the window and the loud woodeny ticking of two clocks outside among the antiques.

"Helen. It's I, Henry Verplanck. Don't you know me?" He sounded to himself like one of the gauche, flabby characters in a radio playlet, the erring son approaching the blind father, the nephew cuddling up to the senile aunt. "Helen."

He tiptoed around to the side of the bed and knelt down awkwardly. He took the can and poured two fingers of alcohol into the glass and filled it with warmish water from the pitcher. It was a familiar act, here in this room, and without thinking, he nearly looked over his shoulder, expecting to see Seward, plump, flushed, and talkative, with his feet propped among the papers on his desk. Kneeling beside the bed, he regretted with surprise the death of his friend, of the man who had taken him to be a friend. The face of a house inhabited by unknown secret people once had made him fearful, and even now passing the shut door of a house where he knew no one could provoke the memory of the fear, but a place he could walk into, known and sometimes welcomed, made him—there was no other word—glad. He could pass it in the sun. And now this house had mutinied with Seward's death, and he could not walk down Hudson Street again because of the staring window of the antique shop. It was only petulance, he knew, that made him believe that it was wrong of Seward to die and leave him now no refuge here in this part of town. The emotion was not important.

He noticed that the drink was spilling and he stood up, brushing the dust and lint from the knees of his trousers. He offered the drink to Helen, hoping it would wake her up.

She reached out with her right hand, and flabby and automatic as a baby's, it closed around the glass. She drank gulping without changing the position of her head, and some of the liquid ran down over her chin and dripped on her bare breast.

Verplanck began to be impatient. "See here, Helen. You hear me."

There was no response. She drank again. When the glass was empty, she let her arm fall limp and the glass rolled over once on the bedspread and stopped.

Then what she did, she threw back the old brown bathrobe with sudden vigor. She was naked, fat, and her thick legs were mottled with patches of blue veins. She drew her feet up and opened her thighs and began to writhe. She worked the muscles of her stomach in and out and her thighs and buttocks stiffened and slacked in a rhythm hideous because it was vain. She raised herself a little, braced on her elbows, her hands clutching folds of the counterpane. She drew long, hoarse breaths.

Verplanck was sure this was an invitation—husband dead, not so drunk as she seems, tight little house wanting a new tenant, a technical demonstration to overcome sales resistance, a free sample, solo. Then he saw the tears on her stiff, contorted face; as she rolled her head from side to side, the light struck the long wet streaks.

It was grief.

Verplanck could not admit this quickly because he had never seen anything like it and none of the books he had read covered such cases.

198

In the contraction of her belly, the heave and wriggle of her hips, was sorrow. It was an immaculate votive ceremony to prevent her husband's going, and for her, in this smoky room, loud with her panting and the squeaking of the headboard, Ole Steve was living still.

Learning and amazed, Verplanck stood watching her, snapping the nails of his thumb and forefinger together in astonishment. At last she reached a crisis, held it, insisted on it furiously for twenty seconds, then relaxed abruptly, flaccid, sweaty, and sobbing. Verplanck leaned over the bed and drew the bathrobe over her to keep her from taking cold. She lay quietly breathing in long sighs. Seward was now, at this last, dead.

Verplanck's impulse was to begin to question her at once, to ask her how she had felt, what she had remembered during this long convulsion. What was the imagery that had seized her and was it like the real thing? He, untonsured, living now, had watched the visit of an incubus, heretofore, he believed, a discredited medieval bogey, and with a scientific enthusiasm he wished to congratulate and thank her. Yet some atavistic respect for a church he never entered and something in her frenzied dignity forbade him.

He went over and opened the window. A draft began to whistle under the door. Streams of smoke blew past him and were dissipated in the dirty courtyard. The air in the room freshened. When he turned back to the bed, her eyes were open, and sane. She moved her head and looked up at him.

"Hello, Henry," she said wearily.

"Feeling better?" he asked.

"Some. Give me a cigarette."

Verplanck drew one out of his pack and held a lighted match for her. She inhaled deeply and the smoke curled out of her mouth as she spoke. "Come to pay your respects?"

"I'm terribly sorry I couldn't get to the funeral, Helen. Did everything go off all right?"

"He's buried. This damned town—there were ashes, pieces of coke in what they threw over him." Her eyes changed and she looked away. Verplanck was afraid she might cry again.

"Helen, I know this has been expensive. I wonder if you'd let me help you out." Verplanck reached inside his coat to his breast pocket for his wallet but the edge of the wallet caught on the pocket and fell to the floor in a spatter of cards and memorandums. He bent, gasping, and picked them all up. He laid the wallet flat on his knee and opened it. He took out five new one-hundred-dollar bills. "Will you take these?"

"Yes. I'll take them, Henry. Just lay them on the bed there."

Verplanck placed them, folded, on the bed beside her. She had not escaped him. The experiment with Seward had been expensive and he had made the last payment. The bill was settled. No one could accuse him now.

"Would you make me a drink?" she asked. "It's right on the floor beside you, isn't it?"

"Do you think you ought to?" he asked in a gush of kindness. "Your mother's here, you know."

"Where is she?"

"She went out to get a doctor."

"What for?"

"She thinks you're ill. It's none of my business, but do you want to disillusion her? I mean, the way Seward died, and—well, do you think it's a good idea?"

"What do you mean, the way Seward died?"

"I don't think it would be wise to take up where he left off, do you? About three gallons of alcohol came in here a week."

She looked at Verplanck, opened her mouth as if she were about to speak, changed her mind, and still looked. The soft, low voice of the woman seated on her box said, ". . . *yeesgaddal v'yeeskaddash, shmay rabboh.*"

"You didn't even ask at Bellevue, did you?"

"Why should I have asked anything at Bellevue?" Verplanck said.

"When you came for me at Bellevue the day they took him there."

"What should I have asked?"

"What Seward died of."

"He died of alcoholism. That's perfectly obvious."

She propped herself on one elbow, to peer at him, her face now shaded from the light. "Seward died of a ruptured appendix." She stopped, enjoying the shock breaking the complacency of Verplanck's face. "It's not so obvious now, is it, Henry?"

"This is not true, Helen."

She said fiercely, "Seward's dead, isn't he? Why should I lie?" She lay back on the pillows, drawing the money through her hands and folding each bill over with a sarcastic tranquillity. "The hospital will tell you. Call Dr. Axelrod. When they cut him open, it spurted."

The idea that Seward had deceived him made Verplanck look at the money. She saw him do it and clenched the sheaf of bills in her fist.

"You thought he died of drink. You planned it that way, didn't you? You were so sure you didn't even ask what killed him."

"Helen, you're upset. You're tired. You . . ."

"I'm also a widow, no thanks to you. It's a pity Seward was so tough, isn't it, Henry?"

"This is fantastic. I hope your mother comes back soon. You really need a doctor."

"It was retrocaecal, they said, purulent and long-standing," she said in a high, finical, hysterical voice. "The only effect of his drinking they were able to discover was that the anesthetic worked slower. It burst when they were lifting it out, and he died very soon without becoming conscious again. He was dead when you and I were eating dinner that night, but they didn't tell me. And you were being so kind and soothing because you thought my husband drank himself to death. You knew, oh, you knew then, all right. But the murder went haywire, didn't it, Henry?"

Verplanck hurried to the door as if he were expecting someone. He opened it and looked out through the shopwindow into the darkening street full of whirling snow. It was merely a question of taste. One did not like to have epithets, "murderer," tossed at one, especially when, as it turned out, they were unjustified. He saw nobody. He shut the door and came back to the bedside. "Have you any aspirin, Helen? I think you ought to take one," he said soberly.

"There are no aspirin. Mother is not coming bringing the doctor. No one is coming, least of all Seward. He is not coming through that door any more, but why did you want to stop him? He was your friend. You couldn't help being fat and stuffy, he said, and he was too polite ever to say you were fat and stuffy to your face. What did he ever do to you? All he wanted was to write verse and have a little drink while he talked. What was the harm in that? Is innocence too much for you? What did you want to kill him for?"

Accused, Verplanck could say, as if the question were tiresome because it was so false, "I didn't want to kill him." It was true. He had only wanted to watch and to record. Death was, death would have been, incidental, a petty Q.E.D., barely necessary.

She lunged up off the bed, screaming, "You God-damned son-of-a-bitching liar! You dirty bastard!" She struck him with one fist and clawed his face with her other hand. His glasses were swept off, and he stooped mechanically to pick them up. She kicked them backward under the bed with her bare heel and jolted the back of his neck as he bent down. He tried clumsily to seize her wrists, shouting at her to keep quiet. Chopping her fist down, she hit his nose, a blinding flash of pain, and he grabbed her around the waist. In her fist were his folded bills, the five hundred dollars. He got her arm between his elbow and his ribs and tried to pry her fingers open. She screamed and twisted, panting, and threw her knee up between his thighs. He let her go, holding himself. She shifted the money to her left hand and, throwing her body into the swing, slapped his face so hard he staggered.

"Get out, you . . . get out, you . . ." she shouted hoarsely. She could think of nothing to call him. She toppled back on the bed, breathless, half naked, and she began to cry.

The Jewish woman did not look at them. She had not changed. She was still singing and had come to the beginning of her lament again, "*Yeesbora ch v'yeestabach, v'yeespohahr v'yeesrohman. . . .*"

Blood and sweat ran down his face. He combed his hair with his fingers. He slid the knot in his necktie tight and tucked it back into his vest. Sensing that she was exhausted, he got down on his hands and knees carefully and peered under the bed for his glasses. He saw them. They were far over next to the wall, gleaming faintly. He knew he could not move the bed without rousing her again, and he decided reluctantly to let them go. He put his hat on and threw his overcoat over his arm. At the door he hesitated and faced round again—the money was still tight in her fist. He went out.

It had been worse than he expected. He was so confused that he had walked down Hudson Street and turned into Christopher before it occurred to him that it was foolish to walk in the dark without his glasses. The darkness and the snow blowing against him made the outlines of everything fuzzier than ever. He stopped to hail any approaching headlights on the chance they might be those of a taxi. He picked a scab of dried blood from his cheek and looked at it, startled. Perhaps she was lying. Axelrod was the doctor's name she said to call.

6

I T WAS JUST past nine o'clock. There were a dozen or fifteen typewriters spatting out the news from France, and in the wastebaskets below the news tickers a yard of paper was already coiled. Miles had arrived punctually, not that he valued punctuality for itself or wished especially to give the Agence Havas a full day's work. It was more that he felt himself to be a settled, responsible person for the first time in his life, and to come and go by the clock was a part of the code of behavior of such people. His coat hung on the back of the swivel chair he was sitting in and his shirt sleeves were rolled up to the middle of his forearms. On the top of a pile of papers on his desk lay a cable ready for him to translate, and to look at, he seemed to be pausing in a task he had begun. He was leaning back in the chair with his hands clasped around his knees, with a cigarette stuck in his woven fingers and, as if he were trying to recall a word, he was gazing, serious, abstracted, out of the window at his left. There was nothing in the view to disturb him. Opposite him was one of the long rectangular terraces of Rockefeller Center white in the light snow, its outer edges lined with a row of small green shrubs not yet removed for the winter. A wall jutted blank above it.

In the eye are no thoughts. We see what we have learned to see—the unknown is not visible—and we forget all that is not fastened to our wants and fears. That is true, is it not? It is a belief. But sometimes, once or rarely, is memory such a thing that we have caught and held, we find, the simple picture as it is, untainted with emotion, not infected with ideas? By some flaw in the usual operation do we keep the first reflection, oh, say, once in a thousand times, preserved in its idiot shape and color to haul out and interpret later? The face remembered (from this morning) is merely the outline of the curve of the cheek, the shadow and the liquid high light of the eye. (Her hair swung forward as she kissed him on the forehead, two locks of it, brown and shining.) What meaning must now be inserted here? What conclusions can be drawn from her sober query about broccoli for dinner? Her compliment on the fragrance of his shaving lotion? What must be read into her promptness with the egg, her care (a lustful care?) not to burn the toast? Is it lewdness to suggest an aspirin for his slight cold, one tablet before he goes, with a glass of water? How must he now distort the candid smile she gave him at the door, her light good-by? Were all these simple acts done, even innocently, to lime him into vice?

Miles sat up quickly and began to read the cable. It was the daily military communiqué issued by the French government: *Au cours série d'actions produites journée hier ouest de Sarre un de nos petits postes enlevés par ennemi faisant dizaine prisonniers stop Situation rétablie comme dit au communiqué du 12 soir stop Aujourd'hui journée calme ensemble du front.* An old L. C. Smith typewriter with green rubber caps over the keys stood beside his desk on a little wheeled table. He had commenced to pound out a translation when Sam Broadus came up beside him.

Sam was a short, thick, heavy man of fifty, a bachelor, very hairy except on the crown of his head, which shone a dull pink beneath a light declining fluff. As if to encourage in himself a cheer he never showed, he dressed in bald, flashy colors. He wore a thick magenta tweed suit that stuck on him like clay and he picked little twigs and brambles out of it every few minutes. His shoes were brilliantly polished yellow brogues turned up slightly at the toes. On the street, with a handkerchief to match his socks peeping from his breast pocket and a Homburg hat with a feather in the bow cocked on his head, portly, walking briskly with his toes turned out, his firm, blue shaven jowl quivering slightly at the impact of his steps, Sam seemed to be a man who had made money on the horses, a cut above a bookie, two cuts above a swipe, a man with silks but not a stable barn. Yet he was gloomy; he told Miles he ate only white food; and he had to shave twice a day, once late in the afternoon with an electric razor he kept in a drawer in his desk.

He sat down on the corner of Miles' desk. "Is that it?"

"Yes."

"What's it say today?"

"They jumped one of our outposts yesterday and took about ten prisoners."

"Where was that?"

"West of the Saar, it says. The situation was 're-established' about midnight."

"Does that mean they got the prisoners back?"

"Probably just the outpost."

"Is that all there is?"

"Just about."

Sam walked around and looked over Miles' shoulder. "Hummph. Say, who's Minister of Information, Giraudoux?" He sat down again on the desk.

"Yes, he's a playwright. He beat out Jules Romains, the novelist."

"Is he smart?"

"I only saw him once. He just looked tired. Why?"

"It wouldn't tire him to give out a communiqué like that. My God, here are four or five million men under arms. There must be more action than that. The war must be going on somewhere. You know what I think?"

"What?"

Sam looked cautiously over his shoulder to be sure that the French employees in the office were out of earshot. He bent over Miles' desk and steadied himself on his flat, hairy hands. "There's some sort of agreement. Schneider, de Wendel, somebody, maybe the *Comité des Forges*—and the Germans. There isn't going to be any war. Just a sellout."

"You've got your dates mixed, Sam. You're talking about the last war. Why should they build all these fortifications?"

"If you had steel to sell, wouldn't you like to build forts? It's just a graft for the *Comité*, that's all."

"The Maginot Line is full of troops. Do they all work for the *Comité*? A steel cartel isn't going to such lengths just to color up a swindle."

"Graft in France is a vocation—you gotta have a call to it like a priest. They're very painstaking crooks. I don't know. It wouldn't surprise me. Say, you've seen it, haven't you, *la ligne Maginot*?"

"Part of it. Last July."

"Is it impregnable like they say?"

"They think so."

"Hell, they've got to think so. They spent all that money. What did it look like really, what you saw?"

"I'm not an engineer. It looked all right. An artillery captain showed me the field of fire through a periscope and begged to point out how his post dominated that part of the terrain and the frightful damage to personnel that would inescapably attend an attack in force."

"Military double-talk. You were *journaliste étranger*."

"There were a lot of guns and the steel and concrete looked thick."

"How many men do you think it would have taken to capture it?"

"Sam, how do I know?"

"Make a guess, then, can't you?" He was almost pleading with Miles.

Miles leaned back, grinning, and clasped his hands behind his head. "You worried? You're not French, are you?"

"Me? Hell, no. That's not it. What gripes me is this: here we are working for the big French *agence*. Havas knows everything. And

what do we get? *Journée calme, dizaine prisonniers.* You're lucky.
You've seen the damned thing. You got something to form a judgment on, but me, I got to fight my way out of the news tickers all
around me and I have to ask the eyewitness to find out anything."

"My opinion isn't worth much, what little I've seen."

"It's the only one I can get. You saw it and you got to trust what
you see with your own eyes."

Of course. It was obvious. It was like finding money in the street.
It had been his business to look and to trust what he saw, and what,
now, had he seen in his daughter? Nothing. A young girl, a daughter,
that is, is like a green tree in a meadow. Sheep graze and caper. Sun
shines down. Light, tender airs blow the sweet flag bending and the
grass. There is nothing sinister here.

Yet fear came again. Was he competent? Could he tell it if he did
see it? He stared at Sam, who picked at a fleck of twig embedded,
woven into the cloth of his sleeve. He had not seen small. He had
been spectator to the gross, undelicate event: men at war, like rough,
moving images of stone, staggered shouting and shooting in their fog,
a dark effluvium of coarse horror, easy to feel and turn away from.
Could he change now, shorten his range and peep and squint at the
devious wishes of one young girl? At last Sam removed the little
twig, covered with fuzz, looked at it, and flipped it away with his
plump thumb. Why not? He was adaptable and you did not have
to have newspaper training to observe your children. He had observed these how many days past, and all he had seen was brightness
and a proper filial affection according to her bond. *Journée calme.*

"I didn't make you mad, did I, Miles?"

"No."

"Well, how many, then?"

"That one post? Why, I should say if they sent a regiment straight
at it—which is what they won't do—but if they did, they would probably lose five hundred men before they took it."

"And it runs all the way to the coast?"

"No. Just to Belgium."

"I thought it went to the coast."

"Daladier wouldn't let it. You hear a lot of talk that it was the

Belgians who stopped it, but it wasn't. They brought it up in the *Chambre*, extending the Maginot to the sea, but everybody complained about the expense and that killed it. It was only last summer that they got around to starting something they call the Daniel Vincent Line up behind Belgium."

"Who's he?"

"He was chairman of the Military Affairs Committee in the Senate. His line hasn't got inside plumbing and air conditioning like the Maginot. After Munich, they got in a hurry, so the Vincent Line is a string of light fortifications covering the Franco-Belgian border. They're permanent but they're light."

"But they've got Liége and Namur in front of them."

"Yes, and part of the Albert Canal."

"They're all set then." Sam made the statement sound like a question. "Aren't they all set?"

"They've got the largest army in Europe, they say."

"When do you think they'll attack?"

"Maybe they won't. They might choose to receive the attack. It's a sucker play, but that's what they might do."

"What about the Germans then? I don't think they'll attack until spring. And then, on the other hand, they may be figuring the same way I am. 'The French think we'll wait until spring. We'll surprise them and attack now.' And for all we know, they may have launched a tremendous attack, just a hell of an attack, and your boy Giraudoux is keeping it secret."

"I doubt it. And he isn't my boy. I don't think there's been anything but small local actions, feelers."

"No, neither do I, really. But it gripes me. We're the guys that ought to know. We work for a news agency. People ask me, 'How's it going?' They think I have access to stuff that don't get in the papers. Half the time I play wise and say, 'It's going swell,' you know, with a knowing look. As if I was concealing more than I'm allowed to tell. But if they're my friends, I say I don't know a God-damn thing and they look at me like I was a fool."

Simple Samuel, showing his bowed bald head, a shaggy finger in his mouth, pigeon-toes turned up, shook his chubby trunk from side to side in embarrassed denial before a covey of his friends, tall, exquisite, pale people, their faces contorted in rage and avidity, with luminous eyeballs on stalks like a lobster's, glaring at Sam as if he were a fool.

Miles laughed. "Do they throw vegetables?"

"You don't take it seriously," Sam said with reproach.

"I'm out of it. I translate cables."

"What do you think you're getting in those cables? Do you think all the news is being released? From your experience?"

"No. I don't think it is."

"Well, why isn't it? People keep asking me . . ." Realizing he had said it before, he shook his head as if to dispel any effect the words had taken. "I mean, God-damn it, this outfit is a branch office of the Quai d'Orsay. You know that. Everything that goes on in France, Havas knows . . ."

"Oh, no, they don't, Sam. When you were down at the courts building, did you know all the crimes in town? All you knew were the ones they got arrested for."

"All right, leave out the skulduggery. Leave out who pays Laval. Leave out who pays Daladier. Leave out who the guy is that nobody pays, the one guy, maybe there's two, in France who is secretly honest but has to act like he is being paid so's he can protect himself. Leave all that out. Take just the public news that anybody could see. Do you think we are getting it?"

"Not all. Some is suppressed for military reasons."

"Admit that. Let this Giraudoux have a blue pencil. I mean, beyond all these considerations."

"You think the French and German armies are locked in mortal combat and the Agence Havas refuses to let it out just to raise hell with your ulcers?"

"You never ate white food every four hours." Sam drew down the corners of his mouth and pursed his lips in scorn. "Eggs. A little chicken breast. Milk. Wait till you get an ulcer and you'll see what this business does to you—never knowing your ass from your elbow." The disgust left his face. "No. I don't think it's as bad as that. I just don't believe that two modern armies are facing each other without fighting. I think there's a plot somewhere."

"Don't leave out the possibility of the truth."

"What truth?"

"Maybe there actually isn't any fighting much. There's always a chance that any unlikelihood is true, you know."

The wrinkles in Sam's forehead subsided. He allowed truth to exist. "Yeah, it's possible, but I doubt it."

"Maybe the coverage isn't very good now."

"Why isn't it? It ought to be. Every captain in every army's got paper work to do. He files reports oop to the major, oop to the colonel, oop to the general staff, and finally they get to one or two men at the Ministry, this punk Giraudoux, and one other man because he voted right three times in the *Chambre* or because his uncle comes from Vaucluse, he can cut, kill, or send out. One man, two men tell us all we know."

"Yes. That's it." Miles looked at Sam's necktie, a dark barbaric tapestry braced with fronds of yellow.

Night is when things like this happen. This is too early in the morning, and he looked for confirmation at a bowl of paper clips on his desk shining in the sunlight. This is stuff for the hot pillow, turned three times for coolness; the unfastened coal chute down the block swinging clanking in the wind; the screak and stop, the screak and stop, of the crumpled laundry bill pushed by the draft along the varnished floor; and all these dreadful clocks the sleepless helplessly mark time by. This is not a parable. It is only a conversation in the New York office of the Agence Havas between myself and Sam Broadus, who likes to be in the know because, if he's not, his ulcers hurt him and, if he is, his friends receive him, Mercury, shuffling in from Radio City, sweating under the urgency of his burden. It is nothing, Miles thought. Forget it. It is day, calm, 9:20 A.M.

For Mary is not France. Ipolyi is not a minister of information—his evening clothes fit better, and he has a more candid devotion to women than even a French politician quite dare permit himself. Margery is not his helper, and what they told me are lies because they hate me. (Yet the body of fair France is corrupted by her ministers.

That is an old story to anyone who has been there.) And it is a little too slick and easy to say that what Ipolyi has told you is a lie because he hates you. If Ipolyi had any feeling toward you at all it was one of kindly approbation, and by your consent his immodest rhapsody on Ipolyi hardened into truth for him if only because no one denied it. You made him look good because you kept your mouth shut. And now —recall the lifted arches of his eyebrows—he is hurt if he is anything since you turned on him, he would say, and rudely refused to accept one small fact offered as flattery about a girl he did not know could be your daughter, which he, with a greater sensitivity than you in sexual matters, regarded as established. "In a way not like a daughter" were the words.

And in this matter of sensitivity, would not Margery be keener than you would be, since her waking hours are *frétillantes*, sweetened by the memory and the anticipation of the bed she has left and the bed she will go to? She is an expert and she (and Ipolyi, too) might be expected to perceive an aura of desire more sallow than your eyes could see. To be sure, she called on you to make you jealous of the fat man, Verplanck, whom she is going to marry, perhaps to beckon you to her skirts again, and she was willing then to knife you as pay for your abrupt departure. Yet why should she select that one thing? You can remember yourself and her—she in the doorway pulling on the second glove, smiling, mendaciously fond, and you, shocked, angry, but still, after the shock and anger had supervened, those faint velleities of touching her, of groping deliciously in her magnificent bosom— ah, how sensitive we are—persisted and added to your surprise, and beginning to loathe yourself, you became more impatient with her, and at last, with the door open, turning to go, she looked over her shoulder, one of her best poses, and she and you both knew, and said, "I shall leave you with it," and even then when you were tasting something like horror, an emotion you had thought reserved for others, you could not forbear to toss one last glance at the last ankle leaving, confused and angry as you were. Why should you disbelieve in the sensitivity of these friends when you can see all that yourself in a few seconds?

To hell with sensitivity. Why should I give credence to an old ram and a whore? Flabby and full of sores and weakness of their yen, and eager to paint others to be like themselves? It is all very well to bluster and be moral, but if he is an old ram, then you were his jolly companion, and if she is a whore, you have climbed in bed with her often enough and she is not flabby. And if they see more with those four large, dark, admittedly lickerish eyes than you, it is because they do not gain or lose, here, this one time, by what they see. Their gaze is pure.

You, on the other hand, may have a blindness. Your eye will shut or you will look crooked to avoid this sore. You have thrown everything away for this: a home and the care of your daughter. You fled it all so cleverly for years, a light-foot traveler, but now you have come home to be a bourgeois. And with all else cast from you, you do not dare lose this. No wonder you can't see it. No wonder they can. And as you are thinking this, irrelevantly looming behind your thought like a colored photograph is the house where you were born, the way it looked when you came back to it the first time since your childhood, changed yet familiar, the maple trees still green but smaller than you remembered. The brick was red but weathered more, and the tenants had demolished the carriage house where you played once in the old hay. And the look of it was too much for you, and you got back into the two-bit taxi without making the courteous little speech you had intended, something about seeing the room where you were born, and later, drinking near-beer in the wooden station while you waited for the train, your lip quivered and you said aloud, "It has slipped away. I would have to live here again." And now, here, staring at old patient Sam and thinking this, you have let all Europe and your trade slip away and you have come home to the house to live again to be secure and fat and sober and well, good. Can you believe it might fall down? Is it likely you will see a crack in the foundation if you can force your eye to slide over it, unseen?

The nails on Sam's fat fingers were cut straight across like toenails. He had straightened out a paper clip and was cleaning them meticulously.

"I think I'll ask for a raise," he said.

"It never hurts to try. What are you going to tell them?"

"Ulcers are like clap and lumbago. They're the comic ailments. I can't tell them their policy of concealing all the God-damn news hurts my stomach or they'll laugh."

"What are you going to tell them?"

"I'm going to ask for a raise or a gold watch. I've been with them long enough. I moved them into the other office in the old A.P. building."

"You did?"

"Sure. We used to look in the windows of the Ritz. Some fun. I've seen some fascinating domestic scenes."

"I'll bet. How much are you going to ask them for?"

"You won't believe it, Miles, but I got to go get a bottle of milk in a minute. Every time I see one of their cryptic communiqués like today, little knives go stick, stick, stick, right here." He prodded the bottom button of his vest. "Milk stops it. Damn a war, anyway. You never know what to think."

"A war's a cinch."

"Yeah?"

"A war is one time when you do know what to think. Everything is sliced right down the middle—you're on one side or the other. There's no confusion. Black's black and white's white."

"When all I had to worry about was Stavisky and the Marthe Hanau blowup, I ate red meat. All I know is that now I eat white milk and plenty of it." He shuddered.

"You know what I mean."

"Sure. But what good does it do to be on the French side when they either won't tell you what they're doing or they lie about it—I haven't made up my mind yet which."

"But there's no confusion in your mind."

"Only in my stomach."

"Go get the milk."

"I'll go get a bottle of milk and then I'll ask for a raise. Either that or Havas can keep a cow in here." He turned away lugubriously. "Or you can have that punk Giraudoux send something about a battle," he said over his shoulder.

Miles began again to type out his translation of the communiqué.

He had got as far as "The situation was re-established," when he hit several wrong keys with his middle fingers. He picked up a circular rubber eraser with a little black brush attached and started to rub out the misprinted letters.

You cannot damn her by report, no matter how expert and sensitive the people are who make it. You must watch her. She will not know the manner of her love and so she cannot tell you. With misgiving and disgust, you must rig little baits and lures to get her to betray herself and you. Crumbs of rubber fell into the typewriter, and he went on erasing until he had worn the paper through.

7

T HERE WAS a tall young spruce tree in the corner, scintillant against the drawn pale-gray curtains. The star that flourished at its peak reached into the coffers of the ceiling and its motionless branches had been coated white, dipped in calcimine perhaps. White electric lamps glowed among them, their bulbs crudely molded to resemble somewhat the still flames of candles. Blue iridescent balls and a dozen tin angels, each with a yellow nimbus and a painted smile of irrelevant Gallic coyness, dangled sorted at exact intervals, some revolving slowly. Around the tree's base, to hide it, a gigantic bow of colorless cellophane had been tied and handfuls of artificial snow winked and shimmered dryly on the branches and on the floor around. The Christmas tree had been set up and trimmed by servants and the effect was one of stateliness and frigidity. There were no gifts under it, no disorder.

When the list had been checked and she was sure that all the

216

guests had come, the hostess had ordered the lights on the Christmas tree to shine and the other lights to be subdued, and with little cries and jolly commands, she had marshaled all the guests and made them sit right down on the floor, tail coats and all, while the gifts were given. Such quaint, such drolly satirical, such mocking gifts. Sly, they were, and inexpensive. An aging dramatic critic had played Santa Claus in a garish cardboard mask and hempen beard from a dime store. He had scratched his heavy stomach before them all, saying that his truss hurt him. He bent grunting to the heap of packages, straightened, read the inscription and called out a memorized insult to the recipient, and flung the gift out over the heads of the seated guests, their faces blanched in the pallid light from the tree. When there were no more presents, dancing was begun in the ballroom. Two quiet maids cleaned up the mess, all but a few strings and ravelings left beneath the tree. Miles had been tossed a parchment scroll, tied with red ribbon, which, unrolled, bore the complete poem, *America the Beautiful* in fancy lettering. The Santa-critic had squealed that it would make a guidebook to this so-strange land, that unknown mother o' Miles. (Laughter and applause.)

Two hours before, as Miles had thrust the gold studs into his shirt and knotted the ties of his white waistcoat, whistling a waltz tune and calling jokes to his daughter dressing in the next room, a Christmas party had seemed to be a pleasant gathering, homely and convivial. Now he stood against the wall with a glass of champagne untouched in his hand, encompassing the room before him full of strolling guests in a gloomy stare, whose vacancy precluded any greetings from his friends, some of whom thought he was drunk, and he divined the mistake he had made earlier in the evening. When he and Mary had been invited to this rich man's huge apartment for a Christmas party, he had been enthusiastic. He had insisted that they go, and he recalled now that the little phrase had been linked in his memory with the dark sheen of red apples, Spies and Jonathans, the rich smell-taste of popcorn, and the smell of smoke from a fire of hickory chunks, a smoke that rose in grayish puffs before a fireplace with an arch of black molded iron, when the wind was wrong and the chimney would not draw, Uncle Rob's fireplace. He had always been taken to Uncle

Rob's for a Christmas party when he was a little boy, nine miles into the country, sometimes in a double buggy through tan-colored slush, or in a cutter where he sat hunched down against the cold, covered with a molting buffalo robe, listening to the chime of the eight bells that jingled, four on each shaft, delighting in the plumes of the horse's breath in the wild air, the woods and farmhouses still, cold, delicate, and far. When they arrived, he had been hurried to the fireplace to stamp the numbness out of his feet, and have his nose blown while his father put up the livery horse. Then Uncle Rob gave him the apples and popcorn and he saw his cousins, and if the wind were wrong, the gray smoke from the fire, stinging and delicious, puffed out into his face and upward.

None of the beanfeasts with his colleagues at Foyot's or Horcher's had superseded this, not *Noël*, not *Weihnachtsabend*. Well, that was understandable. He could honestly say that he had not expected a hickory fire on a hearth whose floor was occupied with a spotless electric heater that gave warmth from a ladder of stern red bars. He had not expected apples or popcorn. The champagne was very good. What had he counted on then? Why had he been so sure that he and Mary would enjoy this evening so much, that somehow a Christmas party was precisely the place to bring his daughter?

Among the passing guests, he saw a woman he knew coming in his direction, apparently on her way to the ballroom, yet sauntering, glancing to one side and the other, clearly willing to be stopped. Miles began to sip his champagne so that he might bend his head and not have to recognize her. Certainly she, a gabby widow, was not part of the anticipated furniture of a Christmas party. *This* Christmas party, yes, perhaps—he had known beforehand the sort of people who would be here, the busy, well-paid folk who had not been born to the city, had been reared elsewhere (like himself, like himself), who, even, as late-comers, assumed a proprietary air toward the city, acted as if they were certain they were its ornaments, hustling, while they denied it, after its meager fames. And if you were eminent, however short the height you stood on, they were friendly. Unknown, you were ignored. If you were only trying to make a home for your daughter and live quietly, honestly, and peacefully, they would laugh at you, he thought with a self-righteousness he marked as soon as the laughter echoed faintly inside him.

"But damn it, I knew all this before I came," he said aloud, irritably.

Something still escaped him. Grant the phonies and the whitewashed Christmas tree. Admit that there are no apples and no pretty little cousins. What remains in common to a childhood gathering at your Uncle Rob's and this smart rout?

The widow, with yards of tulle muffling her fat shoulders, was coming back, stalking him. She meant to be talked to, evidently. And Miles at last knew why he had come. He had been circling the reason as the widow was circling him. It was like a bruise that hurt to touch. He had brought Mary to the party because it would be *healthy*. Because it would divert her. The gaiety of the crowd, the dancing, the rill of excitement that flowed through any mass of people enjoying themselves, would absorb her attention and draw it away from where, he was shocked to discover, he believed it to be—from himself. This final exactness of his thought disturbed him. With too brassy an assurance, he had tried deliberately to keep from accusing her, but now he knew that, in a skulking, covert way, he had thought with a fear equaling a conviction that she had been guilty all along.

"Carol!" he called above the talk and the music.

Loitering at the border of his glance, carefully aloof yet near, the widow heard, turned, and approached him.

He welcomed her with hidden distaste the way a hungry and malnourished man would relish catmeat. However, he was relieved to have someone to talk to.

"No, Carol, I haven't been hiding," he said.

"But three whole months! You just said you've been here since the first of October. Four months nearly."

"I know. I've been terribly busy."

"People kept telling me they'd seen you, but you never rang me up. I knew you were in town and it's absolute nonsense to tell me you work twenty-four hours a day. What've you been doing that you're so busy?"

"Oh, I had to look for a job."

"Job," she said with disdain.

"And I've set up housekeeping."

"You aren't married again."

"No. I'm living with my daughter."

"Daughter? Why, I've always thought of you as a bachelor. But"—Miles could see her remember his divorce and politeness as a muscular twinge of her whole face forbid its mention—"of course, I remember." Immediately, sweetly, she asked, "How old is she?"

"I just danced with her a little while ago. She's here somewhere. Seventeen." Miles looked around, and then toward the doorway of the ballroom through which he could see the dancers. A father's pride in which there is nothing of love made him wish to see her that he might point her out.

"Seventeen!" Her voice had a jealous sound, for, at forty-five, no artifice could keep her cheeks from drooping slightly on each side of her chin. "And you two live together? That's wonderful for you, Richard."

"Yes."

She sighed. "I'm living with a refugee." Pausing, she seemed to wait for a compliment to her kindliness and generosity.

Miles merely said, "You are?"

"I'm sure Hitler will be beaten in the spring, aren't you? The French and British are frightfully strong, aren't they, because after all—the British Empire. I told Anna that it was practically certain she could get back to Stuttgart by fall. November at the latest."

"What did she say when you told her?"

"She just looked at me. She's very strange. Not affable the least bit, but then, of course, she's an older woman—she must be nearly fifty-five. Her name's Anna von Behr."

"Noble, eh?"

"She insists that's her name. And she's got one of those international League-of-Nations passports and it says *von Behr* on that, but if she's not Jewish—you know how they eat. Well, you should see her. And close and grasping? I didn't know her. I'd never even seen her until this committee sent her up to me and there she stood in front of my door. She had everything in one bag. It was made out of some kind of knitted stuff just like a rug. Have you been into the Pierre for a cocktail lately? You used to go there, didn't you?"

"I hear it's full of titles who lammed out of Europe. I haven't been in since I got back."

"You see, I just picked her name off a list. I thought with the 'von' and all that she'd *be* somebody, well, smart at least. You know, one of the small German courts, somebody like that. And there she stood with this old rag bag, and of course I had to be charitable and take her in. She's had a perfectly gruesome time and it desolates me when I think of it, but—I know at a time like this we should all pitch in and help—but, really, Richard, the criticism. Nothing suits her, my friends, my food, the way I dress, the hours I keep, nothing."

"She may have suffered a good deal, Carol. This country must seem pretty safe and luxurious to her. Not that safety isn't a luxury, too."

"Suffered? Of course she's suffered. All refugees have or they wouldn't be refugees, would they? Anna's husband is in that horrible camp at Buchenwald and *she* just barely managed to get out of Germany. I don't deny she's suffered, but I could stand a soupçon of gratitude. It isn't as if I'd had to take her, you know."

"Oh, hell, Carol, she's a human being. Maybe griping about the food is the only pleasure she's got left. If your husband was in a concentration camp and your home was broken up . . ."

"I would certainly have the decency not to pick my hostess full of holes. Let's sit down someplace. This isn't a reception. We don't *have* to stand."

"Well," Miles said. He steered her through the crowd, passing by the door of the ballroom, and they sat down on a small sofa covered in pea-green satin.

"I wish I could see your daughter," she said.

"She's in there somewhere," he said, nodding toward the ballroom. "I danced with her once and then some kid cut in. He seemed to know me. I think it was Herb Cairns' boy."

"He's here. He's home from Princeton for Christmas." The widow, indulging him, asked, "Is she fair or dark?"

"She has brown hair and eyes."

"Like yours. That's marvelous." She sat herself erect and pivoted toward him almost formally. Her face became sober. She was changing the subject. "You know, Richard, the reason I wanted to see you, you're the only one I know who has seen this dreadful thing. There are a lot of other people—well, like Anna—but you are the only one whose opinion I can trust."

"Oh, you mean the war?" Everyone asked him about it. Certain questions were inevitable, and he had prepared the automatic answers. It was dull, like trudging uphill. Did they want to taste violence safely, become pseudo-participants, or was it only to keep posted that they asked him—"I was talking to Richard Miles the other day, the correspondent?" Miles made ready with his first answer.

"Yes. Do you think it will last long?"

"It hasn't begun yet, Carol."

"But doesn't Hitler *know* he can't possibly win? The British have the largest fleet in the world and the French army—well, when I was over two summers ago, I saw some of those Negro troops and they were the finest-looking men I ever saw in my life."

"I daresay," Miles said calmly, looking into her eyes.

"They have the largest army in Europe. Now please explain to me just how the Germans think they have a chance. They talk about bombing London. Can't they realize that the British will bomb Berlin? It will just cancel out. What do you think? You've seen it. You must know."

Asking him things. How could he whittle it down to something she could swallow and digest, a little gobbet to oil her voice box so she could tell it around, appeased, consoled, and knowing. Miles was conscious that the edge of his collar, starched stiff, was rough, and in the dark heat beneath his shirt bosom, he was perspiring. Once he would have replied seriously, glad to air his views, to appear learned and sophisticated. Now it was silly and he wondered if he could say anything that would riddle the ignorant calm of her face and make it color up and jiggle.

"Why do you care?" he asked her.

"Why does anybody care?" The notion of being affronted had occurred to her.

"Is it just that you want something to talk about when you are out evenings or have you got some French bonds or what?"

"Now, Richard, don't get angry."

"I'm not angry. I'm just asking why you want to know about the war. Why, really."

"I think it's our public duty to keep ourselves informed."

He could not answer that one and it was impossible for him to tell her why he was sure the war would be long and terrible, because it was a certainty that was built upon too many small details, some of which were inconsequential, some he had forgotten, the feathers that made a heavy quilt—the old, old Martini-Henry rifle he had seen a French private cleaning lovingly; a profiteer picking his teeth loudly in a café in Prague, reading the menu, while Henlein shouted on the loudspeaker and the Germans were marching in; the expectant, stead-fast look on the faces of Jews in Warsaw; the wrangle about van Gogh he had overheard in a pub in Oxford, students, inchoate rulers of the Empire, whey-faced and effeminate. There were many more memen-tos. It would do no good to drag these out, for he himself did not know why they weighed so heavily. And now returning in the quick skates and flashes of his thought, hearing her squeaking sentences, he did not know which catastrophe he feared, the one that would ruin Europe or the little comber that would wreck his safety and his peace. He had not been able to submerse his doubts about his daughter. They lay always just beyond his attention, shapeless worries that he did not want to think about, always present, chronic, and ominous. He could no longer distinguish between the general ill that he and every-one could brace themselves against as soon as it was fully known and this unique personal apprehension of a trouble that he did not want fished up and made clear to him in any light. Perhaps the two had mingled. Listening and speaking vapidly, it seemed not improbable in the vague, childish reaches of his mind behind his tongue that the two chief anxieties had combined, through malign intelligences of their own, to oppress him doubly and more sharply. He wished Mary would walk by. It would relieve him to see her pleased, and by introducing her, he could keep from talking about the war. He bent forward to see if he could pick her out of the stream of people going to and from the dancing, her hair or the orchid at her shoulder.

"You're not listening to me, Richard," the widow said pettishly.

"Oh, yes I am. You said Hitler was crazy." He sat back, relaxed, to prove that he was listening. "I thought I saw Mary over there. I want you to meet her."

"Oh, I'm mad to. But she's young. She won't stop dancing yet. She's not like us. We're old and we have to talk about serious things." She said this with such a pout and such an egregious coy sigh that Miles, as well as he knew her, nearly laughed.

"Don't you think Hitler's crazy?"

"No. He's a fanatic but he's not crazy."

"I still maintain that no man in his right mind would provoke England and France into war. Why, Germany hasn't the industry to support a war." This last statement she considered a gem, exactly the thing to say to a man, a shrewd observation that showed an alert care for the facts.

Was this the place, Miles thought, to mention the decade of *Rationalisierung* in German industry, to speak of Willy Messerschmitt and his factory at Augsburg, to ring in *raffendes* and *schaffendes*, the meeting between Hitler and Thyssen, the faithful, sinister machinations of von Seeckt, or the number of smokestacks and the skirt of smoke you could see from a Rhine steamboat? No. It would only confuse her.

"Have you ever read *Mein Kampf*, Carol?" he asked.

"Didn't they have part of it in *Reader's Digest*?"

"Have you ever read it all?"

"Well, no."

"Read it. Hitler wrote it and you will see he's not stupid. He's a fanatic who makes the typical Germanic error. They always make it."

"Oh, what is it? They're such specialists. They're so expert that . . ."

"They don't know enough about what a human being is."

"Oh." She seemed disappointed.

"You see what I mean, don't you?" He plodded on to explain. Not that she would comprehend, since she, like the Germans, had never considered people as human beings entire, rather only as they showed themselves to her, assisted her small purposes or failed her, as friends, little snips, heels, or kinfolk.

Opposite them, across the room, a kind of alcove had been let into the wall. In it, a large mirror with a carved wood frame reflected a divan and a few hired gilt chairs. Miles was droning steadily to the widow, and once he looked up, trying to think of a word, and a movement of the image in the mirror made him look more closely. He was almost certain he saw Mary and the young man who had been dancing with her. She must have passed in front of them unnoticed or perhaps there was a doorway from the ballroom into the alcove. Deliberately he looked toward the mirror as he talked and he saw the graceful lift of her hand and forearm as she smoothed her hair. It was Mary and Herb Cairns' son.

He was a tall youth with close-clipped hair, a buff color, from this distance a head of suede. He was immaculate with the fearful precision of the very young, in a tail coat, with a red silken carnation at his lapel. Very likely he was in his freshman year at Princeton. He was sitting back comfortably, one knee over the other, lifting a hand from his folded arms for emphasis, exactly, Miles thought, the pose he would take thirty years from now after dinner with a cigar in the emphatic hand. Mary was sitting erect, listening to him intently, sometimes nodding her head rapidly and smiling.

At first he had an impulse to call to her or to go get her and bring her over to be introduced. Then he could preen himself upon his daughter's loveliness and bask in the widow's compliments, but he sat still, trying to look thoughtful. Now that the moment he had waited for had come, he excused himself facilely, pretending to himself that he was too young to have so old a daughter, and in his mind the image of himself rose up, undistorted by reality, a youngish man, handsome, mature, intelligent, too strong to have a backache and too shrewd to have a child—in fact, the former, the transatlantic Miles, responding to a widow.

"I don't care what you say, Richard. He's a vegetarian and they say he never has anything to do with women."

"All right, he's crazy, he eats walnuts and lettuce, he's a fairy . . ."

"Don't use that word."

"What do you want me to say, homosexual?"

"You don't have to say anything. All I am contending is that you—and everybody, for that matter—are taking Hitler too seriously. You'll find that one fine day the French will attack, and Hitler's government will fall like a house of cards and then there'll be peace and you'll have had all your fuss for nothing."

"Carol, you're wrong. Every time you talk, you hope, and every time you hope, you talk, and whether it's the hope that makes you talk or the . . . you just don't want to miss the Paris spring collections, that's all. You're as wrong as you can get."

"Am I?" she said with a fawning girlishness twenty years too young for her. "Tell me why? Why am I so wrong?"

To be insolent was simply too much trouble, and, besides, he once had liked her. If he said he was hungry, famished for some of the *foie de volaille* being dished out at the buffet, he would have to bring her a plate also. If he stood up and started to walk away, she would follow him. He was almost certain that if he excused himself to go to the men's dressing room, he would find her genteelly lurking near the entrance to the corridor when he came out. Since he had found Mary, he wanted to watch her, secretly, to spy into the alcove looking glass, and the divan where he sat was the only spot unoccupied in the room from which he could see his daughter's reflection.

"Well . . ." he began, staring straight ahead of him (into the mirror) gloomily, as if the untangling of the origins of the war were a painful and depressing task. Although he had only read of him, he decided to start with Clemenceau and the wreckage of the peace, then to proceed slowly through the inflationary period on the Continent, the British General Strike, with appropriate asides about the Munich *Putsch* and the Landsberg fortress, and to bog himself down a long time among the Nazis, the Social Democrats, the Stahlhelm, and *Kommunismus*, meticulously accurate and painstaking, supplying sketches of von Hindenburg, the serviceable Meissner, von Papen, and of course *der schöne Adolf*. Eventually he would have led her, yawning and unenlightened, up to the present, and by that time, he would know from his patient scrutiny how his daughter fared, whether or not she were amused, entertained, drawn out of herself, whether she were

226

now "healthy." This idea, associated in his mind with breathlessness and pink cheeks—he was still so unused to bearing suspicions of the kind Ipolyi and Margery had aroused in him—was for the moment like a STOP sign. He did not want for any reason to inquire what "unhealthy" would mean, partly because it was necessary to give some attention to the tale he was telling the widow but more because an inquiry would threaten too much he felt he had made safe.

Clemenceau had large white walrus mustaches, and in the looking glass, Mary was no longer sitting bolt upright, fascinated. She was leaning back against the cushions of the sofa, talking yet looking downward as if she were being modest. It was her turn now. At first young Cairns had undoubtedly talked about himself, offering her with calculated nonchalance the tally of his feats, ignoring the insignificance of his freshman year in college, and returning to his last year in prep school when he was prominent, a Lawrenceville halfback perhaps who had made a neat thirty-yard run against The Hill or had launched himself into a miraculous shoestring tackle in the last three minutes of a game. Miles could almost hear him. He had done it often enough himself, offering other feats, other triumphs. It was formal, a ritual. And Mary, having listened, having been impressed, was now at his entreaty talking of herself.

For the boy, Miles felt a nostalgic sympathy. To ingratiate oneself with a girl, to say exactly the right things to create an atmosphere, a tension, in which to ask for a kiss with any hope of getting it, these were complicated, almost insuperable problems when he was seventeen. And, to be sure, Poincaré was a scholar, yet he was a worldly fellow, too, and the only course open to him was to reduce the value of the franc. It is not only sympathy, Miles thought—it is encouragement. He actually hoped the boy would say clever things, be sufficiently offhand to be charming when he mentioned his trinkets—his sports, his favorite actresses and actors, and his dance bands. To her, boy. Brag well, strut yourself proudly, for if you do that—then—as a result, Mary will like you, and you will come to the apartment and they will go places together, caroling, "Good night, Father. Good night, sir," and I shall wave the stem of my pipe at them, sitting in slippers before the fire. (I must get a smoking jacket with braid along the edges.) Miles even leaned forward, squinting to see if he could tell whether the boy's expression were lively and his daughter's rapt. And it was true that, at one time, a bushel, the devil, a wagonload of marks would buy only a loaf of bread or a liter of beer.

With this boy Cairns helping him, he could sleep at night, the whole night. He would not have to eye his daughter any longer when she did the least thing for him, to frame a glance that asked the question, "Do you hold my coat like a daughter? Or is there something else in it for you?" or "This special dish, these eggs *soubise*, so luscious in their ramekins? What do you expect from them? Does it give you an impure thrill to see me so well pleased?" Cairns could heal him of these fears. Cairns, this handsome, promising, brilliant youth, could fix it so he could sneer at Ipolyi and cuss out that slut for a God-damned meddling gossip. And Stresemann was earnest but purblind and about then we had all those conferences. There! the ally laughed. He threw back his head, shaking. His daughter had been witty, he thought, in a welling of pride.

"No, they couldn't have stopped it then. The Nazis were too well organized by that time. But earlier they could have."

"But they were so discontented, you say."

"They were, all Germans were. And every one of them who let his discontent run him—the guys who were too apathetic to vote in the elections or the ones who were suckers enough to believe what Hitler was saying—all of them are to blame. We are fighting the German people, not a regime. One man, one vote. If you believe in democracy, you've got to believe in that. Who makes up the army, the Luftwaffe, the Gestapo—men from Mars? No—Germans, the fathers and sons and brothers; in fact, the German people."

As the widow began, as a reply, a long, pointless story about a servant she had once had, Miles looked again toward the mirror, even craning his neck surreptitiously. What were they doing now? Some liaison had been established, a subtle rapprochement that made them regard themselves as separate no longer. They were a couple and together they looked scornfully to the left of the mirror, where there was obviously an open doorway of the ballroom. Probably they were making fun of the dancers they could see.

Suddenly the boy called and beckoned with his hand. He turned to Mary and asked her something. She shook her head. A waiter came into the alcove carrying a tray on which there were glasses and a silver bucket with a bottle of champagne in it. The boy looked inquiringly at Mary again, and she shook her head a second time. He took two glasses of champagne anyway and set one down on the floor beside him. Then he lifted the other, toasting her with a solemn face, and she bent her head in acknowledgment, smiling. He drank the champagne. They seemed to be getting on well.

This was exactly what Miles wished. It was the reason why he had brought her to the party. It was "healthy." Yet he felt a pang because he knew he had given the push that had started his daughter away from him. Cairns or someone else. And he would be alone again with no new friends. But this would be some years yet, and to think of it was only an irritant that enhanced the pleasure he enjoyed in watching his daughter.

"So you see, Carol."

"Yes. It's part of a tradition."

"Germans are sentimental about war. Frederick the Great taught them how. In peacetime the army is a symbol, and every private rebuff, every frustration that your individual German suffers, I guess he looks at the nearest *Offizier* and squirms with glee when he thinks how his sufferings will be wiped out on someone else when the army marches forth to conquer. Hitler has just tapped this well of military emotion and let it loose. It's always been there."

"But this *Lebensraum* . . ."

"It's a cause this time, all right. Germany needs more room, but it's not the basic cause—it's only his excuse."

"Richard, I can't tell you how fascinating this has been but I'm just starved. Do you think we could get some supper?"

"And a drink, perhaps?" Miles said. "Come along, Carol."

They stood up, and as Miles paused to let her pass in front of him, he looked again toward the mirror. It gave him back only the sofa where they had been sitting. It took him a second to recognize his daughter standing in the doorway of the alcove. She was pale and agitated, and she was glancing nervously into the crowd. She saw him

229

at last and started for him with almost a lurch. She walked straight toward him with her head down and a light flash on her cheeks showed him she was crying. When she reached him, she threw up her head.

"Can we go now, Father?"

"Why, yes. But don't you want some—supper?"

"Right now. Please, Father." Her hands were fists at her sides, her head was down again, and she was trembling.

"Sure thing. Excuse me, Carol," Miles said and took his daughter's arm. Everyone near them watched. He heard Carol say, "Poor darling," and out of the corner of his eye, he saw the Cairns boy hanging around shyly.

He made no apologies to the hostess. He left her at the door of the ladies' dressing room and went to get his coat and hat. When he returned, she had not yet come out. As he stood waiting, he was more amused than perturbed. It was, he was certain, the first time anyone outside the family had tried to kiss her. She had been brought up by the nuns and her grandmother. The nuns despised the flesh on principle, and Emmy, prizing virtue as a marketable commodity, had probably been a strict trainer, who would allow kisses, if at all, as come-ons, baits, decoys. Damn it, the girl was growing up. He would have to tell her she would have to expect a tousling once in a while. He chuckled a little and lighted a cigarette.

Yet when he saw her come out, still pale—she had put on no rouge or powder—he was astute enough to realize that what she remembered, the little moment that had made him jocular and her to tremble, was not romance. The rigidity of her face as she passed him, hardly looking at him, showed him that it had been a loathsome marvel, unforeseen, and never yearned for. And in the taxi, when Miles, now sympathetic, put his arm around her, he could feel her shudder.

"He tried to touch me," she said. "To kiss me." She began to sob, hopelessly, with her head on his chest, and Miles, prickling with a terrible apprehension, smoothed her shoulder with his hand awkwardly and kissed her on the forehead, muttering consolation.

Suddenly she pulled his head down and kissed him softly a long kiss on the lips, the kiss, he knew at last, that she could not give elsewhere.

8

THE REST OF the way home he sat stiffly upright with his arm motionless around her shoulders until it began to get numb, as if he were pretending she had been taken ill and needed quiet. He did not see what he was looking at, and she kept her head on his breast so placidly that he could not tell if she were still crying or only snug.

But going up the steps to their doorway, she said, "It really was a nice party." It was a statement which sought to weaken a present tension and to forestall, timidly and apologetically, a later crisis. It was also polite. She had been, ha-ha, well brought up.

"Yes. I thought so," he said in a firm, false tone. He unlocked the door and followed her slowly up the stairs in the dim night light of the hallway.

In their home, she laid her wrap on a chair, to hang up later, and passed through the room, lighting the standing lamps, and into his bedroom, where he knew she would turn down the bed, gather the linen between her fingers, and pull and smooth the sheet. She would open his place at the book he was reading. And lay out cigarettes, matches, and the dish for the ashes. All done in love.

Miles lay in a chair before the fireplace, with his knees bent and his feet flat on the floor. The upturned collar of his overcoat chafed his neck and he did not fold it down. His hat lay on his stomach. His elbows were braced on the arms of the chair, and sighting over his gloved hands, he stared into the nearly darkened fire. He could hear her making it ready for him to be comfortable in the bedroom. In a minute she would come out and hang up her wrap, carefully, because he had given it to her.

She entered and saw him sprawled out dull before the ashes of the fire.

"You look tired," she said kindly.

He lurched and straightened. "No, not a bit. I'm fine." He stood up, settling his white muffler. He pulled at the flap of one glove, looking down, not at her. "As a matter of fact, I think I'll take a little walk. It's early yet."

"If you'll wait just a minute and let me change my shoes . . ."

With alarm and yet a forced calm he said hastily, "Oh, don't bother, Mary. I was just going around the corner to get a paper."

"Well. I think I'll go to bed." She turned away, about to go. "Your bed is ready when you come back." She turned and faced him anxiously. "Father, you're not angry about tonight?"

This is what the weather will be: lies, untruths, fibs, evasions, all to hide her, all to cover her and keep her from herself. Break all looking glasses. Be prompt and clever. A lie's no good unless you brandish it. "Oh, nonsense, Mary." He even took her hands and kissed her on the cheek. "You were right. I don't blame you at all."

"You don't mind coming home so early? It's barely eleven." She looked down at the watch on her wrist. "But honestly, when he pulled me over and tried to kiss me, I just couldn't . . ."

"No. Certainly not," Miles said coldly, jerking the corners of his mouth upward. He let her hands go. "I won't be long. You'd better go to sleep."

She smiled. "I will. Good night."

"Good night," he said. He looked at the hat in his hand, dull-black ribbed silk. He put it on his head. He walked out of the place.

Going down the stairs slowly, with blind precision, he cursed himself for his exit, maladroit, shambling, not at all up to the demands of the part. He was not, however, what you could call a quick study, and it would be a certain time before he could make his entrances casually, avoiding all the furniture of what was now, surely, only a stage for his performance. And having entered safely, poised at the mantel or lodged in a chair, it would be hard for him to pick up his cues and remember the wording of each speech because—it was perhaps a fatal defect in an actor—he had never been able to tell what was happening while it was happening, and in this ignorance, gesture was impossible, his diction would be flat, and obviously, under these handicaps, no sincerity could be permitted him. He would simply have to boggle through speeches to fit situations as they ambushed him.

It must be an illness, he thought. He plodded across the Square, and with an animal's wariness he kept to the empty walks and skirted the puddles now filling with slush from the light snow. The immense symmetry of the darkness and the heavy, massive equilibrium of the buildings before him and to his right and left answered subtly the first articulation of his thought: if she was ill, it was a hopeless malady. He lifted his head, startled, as if someone had spoken to him. Why was it hopeless? In an illness, you called a doctor, a man in a white jerkin that buttoned up over the shoulder to a round collar. On his forehead gleamed a circular reflector. This man ordered your teeth pulled out, gave you pills with a sweet coating, and exclaimed confidently that you would be all right. And in a week or two, Mary, pale as the bed she lay upon, the poison draining, still a little weak, yet eager, smiling, would be up and around, and he would bring her flowers and tease her, purged now and uninfected, as he used to do. This was not hopeless.

While this cheery phantasm protected him, he threw back his shoulders and marched into Fifth Avenue as if he really were on his way to buy the morning papers. Then his good sense forced him to remember his wife. An illness, he knew very well, was as silent and unprincipled as snow. In Constance's lungs, bacteria had soughed their way, riding pellets of moisture, to feed upon the tasty septa of the air sacs and the capillaries, drenched at intervals by the angry blood and bumped and jostled by its corpuscles, but, steadfast, firm, insistent, they form in the steamy darkness colonies and cities full of faithful gourmands browsing without glut—perhaps with a sound like feeding silkworms—until the lungs spring leaks and holes and Constance dies. That was an illness and it was hopeless. Although she was your wedded wife, endowed with the spectacular virtues of beauty, fidelity, and public honor, the bugs got her. Neither that her state was licit nor her character without any but fairly minor blemishes protected her. And there were several doctors, even with stethoscopes, but in the end there was the priest. So less of this facile chat that illnesses are easy.

It was snowing hard. It came down in soft, flat flakes. The snow trucks were out, clanking and swishing, and here and there a late doorman was sweeping a path to his particular door. Miles, humped over, with his hands nearly to his elbows in his side pockets, splashed on in the melting snow. His patent-leather dress shoes were soaked and leaking, and the doormen and the few late walkers stared at his silk hat with the brim full of snow. It was nearly midnight and little Christmas trees and holly wreaths were still illuminated in the windows of shops and apartments.

He was irritated that he should waste time encouraging Mary's convalescence and talking politely to the doctor with the mirror on his forehead, or as a homunculus inside his wife's lungs watching, maybe leaning on an alpenstock (for the lungs were craggy like mountains), their destruction. There was no time to waste. In justice to himself and his new habit of life and, for that matter, in justice to the girl, he wanted to make a broad plan, a master plan, omitting none of the factors, fixed or variable, immediately operating, to facilitate her recovery. A conference would be held for the purpose of clarifying procedure, the election of committees, and the drawing up of specifications prior to the reception of sealed bids. Specialists under contractual commitment could be summoned, and charts indicating progress might be thumbtacked to the wall. Instructions, naturally, to be issued in triplicate (one bond, two onionskin). Optimum efficiency thus secured (by placing matters on a sound, businesslike basis), timesaving could be effected by the elimination of attention hitherto directed at data extraneous to the case in hand, i.e., *in re* Mary Miles. "Yours of even date received and contents noted. Would say in reply we deeply regret our product cannot continue to supply satisfactory service at our former rates. Certain changes fundamental to the nature of the product necessitate . . ."

What he really wanted was to run away. Flight now. Walk uptown, buy ticket, board train for, say, Boston, wire from Copley-Plaza CALLED AWAY RETURN GRANDMOTHER, dicker with N.E.A., U.P., somebody, and go back to France, a salamander safe in the war, without the supplications of kin or friends. Too complicated here. A game better to watch than to play. In France I know myself. I eat Chateaubriand with cress and drink a bottle of Musigny. I say *Bon jour*, and the concierge smiles at M'sieu Meel even if I am reading letters and do not see her. I go *luxus* with a pocket notebook to Toulon and look at the warships. I know myself. I am defined. I end with my skin. The only problem is what to do with the evenings. . . .

He fished in his pocket and brought out a leather cigarette case. He stopped by a lamppost and lit a cigarette. He was in a side street. He had turned off the Avenue without noticing it. He estimated that he could not be far from Sheridan Square. A bar would be open there. It was stupid and romantic to wander around with wet feet in a snowstorm in the middle of the night. It was shock that had sent him out. It was the shock that filled his mind with this dreamlike hurly-burly and kept him from thinking accurately. He puffed strongly on his cigarette and hurried toward the shuddering neon signs at the end of the block.

Or if she would die. That would get him out of this. He slopped and splashed in a hasty quickstep as if the lights, to come out of this dark street, would free him from these thoughts. He did not mean it— it was the shock. He was a swine to think of it. Yet like a scene from a movie he could see her about to cross the street. In the crook of her left arm was a paper sack of fruit. An orange began to spill. She looked down to retrieve it and she did not see the taxi. There she lay, her dress hiked up above her knees, one knee lifted, moving back and forth automatically. They would call him at Havas, and shocked, working his overcoat up over his shoulders in the elevator going down, he would rush to the hospital. There would be the white screens; the friendly nurse and the sad, impassive doctor. Dead. She had been ill but now she was dead. And in this unlikely, this nearly impossible event—yet many are killed in the streets each day—he could foresee himself in the hospital reek, head bowed, murmuring sincerely the platitudes of grief, and masking with a decent sobriety, emblem of fortitude before others ("He will break down later, at home," they would say), as he would mask an untimely smile, the joy of his release, his freedom.

He began to run.

The bar was bright, quiet, and almost empty. An old man with a drooping mustache leaned talking to the barkeep. He looked poor, and his feet were wet, too. As Miles put his foot on the rail, he noticed a haze of smoke as if several people had been there but had just gone. The mirror back of the bar had been shined up and a Santa Claus and *Merry Xmas* painted on it. Miles took off his hat, snapped the snow from the brim with his middle finger, pushed it shut, and laid it on the counter.

"Bad night," the bartender greeted him.

"Bad enough," Miles said. "Double Scotch."

"Just Scotch?"

"Black and White Water on the side."

"Black and White, water on the side, he says." The bartender turned around and picked out one of the beautiful bottles.

He poured Miles' whisky into a short glass and set a glass of water beside it. "You must have walked quite a piece."

"Yes," Miles said. He did not feel like talking. He drank the Scotch and some of the water. "Give me another."

The bartender smiled as if he understood something. His lean, old dry lips curved between the heavy, motionless red cheeks. "You take it," he said, and set the bottle in front of Miles courteously. "I'll git yez some water." He filled a small glass jug with ice water and put it beside the whisky. "There. All set? Morning paper?"

"Yes. Let me see it."

"It's only the *Times*," he said apologetically. With a sigh he stooped and reached for the paper under the bar.

"Thanks." Miles took it and spread it out in front of him.

FINNS PRESS RETREATING FOE
ROME HEARS OF PEACE TALK
NAZI FLEET REPORTED AT SEA

He read the headlines over and over, trying to make them mean something. He took another drink and read the stories under the headlines carefully all the way through, almost moving his lips. None of the reports attached themselves to anything he knew. He recalled a large, arid, yellow area, inlaid with irregular patches of blue and clearly marked with the names, *Helsinki, Ladoga, Petsamo*, and *Kronstadt*, but no men in long greatcoats ran through the piny woods, turned to fire, ran, paused in cover, searched behind them, fired again, ran bending nearly to the next tree, lurched and fell, shot through the throat, and died in strange attitudes, quick frozen like packing-house beef. There was just a map, and for the Roman peace talk, he got a picture only of the Italian near Washington Square where he sometimes bought Parmesan and zucchini. The fleet was the last newsphoto of a cruiser he had seen, any cruiser.

He was trying to do what he usually did in a bar, but the touchstones of drink and the newspaper did not work. The whisky did not seem to warm him and the news awakened nothing. Certainly he did not want to go home yet. There were too many things he had to figure out before he could wake up and come out of his bedroom with any composure, but what the things were that had to be assessed and clarified, he did not know or want to, and the strain of beginning the process, the reasonable process, the thinking, was too great. "It is an illness," he thought doggedly. He leaned further over the bar and began to read the labels on the bottles. He had always liked to do that.

". . . in those big valleys out on the West Coast, but did you ever eat one of them West Coast apples? They look like they're made out of china painted, all perfect. But they don't taste up. They taste like the insides were out of cotton. No, sir, you don't find 'em like that. Right out beside the house. Must have been twenty trees." The old man was talking earnestly to the bartender, who stood with his hands wide apart, grasping the edge of the bar, nodding all the time. As the old man was talking, he was shaking a bottle of mulligan and the drops squirted into his beer. He would look up at the end of a sentence, still shaking, and the drops spattered on the bar. The bartender wiped them up automatically with a rag, and then resumed his original stance, and nodded at the right places.

"Like at Port Jervis. You know where it is?" The bartender did not wait for an answer because the old man was drinking his beer. "Well, I had this place. Four acres. They was a house went with it. The whole thing for two grand. I'd saved up the money, you understand. And so I buy this nice little place outside of Port Jervis for two grand cash, and I was gonna raise squabs. . . . You got too much pepper in that, didn't you?" he asked as the old man set the beer shell down and coughed.

The old man waved his hand in front of him to show it was nothing. He began huskily, "I can remember every one of them trees. Right near the fence corner was a Greening. Then come two Spies and a Winesap. In the next row was a sheep's-nose, a Spitzenberg, and two trees of russet apples. Row three was all Spies except the last tree, half Pound Sweets and half Winesaps—it was grafted. The fourth row had four Grimes Golden. And the fifth row started with a Spy, no, it was a Tallman Sweet, then a Spy, a Gravenstein, and the last tree in the orchard was a snow apple. They took fifty barrels of apples out of there every fall. Why, there was coopers all around the county, farmers, just farmers, split out their heads and staves by hand, barrels stacked up everywhere. But all that went." The bartender drew another glass of beer, cut off the rising foam with a bone knife, and slid it across the bar to the old man, who held it and started shaking mulligan into it.

"Like me at Port Jervis. . . ."

The old man stopped in the middle of a shake and looked up sharply. "Like everybody. Not only you. Why, he used to take me and my brother in the wagon, my old man did, in the winter, the wagon box full of straw, and we'd go to town, the two of us hunched down in the straw fighting, and he set up there on a spring seat wearing a

238

dogskin coat and a cap with earlaps. In town he'd buy us each a suit of clothes and he'd shop all day doing it; two bucks and a half, he paid. That's unusual, isn't it? For a suit of clothes. And when he got done, he'd go have a hair trim in the Gibson House barbershop and get his mustache dyed black and we'd come home. We had to come west and generally he'd get what wind they was and his mustache'd freeze. He'd go stomping into the house and tick the icicles off on the stove and they go ssss. . . ."

"It was the same at this place I had up the river. . . ."

"Did you get icicles on your mustache raising squabs at Port Jervis?"

"No. . . ."

"Then what you trying to prove?"

"I mean, you say you lost your savings. Your father lost his farm. I had all this dough saved up from eleven years' tending bar. Why, Jesus, I invented the Zipper cocktail, one part rye, one part Spanish brandy, one part lemon juice on a lump of sugar. And I take it and buy this little place to raise squabs for the hotel market, a nice little country place, with roses, and what happens? I get sold out."

"Lock, stock, and barrel. That's what I say. My old man farmed early, farmed late. He was smart. And he was mean. Not that that cuts any ice, but my old man was meaner'n hell. Look at that." The old man set down his beer and thrust his right hand open across the bar. Miles could see a long white scar running from the notch of his thumb across the back of his hand. "You see that? He sent me out to plow with a broken-back horse when I was seven years old. He was a horse jockey—always trading. He traded for the fun of it and he got this one somehow and he sent me out to plow with it. It had a vertebray out of place or something. Couldn't draw a straight furrow with him because his back hurt and he was skidding around trying to go ass-end to, half the time. My old man come to see how I was doing. He was plowing another field with a three-horse team and he had the whip with him, black-snake whip. He took one look at them crooked furrows and he come for me cussing like who-laid-the-rails, and when he got up close he let go with the black-snake. Took me right across the hand there, see?"

"What the hell was the matter with his head, sending a kid seven years old out to plow a field?" the bartender asked.

"He was mean," the old man said proudly. "All of us kids went to the field young. We worked, I can tell you. Later on, several years later, it was on a Sunday, he was talking. Said something about his being my father, the way he brought me up, I forget exactly, anyhow he said, 'The kind of father I am'—I forget the connection. And I said to him, 'Father? You never were a father to me. All you were was my sire.'"

The bartender whistled. "He sock you?"

"No. I was too big then. But you see what I mean. You see how I felt about him. He was a hard, tough man, sharp, hard-working, and my old man was honest, you could always say that. Now you'd think a fellow of that caliber could make a go of it. But he couldn't. He couldn't cut it and they sold him out."

"That's what they done to me."

"Sure they did. You bet they did. And now look at you."

Miles turned to the two men. "You gentlemen think you've got trouble?"

The old man jerked his head toward the bartender. "Look at his feet. Go on, stick your foot up there."

The bartender heaved a foot up onto the counter behind the bar. The toe of his shoe had been sliced four or five times lengthwise.

"He does it with a razor because his feet swell from standing on them. Every pair of shoes he owns. Fact?"

The bartender said, "That's right."

The old man turned squarely to Miles. "Would you like to buy some Christmas cards? No, I thought you wouldn't. That's what they all say. Now I don't know your name, but you come in here in a plug hat and ask if we think we got trouble. Here we are, two old men . . ."

"Ah, I'm not but fifty-eight," the bartender protested.

"And he stands there with his shoes all slit and I peddle Christmas cards and stationery and birthday cards, Mother's Day, Father's Day, Easter cards. For every damn day, I got cards to peddle. Why? Because I got sold out. My father got sold out. *He's* still pumping beer because he got sold out. What do you want for trouble? And I live with my son-in-law, works for the B.M.T. What's trouble then?"

"How would you like to have your daughter in love with you?" Miles asked, his face stiff.

"Huh? How's that?"

"How would you like to have your daughter in love with you?"

"Oh, my *daughter's* all right. It's that God-damn son-in-law," the old man said.

"No. I mean . . . how much do I owe you? Here. Here's five dollars," Miles said. He turned around and walked out.

It had stopped snowing. He left the Square by Christopher Street. He was not ready to go back to his place yet. He decided nothing, concluded nothing. What had he expected to impose on the faces of the barkeep and the beer drinker? Sympathy? If he had gone on to explain, stopping, beginning over, repeating himself, dragging, as they would think, something unclean, a shadow of nastiness, over the conversation, kept on and kept on until they understood why he had spoken in the first place, would he have wanted, sprouting from their embarrassment, their sympathy? Or had he only wished to brag that his trouble was greater than theirs and since he could bear it, classily dressed, drinking high-grade Scotch and sporting a plug hat, he was more of a man than they? They were strangers. Why did he desire either their approval or their pity? Earnestly addressing himself, pretending that it was an all-important question, almost consciously pretending, pretending by reflex as you would jump to avoid a car, he talked to himself all up Christopher Street. And a little removed from this lively debate sat his daughter, Mary, almost as if he could see her out of the corner of his eye, statuesque, ungreeted, yet demure.

Yet they were not strangers to one another. He, the barkeep with the slit shoes, and the old man with the scar on his hand had their troubles in common. Had he wanted on overhearing them merely to join their fellowship? Why was it a man can bear disaster better if he knows he is not alone in it? Where lies the comfort in another's suffering? Perhaps to stiffen, to brace the heart against pain distorts the look of his face (yet he had been recognizable, nothing changed, in the bar mirror), cramps his will and the way he answers to his will. It may crystallize and deaden what is human. The organism threatened, the moist and simple tripes and glands and coiling guts that guarantee its repetition, its continuance afar, it withdraws its outposts, the human graces. The man with angina pectoris or the man whose daughter wrongly loves him may during the crisis of his pain suffer an exile. While the twinge holds him and the fear, he retreats from his humanity. He is a doll, much like a man but with less judgment, no feeling he can spare, incapable of love. And at this time if he can find another man in trouble, it is comforting because they can sit down and talk it over, take the nap off it by making it familiar, or they can stand up at a bar and have a drink together. Yet, all the time, they are peeping for signs of the bond that ties them, asking themselves, "Since he is dished like me, how much has it dried and warped him? How much of himself remains straight, undesiccated? Much? If so, then much remains of me. Now there, that was an acute remark he made—can I do as well? If I can, I have not been sent too far away by this. Can he, do I (glancing into the bar mirror), recognize me as the erect, mainly hairless creature, flabby, with misshapen feet and plugs of metal in his teeth, but still a man who can wince and shrink from the next one, speak, complain, and cherish now and not in the flitting of hope and memory a calm he has hacked out of these weeds? Still a man, a guy, a fellow, one of the boys, a customer, a patient, a lover? For if he, I, am something less, I cannot stand this alone. You cannot talk to a horse, however faithful, nor can he comfort you with soft, well-intentioned neighs, tapping with horny hoof upon your shoulder."

These weeds in which Miles was tramping, the dark house fronts, and the few selected trees of Christopher Street remained, he noticed sheepishly, impassive before this fine talk. It had always embarrassed him to indulge his emotions even privately, yet he knew that all in his silent ranting had been true and it had worked off the shock. He was in trouble, he could see that, and tomorrow morning he could figure out something. He saw that he was approaching Fifth Avenue again. He had gone around in a circle and he was walking up Ninth Street. It would be, he thought boldly, nice to drop in on Margery for a minute. She ought to be home by now from whatever festivities she had visited. Although he continued, as it were officially, to think about his daughter, a warmth, a sneaking relaxation, filled him as he decided to call on his mistress. It was only around the corner on Tenth Street. She would be angry at his coming at this hour. She would haggle about letting him in. It would all be smooth and familiar.

He quickened his step. He was thinking about his daughter. At the same time he anticipated, the anticipation accompanied by a complete set of images of thigh and silk and once-forsaken breast, the pleasure he would have with Margery. Not immediately, of course. It would take an hour to undermine the objections she would raise to shield her pride, but at the end of all his talk, she would capitulate and he felt he deserved an hour of this enjoyment as a reward. It was as if he were pleading before some vague tribunal. Not an open court, not public— he was actually devoting all his time and all these soggy footsteps to thinking about his daughter. That's what he was really doing, yet, in a way, in a minor, a sort of subordinate way, off to one side, so to speak, he was arguing his case: "Here I am suffering. It is my main activity just now. Am I to have no relief? Not even the short half-hour this little business will take? Oh, come now, Judge, we are men of the world, you and I . . ." Miles shuddered with disgust. He was not certain that he was even suffering. His mind ran around in circles, that was all, and you could say what you liked, it would stop running around in circles if he could lie down with Margery. He looked up toward the second floor of the building where she lived and he could see the lights on. She was at home.

In the little foyer, he looked into the glass of the inner door and settled his tie. He stamped his feet to shake out the snow that had stuck around the soles of his shoes. He was about to press the button under her name when he noticed that the inner door was not locked. It was on the hinge. He pushed it open and entered. He would surprise her.

As he mounted the staircase, he could see between the banisters around the stair well that her door was ajar. Perhaps she was having people in. He could listen quietly at the door and if he heard guests he could sneak away again. He walked carefully until he stood before her door. He listened but he heard no strange voices. Someone was moving around a little. He knocked.

"Yeah? What do you want? Come on in." It was a man's voice.

Miles went in. Margery's flat was empty. The walls were freshly papered. Miles remembered he had smelled the drying paste as he came up the stairs but he had not marked it particularly. The man was pale and thin. He was in his shirt sleeves and a dead match rolled in the corner of his mouth.

"The joint's rented," he said.

"I was looking for Miss Elliot."

"Well, she ain't in the bathroom, mac." The man looked all around and above him. "Ain't this a hell of a note? Them damn paperhangers just got out of here it ain't ten minutes ago. They belong to a u-nion," he said sarcastically. "Get double time for working nights. What do I get? The insomnia."

"When did Miss Elliot leave?"

"Friend of hers, huh?"

"Yes. Are you the caretaker?"

"Thanks, mac. Yeah, I'm the janitor. Why, I'll tell you, Miss Elliot, she moved out day before yesterday, so in two days I got to get the place redecorated because the boss is in Florida taking the cure and . . ."

Miles interrupted him. "Do you know her new address?"

"I could tell it to you, sure, but I wouldn't advise you to go ring the bell there this time of night. She *married* out of here."

"Oh."

"He came down to help her pack up. Kind of a fat guy. It was a name like Grant."

"Verplanck?"

"That's it. You want the address?"

"No. I know what it is." Miles settled his overcoat, ready to go.

"You sore?" The man rolled the match to the other side of his mouth. "She run out on you?"

"Oh, not exactly."

"You don't have to be cagey. You'll never see me again."

"All right. She ran out on me."

The man looked at the frayed end of the match he had been chewing and threw it on the floor. At once he bent over and picked it up and dropped it into his vest pocket. "Christ," he said in a complaining

244

voice, "keep the place clean. They'll be moving in in the morning."
He looked at Miles. "As nice a looking dame as I ever saw, but I'm
the janitor, see? I sit downstairs there where I can look out over the
sidewalk and you get to know the sound of the buzzers. Know every
one of 'em. And let me tell you one thing, mac, if she ran out on you,
you got lots of company."

"Yes, I know."

"Miss Elliot was widely acquainted with the opposite sect."

"Well, thanks," Miles said.

"No use standing here." The janitor followed Miles to the doorway,
switched out the lights, and walked downstairs with him, talking.
"You don't get a tenant like her. She was put together. They wasn't
nobody at the old Irving Place as good as she was." They had reached
the bottom of the steps. "I got a peek at her once. I had to call on her
about the kitchen. There's a fire ordinance all places where food is
prepared got to have an outside exit. We ain't got no exits, so I went up
to tell her, tip her off, see, that she better keep the kitchen very clean
just in case. No copper's going to bother her after he sees her, but one
of 'em might start up the stairs with the idea of bothering her. But,
ah, what the hell, come clean, I didn't care about the ordinance. I just
wanted to look at her, you know how it is. So I knock at the door,
bing, bing, like that. She don't ask, 'Who is it?' like most dames; she
opens the door. She's got nothing on but a black satin kimono. Tight.
It's pulled tight. What do you want? I stand there. Can't talk with
those big dandies looking at me. My tongue sticks in my mouth. She
knows. Oh, boy, but does she know what's underneath her chin, and
she just laughs. She stands there laughing at me look." The janitor had
been staring thoughtfully at the floor. He looked up at Miles. "It was
genuine beauty, that was. Son of a bitch."

"She's beautiful," Miles said. "Thanks a lot. Good night."

"And Merry Christmas." Miles had the door open and was just
stepping into the street. The janitor called, "Say!"

Miles stopped, holding the door open. "Yes?"

"Man to man. You don't mind if I ask you. What the hell, she's gone.
Gone from you. Gone from me."

"What do you want?"

"Man to man now: were you getting that?"

It was too much trouble not to answer. Miles knew what this pale, thin man would do with his reply, down in his little cellar, turning it deliciously over in his mind. "Yes. I was. Once."

"Mellow, huh?" He clucked. "Brother, my hat's off."

Miles shut the door and began to walk toward Fifth Avenue. He was tired. It was late and time to go home, if you could call it that, and go to bed. Linked by trouble, linked by love. He was confrere to the pigeon raiser of Port Jervis and the old bankrupt greeting-card peddler, and now he was called brother by this pathetic janitor. He had better end this night walk before he got cozy with every bum in town. Besides, it was turning colder and the wind was beginning to blow. He turned up his coat collar.

The upshot of it was: he was not invulnerable. He had been overtaken. It was like driving at night in a thunderstorm. He remembered driving to Maidenhead one wet night in an old rented Daimler. The road ahead was lighted clearly by the headlights. He knew the curves and the stretches before he got to them. It was safe driving even in the rain. Suddenly there had been a crash of thunder and the quick white lightning. And there all around him, unseen in his darkness till now, was the countryside, new and strange and somehow dangerous in this glare. It had been curious to think it had been there all the time.

He had helped people. There had been times he had watched the deaths, the fevers, and the sweats of others with an agitation he had believed to be sympathy. He had paid off doctors, bribed policemen, and had listened unendingly to the painful recital of casual acquaintances, always ready to loan money, to importune influential men, to be as kind as he knew how. Maybe it had been pity, but it had not been sympathy because he had never suffered anything and he had taken it for granted he never would suffer anything. Calamity struck other people, not himself. It was the sort of thing you read about in the papers. But he, Richard Miles, was fundamentally immune, mystically immune.

Well, that was all off. He was not immune. An inroad had been made upon him. This had come—maybe it was only an illness in her—yet it was clearly the sort of thing that did not happen to him. Europeans, yes, naturally, Texans, people living around the corner in Cornelia Street, but to him, no. Nothing had prepared him for this. It seemed wrong to feel it as unjust now that this shock, this insult, the illness to his daughter, had occurred, but he might as well be truthful.

Suddenly he felt insecure. Anything might happen now. He was passing the pale archway in the Square, and as he looked across the snow, through the trees, to have a safe place in sight, as if he might fall or be robbed all at once, he saw in one window the light his daughter had left for him.

9

DEAR DODIE,

It was sweet of you to send me the cologne, and you're right—I'll have to write to you now. I haven't written you a letter before because you would have been so disappointed with it. I know what you think New York is like. It's all lights and store windows full of mink and caracal, and restaurants with actors "dining" with diplomats and refugees and Brenda Frazier, and at night there are big musical shows and dancing at the Rainbow Room and in the morning you have breakfast in bed at your hotel with the orange juice in a silver bowl of ice. And if I tell you how I live you'll think it's weird and stuffy. Actually, except that there are no lawns, it's the same way the people on Broad Street live when you go into town on Saturdays in the station wagon from school, older people.

I won't be wearing the cologne on dates because I don't have any.

I don't have the time. Do you care how much porterhouse steak is? Do you wonder how to tuck in a sheet so it won't come out at the foot of the bed? No. Not yet you don't, and if you are lucky the way you want to be lucky, you never will care. But I have to run our apartment. Father let me pick it out and we have a big one on Washington Square. I can look out of the window and see the arch and all of Fifth Avenue beyond it. I have my own bedroom next to his and there is a living room, dining room, kitchen, and bath. Mornings I am up before eight to get breakfast and see him off to work. Then I drink a second cup of coffee and read the morning papers. We take both of them and he likes to have me read them so I can talk to him. After that I do the dishes and make the beds and sweep and dust a little. I used to get tired at first, but now it's easy and I can usually get the marketing done before lunch. In the afternoon I go to the movies sometimes or I take a bus uptown to the Museum of Modern Art or the Metropolitan or somewhere, but I come home before five to get dinner. It took me a long time before I had any confidence in the kitchen, but now he says I am practically a *cordon bleu* (look it up in Larousse). After dinner we just talk or we go out to a play once in a while, that is, we used to, but tomorrow night I am beginning to take drawing lessons in an art class. I remember how you and Sister Mary Fabian sneered at my efforts, but he thinks I have talent and it will give me something to do evenings because he is having to work nights since Christmas and I hardly see anything of him. If you ever run into my grandmother when you're in town, make a special point of telling her that Father is working at Havas. It's a news agency and he translates French cables. He turned down a wonderful offer (financially) to lecture on his war experiences.

If I wanted to be nice and polite I could ask what you are doing in dancing class—how are you and the *entrechat?*—or about the concerts or Sister Clare's headaches, but I can't really because the whole school and everything I did seems rather vague and childish now. It's funny and you will be offended but you seem to be a little girl and as I remember myself before I ran away, I was a little girl, too, and all the cat sessions and the cigarettes we sneaked in the third-floor john are like the things you did on a summer vacation three or four years ago

—just silly. I can see you laughing but it's true. And it is all right for you to laugh as hard as you want because when I ran away I ran a long way away, and the things I left, I have gotten over—like an illness— and the best thing I could wish for you would be that you could have something happen to you like this. It would have to be something else, different, for you. You couldn't run away from school and go home and suddenly take up cooking and housekeeping. Your family would think you were crazy and they would have to let Elsa go and that would kill your mother. So stay where you are, Dodie, and get A's in everything and pray for me every night in chapel.

Love,
MARY

PART
III

I

THE QUARREL had begun at dinner. It started, continued, paused, and started in a slow, monotonous rhythm. As they were having a furious exchange of accusations and replies, old Charles would enter to offer the bread or the silver dish of peas, and they would break off abruptly. Verplanck would take a sip of wine and Margery, refusing the peas with a smile and a little movement of her head, would eat a piece of the roast while the old Negro limped politely around the table. As soon as he shut the door, they would begin again, loudly, sarcastically, knowing that old Charles, deaf, could not hear them in the pantry.

Verplanck was genuinely angry. It made him awkward at table. He spilled things and dropped his fork. They had bickered in this way for two or three days. At night alone in his bedroom, as he smoked a cigarette in the darkness just before he went to sleep, Verplanck pondered the rare sincerity of his anger, trying to discover why this woman, his wife, could unfailingly make him lose control of himself. It had not happened in years. It was degrading. He was too drowsy at these times to conduct a full analysis of the situation. He would try to weigh and dissect reasonably, but then his hand would jerk from the hot ash of his cigarette, and full of a dull retrospective wonder at his own wrath, he would turn over, mash the butt of his cigarette in the ash tray on the side table, and go to sleep.

Every day since their marriage, Verplanck had mentioned in one connection or another this trip through South America which was to be their honeymoon. He said she did not need, nor did he offer, a honeymoon as an emotional stimulus, no. He could compliment her that she was neither conventional nor sentimental. She would not cherish the memory of a honeymoon because she was too adult, too sophisticated a person to feel lost without these amatory keepsakes. (In this way, he put himself in a favorable light—by assuming that, had she been sentimental, she would have treasured the moments of their first intimacies.) But they were, both of them, debilitated by too long a sojourn in the city. She had been working at a job and he also had been engaged in difficult and enervating research, and, moreover, she had agreed to the journey just after they had become engaged. Thus to sail—she was, he said stoutly, growing a little sallow—would be wise if only for reasons of her health and, he left the inference, it would be honorable. Why had she changed her mind?

At first she had put his questioning flippantly aside as if it were a joke that grew tedious, but when she saw he intended to persist, she had become unexpectedly angry, and every day as they were having cocktails before dinner, he found it harder to speak of the trivia of the day because she was sullen. She came down in negligee, would drink five or six Martinis one after the other (and all his cocktail glasses he bought large for his own personal reasons), lit each cigarette from the last, and said nothing. She seemed to be waiting for him to bring it up. And he always did bring it up. That was one of the things that worried him most as he lay smoking at night—he always brought it up in this ridiculous helpless way, and by the time dinner was served they would be fighting and—it might have been only the cocktails—she would call him insulting names. And what was worse, he would forget himself and call her names right back—and spill the wine and sweat and drop his fork. It was disgusting, surprising, and, in a curious way, a little frightening.

Verplanck was methodical. He had not asked Margery to marry him until the plans for his study of her were complete, even to a list of chapter headings. In the months he had courted her, he had imagined dozens of approaches, ways to wheedle, feints that would extract the information he wanted without her knowing it. In his imagination, all of this activity, the jotting of notes and the intricate tabulations, took place in South America. South America was still peaceable and open for travel, and he had chosen it first because a foreign country would unsettle her, and weighing an exotic fruit or inspecting a rubber tree, she would offer less resistance than she would in New York. He had counted on this honeymoon so long that a tropical setting was necessary or he felt he could not begin. He had expected checks, rebuffs from her, even a little hysteria perhaps in Bahia or São Paulo, but never to come to these routine difficulties at all, to be balked at the start, it was unthinkable.

And it troubled him, he found, that she would break her promise. It made people very hard to deal with if they were not honest, and he laid great stress on the keeping of a pledge, no matter how gaily it was given—she had laughed when she said the honeymoon was all right with her. It was not a question of the moral sanctity of speaking the truth, not at all. It was only that if they lied, they became slippery. You never knew what they would do. It was impossible to make plans.

She had so far given no reasons for refusing to go and she upset him by making, for what he considered merely tactical excuses, "counterdemands." She wanted him to take a penthouse apartment uptown in the Seventies or Eighties or some such district which was much too expensive. He was not a rich man. She taunted him with the luxuries he had promised her on the honeymoon. To stop her (reasonably) he had been forced to show her his bankbooks and a list of fully half his securities. Apparently this convinced her, but he had hardly shut the bankbooks up in his files when she changed again. Now as a concession she demanded a complete redecoration of his apartment where they were now living. She had no dressing room, no boudoir. She refused to live in a cubbyhole and she even suggested that they have the partition of his library torn out and a new wall set in to give space for this gigantic tiring room. His library and work-room would then be only ten feet wide. Did she want him to sit on his books?

It was at that time she first called him names, lard-tub, *Schmalz-gesicht*, and other foreign and domestic insults. Usually he would not have minded. People had tried to humiliate him before and he had gone on talking and smiling imperturbably. But now it was different. He wanted to reply. He found himself pointing his knife across the table at her for emphasis and, as he did it, he knew it was a dreadful waste of time to quarrel. It held up his work, and bending his head to eat—he scarcely tasted the food—and to shut out her stream of epithets, he thought perhaps the friction might have arisen from their close association, because they were living together and he saw her every day. He had never brought one of his subjects into the house before. It was very discouraging.

"Would you consider going to Rio . . ." he began with a calm he did not feel.

"You fool, I told you I've been to Rio."

"I mean, would you consider going to Rio, nowhere else, just down there and back, while we had the place redecorated?"

"You're too poor," she sneered.

"No. I could afford that. I had planned a longer trip."

She seemed tired. She turned her head away from him and said in a disgusted voice, "Quit making me offers, Henry, for God's sake. I'm not going."

"It would save you all the bother. You could leave your instruc-tions with the decorator. Really, Margery, you ought to have a vaca-tion. You've worked all these years and I think you're unable to relax yet. You're wound up. You're thin. You look pale."

"So I look old." From her tone she expected him to agree.

"Oh, no," he said suavely. "You look run-down. A sea voyage . . ."

"Has it occurred to you there's a war on? We might be torpedoed."

"Oh, there's not a chance of that."

"You're so pigheaded you'd tell me that while we were taking to the lifeboats."

"Have you heard, have you read, of a ship being torpedoed?" he asked coldly.

"No. But I will. Any day now, and I'm not going to be on it. I may be old and toppling but I want to live a while longer."

Charles entered quietly.

Margery turned to him and asked, "Charles, will you serve my coffee in my room?"

"Yes'm."

"And bring some brandy with it. You might bring the bottle."

"Yes'm, I will. Mist' Hinry, there's a gentleman downstairs wants to see you. Mr. Miles."

"I'll go right down, Charles," Verplanck said.

"All right, suh," Charles said and limped out.

Margery and Verplanck got up from the table. Verplanck said righteously, "I did not say you looked old. You are deliberately misrepresenting me."

"Oh, shut up. Go see what Dick wants."

"You'll be joining us, I suppose?"

"Like this?" She opened her hands and glanced down at the negligee. "I should think not." With a rustle of satin, she walked out of the dining room.

Verplanck obdurately wanted to continue the wrangle. He was more angry than ever to discover this, that there was something about this woman that could trick him out of his composure and make him like the trick. He felt naked without his composure. As he left the room to go downstairs, he was not curious as to why Miles had come. He was resentful that he had betrayed himself again and when he saw Miles standing near the foot of the staircase, he was, in his confusion, far more cordial than he would have been otherwise.

"Why, hello, Miles," he said. "We were just about to have our coffee. Won't you have some, too?"

"Congratulations, Verplanck. I haven't seen you since the wedding." Miles did not hold out his hand. "I wanted to talk to you alone."

"Margery's not feeling well. We can go up into the library."

Miles took off his coat and laid it on a chair and put his hat on top of it. They walked up the stairs in silence. In the library, old Charles had set a silver pot of coffee, a brandy decanter, cups, and glasses on a side table.

Affected insensibly by Miles' silence, Verplanck had forgotten his wife and had grown curious enough to be bland. "It's been quite a long time since our little dinner together. I intended to ring you up but . . ."

"I know. Your marriage," Miles said.

Verplanck glanced up a little sharply over the flowing spout of coffee. Miles was stolidly watching the demitasse fill. Verplanck said jovially, "Yes. She accepted me rather suddenly so—— There. Sugar? Cream?"

"Black, thanks."

". . . we married rather suddenly," he finished. He sat back in his deep chair, stirring his cup of coffee. He seemed to be waiting for Miles to lead off, now that the formalities were over.

"I came to see if you could tell me the name of a good psychiatrist," Miles said.

Verplanck, wary at once, took a sip of coffee. "There are a number of them. Just what do you . . ."

Miles said impatiently, "It's not me."

"Oh," Verplanck said without inflection.

"It's my daughter."

"What seems to be the trouble?"

"She doesn't know there is any. She's perfectly happy. She's in love with me."

Verplanck's cheeks began to bulge as if he were about to smile. Then they drooped circumspectly. "In love with you," he murmured. "Incestuously, you mean?"

"Yes. Who can I see about it?"

"These states are difficult to recognize. How can you be sure? What are the signs of it? What is the evidence?"

"I've got plenty of evidence. What can be done to cure it?"

"Cure? You regard it as a sickness . . ."

"Certainly."

"Yet it is one only in respect to the morals of our society," Verplanck went on, smiling now a little. "My dear Miles, why do you . . ."

"See here, Verplanck, I don't want to hash it over. Tell me someone I can see about it. I'm tired of sitting in the Trans-Lux."

"Sitting in the Trans-Lux?" Verplanck asked.

Irritably, as if he had said more than he had intended, Miles explained, "I've just come from there. I go there every day after I leave the office. It's so I won't have to go home. I don't want to see her, so I tell her I'm working nights, and then I go to the Trans-Lux and watch the newsreels."

"Aren't you being a trifle severe? She is no one to be afraid of."

"I'm not afraid of her. It's just that . . . I don't know," Miles said. He was conscious that he seemed ignorant and immature.

"You feel perhaps a certain repugnance?" Verplanck asked lightly.

"Yes, I guess that's it," Miles said slowly. "But, look. I don't want to talk about it. If you can't tell me someone . . ."

"It might make you feel better if you did talk about it," Verplanck interposed smoothly. "If you will pardon a personal opinion, I think you are exaggerating the whole matter. It's not at all as serious as you seem to believe."

Miles flinched as if someone had hit him. "What do you mean?"

"Why, the cure as you call it is very simple. To remove your daughter's . . . unwelcome affection, you have only to remove your daughter. Send her away. Didn't you tell me once that she was in school?"

"Yes."

"Has she finished?"

"No."

"You must have taken her out of school to bring her here, didn't you?"

"Yes." Miles was looking at the floor, following Verplanck's thought. For the past ten days, he had been lethargic. He had avoided his daughter as much as he was able and he had spent his free time in movie theaters. There in the darkness, titillated by the racing images of love and war, he could forget his daughter a little. He did not wholly forget her. The fact was always there, heavy and inexorable, and moving restlessly in his seat, he sometimes reproached himself for his laziness, but then the guns would fire before him or the girl would be kissed and the reproach would be dissipated. It was only this evening that it had occurred to him suddenly to come to Verplanck for advice. His trouble had appeared to him complex and terrible. He had been at such pains to shun it that to be told offhand that it was simple seemed unjust.

"Surely it would be very easy to send her back to school."

"Yes. It would be easy, but I can't do it."

"If you let her go back to school and recommend to the headmistress that she be allowed a little freedom, a modicum of extra-curricular freedom . . ." Verplanck seemed delighted by the phrase, ". . . with young men, a few dances, parties, that sort of thing, why, in a year she'll have forgotten all about you except as the source of her allowance."

"A *year?* No, I can't send her away." Miles straightened up. "Can you tell me a good psychiatrist?"

"Are you worth a lot of money?" Verplanck said coarsely. "Forgive me, Miles. I know you are worried and distraught by your daughter's, shall we say, bias? It seems monstrous and terrible. You want it remedied as quickly as possible and naturally you think of a psychiatrist."

"What else is there?"

"Nothing except time, which you are not willing to spare. I mean, you think hastily of a psychiatrist now as you would think of a surgeon if, say, your appendix ruptured, but it is not the same thing. You probably want her analyzed, not that this is necessarily indicated. Psychoanalysis is popular. Everyone has heard of it. Men have themselves analyzed for the same reason they once drank beef, iron, and wine—as a tonic. But do you know how long an analysis takes?"

"No."

"Six months to a year. Do you know how much it costs?"

"I've heard twenty-five dollars an hour."

"Just about. Four or five hours a week. That's a lot of money."

"That's all right. The money is nothing."

"More coffee? Some brandy?" Verplanck poured the coffee and ran a little brandy in Miles' glass, subtle hints that money bought these luxuries as well as peace of mind, and to get the latter one might have to forgo much.

"No, I can stand the cost. I just want to know someone I can take her to."

"I was wrong then. I assumed you did not want to put her back in school because of the cost."

"No. I've got the money."

"I am being too persistent but—why can't you isolate her for a year or so, from yourself, I mean?"

Miles had been sitting bent forward with his elbows on his knees, staring into the coffee cup he held in his hands. When he looked up to answer, his forehead caught the light and Verplanck could see he was sweating.

"I can't," Miles said. "There are personal reasons. They are private. I've got private reasons."

"It's not that you return your daughter's affection, I suppose?"

Miles jumped up. "God-damn it, Verplanck, all I want is the name of a doctor. If you don't want to give it to me . . ."

"Oh, please. Please sit down, Miles . . ."

"Why the hell should I? I ask you for help it's no trouble to give and you . . ."

"You should sit down because you must not get angry," Verplanck said, as far as Miles could tell, sternly. "Any psychiatrist will ask you that. It will be his first question. How far do you think he will get if you start jumping at his throat? You must first of all rid yourself of any desire for privacy. You can withhold nothing. That is precisely why I asked you that question. You insist that you cannot send your daughter away for personal reasons." His voice became wheedling. "I merely wanted to show you how open you must be if you want to help your daughter."

"I know. I'm sorry. This has been on my mind."

"Naturally. It couldn't help it."

"But I don't like this telling all. You said a minute ago that an analysis wasn't necessary, didn't you?"

"From what you have said, not a formal analysis, no."

"This goes on too long. I want to know what to do. This is no life as it is. You say formal analysis—are there any other kinds? Who gives them? You're too slow, Verplanck. You don't tell me anything."

"*I* am not exactly a charlatan, Miles."

"How do you mean?"

"I have a medical degree. I don't practice but I have it. And I have spent ten years in psychological research. If you would care to put this in my hands, I would be glad to help you."

"Oh, no. No. All I wanted was . . ."

"It'll be no trouble, if that is what you are thinking. I'll be very glad to do it. Because, frankly, it would be fascinating from a professional viewpoint. I don't want you to think it's pure altruism."

Miles said nothing.

"Is it my credentials you want?" Verplanck asked jocosely.

"No. You're perfectly competent probably. But—what would you do? What would the treatment be?"

"How old is your daughter, seventeen?"

"Yes."

"Seventeen is a little young for a routine analysis." Verplanck brought out this lie with caution, alert to see if Miles could tell it was a lie. "It is sometimes a harsh process, dipping down into the memories and dreams, you might say to the bottom of the psyche. And once the turning point is discovered, the point in her life where she began to—ah—deviate from the accepted norm, you understand, it is necessary to make this conscious, to induce her to recognize and to accept it, and sometimes the results are shocking. One's character has to be sufficiently stable to face the conclusions that must be inevitably drawn, and my only thought is to spare her that moment. But 'spare' is hardly the word. She cannot be wholly spared it. Rather my objective will be to bring her to it in a different manner than usually is done."

"What is your method?"

"Why, it's very hard to say—to a layman. Eclectic, I think it might be termed. I combine my own theories—tested, of course—with the most fruitful results of other leading psychiatrists. I shall talk to her at great length, of course, and you will have to help me all you can. Which you would do, wouldn't you?"

"Yes. Certainly."

"Then shall we consider that I'm to be . . ."

"I don't know. This isn't the customary way . . . how much would you . . ."

"Nothing. Not a thing. You can buy me some books that I need if you like."

"But if you take the case, you ought to get more than that."

"It's hardly a case, my dear Miles. I shall be very glad to help you, and it's not mere paltry generosity. I'll be learning a great deal myself as I work."

"But are you sure you can—well, straighten her out?"

"I am perfectly sure."

"Why do you say it's hardly a case?"

"I am not orthodox. Sometimes I flatter myself I am too logical for my colleagues, but—a case implies illness, doesn't it? You yourself regard your daughter as ill, don't you?"

"Yes. What else is she?"

"What is an illness? It is an organic disturbance detrimental to our bodies. A disturbance, or it can be a deterioration—smallpox, cancer, you see? Now in this sense is your daughter ill? Has she been infected? Is she suffering? Obviously she isn't."

"But she is not normal."

"Forgive me for taking the long way around." Verplanck poured himself some more brandy, sipped it and rolled it on his tongue, swallowed, and exhaled. "I have just spoken of organic illness. Now consider illness of the soul."

"Soul?" Miles said, startled to hear Verplanck use the word.

Verplanck lifted his shoulders and put his head on one side deprecatingly. "A convenience to indicate the nontangible. *Psyche* is Greek for 'soul,' you know. From one point of view, there are two kinds of psychic illnesses, those that cause the patient great personal unhappiness or, in extreme cases, like the old classic dementia praecox, end in utter failure of the so-called mental powers. Idiocy, you might say. Then there is a second kind, the illness where the patient is at home with himself—happy—you see, but where the details of his conduct may distress or actually injure society. Certain kinds of insanity, manic states characterized by wildly euphoric feelings sometimes issuing in violent acts. Now do you think your daughter morose, pathologically depressed? Is she a menace to others? No. She is not, is she?"

"No. Not to others."

"She is healthy and happy, pursuing, as far as any third person can tell, a normal round of life."

"As far as a third person can tell, yes."

"Very well. From what you say, she is enjoying a perfectly normal affection. Subjectively she is innocent. She senses nothing unusual, and here is what you object to: her affection has what may be defined as an abnormal goal, yourself. You are the only one who suffers. The moment anyone else suffers, the moment she transfers her love from you to another man, the trouble ceases. Briefly, you are what is wrong with your daughter. I am not trying to be facetious. You have come, returned, into her life just at the time when she has emerged, as they say, a woman. She has undergone the physiological changes that make her capable of bearing a child, and accompanying these are the usual intensifications of the sexual feelings. You are nearly a stranger to her. Is it hard to conceive that she should fall in love with you? As I have said, the simplest remedy is to remove yourself from the scene. Then she will find another person." Verplanck watched Miles very closely as he said this. He did not think there was any danger of Miles' agreeing to go away from his daughter but he wanted to remind him of the possibility one more time because his frequent references to the simplicity of the remedy would irritate Miles and make him call to mind more clearly the reasons he had for staying, whatever they were. Verplanck was convinced by now that this father-daughter relationship would be a magnificent subject for his attention and study. It was dramatic. It provided an interplay of character that would swell, diminish, and change under his eye. A woman, one single woman, his wife, was static, and he could turn to her any time.

"No. I am not going away," Miles said, as Verplanck expected,

264

irritably. "I want to keep things as they are. If you can cure her, go ahead, only I wish you would set a figure."

"I wouldn't think of it, my dear Miles. It will be a pleasure." He settled back in the chair comfortably and folded his hands across his stomach. "Now, since you've agreed to let me 'straighten this out,' will you tell me why you object to going away so strongly?"

"What has that to do with Mary?"

"If I am to take nearly all from her, I must leave her something. You don't want her to hate you when I am finished. It is necessary that she know—and I shall have to know first so I can tell her—just what is the depth, the texture, the shading, of the affection she can count on from you. You must tell me how you feel about her. Now, it may be that the reason you must stay near her, keeping everything as it is, has nothing to do with her, but I rather think it has."

Miles had begun to see that Verplanck was not so stupid as he had appeared to be the other times he had seen him. "You're right. It has. A whole lot."

"Now, you understand, Miles, I am not trying to pry into your personal beliefs, emotions, convictions—whatever you want to call them—except to clarify the situation. It is a technique I must use and you will have to help me by your candor. What does your daughter mean to you? Don't try to be too coherent. Say whatever comes into your head first."

"Why, I don't know—her hair, I guess."

Verplanck wanted to cry "Bravo!" and clap his hands. Asked that question, so many people would have answered deviously out of diffidence or shyness. They would have tried to hide the blunt fact under a statement like, "Because I want to keep the home together," or similar pompous rot. But Miles had been completely frank, had gone straight to the essential. Probably his newspaper training, Verplanck mused.

"Anything else?" he asked.

"The way she moves her hands," Miles said.

"What are the conditions that make these things valuable? You realize that you could say these about any woman, don't you? There is nothing fatherly in liking a girl's hair and hands." -

"Yes. I knew that when I said it, but you want candor."

"I do and I am very grateful for it. Please go on, if you don't mind. Tell me, what is your daughter doing when you see her hands? Where is she when you notice her hair?"

"In our apartment. She likes flowers. I see her with flowers in her hands, arranging them. Whenever I think of her casually, without any reason, that is what she is doing. And the sunlight is always shining on her hair."

"Through the window of your apartment?"

"Yes."

"You never have a pictorial image of her, say, in the park or walking in the street in the sunshine?"

"Not if it just comes into my head."

"What is the apartment? What does it stand for?"

Miles smiled. He felt easier now because he believed something was being done. The cure had been started. "I see what you're after. Off-hand, I don't know as I can say what the apartment means. It's not Europe."

"And you like it for that."

"Yes. And it's not the town where I grew up. I didn't like it there either, except as a kid. I always wanted to get away."

"Is it New York? Positively, I mean."

"No. The only reason I settled here was because I knew I could get a job." He had also, he remembered, settled here because Margery might have married him, but he did not think it discreet to mention it now. "Somehow the apartment is a safe place. I don't mean it's anything in itself. It isn't beautifully furnished or even very convenient. My neighbors mean nothing—they never do in a city. It's not so much a home as it is a place to hide in, I guess."

"What are you hiding from?"

"We talked about the war once. Didn't you believe what I said?"

"The war," Verplanck repeated. "What else?"

Miles did not speak at once. He waited, then replied, "I don't know as I know. It doesn't seem to be right on tap. I'm not conscious that there's anything, yet . . ."

"Let it go for the moment. Let me ask you this: couldn't you hide alone? Why is your daughter necessary?"

"I like her."

"Go on."

"I like her because she makes no demands on me. That is, and this sounds pretty callous, I have to have a place to live and I have to eat . . ."

"And as long as you're at it, you might as well share with her, is that it?"

"Yes, just about. She doesn't keep after me to make more money. She doesn't beg for new clothes. She doesn't want to move in society. She doesn't care if I'm respectable or not. If I want a drink or two, it's all right with her. She doesn't bother me."

"Who did?"

Miles laughed at Verplanck's shrewdness. "You're right. My wife. We never wanted the same things. We both came from the same town. I wanted to go and see things. She wanted to stay and join the country club."

"I see."

"But Mary asks nothing, and because she doesn't, I want to do everything I can for her. We had a good time together before this came up. She's intelligent. She laughs at my jokes and she's a wonderful cook."

"Does she resemble your wife in any way?"

"Her eyes. That's all. No traits inherited from her that I can see."

"How long had it been since you'd seen your daughter before your return?"

"About seven years, but we wrote regularly back and forth."

"Then you couldn't have known much about her really until you saw her."

"Only from the letters."

"Hmmm. I hope I'm not tiring you with these questions." Verplanck patted the coffeepot and clucked in disappointment. "It's cold. Would you like some more? I'll have Charles make some fresh."

"No, thanks."

"It's no trouble at all."

"No. I've had enough. Thanks very much."

Verplanck leaned back again in his chair. "Was it your intention to live alone in New York when you came back or were you going to bring your daughter here to live with you?"

Miles hesitated. "I was going to bring her here this coming summer. She would have finished school by then. But she fooled me. She ran away from school as soon as she knew where I was. And when I saw her and talked with her, I knew I couldn't play the heavy father and send her back. I liked her too well."

"Quite." Verplanck hunched forward heavily in his chair, looking sharply at Miles. "Now, can you isolate and present the reasons why you, still in Europe, decided to come home and adopt a daughter whom you knew only from her letters, who was adequately provided for as she was? I assume, you see, that the intervening seven years had made her a stranger. Can you do that?"

"I felt worthless."

"In what way?"

"I said something about it the last time I talked to you, I remember. Europe was so full of blindness, complacency, and graft when this war was blowing up that Europeans seemed to me to be stupid little people, and for me to hang around and describe them would have been stupider. I had to get out. I was alone and I had a little money. Mary was my daughter, and I guess I thought I should support her. Maybe I wanted responsibility for someone beside myself. I was tired of being alone, too, good and tired."

"At once an occupation and a companion."

"I wouldn't say occupation. She was somebody to work for, and I was under an obligation to her anyway."

"I see. You have been very co-operative, Miles. I don't think there's any more I want to ask you this evening. This is adequate for a start. Will you come again soon?"

"Me? I thought maybe you would want to see Mary."

"Not yet. There are some other things I want to ask you. How about day after tomorrow—about eight?"

"That'll be all right." Miles stood up. "Have I told you anything? Anything you can use to help her?"

"Yes. Quite a lot."

"I'll see you Thursday evening, then. I'm really grateful, Verplanck." To his surprise, he nearly put out his hand to Verplanck. He caught himself in time.

"It's nothing, Miles. I'm very happy to be able to do it. Good night. And don't worry about this."

"I won't. Good night."

At the last glimpse, Miles saw, in a pool of light from a table lamp, the gleaming black shoes and wrinkled trousers and, above them against a background of books, Verplanck's plump face smiling, and he wondered how he had ever thought him dull before. Actually, get him on his own ground, he was brilliant.

2

B ELOW, VERPLANCK HEARD the street door close behind Miles. It had been a very good evening. He was exhilarated. He seized the brandy bottle, uncorked it, and guzzled three swallows. He let his fruity breath escape in a giggle and rubbed his stomach with one hand. If he had known how to caper, he would have capered gracelessly alone in the silence of his house. But his eye caught the brandy glasses and the coffeepot and cups. He went to the bellpull beside his desk and rang for Charles. He switched on his desk lamp and economically put out the rest of the lights. He was about to sit down at his desk when he remembered his wife. The stain of the quarrel was gone.

He hustled his knock-knees down the corridor but stopped short before her closed door. She had been superseded. There was really no point in regaling her with a painstakingly bogus tale of Miles' visit, since it no longer mattered how she took it. If she wanted Miles for a lover now, she would damned well have to hump herself and snare him alone—he, Henry, the *Schmalzgesicht*, would not play Cupid any more. Why, then, go in at all? Yet as his hand was on the knob, the hinge beginning its murmur, he acknowledged himself jauntily a male. Margery was a beautiful woman. What harm to indulge himself even if there were no profit in it?

Hung about with stale, smoky air, she was sitting naked on the edge of the bed, one heel on the mattress, drawing a finger lightly across one scarlet toenail.

"It's nearly dry. I've been painting up my feet."

"You have beautiful feet, Margery."

She threw up her head and looked at him. "Well, I'll be damned," she said in mock astonishment. "I thought I was an old bitch, and here you come creeping in, all quivering and tender. What's the matter—too many oysters tonight?"

He glanced at the brandy bottle sitting on the floor beside the bed. It was nearly empty. She followed his glance.

"All right, what the hell of it? I've got to do something sitting around this ratty old flea-bag."

"You talk so coarsely, Margery," Verplanck complained.

"What did Miles want?" she asked. She straightened her leg out in front of her and wiggled the toes, saying in a cute voice, "There. All dry. Pretty? Smells like bananas, doesn't it? What did Miles want?"

"I think he came to pay us his respects and give us his felicitations."

"He didn't punch you in the nose, did he?"

"Why do you say that?"

"Dick felicitate us? Don't be funny. He isn't that kind of a guy. Not Richard Miles." Verplanck saw a sly look mold her features. "On the other hand, why not? Maybe he did at that. Did he ask where I was?"

"He did—very kindly."

"What did you tell him—'My wife is in the bedroom, barrel-house drunk'? I can just hear you."

Stiffly Verplanck said, "I told him you were not feeling well."

"Stout fella. A lie well stuck to is as good as the truth. You are a liar because I'm feeling wonderful. Have a drink?"

271

"I've had one, thanks."

"You've *got* a book, huh? Well, I'-l-l have one. I think I'll have just one short pour. One little drink." She bent forward, Verplanck eying the swing of her breasts, picked up the bottle, and poured the drink into her glass. She was unsteady and the brandy gushed out and spilled over the rim. She paid no attention. She drank the glassful neatly. "I'll tell you what, husband mine. You can lace me into my corset. I bought a corset today. It cost sixty dollars. Do you care?"

"But with your figure you don't need a corset, Margery."

"Oh, reason not the need. I *want* a corset. Everybody's wearing them." She thrust her feet into a pair of high-heeled mules and ran teetering to a table by the window. She tore the wrapping off a box, strewing it on the floor, and from the box she took the corset. "Black, see? Black satin."

"Margery, I'm not going to lace you into that thing," he said firmly.

"No? No lacee?" she trilled in soprano. Then she said in a hard voice, "Oh, yes, you will, my dove, my little pouter. You'll lace me and you'll pour me baths of Walker-Gordon milk. Because . . ." She pirouetted, singing, round the room, the corset flapping from her outstretched hand, ". . . I'm going to be like Anna Held. The teeniest waist in Gotham." She stopped, panting, in front of Verplanck. "What do you mean you won't lace me up? Certainly you'll lace me up. I know what you married me for and what you married me for will not, as we say in the magazine business, be available unless you do as I say. Give me a cigarette."

Verplanck handed her a package. He was suppressing a smile at her confidence. She could not know that in the last hour she had become a superfluity. And as to what she had available, he could get that anywhere. There was a certain small advantage in having it in the house, that was all. And, of course, she was beautiful. He struck a match and held it.

"Don't nag," he said.

She puffed. "I abhor it." She puffed again, straightened up, and blew the smoke in his face. "Darling," she said in a kindly, throaty voice, "lace me up."

"Well," he assented, "but I fail to see why you should confine your beautiful belly in whalebone and steel."

"An heap of wheat, punctuated by the large, the European navel. And corsets are not made out of whalebone and steel any more, chum. Here." She thrust the laces toward him and turned her back.

The laces were looped in a simple knot. Verplanck fiddled with it and at last untied it. "Now what do I do?" he asked.

"Have you always worn button shoes, stupid? Just lace me up. Start at the top and come down and don't start pulling until you've got the laces through all the holes."

Verplanck crouched. He dropped the laces two or three times. He wet his fingers as if he were threading a needle and guided the ribbons through the eyelets with slow, finical care.

"You should have been a watchmaker, Henry," she said over her shoulder.

The muscles in his calves had begun to flutter from the strain as he finished. "There. Now what?"

"Start at the top and pull it tight. Good heavens, it's perfectly simple. Only pull." She took three deep breaths and blew them out. "O.K. Now pull hard," she said through her teeth.

He drew up the slack timidly in little tweaks.

Her breath came out in a loud puff. "My God, *pull*. I'm not double-jointed or I'd do it myself. Put your knee in the small of my back and heave. Only wait till I get the wind out of me." She breathed in and out again. "Pull," she whispered, choked.

Verplanck pulled until his arms ached. At the foot of the column of laces he tied a bowknot in the ribbons. "How's that?"

Margery exhaled. She ran to the bureau and pulled out two drawers and rummaged through them. "It's tight this time." She found what she was looking for, a tape measure. She ran back to him. "Measure me," she said brightly.

He slid the tape around her waist and drew it tight.

"What is it? Hurry up," she said, jiggling up and down in eagerness. "I'm only twenty-three normally. What does it say?"

"Just a second. Nineteen. Nineteen and a half."

"Oh, that's not bad. How do I look, Father Time? Can I be your hourglass?" she asked coyly. She ran to the bureau again and found a pair of black silk stockings. She sat stiffly down on the edge of the bed, crossed her knees, and began to slide one of the stockings on.

Verplanck watched. Although he was uneasily enduring a vague surmise that this display was not for his special delectation, that there was some other perhaps narcissistic aim, he was by no means insensible to it. He enjoyed it. He was filled with a voluptuous excitement and it pleased him to identify precisely the stimuli that aroused it. From her leg, long, gleaming, rounded, tense, as she stretched it out to fasten the stocking to the garter, from the rich, debauched contortion of her waist, he could and did abstract the quality that was nourishing his unseasonable desire. It was pressure, the apparent pressure of the stocking, the real pressure of the corset, taut and shining. Whatever was compressed by shoe or corset, glove or stocking, imitated, did it not, symbolized at least, a tumid phallus. Kid gloves compelled the future. To watch a woman climb on a bus was a foretaste of the paroxysm. At least Freud said so. Or did he? He must look it up. She stood up panting, with one leg bare, and reached for the brandy bottle, and Verplanck was puzzled again. Her florid bosom spilled lightly from the black lace border of the corset. Why was this sight inspirational? There was nothing squeezing them. Was it the old infantile memory of sustenance? Were they aphrodisiac because every man had sucked them (unless, as now, he was being raised on a formula)? Nonsense. They were not udders, definitely. Perhaps it was because, in this context, they were unconfined and drew his eye out of sheer contrast. They were the flowers that burst from this slim stalk. He noted, with a tingle, that he had vaulted into poetry—she was a powerful woman. Even so, silly as it was, there was no sense in denying one's aesthetic impulses. Many were undoubtedly valid.

She had just fastened the other stocking. She picked up her cigarette and poured herself another brandy. With the cigarette in her mouth and her head back to escape the smoke, she said, "There now, do I look so aged and infirm?"

Verplanck lurched toward her. "Margery, I never said . . ."

"You hurt me at dinner."

"But you misquote me. I didn't say you looked . . ."

"Do I look so run-down?"

"You look marvelous, darling. May I . . ."

She raised one finger and waggled it from side to side. "*Oh,* no. Not in this outfit. Why, these stockings are one-thread. You'd tear them all to pieces. And besides, it's only Tuesday. What's got into you?"

"I know but—damn it, Margery . . ." He reached out clumsily and pulled her to him.

In his embrace she looked up at him coldly and said, "You're not cut out for a rapist. Let me go."

Verplanck dropped his hands.

Mockingly, pouting falsely, she cried, "Oh, now, *you're* hurt. Did Wed-Hot Henwy wanta see mamma evwy night? Did-um?"

"Oh, stop that disgusting baby talk."

"All right. I'll tell you what," she said nonchalantly. "You go work or putter or something and come back after a while. I've got to do my face and hands. You come back in an hour and knock and we'll see."

"But, Margery, why not now?"

"This is highly irregular. This is not in the bond." She spoke as if he were a little boy. "Now, run away or I'll give you a good sound birching, yes I will."

"But . . ."

She yawned. "Will you kindly get the hell out of here?"

"Well, all right," he said uncertainly. He went to the doorway, turned, and looked back. She was already seated at her dressing table, peering into the glass, twisting and stretching, smoothing her waist with her hands. She cocked her head on one side, smiling.

He ran back to her, "I'll come back in an hour."

She scowled and looked up at him. "Run along, will you?"

Verplanck left her room, closing the door softly behind him. On his way to the library, he pondered his wife's self-adulation, choosing it as a more satisfactory theme than the embarrassment of his own defeat. He was inclined to doubt that it was true narcissism. Hadn't Rohleder, he believed it was Rohleder, said somewhere that the narcissistic impulse was due to a defect in the "sexual center" (probably meant the anterior lobe of the pituitary) of the brain? Ellis had dodged the issue and merely quoted other authorities, he seemed to remember. The mirror was, of course, important. In the library he glanced up at the rows of books, with the half-formed intention of looking up a few definitions, but he drew out his desk chair and sat down firmly. Confidence returned. That Margery admired her body was surely only an ingenuous offshoot from an intense but normal sexuality. She gave it the care and took pleasure in the care that a carpenter gave his tools or a painter his paints. She was proud of it because it was expert. Narcissism, faugh!

While he was musing in this way, he had taken from a drawer in his desk a new notebook and opened it to stretch the binding and make it lie flat. He rubbed his fist over the open page. He picked up a pen, tried the point on the blotter, wet it with ink, and at the top of the first page, he wrote *Preliminary Notes on Richard Miles* and under-lined it carefully. Then he sat back, lit a cigarette, and looked at the nails of one hand, clean, broad, with a raised plump welt of flesh around them. It was amazing how things turned out: he had expected to deal with Miles as Margery's lover, an accessory really to the study of his wife, and here he was through sheer luck beginning a notebook on Miles, a study in his own right. He moved his chair closer to the desk, picked up the pen again, and began to write:

To the unprejudiced observer, Miles exemplifies the dilemma of the modern educated man. He is thoughtful but wastes his thought; informed, but his "facts" are irrelevant; he is cultured but his culture is a gloss, an overlay that he has consciously selected like a cosmetic from a litter of artifacts made by men who created them inevitably and without choice; he is "good" only out of respect to the police sergeant, without moral beliefs. (He discovers what actions are morally impossible only when they are forced upon him. Then the dormant, scarce-remembered, hitherto inoperative taboos instilled early by his parents and more recently and weakly by society stir sluggishly within him and make him say "No" without knowing why.) He is not irreligious, nothing so positive as atheistic; he is, rather, almost schooled by his environment to ignore religion, and any intimations of a power beyond himself reach him faintly and unrecognized if at all. He is a free-standing figure, without—even—any attachment to his pedestal other than his weight. When he moves, it is in utter liberty, but the movements are random and disordered. He would call himself, proudly, if challenged, free, but free how? Free from what? He has forgotten. In the most literal sense, he does not know how to act.

In the senseless elaboration of his comfort, by constantly embroidering what is in fact only a pillow for his bum, he has as a type stultified himself, become unrecognizable to an observer, because he has lost his spirit, i.e., a sense of focalized order originating outside himself. (Discuss historical causes of this later.) Day and night, his heartbeat, the rhythm of the moon, the natural succession of the seasons—all of which he can slow down, accelerate, or deny—no longer signify the fundamental dynamics of life. They are inimical because he can control them, manipulate them mechanically for his pleasure, a poor sensual pleasure which, when it has been achieved, is only superficially gratifying. Ra of the Egyptians is eluded by air conditioning. Since his perceptions have become so blunted, only hints reach him—as they have reached Miles—of the chaos in which he exists. And sitting in the darkness on his pillow, he sees nothing valuable until, like Miles, he is overwhelmed.

Since his departure from Europe, Miles has not represented the type in its full ignorance. He says he felt worthless, and this feeling, probably not with the clarity of the statement, intruded upon him while he was still in Europe working as a correspondent. It is this intuition that separates him from his fellows. He is further differentiated by the fact that he is alone, and when applied to him, the word has a fascinating richness of meaning.

As regards family, it may be assumed that his parents are dead. His wife is dead. And it is unlikely that there are avuncular relatives or other sibs who see him with any degree of regularity or influence him in any way. The only blood kin with whom he maintains relations is his daughter, and this relationship is threatened.

He belongs to no caste, such as the military or priestly, whose tenets might sustain him now in return for his allegiance, and it is doubtful, since he has given up working at his profession to its fullest extent, whether he is friendly with many journalists. If, as he says, the profession seems stupid, then its practitioners are equally so and he *rejects them because of it. In fact, it is probable that he has no close friends whatever because of his long stay abroad. This probability is corroborated when one considers that he spends his evenings alone at the cinema. If he had a close friend, he would seek him out especially at this time.*

Miles has been a wanderer. Like many Americans, he was born and reared in a small town and whatever affectionate memories of "home" originate there. Yet, like many Americans, he left it dissatisfied. (Inquire precisely reasons why.) He forsook Europe, the adopted continent, in fear and disgust, fear of war as destructive of a way of life he had found romantic, disgust because Europeans did not share the fear. Now he has come to rest in New York. In his travels he has not had the time to be a citizen of any one place. He has not accepted civic responsibility and has not allowed himself to form the indefinable yet comforting ties that are the fruit of this acceptance. Places have been merely coigns of vantage where he could perch to watch the news take shape, and their inhabitants were never neighbors. Now, as a resident of a modern metropolis that is too big, too complex, and too confused to permit a communal solidarity, he cannot enjoy the reciprocal kindly interest in his affairs that a genuine community might take. In short, he is a stranger who has taken root nowhere, without place, trade, friends, or family.

He has been trying in a fumbling manner to discover an environment, a relationship and a duty that will work. He does not ask that these delight him or provide any deep satisfactions particularly. He wants only the security of negation: to live without the perpetual gnawing of fear and disgust, without a conviction of personal worthlessness. For "home," he has substituted "a place to hide in." He has no longer any pride in his work; anonymity and pay are sufficient rewards. He counted on his daughter to replace his friends, and by shielding and cherishing her, providing for her and presumably educating her, she would inspire his remaining slight ambitions. Since few of our contemporaries attempt to realize their widest potentialities by the fulfillment of a preconceived plan or theory, it may be assumed that Miles constructed his program, this ascetic pattern, by trial and error, empirically, almost by chance. Yet at the moment that he seems to have become fully conscious of these vague aims and wishes as a program, it is destroyed by his daughter.

It is clear that he does not think he regards her as sinful. He says she is ill and speaks of a "cure," but his attitude toward her exhibits, to a rational observer, a curious yet typical dichotomy. She is ill, and yet he will not go near her if he can help it and he spends his free time away from her. He feels, he admits, a certain repugnance. It is not as if she were suffering from leprosy or as if he had learned that she were coprophilous. There is nothing disgusting in her appearance or behavior. Then why the repugnance?

It is hardly to be doubted that the subject is undergoing the belated emergence of a moral sensibility that even now he would very likely deny. ("Moral" as here used does not mean an innate mystic ability to distinguish between an absolute Right and an absolute Wrong; rather it means the ability to recognize and comply with the customs and behavior patterns of a given place and time.) What we have here is a survival of Miles' solid bourgeois upbringing, a survival vitiated by disuse, but still retaining enough strength to prompt him, even to direct him now. In fact, it would not be surprising to find him, under the pressure of this crisis, returning and clinging to a scheme of values instilled in him as a child. Although he knows he has come to the end of something, i.e., his old way of life, he will not command the detachment or perspicacity to formulate a new code of values, partly—if he is typical—because his introspection has not been contemplative, only fretful, and partly because he is confused. It will be easier to resume an obedience once enjoyed, now half remembered. He is throwing himself backward in time to his mother's knee.

When Miles was a boy in the early years of this century, perhaps two hundred years had elapsed since any votary had publicly died for his religious faith. "Sin" and "virtue" were hardly the paramount guides to behavior except in rare cases. However, they were not yet words devoid of any but historical connotations. Among the great Protestant middle class that nurtured Miles, they could be taken seriously as dim atavistic qualities, never weighed or examined directly but given a certain hasty respect. What had once been living, austere, intense, the symbols of divine command or punishment were now

279

revered as monuments. Going to church was still approved socially.

It is obvious that this code of morals, if it can be termed that, had its origin in a Protestant Christian religious faith and logically can be binding only if it be informed by that faith. When one considers that Miles' parents and those in charge of his upbringing were not especially pious (N.B. Ask if his father played golf), then how much greater will be the dilution in Miles himself? He is certainly not religious and he is oblivious to his present submission to the saws and edicts inculcated in him as a boy. But he does obey them. That is the important thing. In whatever guise he remembers them, however weakly they prod him, he obeys them. Thus his "repugnance" undoubtedly rests upon a sense of sin which his daughter has violated. In his eyes, she is actually wicked, although the spurious tolerance he has acquired in his adult years would not let him admit it. It is as a man familiar with the methods and techniques of his time that he brings his daughter hopefully to a psychiatrist to be "cured," yet unconsciously his attitude toward her is motivated by this anachronistic belief in sin which expresses itself in a "repugnance" that he does not try to explain.

Before proceeding further, it will be necessary to test the strength of this newly burgeoning belief in order to determine whether it is in fact a resurrection of nearly vestigial moral perceptions or whether, improbably, Miles has been frightened by the war and more recently by his unwelcome discovery of the character of his daughter's love into an intellectual reconsideration of his conduct, i.e., decided it was time for him to overhaul the foundations.

Verplanck frowned. The last sentence was flippant. He was tired and decided to stop writing. He moved his chair backward a little and rubbed his eyes under his glasses. He wanted to evolve some way to try Miles, to test him, as he had written. If he were to continue to observe Miles under stress and to determine the stress, he must know the weight of the forces that opposed him. But how to find out? He slumped down, thinking. The pen in his right hand was automatically drawing little symmetrical figures on the blank page of an engagement calendar. Verplanck bent over to look at them. They resembled hourglasses. Carefully, smiling, he drew ineptly the outline of Margery's corset.

Abruptly he snapped the notebook to and laid it in a drawer of his desk. He got up, left the room, and went down the corridor to his wife's door. Softly he listened, almost willing to put his ear to the panel. From the room a gentle susurration issued, grew louder, and swelled into a long strangling whine. Margery was snoring. Verplanck had never heard her do it before. It was really too inconsistent, a lovely woman like that.

He turned away disappointed. He did not want to wake her up. She might waken with a headache and their quarrel would begin again. Anyhow, it was late. He began to tiptoe down the corridor. Suddenly he heard a giggle. He stopped, bending and craning to listen. He was sure it was a giggle. It was Margery laughing at him. Was he, then, somehow ridiculous?

3

IF THIS HAD HAPPENED some few years ago, it would then have been right for him to spy on her, to ask these innocent-seeming questions that drew her out, to watch. It would have been right because it was expedient. Years ago, if they had been living together in a flat in Bayswater or off the Kurfurstendamm, Wielandstrasse perhaps, with trees planted in the sidewalks. Then wouldn't he have been clever, Machiavellian, sly? In two or three evenings, without a second thought, he would have yerked the whole thing out of her, puzzled her maybe, made her fearful, damaged her, but, by God, he would have dug the simples out of her to cure her bingety-bang without any of this tenderness or horsing around. But now he found he was reluctant, kind, and slow, not thinking of himself, and, if he asked a question whose intent was hidden from her, stammering with shame. He held up a dish.

"Where does this go?" he asked.

With her hands to the wrists in the soapy dishwater making a metallic clatter in the pan, she nodded to the right. "There, in the cupboard beside you. No, I've never even thought of it."

"You will. Wait and see." He took another dish from the drying rack.

"But I'm too young to get married, don't you think?"

"Oh, I don't mean now. Later."

"Later," she said, as if that were a long time away.

"Take last summer now," he said, polishing vigorously and looking at the dish. "Didn't you have any dates?"

"You forget. I was living at Grandmother's."

"Didn't she let you out at all?"

"Once. With Oliver Channer. We went to a garden party."

"Garden party? My God, do they have garden parties there now?"

"Yes."

"Too many English movies. Tea, I suppose."

"Yes. We had tea, and we could move around and admire the herbaceous borders."

"And I can remember when the only interest that town had in growing things was in dollar wheat and the Grange exhibits at the Fair. Who's Oliver Channer—Ted Channer's son?"

"Yes. He goes to Culver. He was a member or a corporal or something in the Black Horse Troop."

"And Emmy sat on an iron chair in the background . . ."

". . . with Mrs. Channer and said, 'What an ideal couple.'"

"Ted Channer must have done pretty well."

"He's a real-estate man. He owns the Willow Grove subdivision."

"Where's that?"

"Out where the boom lots used to be."

"And the garden party was your one brief burst of glory?"

"That was all. Grandmother told me she was willing to let Oliver come to call. But he never did. He must not have taken to me."

"He was the only one she'd have in the house?"

"I was definitely not going to become one of these young girls, why, they're mere children, hanging around saloons and beer gardens half the night."

"Emmy sure is hell on other people drinking." So that he would not have to look at her, he bent over to slide the skillet into the cupboard beside the stove. "But didn't it bother you not to have dates like your friends?"

"I never wanted dates. Boys are silly. All they do is talk about themselves."

He stood erect, smiling, "Yes. They never get over it."

She did not answer. She wrung out the dishcloth and wiped the sink and drainboard. He waited anxiously. She spread the dishcloth over the faucet handles to dry and at last she turned around and faced him. "You're always worrying, aren't you?" she said gently.

"I am? How do you mean?"

"You're always trying to get me to have dates. You bring it up very subtly and you're just being generous. You seem to think I'm denying myself, and out of kindness and generosity, you drop these little hints. Well, I'm not denying myself."

"You're sure?"

"Certainly. I could have a date every night if I wanted it, even here. My art class is full of all kinds of people. All I'd have to do is borrow a red crayon."

"All the same, it's pretty thin for a girl your age to do nothing but cook and wash dishes and keep house."

"For my old father. Go on, say it. The dishes are done. Thanks for helping me. Let's go in the other room."

He went into the living room and sat down in the armchair before the fire and lit a cigarette. After she had hung up her apron, she came in and sat down opposite him.

"Old father," she said, "this is pure self-sacrifice. I don't think you really want me to have dates because if I do, you think I might fall in love with someone and marry him and leave you alone again."

"No. That's not it. I . . ."

"You want to be fair. So you encourage me, but in your heart you want everything to stay just as it is, don't you?"

"I like it the way it is, you're right."

"Well, you can stop worrying. This is the way it's going to stay. I don't like other men. I like you." She jumped up. "I'm going to be late." She ran into her bedroom to powder her nose, and in a moment, she hurried out and took her coat from the closet and began to struggle into it. As she did it, she looked like a child.

"Aren't you going to take your drawing things?"

"They're there at the school. We have lockers."

"Here's some money. Take a cab."

"The bus will get me there in time. What are you going to do?"

"Oh, read, listen to the news, I guess." While he was speaking he got up, went over to the window seat, and turned on the radio.

"Well, I'll see you." She kissed him quickly on the forehead and ran out. From the window he watched her take a bus in the street below. He turned off the radio and waited until he saw the taillights of the bus flick off in the darkness up the Avenue, then he put on his hat and coat and ran down the stairs. He hailed a cruising cab and gave Verplanck's address.

Miles was excited. In the few answers she had given him, he believed he had found something Verplanck could use, and now that he was no longer with his daughter, watching her eyes and the turn of her head, hearing her reply, he was not ashamed of himself. He wanted only to see Verplanck as soon as he could to tell him what he had heard.

When Miles entered the library, Verplanck was sitting at his desk adding a column of figures he had set down in a small pocket notebook. The items that made the total were things Margery had bought in the preceding month. She had been insanely extravagant, yet Verplanck feared to reproach her. She might start one of those exhausting quarrels again. For two or three days she had been pleasant and affable as, he thought, all women are when they are spending money, and he did not want to arouse her. Hearing Miles' step, Verplanck raised his head, drawing his brows together, and peering beyond the circle of light from his desk lamp.

"Oh, hello, Miles." He got up and offered his plump hand. He kept the notebook in the other with his thumb in the place. "I was expecting you. Do sit down. As a matter of fact, I was just taking a few notes on our little problem." He raised the hand with the notebook in it.

Miles sat down in the red-leather armchair. A low table with the customary decanter of brandy and two glasses had been already set beside the chair.

"I'll stay here," Verplanck said. "It's easier to write at a desk and, if you don't mind, I'll just continue to take notes. Please help yourself to the brandy."

"Thanks," Miles said. "Want some?"

"Later, I think."

Miles poured a little brandy into his glass. "I've been talking to Mary," he said. "Only a few minutes ago."

"Anything—ah—significant turn up?" Verplanck asked.

"I don't know what you'll think. I think it corroborates what I told you."

"What did she say?"

Miles had been eager to tell Verplanck all about it but as he began to speak he felt uneasy. He knew he should respect the privacy of their conversation but he had to tattle to cure her. He spoke with a rush in long sentences, using a tone that implied a loathing of the whole business, a kind of whine. Verplanck watched him blandly with his hands folded, rubbing his thumbs together, and occasionally, for the effect, stopping him and turning to write "Now is the time for all good men to come to the aid of the party" in his notebook. Before he had finished, Miles knew obscurely that he was betraying his daughter. He was profaning her, and it troubled him to think that he would remember this moment when he saw her again and it would stain and dim the beauty she had for him.

"I think you are right, Miles. This is definite corroboration. We must not, however, attach too much importance to her grandmother's strictness. Your daughter did not want the company of young men in the first place. It is like a corset—if a woman wishes to confine herself, there is no good persuading her not to, is there?"

Miles was taking a sip of brandy and he did not reply.

"Tell me," Verplanck said rather suddenly. "What kind of man was your father?"

"*My* father? Why?"

"Obviously your conduct as a father was influenced in a dozen ways by the only model you knew intimately. One half of our little prob-

286

lem is that of your relations to her as a father. I told you I wanted to clarify that aspect of it before I talked to her. Do I make myself clear?" Verplanck said with a faint sarcasm.

"Yes. I thought you wanted to talk about her but . . . my father, eh?" He nearly said "my old man." That was how he had always thought of him.

"Yes. Would it assist you if I asked what he did for a living?"

"He talked." Miles paused. Yes, the old man had talked. Up and down the Mississippi Valley, from water to water, in Pullmans in the washroom, in the smoker, in the diner on the Southern, the Santa Fe, the I.C., the L. & N., the Y. & M.V. on the gritty green-pile seats of day coaches, old ones with baseburner stoves and gas lights on the Katy, the Central of Georgia, the Gulf & Ship Island, the N.C. & St.L., the Lake Shore, and the C.H.& D. "He was on the road. He sold fence."

"Fence? Oh, fencing, you mean."

"I mean wire fence. *Horse-high, Bull-strong, Pig-tight.*"

Talking, he went out with the retail hardware owners to show them how to sell farmers the fence he had sold them first, and talking, telling jokes and stories, he leaned over the fences in the Blue-Grass and appraised the mares in foal. He had once eaten dinner, they all wore tuxedos, in Old Man Haggins' horse barn, it was that clean. And out of Pea Ridge, near the battlefield, standing with one foot on the lowest rail, he spied the shy, lithe razorbacks hidden in the pig-weed. And near Ottumwa and Muscatine, he made prophecies, chewing an alfalfa stem, on the price of feeder steers with white faces and curly flanks. And before he left the farm, the farmer bought ten twenty-rod rolls, No. 9 top and bottom, with No. 12 filler, and the retailer bought a carload from the old man.

"You could probably fence off the whole United States with the fence he sold in his lifetime."

"He must have been very convincing."

"He was."

"And friendly."

"No. He made very few friends. He was not intimate with many people. He liked to tell stories. Selling fence gave him a chance."

There was the time when he was trying to find Smyrna, Kentucky. It was way up in the hills. He was in a buggy with a livery horse, right up *in* the hills, and he couldn't find it and he couldn't find it. Well, sir, it run along till almost dark, and finally he see a house coming, just one house, and when he got close he see they was another house set right next to it, and standing on the porch of this other house they was an old, old lady. All bent over. Hair on her face. And he leaned out of the buggy and says, "Excuse me, madam." And she heard him and looked around, up out of that stoop, and says, "Yes?" "Could you tell me how to git to Smyrna?" he asked. And she says, "Mister, if you'll git down out of that buggy, you'll be in Smyrna right up to your hind end."

And then they was the time he and Jim Burrus was traveling together up in North Carolina; Jim knew the country. And they were driving a surrey, uphill and down through the mountains, to see a customer. Well, by four o'clock in the afternoon they see they wasn't going to make it that day, so when they come to a store—it was just a store set on the side of a hill, nothing around it—Jim says they could stay there. So they talked to the fellow and he says they could. They ate supper and the storekeeper took them upstairs to an attic room. They was a big four-poster double bed and all around on the floor was fruit jars, all full, why, devil, they must have been a thousand quarts, mostly peaches. They raised a lot of peaches around there. So the next morning after breakfast, the old man says to the storekeeper, "Would you sell me a couple of quarts of brandy?" All them peaches, you see. And the storekeeper says, "No. I don't sell. But I'll give you some." Well, out in the garden they was forty, fifty stakes with nothing growing up them and he went and pulled up one of them stakes and under it was a jug. He poured out two quart Mason jars full and give it to him but just before they drove away, the old man sneaked in and laid a couple of dollars on the kitchen table.

He had a customer in Lexington, Kentucky, named Jim McDonald, who was raised in the Carolina mountains, and the old man figured he got homesick for that mountain brandy so he packed the two Mason jars in his grip to take to him as quick as he got to Lexington.

Well, he had to make a stop at Nicholasville, Kentucky, big hardware merchant there, and Nicholasville was dry. They had local option. Just as the old man finished writing the order, in come the sheriff, a friend of his, Jack Muir, and the sheriff eased up to him and says private, "Bring anything in with you on your hip?" The old man often brought some brandy or moonshine in across the line and then his customer and the sheriff and a couple of others would have a little poker game. The old man says, "No, Jack, I didn't." Then he had to brag and show off. "Tell you what I have got though. I got a couple of quarts of peach brandy in my grip I'm taking to old Jim McDonald over in Lexington." He could have bit off his tongue for saying that and, sure enough, the sheriff says, "Come on. Let's open it." But the old man turned him down, said he had to take the liquor on to Lexington. The sheriff didn't say nothing. He just turned around and walked out of the store.

Well, it wasn't but a few minutes when one of them big, ole, long boys come into the place. He had a star as big as your hand pinned to his vest. He says, "Is they a Mr. Miles in here?" The old man spoke up and the deputy unloaded a warrant for his arrest. It was a real warrant signed and sealed. The old man looked at it and he says to his customer, "This is a hell of a trick for Jack Muir to go and pull on me just because I wouldn't give him a drink." And he says to the long boy, "Lead the way."

Well, court was in session, and when they went into the courtroom, the judge stopped the proceedings and says to the deputy, "We'll dispose of this case right now." Old Judge Williamson, and many's the time he drank out of the old man's bottle. He set there, had his robes on, and he looks down over his glasses and says, "Mr. Miles, you're charged with having in your possession at the Nicholas Hotel two quarts of brandy. Do you plead guilty or not guilty?" They wasn't nothing for it so the old man says, "Well, judge, I got the brandy. I guess I'm guilty all right." And the judge says, "Do you mean to say that you have in your possession at the Nicholas Hotel two quarts of old North Carolina mountain brandy?" And the old man says, "Uh-huh." Bang! the judge smacked his hammer down. "Court's adjourned. Let's go git a drink." And that was all of the mountain brandy.

As he recalled the stories, his father telling them and the pantomime, Miles stared past Verplanck, smiling.

Verplanck said, "They must have been good stories."

"They were, and he had a gift for telling them. You see, he wasn't paternal. As a father, he never did anything I have done as a father. He was just a big red-faced man with blue eyes who came home every now and then with presents for me, and while he was away he wrote me letters."

"And while you were away you wrote letters to your child."

"Mine were only from Europe, but his were from the Peabody at Memphis, with the hotel building engraved two inches high on the envelope, and the Battle House at Mobile and the Grunewald at New Orleans and, oh, the Gunther at San Antone and the Royal Palms at McAllen, Texas, and the Muehlbach in KC and the wonderful Jens-Marie at Ponca City. Now don't tell me that some cheap French crib like L'Hôtel de l'Universe et Brasil comes up to these."

Verplanck smiled indulgently. "No, but your habits were the same. Was he away much of the time?"

"Most of the time, as I remember. Sometimes as long as four or five months. In those days it was a serious journey to go from New Orleans to Chicago even if you were a salesman. When he came home, it was an event."

Watching him climb out of Poopy Holloway's station hack, Miles, six years old, had run tumbling down the porch steps, out under the maples in the front yard, screaming, "Daddy, Daddy, what'd you bring me?" And once he had brought him Creole pralines in a box like a bale of cotton, bound in burlap with cotton fuzz sticking out of the ends.

"Was he, as they say, a good provider?"

"Yes. He worked on salary and commission and he made pretty good money. We had ups and downs, but I never knew any hardships."

"You had a car?"

"Yes. It was a Mitchell. It had white wheels and a one-hundred-and-twenty-four-inch wheelbase. My mother was afraid to drive it, and it sat in the garage all the time he went away on trips."

"Did he play golf?"

"He took it up after the war. By that time his customers were big wholesalers. He began to carry a dinner jacket around with him, too."

Verplanck got up and poured himself a drink of brandy. Standing, looking down at Miles, he said, "I think I see your father quite clearly—essentially a hedonistic wanderer, wouldn't you say? It seems to me that you are very much alike."

"Why? Because we are hedonistic wanderers? Nobody ever said we were alike, but if you're right, his wandering lasted him all his life. Mine didn't."

"It lasted him long enough to influence you perhaps. If only from his stories and the letterheads of all the hotels he patronized, you might have acquired an early love, admiration is better, for travel."

"That's possible, but I doubt it."

"At what time did you cease to worship your father?"

"Worship him? I never did that I know of."

"Am I wrong to suppose that in any family the mother rarely appears to her children as a separate person with traits and private habits of her own? Her care, affection, and discipline are too deeply integrated with the child's own life—in fact, they form it. As a result, the child knows only the warning, the kiss, and the reproof. He does not reflect that the common center from which these emanate has a shape and a style of its own. A father, however, is different. He sees less of the child. It is oftener the mother who does the spanking, and the child has few painful memories of him. He comes only on occasion, bigger, louder, rougher than the mother. To a young child, he is larger than life size, a figure perhaps a symbol of power."

"You mean there was a time when I knew my old man could lick any man in the block and I worshiped him because of it? Yes, maybe you could call it worship."

"And later this image shrinks. The awe once inspired by its supernatural power dries up and sometimes between the time of puberty and his social acceptance as a man, the youth learns that his father is only a man like other men."

Miles chuckled. "That happened to me the first time I heard the old man tell one of his dirty stories. I was quite chaste at the time."

"Undoubtedly it was a shock. Now consider the last stage—your father is dead, is he not?"

"Yes. Died of a heart attack eight years ago."

"Am I wrong in supposing you were admitted to be head of the family long before his death? Didn't he abdicate and even willingly? As he grew older didn't his influence over you grow less, his orders tolerated rather than obeyed? . . ."

"Smaller than life size finally?"

"To you, yes. We have no patriarchs any more. Youth and its qualities are too much prized. The old have no dignity because they try to be young and their wisdom is flouted," Verplanck said with sententious regret.

"You're right, but so what? Where is all this leading? Do you mean that my daughter worships me in the same way I did my father?"

"In a sense, yes."

"I don't know. Women worship where they may be of service. Men because of envy."

"Precisely . . . 'where they may be of service.' That's an excellent aphorism, Miles. Very sound. Brilliantly put. Just let me write it down," Verplanck said, and thinking of his to-be-published study of Miles and his daughter, he actually did write it down. Apt as he knew it was, it set his teeth on edge because he did not know enough about women to have said it confidently himself.

Miles had been diverted by the memories of his father. At the mention of his daughter he felt the ache begin again. "I don't believe my daughter feels as she does merely because I am her father. The origin of her, well, affection is not filial."

"Fatherhood is a mystic state. It would, it can absorb many kinds of love."

"Mystic state? Why?"

"You know there is a tribe in Australia which has not yet grasped the connection between sexual intercourse and childbearing. A native woman may be digging roots in the bush. Suddenly she is seized with the pains of labor and shortly bears a child. It is her belief that the spirit of the place has entered her and caused the birth, and the

292

symbol of the spirit, an animal or bird, becomes the child's totem. Where is paternity, then, in our sense?"

"It may be mystic to a tribe in Australia but it is not mystic to us. I am the wise father, you might say."

"That thou art my son, I have partly thy mother's word and partly mine own opinion, as Falstaff has it. I would say that it is only because of the sanctity of property rights that the family has grown sufficiently stable to guarantee the positive identity of children, and, even now, as you know, mixups are possible. It is not unheard of for one child to be substituted for another in a hospital—a mere slip or oversight—and if the four parents and the two children are of the same color, no one is the wiser."

"But children look like their parents."

"And if they don't, a grandparent will serve for the likeness very easily."

"Are you trying to insinuate that Mary is not my daughter?"

"Not at all. I am contending only that fatherhood is a mystic state. You cannot count the genes that make you your father's son. His blood is not in you, actually. That was chemically supplied by the milk and eggs and beefsteaks eaten by your mother in her pregnancy and it is renewed and freshened by the same fodder, only now you eat it. What did your father give you, then? What are the heirlooms? A name? Once kept hushed as the label of the soul, it is now a mere tag, something to put before a telephone number." Verplanck had risen again and was standing over Miles. "Life-insurance money? An uncle can do that. Did he educate you? Not much. You said he was away most of the time."

"Yet I am like him in many ways."

"He came home sometimes. You would have been like him in many ways if you had been a foundling. All men are like enough to have it mentioned lovingly by an aunt. No, Miles, you can prove no connection with your father other than that of the spasm of your conception. You or any son. There is a greater evidence than any I have mentioned. Think of Christianity a moment. Who is the father of Christ?"

"God is the obvious answer."

"Certainly, but how shown? How manifest? In the gross flesh? Was Mary surprised and tumbled in her cottage by a priapic deity like Zeus? Ah, no. It was done with more finesse than that. Conception was immaculate. Was it because Yahweh was detained elsewhere by press of business and sent the dove as a surrogate? Was he afraid to manifest himself? No. To the Jews he was omnipotent. Why, then, did they construct this elaborate myth if it did not symbolize a fundamental truth? Paternity is a mystic state."

"But why must I believe it? Why is it so essential?"

"You must see that a father is only an economic convenience. Beyond the economic, his first and final task is to supply a moment of pleasure as a beginning to nine months of trouble that culminates in agony. Compared to a mother he is nothing. Paternal kinship is nothing." The brandy glass in Verplanck's hand was untouched. He was intent on what he was saying, watching Miles, looking him in the eye, and making loose, awkward gestures.

"Well. If I admit, if I am convinced—then what?"

"Then you can do a great kindness."

"How?"

"You can sleep with your daughter."

Miles said nothing.

Verplanck had given his argument very rapidly. Miles had been thinking affectionately of his father as he had seemed when he himself was a boy. It was at the same time he had learned about God in Sunday school, he remembered, in the basement of the church, the heating pipes banging overhead during the lesson. There he had been given a card that showed the Virgin kneeling in astonishment and a small white dove fluttering above her. He liked to remember this time of his life when everything was simple and happy, and so the argument which aroused these pleasant memories seemed for the moment plausible.

It did not at first seem strange or repugnant to imagine what Verplanck suggested. It was undoubtedly a solution. It would be a kindness, so he thought. He could see himself in pajamas, see her in her nightgown. She got into the bed first, then he, and he reached to turn out the light on the side table. Fathers have got into bed with daughters, not meaning any harm. Tense, he waited for the plot to move. How would he act now? It was all darkness. Nothing. Yet he did not turn and kiss her, sliding his palm easily over her young shoulder. He could not. With a relief he could not fathom, he knew it was wrong.

"Oh, I can't do that," he said to Verplanck in a tired voice.

"Nonsense, Miles. What keeps you? Who would know?"

"I would."

"It's immoral, is that it?"

"Yes. I guess so."

"Haven't you ever done anything immoral?"

"What other people said was immoral. Things I did with the best intentions that turned out later to be immoral. I can't do this."

Seeing failure coming, Verplanck flounced his shoulders heavily. "These petty scruples. You're a man of the world, Miles. Don't you see what you would be doing for your daughter? Never in her wildest dreams has she imagined a fulfillment like this."

"You're right. She hasn't. She wouldn't do it, either."

"Ah, but you could persuade her. You want to remain with her. Why not keep her with you under the happiest circumstances for her?"

"Even if I would do it, she has had the nuns at her back for five years. She knows what sin is."

"I doubt if the nuns have discussed precisely this relationship with her," Verplanck said dryly, to vent his annoyance. He turned back to his desk and sat down. Failure had come. He had met Miles too late. A year ago, perhaps, he might have carried him. He glanced down at his hands. They were almost trembling. Where the hairs entered the skin, light beads of sweat had seeped out while he talked. It was an effort to go on. He was tired, yet he said with suave kindness, "I think you are making a mistake to reject the simplicity of my proposal. In one light, you are even selfish."

"I'll be selfish then."

The strain of his excitement was ebbing, yet Verplanck still held to the failed plan. "Maybe you're right. It requires courage to shout one's conscience down, more courage than some of us have. That is, providing you still give house to that ancient bogey . . ."

"All I know is: I can't do it."

"That is why I wanted to talk to you at such length. This seemed to me to be the arrangement that would promise most. It would satisfy your desire to continue to live with her and it would satisfy— ah—her desire," Verplanck smiled at the feebleness of the redundancy. He went on more briskly. "But since you assure me that she would not comply and since you refuse to make the effort, perhaps I had better talk to her."

"I don't know. I don't like this, Verplanck . . ."

He took Miles up smoothly. "It disgusts you, doesn't it? It goes against the grain. Certainly. You must expect it to. There are, alas, no easy pills or surgery for an affair of this sort. A cure, that is to say, the proper readjustment or reorientation, comes slowly after endless labor. There will be many times in the course of it when you and she will be bored, you will be hurt, shocked, and perhaps even frightened, but you must let none of these interfere. That is, not unless you are indifferent to her happiness and your own."

"I'm not. You know that. Asking what you did seemed a little raw, that was all."

"Of course. Yet it was a necessary step."

"I want to go on with this, Verplanck, even if I don't like it much. Do you want to see me again or . . ."

"Your daughter the next time."

"How will we work it? I can't say, 'There's a man wants to talk to you.'"

"No. That would hardly be tactful. Would you care to come to dinner, you and she? Then afterwards, perhaps, while you talked to Margery, I could ingratiate myself with her."

"She might talk to you. I don't know. But that's probably the best way. When?"

"Would Friday do?"

"I think so. She'll have to miss one of her art classes, but that'll be all right."

"Friday then." Verplanck stood up. "I'm sorry about this evening but, as I say, it was necessary."

"Good night, Verplanck."

"Good night." He waited until Miles had started for the door and then sat down again. At the door Miles stopped and looked back as if there were something more he wanted to say, but he did not speak. He opened the door and went out.

When he was a boy, he was on his uncle's farm on a wet day in September and had gone to the woods to get the cows. The trees were maple, basswood, oak, and once in a while a hickory. The leaves had begun to turn, so that around him in the cold breeze of sundown there were patches of red, yellow, and brown among the varying shades of green. In the woods was a low patch where flags, cattails, and marsh grass grew in hummocks out of water that was oily and full of iron rust. In a weak green light from the west, he remembered the bluish film of oil on the water near the dry grass of the hummocks. He had called the cows and he could hear them coming, the snapping of dead branches as they stepped on them. They were coming too slowly. He was running around the edge of the swamp to hurry them and suddenly he stopped short. On the ground in front of him he saw an eye. It was large and dark and the lashes around it were gummy, stuck together. It was set in no face; no ear or snout was near it. It lay on coils of shining raw flesh, pink and striped with blue and purple, a pool of limp wet flesh. At one edge a neat black hoof protruded, and there seemed to be a rim of hide around it covered with brown hair. He had swallowed hard and kept swallowing as he tiptoed away as if it needed silence. Before he went far he saw a cow grazing, and trailing from her was a rag of afterbirth. All he had seen was a calf that had grown wrong in the womb and had been born there at the edge of the swamp, spilling out as a liquid spills, leaving that one staring eye on top. Miles had seen it in dreams many times since. And at the doorway, looking backward at Verplanck, he remembered it again.

There was a door in the corridor opposite the stairs. As Miles was turning to go down the stairs, the door opened and Margery came out. She was dressed in a black negligee, new; he had never seen it before. Her dark hair was elaborately done up high on her head. She stood with one hand high against the side of the doorway and the other on her hip. The pose was a little mannered, but she looked as she always did, lush, acquiescent, and beautiful. She always looked like that, angry, sad, jubilant, or drunk.

"You're a fool, Dick."

"Hello, Margery," he said with deliberate stupidity.

"He's a fool, too," she said, bending her head toward the library door.

"Why did you marry him then?"

"You said we were through and . . ."

Miles laughed. "Don't tug at my heartstrings, Margery."

"He's a good provider if you can shake it out of him. Don't you like my new clothes?" She opened the negligee and Miles saw that she was wearing a black satin corset. Her waist was very slender.

"You'll have to use a blackjack. I'm not having any. This isn't like you, Margery, hawking this way. You'll have to set up your pitch in another street."

"Oh, honestly, Dick, be decent. He's out every afternoon, either at Columbia or the Public Library. Then is when I take long, wholesome naps. Evenings he works in there and I can curl up with a good book. I've even joined the Book-of-the-Month Club. I ask you, is that a life? We're not getting any younger."

"You don't read all the time. You've got a breath you could hang your hat on."

"Well, is *that* a life?"

"It'll last a long time if you put a little water with it."

"Oh, now really, Dick. Come and see me. I'm perfectly willing to let bygones be bygones."

"So am I."

"Why do you come to see him? You were here the other night."

"Oh, we talk. I'm making new friends, you know."

"Do you think it very kind to make them in the house where the old ones live?"

"I hadn't thought. By the way, we're coming to dinner next Friday."

"We?"

"Mary and I."

"Oh, that'll be jolly, a little family gathering. You are the most ungrateful brute I ever saw."

"I must be pretty ungrateful then. Good night, Margery."

As he started to go, something light took his eye to the left. At the end of the corridor, Verplanck was standing in the library doorway. He was out of earshot. Margery did not see him. He was just standing there, smiling, silent, and benign, watching them. Miles went on down the stairs.

4

H E WAS twenty-two years old and all he wanted to do was swim. He had been on the team at Detroit Northwestern High School and he had been the number-two sprint man for three years at the University of Michigan. He was not really very good. At public bathing beaches, where he did not like to swim, a crowd would always gather to watch him and even the lifeguards would nod to each other, but in the Payne Whitney pool or the Iowa pool, other swimmers would take one look at him and go on talking. He was strong in the shoulders but had little natural buoyancy, and he was as good as he would ever be in his senior year at Michigan, when he swam the last leg of a medley relay in :52.2 against Ohio State. This is fast time even considering the relay start which allows you to time your arm swing smoothly by watching the man coming in at your feet. It was fast enough to have made him the number-one sprint man at any college in the country but Yale, Michigan, and perhaps Northwestern or Ohio State in the odd years. He was not a great swimmer though.

He was six feet two inches tall and weighed a hundred and ninety in his silk tank suit, and when he was swimming the muscles of his upper arms and shoulders looked huge through the breaks in the foam. He carried a Spalding annual around with him, and the page was very dirty where the world's records were listed, and he had drawn a ring around the line where it said: *100 yds. (75-foot pool), 51 seconds—John Weissmuller.* He had never doubted that someday he would climb out of a pool, everyone shouting and his chest aching, and an assistant timer would run up to him and scream in his ear, "Fifty and eight! Fifty and eight!" He had decided to try his first champagne on that night, but in the showers immediately afterward he would be modest, merely saying thanks and sticking out his soapy hand. He was sure he could break the record if he worked hard enough and so was his girl, Joan Hinkman, a Delta Gamma at Michigan, but nobody else considered it probable.

When he was in high school and in his freshman year at Michigan his family sat in the reserved seats at swimming meets, with splash curtains drawn up over their laps, very proud of their son. His father wrote down the first, second, and third places and the time for every race in pencil and kept the programs in a drawer in his bureau. His mother, when she caught a glimpse of his face as he turned his head to breathe, would repeat softly to herself, "That is my son, the flesh of my flesh," and a heaving, swelling feeling would come inside her breast as if he were in danger, and she would twist her handkerchief into a knot in her lap. She also kept a scrapbook of newspaper clippings for him with great neatness, spreading the newspaper out on the dining-room table and cutting the story or the photograph out of it with her best dressmaking shears, to paste carefully in the scrapbook. With a deprecatory manner, she would get it out of the bookcase and show it to anyone who came to call. Once she showed it to the iceman. Her son, Stanley, was a marvel to her, she said, because no one in her family or on Mr. Dinsmore's side either had ever taken to the water, and when they had lived in Adrian before Mr. Dinsmore had gone into the automobile business, Stanley was forever running off to swim in the Raisin River. It was a very treacherous stream and a great many people, some of them grown men, drowned in it every year. But even when Stanley was a little boy, not more than eight or nine, he had shown this mysterious ability in the water. Then she would lean forward toward the visitor and point out the photograph taken of Stanley after he had won the fifty-yard dash in the city high-school championships.

After his freshman year at Michigan, his family's pride in his swimming grew less. They stopped driving out to Ann Arbor for the home meets, and Mrs. Dinsmore began to let the scrapbook go. She saved the newspapers that contained the clippings just as faithfully but she let them pile up in the bookcase. Both of them wanted to see signs of a talent in Stanley or at least an inclination toward some profession. (Mrs. Dinsmore yearned for him to become a professional man, a doctor or a lawyer, because it had—a word she now hesitated to use publicly—more *class*. Mr. Dinsmore, who had never heard his wife's hopes even when they were talking in bed at night, assumed that Stanley would get a job as a service man at the Rouge plant in the summer before his senior year and go into the sales end when he was graduated.) Stanley was a constant disappointment. He talked only of swimming and he went into the bathroom every few minutes to wet his hair and comb it.

Mr. Dinsmore was fifty years old. When he was forty, he was making twenty-five thousand dollars a year as a lesser member of the Ford hierarchy and his salary had not been cut during the depression. He spoke easily of "Edsel," "Sorenson," and "Harry Bennett," although he never spoke to them or they to him because they did not know who he was, and the Founder was always "Mr. Ford." After his salary was raised, before Mrs. Dinsmore really knew about Grosse Pointe, he bought a new house on Oakman Boulevard, a red brick, "Georgian-type" with an arch of brick thrown out over the driveway that led to the garage in back. They sold nearly all the old furniture they brought from Adrian and bought new. It was heavily over-stuffed and there were seven floor lamps on the ground floor. Mr. Dinsmore was very happy in the new house, yet it seemed to lack something, a last touch of the opulence it deserved. One day he had an electric organ delivered and installed. He was unable to say why he wanted it, as neither he nor his wife could play it, and Stanley had gone no further than Chaminade's *Scarf Dance* in his piano lessons. Yet there it was standing at one end of the living room, its console a soft gleaming mahogany. No one touched it except to polish it, but occasionally when Mr. Dinsmore had some of the boys from the plant in for a drink, he would solemnly pull out all the stops and lay his forearm on the keyboard and press down. A vast blurred sound would shake the house. "Cost me fifteen hundred. Makes a hell of a racket, don't it?" he would say proudly. At such moments he felt that he stood on the pinnacle of life and he would urge everybody to finish their drinks so they could have another.

He drove a Lincoln Zephyr. He belonged to the D.A.C. and he lunched there as often as he could, eating tenderloin steak and deep-dish apple pie, smoking rich Corona cigars and reciting the lore of the automobile business with his peers. He owned a summer cottage at Pointe aux Barques. He had fifty thousand dollars' paid-up insurance. His wife had a mink coat and a God-awful number of dresses. His son was in college and belonged to a fraternity—not one of the best, maybe, but Calvin Coolidge had been a Phi Gam—and the boys at the house were such fine fellows that Mr. Dinsmore was a little afraid of them when he went out there on football Saturdays. Or if it rained, him and Mrs. Dinsmore listened to the game over the radio. It cost seven hundred and fifty. They didn't have to go out in the sopping wet. They could take it easy. That was the point: they weren't rich but they could take it easy. And while he did not know that he regarded his wife and son as scarcely sentient trophies wrung from a life to which he owed a duty to embellish further, he waited and searched to see if his son would not spontaneously discover the virtue of his life and begin to emulate his father on his own hook. There was nothing else the boy could really want, was there? But Stanley was apathetic to the point of defiance.

His father sounded him shrewdly to find out if any of those long-haired professors out at Ann Arbor had been putting funny ideas in his head, radical ideas about unions and things. Stanley said they hadn't. Mr. Dinsmore asked him if he didn't want to transfer to the

Engineering School. Stanley said, no, he didn't think he did. He was getting along all right in the Lit School.

"Have you been thinking what department you want to get into when you graduate? They could probably use a college man in Sales."

"Why, I sort of thought of going to New York if I could."

"Hell, they wouldn't put you in the New York office right away. You got to learn the business first, boy. N-o-o, sir," he chuckled. "Start at the bottom of the ladder, that's what you'll do. Then if you work and keep your nose clean, why, five, six, eight years, you might make Export and you can go to New York or China or any damn place you want."

"I wasn't thinking about Ford's necessarily."

Cunningly, Mr. Dinsmore did not explode. "What were you thinking about? What's New York got that we haven't got?"

"The New York Athletic Club for one thing."

"And what's the matter with the Detroit Athletic Club?"

"I'm getting tired of Pinkston. He always wants to develop a diver. He doesn't give me any coaching."

In the effort to keep his temper, Mr. Dinsmore nearly bit through the end of the unlit cigar he had in the side of his mouth. "Oh, so you want to keep on swimming?" he said. "You've been swimming in meets for ten years, ever since you were twelve years old. Don't you think it's time you started figuring how to make some money?"

"Oh, I intended to get a job there. I didn't mean you had to keep up my allowance. I'll get a job somewhere and work days and swim in the evenings."

"Swim in the evenings, huh?" Mr. Dinsmore had been right for so many years that he could not admit suddenly that he had been wrong in the way he had handled his son. Yet the idea was there. This smooth tanned face was the face of a stranger. "When I was your age, I'd been working five years painting screen doors at the Prentice Screen Door factory in Adrian. I had four hundred and twenty-three dollars in the bank saved up."

"I'd just as soon save all the money I could."

"But, for the love of God, how long you going to keep on swimming?"

"I've got five or six good years yet. Look at Walter Spence. I bet he was thirty-five years old before he quit. That record of Weissmuller's can't last forever."

Mr. Dinsmore could see they didn't mesh. And worse than that they weren't going to mesh. His only ace was to order him to go to work at the plant. Stanley would do it. He had always been obedient, but he bet, by Christ, that if he did get him a job in the Service Department, he would swim noon hours in the Rouge itself, eat in ten minutes, swim twenty in the dirty little river in the mud and muck and coke dust. He bet, by God, he would.

Mr. Dinsmore hated to argue. He hated people who knew their own minds when their minds were different from his. He wanted things neat, not wishy-washy. He gave the order. After all, when you consider it, he made twenty-five thousand dollars a year. He knew best.

"Well, young man, you're going to work in the Service Department. When's graduation?"

"June seventeenth."

"June eighteenth there'll be a job waiting for you. New York's out." Mr. Dinsmore stood up and walked quickly out of the room. Since his son was a possession that represented a sizable investment, he suffered no hesitation in commanding him to work at Ford's. And having commanded he was sure obedience would be forthcoming and he thought no more about it.

When he is seventeen, a boy has done nothing. All things are possible. And out of all the possibilities he will, with the natural optimism of youth or maybe the natural optimism of American youth, pick the things he wants the most. The future will bring him wealth and honor. He will never, in rags, shoot snipes in the gutter or go to jail and yell out of a cell window at a passing seventeen-year-old boy, "Hey, bud, go get me a deck of butts, will you?" Since these things are certain—the honor, the money, and the great abilities—in the future, in just a little while now, can he be blamed for borrowing ahead of time some of the prestige, a touch of the arrogance, that, granting only the accomplishment, will come along pretty soon? Young kids are snotty bastards. They don't treat their elders with respect. They are contemptuous of people who work at dull jobs because they know themselves are princes.

Stanley Dinsmore was twenty-two years old. Out of the zodiacal scheme of possibilities that lay before him, he had adopted one. He had not chosen it exactly. As a skinny little boy, he thought swimming was the only activity worth putting any time on, and in the heel of boyhood, when the choice or the strong, strong wish is made, with his voice changing and the first light beard hairs shining on his face, scarcely knowing he did it, drifting easily into it as if he were borne on water, he became a swimmer and he did not wholly know or his father at all that he had chosen anything or how deep the choice was.

For there was nothing for him that was not linked with swimming, nothing desirable. If he thought of money, having a lot of money, it was only to use to pay Matt Mann or Bob Kiphuth for coaching him privately, and once having broken the record, he could use money for railroad tickets and steamship passages to cities where he could swim and conquer other lesser champions. Fame was the flash of the bulbs of news cameras (the water of the pool would show at his feet) and columns in the newspapers about him, his stroke analyzed, his kick admired by Corum, Cunningham, and Salsinger. Fame was also the dull gleam and distorted bas-reliefs on medals, big as silver dollars. Health when he thought about it at all was a little vague anxiety about the tone of his muscles—he often rolled his shoulders as if he were trying to settle his coat collar or he would stretch out his arms and shake his hand loosely at the end of it. Girls would like him automatically when he was the champion, tanned, modest, dressed in a white jacket with a wine-colored bow tie and a boutonniere to match. It would be simple to take them out on the verandas of a dozen country clubs and kiss them, beautiful girls like Gloria Callen. Of when he grew old, when his wind went back on him and the fat set in his muscles, he seldom thought.

In the history lectures at college, France held his attention briefly as a small area, almost square, filled with trenches and cathedrals, in whose porches stood, meek and awe-struck, the great personages all together, the Henry kings, the Louis kings, Joan of Arc on a white horse, the cardinals each in his scarlet biretta, Richelieu and Mazarin,

Napoleon, Pasteur (with Paul Muni's face), Mme Curie, Charles Boyer, and foreground, front, and center, in a glow of brightness, larger than all these was Jean Taris, the Olympic 400-meter swimmer, in a water-polo cap with his ears sticking out. On the English cliffs, Drake did not bowl, rather, at the foot of the cliffs, Captain Webb was forever setting out for Calais swimming breaststroke. The rest of the island was a jumble of relics, ghosts, and dates to remember. Germany was a dark vicious plain and on it in a clump stood Bismarck, Kant, Beethoven, Hitler, Göring, and Goebbels, and Henry the Fowler, all drinking steins of beer, and at the rear a file of persecuted Jews slunk heavily away, but again in the foreground, clad only in a swimming jockstrap, was the stocky frame of Erich Rademacher who won the breaststroke at Amsterdam in 1928. Before the town hall of Stockholm (a picture of which he had seen in the *National Geographic*), Charles XII, the Bernadotte family, Gustavus Adolphus, and Garbo feasted at a table laden with smörgåsbord (which he had eaten at the Stockholm Restaurant on East Jefferson in Detroit) and at the head of the table, gaunt and lean, sat the great Arne Borg who had once held every world's record from the 220 to the mile. The other nations of the earth were dim and dull except for Japan, where Koike, Makino, and the others came from, the tireless children, fourteen years old, who dishonestly pumped themselves up with oxygen at the Los Angeles Olympics, and winning, received congratulations from the Tenno. Stanley Dinsmore, if anyone had cared to ask him, could have explained that his geography and history were mixed and spangled. He could not help it. He would not have apologized for it because his education had not led him to think that his aims were mean or petty. He would have explained it all with dignity and confidence, knowing he was not ignorant because he was a college man, and with a certain earnest charm.

What he could not explain, what he knew with sureness, as his blood knew the pipes of his body, in the way his eye picked out near from far, as real as his teeth and never thought upon, was himself in water, himself before water, himself after water, water and he. Solemn, fascinated, a fat baby, he had sat in a white tub slowly opening and shutting his fingers upon the slender, this beautiful, the wild, wild water, trying to grab it. Older and under it, holding the willow roots against the haul of the current, frightened of the silence as if it had a secret in it, he had opened his eyes and looked out through the still brown murk toward the light glow where the sunlight struck the surface and bent, descending, diffused. And in the circle against the darkness he saw a fish, his companion, swimming to stand still, he and the fish, alone, he king over the fish and the flow, and he had come up breathless with his eyelids stinging and full of mud among the dull grasses of the riverbank.

And now. The coach sang, ". . . a nice easy hundred, Stanley. Keep y'head up. Get 'em in and get 'em out and re-lax, boy," and lifting his bare feet up and down nervously, curling his toes over the edge of the tiles to get a firm grip, he would be thinking how he would launch himself outward over the water at the coach's signal, duck his head as he entered, and after he had glided for a second, start his kick and lift his head and when he felt it break water, pull one arm down under him in a strong sweep. From then on he would keep his head high, and fling his arms loosely and accurately in front of him, not pulling hard, re-laxed, breathing seven times in the twenty-five yards between turns, and when he rolled his head sideward to breathe, he would see the coach running naked along the edge of the pool, sweeping his arm forward to make him go faster, his mouth round, tense, shouting but unheard in the thunder of the foam.

Almost smiling at this unseemly superficial commotion he was making on the surface of the green water, almost but never quite knowing that it was unseemly, superficial, he would finish the distance and hang onto the edge of the slop trough, panting and tossing his head to throw the long yellow hair out of his eyes, looking anxiously at the coach to hear how long it had taken him, how long over fifty-two seconds. But if he could have only the water, the green water, this fluid mirror of breaking images, always bearing him softly with minute and gentle pressure or flowing past him or above him as he sank with his hair waving a little, as he sank alone, given this, he would never have cared to race anyone, a man or a watch. He would not have agreed that this was true. When he talked of swimming to a girl or to other swimmers, he said he wanted to race, he wanted to beat the record more than anything else in the world. But it was not true and he almost knew it, for the water was his own place, and at night in dreams he owned it all, pond, pool, lake, and the little elbow reaches of the sea. Neptune he did not believe in, one of those old Greek gods in white statuary, in hard poems. The myths and stories of water were nothing to him. Water was a place, a kingdom where he could live, solemn, fascinated, a secret in it, alone, without sound or time or anyone to bother him.

One day at the end of summer, he met his father near the Rotunda. They drove home together every day.

"Pay day, huh?" his father asked.

"Yes." He held out a folded wad of money he had been carrying in his hand. "I've just quit." He looked straight ahead through the windshield at the road. "I'm going to New York."

Mr. Dinsmore did not speak all the way home. Nothing was said at dinner and Stanley did not watch his father to see how he was taking it, and he could tell from the conversation that his father had not told his mother. After dinner he went out to say good-by to a girl and when he came back his father and his mother were planted in the overstuffed chairs. They looked as if they had been waiting. His mother had been crying.

"I'm not trying to disobey you. This isn't a revolt . . ." he began.

"We just talked to Ben in New York. He says he can make a place for you in the agency," his father said.

"We thought it would be better that way. It's not so hard to start out if you have your family behind you, and your Uncle Ben is a very successful man," his mother said. He saw that they had been hashing it over and they were reconciled to it. His mother's voice did not quaver when she spoke, although the rims of her eyes were still red. He had been nerving himself for an angry scene of recriminations and when he found they had accepted his going, he became almost apologetic and gave them the reasons eagerly, reasons they had already heard but could not comprehend.

He left for New York two days later. He had read enough novels in college to recognize it as a cliché when his mother told him to wear his overshoes on wet days.

He began work in his uncle's advertising agency at thirty-five dollars a week and he was no good. His uncle had not needed a new man and had hired his nephew in response to family pressure. To reassure himself that it had been a smart move, he began to praise Stanley to his associates even before he had arrived, and the office personnel, even to the stenographers, expected a brilliant newcomer. His uncle set him to writing copy at once. His advance notices were so solidly founded and his uncle was so unwilling to disbelieve them that it took him two weeks to learn that Stanley had only a dim conception of what he was supposed to do. He was not properly excited when he thought of soup mix, dog food, shoe polish, or even women's silk hosiery. He was awkward with words, and he stubbornly wanted to tell the truth. In disgust, his uncle gave him the job of checking radio shows the agency handled, and Stanley sat quietly, even contentedly, in a chair of chrome and plush, looking through a window at the actors, comparing the lines of the script with the loud, unnatural voices that came out of a grille above his head.

One day his uncle found a pile of scripts that he had checked. The margins and the blank back pages were covered with sketches in pencil—a girl's head, a microphone drawn in detail, and the head and waving arms of a man whom he was able to recognize as a director of one of the radio shows. Hopeful of discovering a useful talent in his nephew, he told him he was an artist in a voice buoyant with false professional enthusiasm. He called in the agency's art director, asked him the name of a good art school, waved him away, and got on the phone at once. In two minutes, Stanley, a little bewildered, was enrolled in a night art class at his uncle's expense.

He did not care one way or the other. He had always made little sketches in pencil, not very aptly. The flyleaves of his schoolbooks had been full of them. They were fun to do, but he knew he was no artist. It would make him hustle after five o'clock every day to get in his swim at the New York A.C., eat dinner, and get downtown in time for his art class. It would also give him something to write home about.

He had visited New York three times before, once on an automobile trip with his family, twice with the university swimming team. He had seen the sights. He had risen to the top of the Empire State Building. He had taken the ferry to Staten Island. He had stood gawking at the imitation sky in the Hayden Planetarium, and he was no longer curious about the city. He had taken a room in a small hotel on East Fifty-sixth Street and shared a bath with a middle-aged doctor who was doing research on cancer at the Medical Center. Occasionally they would meet in the little hallway by the telephone and they would speak cordially. One evening the doctor had knocked at his door. In his hand was a glass photographic slide. Held up to the light, it showed a picture of a small mouse, dead, sliced accurately down the middle with the skin retracted to show the guts. The doctor pointed with a pencil at a small dark sac near the stomach. "Melanoma," he said.

Stanley was disappointed in the attitude of the swimmers at the N.Y.A.C. It was true that most of them worked and so could not give much time to practice. He could make allowance for that, but it hurt him to find that they did not take swimming very seriously. Some of them drank and they all smoked, and they said that the college teams were going too fast these days. Sometimes after swimming, and hearing this kind of talk in the dressing room, he would cross Fifty-ninth Street and walk in the Park for a little while dispirited. He had expected somehow that it would be like entering another college—the same eagerness, the same tension—but they were not there. His ambition remained unchanged. He swam hard every day. But he had been fooled somewhere.

On week nights he was tired and ready to go to bed after his art class. Saturday afternoons and Sundays were the worst days of the week because he was lonely. His uncle had asked him up for Sunday dinner at his apartment in Central Park West the first two or three Sundays. Then he stopped, and one day at the office he said in a quick, apologetic mumble that a boy ought to get his legs under him by himself, no sense in family interference. Stanley knew that the invitations had been stopped because he could not write acceptable copy. His uncle did not want him around.

Saturday afternoons and evenings, Sunday afternoons and evenings, he went to the movies. They palled on him after a while because they made his head ache. He tried burlesque shows, glancing around him a little furtively as he bought his ticket. Then he began to go to the restaurants off Broadway with big floor shows full of girls dressed in shoes and G-strings. He liked them because he could see them up close. He sipped one lemonade after another nervously. He wanted to meet a girl. None of the stenographers at the office were pretty. The one who was passable lived far away in Flushing, and he was too shy and too new to the city to think of taking her home in anything but a taxi and a taxi would cost too much. He thought of stopping at a liquor store and buying a bottle of whisky in the hope that if he got drunk something would happen. He would become clever, suave, and knowledgable and thus inevitably meet and charm a beautiful girl. It was only a thought. Drinking cut your wind.

When he began to go to the art class, he planned on getting to know someone there. The class met in a big studio on West Twenty-third Street. It was a long, narrow room full of kitchen chairs. There was a big, slanting north window, but at night the light came from rows of drop lights. Scattered along three walls were busts and life-size models of classical statues in plaster. A line of green metal lockers, like the lockers in railroad stations, stood against the fourth wall. The teacher was a young man of thirty with hair not long enough to look arty. It looked uncut. He wore flannel shirts and tied his tie with a wide knot. When he talked of Chardin, he would include the green bottle, the melon, and the apples he had set for them to draw in large plastic gestures, and his voice would quiver in a lyric expansiveness. His comments on the students' drawings were acidulous.

The students were all kinds of people, some of them as old as his parents. Among them were seven or eight girls whom he did not think were any older than he was. They seemed older. They were sure and confident and they talked loudly in what he took to be a Brooklyn accent, arguing fiercely about politics and Fascism. He had seen girls like them in his classes at college. He would not have minded joining in the arguments—he remembered several opinions his professors had stated—but they made a group without him and he was too diffident to break in. He contrived to sit next to one of the pretty ones, and during a recess, in the heat of a discussion he did not follow, the girl turned to him unexpectedly and said, "What do you think of Bill Gropper?"

"Who?" he asked, startled.

"Bill Gropper," she said.

"Who's he?"

She jerked her head toward him and said to the girl next her, "Never heard of him, he says."

"Politically undeveloped," the other girl said.

"Say, what do you do? N.Y.U. boy?"

"I work for Dinsmore, Ludwig & Coles."

"What do *they* do?"

"They're an advertising agency uptown."

"Advertising agency, huh?" She spoke to the other girl. "You're right, Mahnge. He's not politically undeveloped. He's politically still-born." She turned her back on him. Her nose was shiny.

It was all right, he thought. He knew nothing about politics or Bill Gropper. He wanted to break the hundred-yard short-course record. He had come to New York to attach himself to the swimming team of the New York Athletic Club, and although the fellows there didn't seem to have much fighting spirit, he thought he would do all right when the A.A.U.'s came along in the spring. Meanwhile he had to make a living, and if his uncle thought he could draw pictures, he would try to learn. It would keep him his job, and it might come in handy someday when he was old and could not swim any more. He might, then, even want to be an advertising man.

He did not really worry about his swimming or his job. He worried about his loneliness and he knew it was loneliness he was worrying about. When he woke up in the morning and saw the same old apartment building in yellow brick across the street, when he heard the el banging down Third Avenue, and knew that after he had shaved and dressed he would have to go through the chore of selecting his own breakfast, it made him angry. It seemed unfair. He wanted a girl to talk to, as he had talked to Joan Hinkman on the porch of the Delta Gamma house. He wanted to tell her how his shoulders had felt that day during his workout, and to kiss her several times before he left. If he had not been after the record, he would have liked to have an "affair," where you went to bed with the girl, but his father had always told him to keep his pecker in his pants and anyhow that kind of thing weakened you. All he wanted was someone to talk to emotionally, sort of. It seemed very little to ask. He began to buy *Liberty* and *The Saturday Evening Post* and to lie on his bed Saturdays and Sundays and read them. He thought he might pick up something about politics, and the magazines made the place look more homelike, lying around.

One evening early in February a new girl came into the class. When he saw her, he wished he had put on a clean shirt and not tried to make this one do. He wished he had combed his hair in the men's toilet before class. With unobtrusive care, he leaned back in his kitchen chair and thrust his hand into the left-hand trouser pocket so that the coat would fall away and expose his vest. She might see the fraternity pin if he leaned back far enough for the light to hit it.

She had beautiful hair and eyes and, as she took off her coat, he could see she had a cute figure. Her face was not shiny. She made him homesick to look at her. He felt that he could almost walk right up to her and say, "Hello," without her getting mad, that she would somehow recognize him. He watched her while the instructor assigned her locker, and pointing, smiling, making outlines with his hands in the air, he told her how to begin. On the top of a low cupboard sat a flowerpot with a sansevieria shooting up its spiked, mottled leaves. Behind it was one of the classical busts, an Apollo's head with blank eyes. That was the problem, the instructor explained. It was purely a problem in color values. Holding her block of paper and her crayons, she followed his hands and eyes, listening attentively.

"Just take any convenient chair, Miss Miles," he said.

There were seven empty chairs. Stanley had counted them. None of them was beside him. The girl looked at the chairs, then at the plant and the Apollo's head, and moved to a chair two places away from Stanley. She sat down and began at once to draw.

It would be a delicate business, he knew. He would have to pretend that the light was poor, someone was obstructing his view or something. He waited five minutes, adding a stroke here and there to his

314

drawing. He got up casually, squinting at the plant. He moved a yard or so away from the new girl and shook his head as if he still could not see well. He glanced quickly down at her. She was bent over the stiff block of paper on her knee. He walked slowly to the chair beside her and studied the plant carefully for several seconds. Apparently he had found just the angle. His face relaxed into a smile and he sat down in the chair beside her, safe, his heart pounding. He did not think anyone had seen his maneuver.

The studio was quiet. People occasionally spoke to each other or to the teacher in low voices. Stanley worked conscientiously for three or four minutes before he began to look at her again. She was not wearing cheap clothes. She had nice hands but they were thin and she was not wearing nail polish like the other girls. She knew something about drawing because she had already laid out the whole composition the way the instructor had told them to do. He liked her looks and he did not want to risk anything by speaking too soon.

The instructor came to stand behind his chair and looked over his shoulder at his drawing. "O.K.," he said. "A little stodgy right there. Look." He took Stanley's crayon and touched the drawing two or three times. "Now, just keep going."

He looked over the girl's shoulder. "Oh, that's very nice. Talent, very possibly. You got it blocked out swell. Wait, now. Those mottlings. You're not looking. You're not observing sharply enough. You've seen sansevieria before?"

"Yes," she said.

"You know those patches are cream color, don't you? But under this damned electricity—here, Dinsmore's got it. Let me take your . . ."

Stanley handed over his drawing. This was luck.

"There, see? You must put down what you really see, not what you know it is from looking at it some other time, what it is under another light. Color has no fixed value of itself, you know. It's all relative. Depends on the light, see?"

"Yes, I think so." She took some different crayons out of her box.

The instructor gave the drawing back to Stanley and went on to another student.

Now was the time. It seemed as if he were taking a deep breath. He leaned toward her and said, "Don't let him scare you. He's all right." It was all he could think of to say.

She did not look up. "Yes. I know."

"It's only five minutes before he gives us time out. Would you like to go downstairs and have a coke and I'll tell you about him. It's right downstairs."

She looked up at him, smiling a little. "No, thank you," she said.

5

VERPLANCK'S SITTING ROOM was next to his library on the second floor of his apartment. The draperies covering the windows were made of wool dyed a strong delft blue, and in corners and along the walls were ranged heavy pieces of oak furniture, dark and ornately carved, a chest of drawers, a sideboard seven feet high with racks under a rich entablature full of heavy dishes, and near the fireplace a chest. The chairs stood square and thick and upright. It looked like a room that was seldom used.

Miles walked over to the fireplace and stood looking down into it. "This looks cheerful," he said.

Margery had sat down on a long settee. An elaborate silver coffee service stood on a low table in front of it and she was busy pouring the coffee. She looked up over her bare outstretched arm. "Cheerful?" she said. "I think it's ghastly."

"Oh, I don't know. It has a kind of nice formality . . ."

"Dutch, most of it, all Dutch." She held out the cream pitcher toward him. "See the lion? Down by the base." Miles bent over to look. Worked unobtrusively into the heavy floral design was the small figure of a lion. "It's the Dutch label for silver. The chairs, that bureau thing, and the *uitzet* all came from Mynheer Paul. Rotterdam. Henry's uncle. There's a lot more but it went to Guiana. Henry's brother lives there. He got most of it because he's the *Stammhalter*."

"How Dutch is Henry?"

"As Dutch as I am English. Grandparents. He was born here and so was his father."

"What's a *uitzet*?"

"It's a dower chest. God knows how many litters of the Verplanck virgins sewed their eyes out to fill it. Henry says in the Netherlands they start them on samplers as soon as they're old enough to hold a needle. Even if they're well off." She threw her hand out toward the chest which stood against the wall near the fireplace. "That damned thing was hand-carved by a great-great-uncle or somebody. And if you don't think it doesn't catch the dust . . ."

"Yes. I can see." Miles leaned over and picked a little cobweb from the carving of the chest. He held it up, a wisp fluttering from his thumb and finger.

"I'll kill that damned nigger. All he does is pray in the kitchen and chase up to funerals on Lenox Avenue."

"He can cook, though."

"He's Henry's notion of the perfect gentleman's servant. I've tried to tell him that he's got a wife living here now, but he wants everything kept as it is. Especially this room. He raised holy hell when I suggested doing it over. You know how Henry raises holy hell?"

"No. Never saw him."

"Pouts, mopes, and takes baking soda in hot water until he's one long rumble."

"Why the baking soda?"

"It's cheaper than drugstore bicarbonate. Pouting upsets his digestion, he thinks."

"Maybe he has some sentiment about the furniture."

"Sure he has. But try and get him to admit it. Henry, my dear, is an intellectual, self-confessed, and for a guy that makes only with the brain, there's hardly a day goes by he isn't either at the point of tears or all swollen up with rage or . . ."

"I gather he won't let you redecorate."

"This is a straight bill of particulars. I'm not talking about re-decorating. But *look* at the place. Pictures of cows, for God's sake. You see that one over there? A genuine Paul Potter. The happy peasant in the hay is thought to be—the family isn't sure—a real Cuyp. Now honestly, Dick, am I so unreasonable? Do I need a setting of rustic heirlooms? Do I look like Maud Muller?"

"No."

"I want luxury, chi-chi. I want to be smart. You know that even on the pay from that translator's swink at the Embassy, I got my clothes from Schiaparelli, what I had. What's the matter?"

"Did I say something?"

"No, but your face changed. What were you thinking? Come on now, Richard, I can tell when you're thinking."

"You're dated. This burning passion for luxury, all this chi-chi, is old-fashioned. It's almost quaint."

"Oh, hell, I know you've been to war. You've seen misery and death and bloodshed and the very devil and all. But it's other people's misery, not mine. What do I care for a bunch of Polacks who never had a bath? Now don't tell me I ought to care. Maybe I should. But I don't."

"That's quaint, too. Being so tough."

"It's not toughness, it's honesty. Don't tell me it's got to the point where I can't be honest with you."

"You can be as honest as you like, be as tough as you like."

She took a sip of coffee and looked at him over the rim of her cup to see if he meant what he seemed really to be saying, "I don't care what you do any more." She set the cup down with extreme care and tapped it lightly with her forefinger, looking downward, her lids hiding her eyes, smiling. "I still want the chi-chi."

"And you were pretty sure you would get it from him, weren't you?"

"Frankly, yes. I never had a beau who was so lavish with presents—you never gave me a damned thing, but he always turned up with books and flowers and caviar and liquor—just a prince of a chap. He seemed to be plastered with money and he didn't care who peeled it off him. When we went out together, it was just like what I hear of '29 . . ."

"What you *hear* of '29? What's the matter, did you have amnesia when you were twenty-two years old?"

"That's right—twit me. I was merely trying to say that he was apparently a free spender. He left five dollars with the hat-check girl, the taxicab got a dollar tip, he even tried to give Eddy Duchin fifty dollars one night for some tune. Duchin turned it down, but ole Henry made the effort. I saw him. Why, I thought everything was going to be candy. I got fooled. You don't know a man until you see whether he adds up his laundry slip."

"Hmm . . . you don't look as if you got fooled very badly."

She was dressed in a gray velvet evening gown of a curious light tint. It was severe and scant and obviously very expensive. She wore two large garnets at her ears and a crowd of garnet bracelets encircled her left wrist. She wore no stockings. There were garnets gathering the ribbons of her sandals, and her toenails were lacquered a dark red.

"You can't buy clothes like that for nothing," Miles persisted.

She put one heel on the edge of the coffee table. "Oh, clothes," she said contemptuously.

"He'll get you clothes but not furniture, is that it?"

"*He'll* get me? He has no choice. I buy them and they send him the bill. He isn't pleased but I don't think he's quite got the gall to have one of those little notices put in the paper, 'I will no longer be responsible . . .'—you know what I mean."

Miles blew through his nostrils, a faint laugh. "Pretty dismal, isn't it?"

"Oh, don't sit there being facetious. When I think of the men I could have had. Just a few years ago, and I go and marry Henry because he's rich and generous. Generous! As soon as he's fifty he'll carry one of those old-fashioned snap purses. I suggested—I was timid and deferential, you should have heard me—just after we got married I suggested that it would be nice if I had a maid."

"What did he say?"

"I didn't think he heard me at first. I repeated it forte. Then he told me," she said in a mincing imitation of Verplanck, "I was too beautiful, too vibrant, too *young* to need a maid. Maids were for dropsical dowagers. The maid, he said, picks up the reticule. And the battle I had with him about redecorating, o-o-o-h! It went for days. Think what you could do with this place in Swedish modern. You remember that Swedish place at the Fair? Oh, that's right, you didn't see it. Why, it would be marvelous." She stopped suddenly. "Dick," she said soberly.

"Yes?"

"Do you know why I want to redecorate? Do you know why I married him in the first place?"

"Chi-chi. You just said."

She had turned toward him and, leaning forward, had propped an elbow on her knee. She held out one hand and was stroking it with the other. She did not look at him. She watched her hands. "Yes, chi-chi. I've always wanted it. I want it more than ever now."

"Why now?"

"Oh, because everything's so proletarian and sturdy and kind and mean. Sympathy and baby crèches and Bundles for Britain. I'm sick of it. I want to defy it. I want to let my fingernails grow longer." She lifted her foot. He could see a flush of rouge at her heel and a touch beneath the ankle bone. "I want more shoes like this. You can't walk in the snow with these. You can't even walk in them. They're just ornaments. I want to be beautiful and useless. I'm tired of justifying myself. I don't want to prove my value to society."

"All you want is a redecorated apartment."

"Dick, I'm trying to be perfectly honest."

"All right. Go ahead," Miles said cheerfully. "You don't want to prove your value to society was where you left off."

"Oh, stop treating me as if I were an idiot. The only reason I want the place redecorated is because of you."

"I told you the other night I . . ."

"Dick, please." She spoke softly, evenly, and so seriously that Miles took notice for the first time. Up to now the conversation had been only a pastime for him. He had to talk to her while Verplanck was talking to his daughter in the library. "I married Henry because I was sure he was rich enough to give me a place to entertain you."

"A place with a bed in it."

"A large white bed with sheets of Chinese silk. Where you and I can lie. Is it too much to ask? Will it take up too much of your time? You see, I am without subterfuge now. Will you come and lie with me in a perfumed bed? There will be just a dim light with thick curtains that shut out . . . I won't talk about love in this connection. Love is stupid."

"Oh, I don't know. I think there is such a thing."

"All right. Call it love. I drink every night now. You know. You saw me. I drink and then I take barbital, and sometimes when I'm dopey, he comes in, not very often. But he's so awkward and timorous that he brings me to. I can't even imagine it's you."

"Why has it got to be me?"

"None of the others were good enough." She stood up and walked over to the fireplace and looked down into the fire. Miles recognized the dramatic value of the move. "No, that's not it." She turned around and faced him. "I know why. The liver is the seat of love, isn't it? Give my liver a mouth and it would tell you. Nothing would be filtered out or substituted en route from the source. This is the truth, the low-down, the McCoy, and it's horrible that I know it. It's horrible that I have to know it. It has got to be you because you have run away from me, and if you have run away from me, it's because I'm old, and if I'm old, with the cords beginning to show in my neck, and my chest getting thin so the ribs stick out above my breasts, my hips spreading, and the crow's-feet, why then I begin to diet, and take beauty courses at Arden's and Rubinstein's and at last the hot flashes come and I'm just a poor old salty bitch, pulling up my skirt at parties to catch what I can catch."

"That will come, anyway."

"I know, but not now. Please, Dick, not now. There's nothing wrong with me now, is there? Look at me. I've got a while yet, haven't I?"

"You mean I've got to prove it to you?"

322

"You can prove it. If you run away . . . Dick, I mean what I say, you know."

Miles believed she was speaking the truth, but he was not particularly interested in what she was saying either as truth or lie. He was thinking about his daughter, ten, perhaps fifteen or twenty, feet away, through the wall, in the library with Verplanck. He knew most of the dramatic devices that Margery used to arouse his attention, approval, or desire. They were old stuff, and as familiar as he was with them, none of them appeared to be weighted with enough sincerity to embarrass her if she were caught in them. Yet he believed her this time, partly because she was standing up perfectly straight in no calculated pose, and her voice had a timbre he did not recognize, but chiefly because she was standing in front of the fire and he could see through the skirt of her gown. She was not wearing a slip. Her legs were distorted by shadows. Usually she had quick presentiments that kept her from appearing awkward or ridiculous. If she were not intent on what she was saying, she would undoubtedly have one now, and if she were intent, it was probably because she looked silly and did not know it, that she was speaking honestly, as honestly as she could. And the honesty might be a new trick. She might even have practiced the tone of her voice (but not the stance before the fireplace). She knew him well enough to know that once he had never believed what a woman said, only what she did, and if she were no more willing to commit herself than she was habitually, she might be thinking that she could speak the truth with impunity, unbelieved.

"I believe you," he said. "And I don't think you're old. You're very beautiful."

She came away from the fire and knelt down quickly and tried to kiss his hands. "Oh, Dick, you're back. You've come back."

He took her arms above the elbow and pulled her up. "Stop it. Don't be a fool. I'm still through. I'm not seeing you any more alone."

"Why not?" she said in a harsh voice.

"I don't want to. I told you all about it last October."

"Is it because of what I told you about Mary?"

"No."

"It is."

"No, it's not. I was through with you before that. You remember the day I got through with you. Mary wasn't even in New York."

"I was angry when I told you that about her."

"You mean it's not true?"

"Oh, it's true enough from all that I could see, but I wouldn't have told you at all if I hadn't been angry. Don't hold that against me, Dick."

"You're old, so I quit. You can't believe there's any other reason but that, can you?"

"Well, is there? You would see it quicker than I because I'd hate so to admit it. I look at myself every day. I think I'm the same. You're the same. And what we're talking about is permanent."

"Nothing's permanent. That's what you can't see. You're smart enough other ways, why can't you see that? There's more to a man than what he keeps in his pants."

She looked Miles in the eye for two or three seconds. She spread her skirt a little and sat down gracefully. "Will you have some more coffee?"

"No, thanks."

"You really are through with me, I guess." She turned to look at him, as if it would give her words a guaranty of truth. "It's going to take some getting used to, Dick."

Miles knew she was being gallant now, biting the bullet, and however truly she had spoken a moment before, he knew she was now playing one of her old familiar games. "Oh, you'll be all right, Margery," he said jovially. "You can divorce Henry and get a hell of a big settlement. Hurry and you can make that place out in Idaho— what do they call it? Sun Valley?—before the season closes."

"Speaking of Henry, do you think you ought to leave your daughter alone with him this long? From what I know of him after dark I suspect him of leaning toward the *détournement des mineurs*. Big girls scare him. Little girls might not. She seemed to like him at dinner."

"There, that's what I mean. If you are clever enough to do that, to pick out the one way you can hurt me and do it so smoothly and subtly, putting a scene like that in front of me, why can't you see what I'm talking about?"

Margery got up and walked over to a blue bellpull beside the fireplace. She jerked it once. "What will you drink, Richard? Brandy? I'm going to get drunk."

With cigarette ashes scattered over his dinner jacket, his black tie askew, and one foot in its dress pump lying weakly on its side, Verplanck sat in his red-leather chair in the library, calmly directing his conversation with Mary. She was wearing a black dress with white lace at the shoulders and she was drinking occasionally from a little glass of *crème de cacao*, a liqueur he had set out as the one she might like best because it tasted like milk chocolate. He had taken pains to be polite to her at dinner and deferential to Miles, sensing that the deference and politeness would impress her. He was careful when she spoke to bend forward and listen attentively and his reply was never patronizing. With great taste and astuteness, he was pretending that she was adult, intelligent, and charming, and as far as he could tell, she was taken in. She was certainly not reticent.

They were speaking of her school days. Verplanck had finished reading two books on adolescence a few days before and he had noted particularly the emphasis they placed on the development of the ego, the personality that was bursting its cocoon at this period to make its first tentative adjustments to its environment. He had decided then to coax the story of her life out of her because she, a young girl, would find that the most congenial subject. Yet as he watched, and asked and listened, he felt her youth attracting him. He was a little perturbed to find this out, and he sat up straighter in his chair and crossed one leg over the other, assuming a more alert pose, telling himself that this was most unlike himself to lose his detachment and essentially his honesty in the graces of a mere young girl. She was describing for him the faculty of nuns, the tall and the plump, the pious and the ones who would be worldly if they dared to chance it. She talked well. He could see them quite clearly but more clearly than the nuns he saw her speaking of them.

In laying his plans for this interview, Verplanck had placed the chairs and the light before dinner, like a stage director. He had set the floor lamp behind his chair and adjusted it until he could be sure that her face would have more light than his own. Now illumined, her face had a freshness that it astonished him to find touching and, if she turned her head in mimicry of Sister Catherine, a sudden pallor that was ominous. With an irritating vagueness unlike his usual labored precision, he thought she was in danger and a distorted impulse to protect her arose faintly in his mind. As if he stood in Miles' place, or if not there, in the pull of some ambiguous tie, hardly that of blood, avuncular perhaps but—he did not know what it was. It seemed to him, fatuously, that she was like a flower about to be cut down or a fragile vase on whose surface the crack would presently appear. The truth was, he told himself in an effort to pull himself together, she was a vessel and in her forces, liquids, ichors were at work which would soon shatter her, too frail to withstand them and keep whole, this patina, this gloss of womanhood too recently acquired. Of course, in the cracking or the cutting down, there would be pain. The ichor—it was as warm and red and rich as blood—would be spilled and run wasted, loosely and at random in strange places, no longer in its comfortable channels, and simultaneously her father's tenuous fabric of security would be broken, and together they could agonize but, for once, at last, observed in the services of truth. He could record it all. She was little more than jail-bait, really, after all.

"Did these funny women actually teach you anything?" he asked loudly, warmly.

"Oh, yes. I think so. The pious ones studied very hard. They went to teachers' conferences and worked on their doctor's degrees all the time. Some of them knew quite a lot of history and literature and languages and they worked terribly hard to see that we got it."

"And the impious? The worldly ones?"

"Sin. That's all they taught us."

"They were ashamed of their wicked yearnings, do you think?"

"Oh, I doubt if they were very wicked—wanting a beefsteak on Fridays or wondering once in a while if they shouldn't have gotten married instead of taking the veil, but you're right, they were ashamed.

It might be labeled a class in domestic science or chemistry but in the end it was a class in sin."

"But they really didn't know anything about it, did they?"

"Not much firsthand, no. But they knew Saint Thomas."

"And they worked awfully hard to see that *you* got it?"

"Yes, pretty."

"And did you get it?"

"What do you mean?"

"I've talked a lot with your father since he returned. He's an extremely intelligent man, don't you think?"

"Yes. I think he has made a very good adaptation to the contemporary trends of our culture."

"Whew! What's that, some of the sociology?"

She laughed a little, nervously. "Yes. I guess I was showing off."

"It sounded wonderful. But, as I say, I have talked with him quite a bit and although he isn't a Catholic, he was perfectly willing to put you in a Catholic school . . ."

"Mother had something to say there, I think."

"But he could have protested. He knows what a Catholic school would teach you and he must have wanted you to learn about sin, or at least he didn't care if you did."

"Oh, I don't think he cared."

"Well, what did you learn, then? What is your conception of sin? It just occurs to me—this is a very strange subject to be talking about."

"I'm flattered that you'd take the trouble."

"Sin is wrong, of course, but what is wrong exactly?"

"I think you know. You're just pumping me, aren't you?"

"Why, I know something of the official dogma of the Church but probably not half as much as you do."

"Sin is the disobedience to God's commands. That's what we were taught."

"Honor thy father and thy mother, eh?"

"Yes."

"That is fairly obvious, the Ten Commandments. But what about things that are wrong in themselves? Is there any wickedness that is self-contained, so to speak?"

"I don't think I see what . . ."

"I can tell that the nuns were very thorough. What I mean is this: did God cover the whole field? Did He specifically and categorically forbid everything that is wrong, or are there some things He didn't mention that are still wrong?"

"I see. Let me think a minute." Without any shyness, she looked upward with her mouth open, thinking. "I believe He covered the whole field. He made blanket injunctions. If you do something and you're worried whether it's a sin or not and you can't find out if it's been forbidden, you can look it up in the writings of the Church Fathers. They made the definitions. Maybe you don't think that what you've done has been forbidden in any of the Commandments or anyplace in the Bible, but you may find out—the priest will tell you—how one of the Fathers has worked it around under the heading of pride or lust or avarice or something."

"A closed system, then, isn't it? Everything wrong has been forbidden either directly or through later interpretation and there is nothing for the individual to decide. He has only to refer to the proper authority."

"Yes. I suppose that's it."

"And that leaves no room for absolute evil, for if it were absolute, anyone could recognize it by using his own private perceptions, and to do so is to ignore the Church's authority. Such an independent person would then be a Protestant, wouldn't he?"

"I never thought of it that way, but Protestantism means 'to protest,' doesn't it? It's funny but they always seemed to be people in a closet where it's dark and we are people in light. The nuns did that, probably."

"Thorough, as I said. To strengthen or to proselytize, that's their job. Do you believe what they taught you?"

"In my own way. I don't believe it the way the priest says it in church or the way they said it in lectures, but privately I think I believe it."

"And if you sin . . ."

"I'll be punished unless I confess and am forgiven."

"Has hell a mouth like a dragon and little two-toed winged devils flying around with red-hot pincers?"

"I've seen Flemish pictures." She smiled. "I'm vague about the punishment."

"Did they point out to you the paradoxical nature of love?"

"Is it paradoxical?"

"Perhaps not from the Catholic viewpoint. From my own, certainly. Consider the kind of love you are enjoined to have toward God."

"Yes."

"Is it the same kind you would have toward a young man?"

"I have never had any love for a young man. I couldn't say."

"But when you do."

"I doubt if I shall."

"But you would agree, wouldn't you, that if you ever did, it would not be the same kind of love."

"One would be spiritual, the other fleshly."

"Please help yourself to the liqueur. You'll forgive an old man for not getting up," he said jocularly. The affair was proceeding nicely. He did not want to rush it. She poured out another tiny glassful. "Amazing taste, hasn't it?"

"Just like the first chocolate you ever had."

"Do you want to continue our somewhat ponderous discussion?"

"Yes. I like it."

"Hmm. Fleshly love is the love of one person for another, isn't it? It excludes the divine."

"You know I don't know all the answers to these things, Mr. Verplanck. Some of them I can remember and some I have to guess."

"Does it matter? We're just talking."

"I was just thinking of fleshly love. You're right, I *think*."

"Is the love you have for your father the same as that you would have for your husband, say?"

"What do you believe in all this? You're not neutral, are you? You're making me feel almost as if I were being examined."

"I'm a dog of an unbeliever. I think all love is the same, fleshly and divine."

"That's it, you see. It's not. Because not even fleshly love is consistent. I couldn't have the same feeling for anyone else that I have for my father—and you say it is all the same."

"Hmm . . . I haven't said it very firmly yet, have I?"

She smiled. "No."

"Now supposing you discovered you had a violent passion for some young fellow—discovered it, you see. You didn't know you had it before. An illicit passion, you might say."

"Why is it every man I have ever talked to past thirty years old asked me about my love affairs?" She felt that this was a sophisticated, grown-up speech to have made.

"Oh, please don't take this question personally, Miss Miles. I am only trying to develop an idea."

"I know. It was a silly thing to say. What was it you asked me?"

"Can you sin without knowing, unconsciously?"

"Without intent?"

"Yes."

"I don't think so. There has to be the intent."

"Now, if there were this young man . . ."

"And I discovered I loved him illicitly, you say?"

"Yes. Then what?"

"Saint Paul says it is better to marry than to burn."

"Would you marry him?"

"I don't think I'll ever marry anyone."

"I see." Almost choking with excitement, he said softly, "And if you discovered that you loved your father in that way?"

"My father?"

"In that way. Illicitly."

She stood up, straight as a ramrod, like a soldier.

"You *do* love him that way, you know," Verplanck said, still quietly, although he could feel the pulses in his temples.

At last she said, "How do you know? Why do you tell me this?"

"Without intent, unconsciously, you love him more than anything in life, illicitly, sexually, sinfully. You are discovering it as I tell you, are you not?"

"Yes."

"It's true?"

330

"Yes."

"And since you know it, it becomes a sin for which you must get absolution."

"Yes."

She sat down carefully. She had always thought catastrophe would come in violence, and to find it in a library warm against the snow outside, served to her like a liqueur by a gentleman in a dinner jacket, almost gently, struck her with terror. Her head sank on her arms.

"You must not cry," Verplanck said kindly. "Your eyes will redden and he will ask you about it."

6

IT WAS BETTER to accept it now, in the winter with the soot falling
among the flakes of snow out of a dull sky, black and white together, and the disgusting milk wagon with the unnatural rubber
tires pulled by a dirty horse in the street below. Summer would have
been like last night. In summer she had played with her dolls on the
paths among the flowers in her grandmother's garden. Nothing vile
happened in the summertime, under the green leaves, among the hills,
which, distant, lay in the heavy haze, beside the lakes that looked black
and still and shining under the sunlight. Summer was happy and safe.
(Yet so were books. "Books are friends," the nuns had said. Yet
among books, in a soft chair, drinking a sweet and delicious drink, and
talking cleverly beyond her years, in this light and friendly atmosphere, a borrowed summer, she had seen it come just the same. Perhaps there was no safe season.) "But I did not accept it then," she
thought. "I got home before I cried, and then, alone, I cried myself to

sleep, resisting it, hating it, denying it. But now in its proper place, looking out at winter in the street, I can accept it."

The room had aired. She pulled down the window and turned away from it. She switched on the light beside her father's bed. His impress was on the pillow and the rumpled sheet. She touched the place where his head had lain but it was no longer warm. As she had done a hundred times before, she made up the bed, pulling the sheets tight and tucking them securely under the corners of the mattress in the way the infirmary nuns had taught her. When it was finished and the counterpane was smooth, she looked down at it, in the warmth and gratitude she always felt that she had been allowed, that things had worked out so that she could make a clean, smooth place for her father to sleep every night. A deep, illicit warmth, she knew it was now.

It was funny she had never discovered it for herself. She had lived in it as she had lived in air. "Illicit" was from *licere*, "to permit." God was the one, of course, who permitted or did not. That was His privilege with His creatures. But why? She honored her father in this. It harmed no one. "Sexual" was from *sexualis*, and some of the girls had underlined it in their dictionaries. When she thought of it, she always saw it lower-case in the right-hand column of the page. Surrounding it was a gloom like night, and in the night were glimpses of people, naked, furiously straining, contorted and shining, doing nothing she knew or recognized; cries came out; and mingled with the darkness was a reeking, shameful, marvelous perfume. And now she knew and she accepted it as true that she had seen her father in the darkness and herself, rarely but still seen, at night when she was going to sleep. And this was sinful, a word not in her Latin dictionary. It was forbidden by the Church, a mortal sin. What made a sin mortal? "Grievous matter, sufficient reflection, full consent of the will." She had learned the phrases as a lesson once and the nuns had commended her for learning them so well. The matter was grievous, surely. If she counted the short, barely wakeful meetings of her father and herself in the sweet stench of the shadows, then there had been sufficient reflection. But she had never willed to do this. There had been nothing to consent to. She had lived in it as she had lived in air. She knew she ought to see a priest. She knew also that nothing a priest said could change this.

Without it she would strangle. It was not too hard to live with. She could accept it.

She took the broom and began to sweep her father's bedroom, surprised as she was every time at the dust and rolls of lint she swept off the carpet. Sweeping, she thought, "Nothing, nothing, nothing." She would tell her father nothing. He suspected nothing now. She would tell him nothing ever. Other people might see it in her face, but he would not discern it because he had not known her long enough to see it as excess—whatever it was, an expression of the eyes, something around her mouth. It had begun before he had returned from Europe and it had been there all the time they had lived together, but he had never seen a different look in her face and he would take this betraying smile, this ardor, grievous, sinful, sexual, as the natural thing in a daughter. And if she told him, he could not help her any more than a priest. And if she told him, he would be hurt and shocked. He might withdraw his love (although hers would never budge) or change or even go away again. It was better to keep still about it. She felt stronger carrying it inside her like a beautiful disease whose symptoms were only rapture and delight, bearing it alone, stiffening herself against the punishment that would come later inevitably, and as she formed this in her mind, she seemed to see whatever priest she might have visited near by, Mother Crescentia and the nuns at school, the monsignori and the cardinals, and even the Pope at last in his tiaras, the whole panoply of the Church, turning sadly away from her, all those heads turning at once, as from someone who was lost irrevocably. Well, she could accept that, too. All she wanted to do was to keep things as they were. And having thought this, savored the actual words, it was as if some power beyond her had already made the decision to keep things as they were, never to change them. It comforted her and she swept very hard for a minute or so.

The wine had been the color of garnets and *she* had worn garnets and gray velvet, chiming in a flutelike voice full of hatred, "Oh, do try some" to her of the wine, and commanded the old Negro with her hand to pour it out dark and gleaming, flaunting her intention to impose the garnets on her guests, if they did not have eyes for them, they should have tongues to taste, to drink and admire them, either warm and liquid in the glass, or hard, glittering, implacable, warmed by the various fleshes of her wrist and throat and instep.

This was the woman her father wanted still. *Mrs. Verplanck* was wrong. It did not do her justice. "Mrs." was wrong because she did not, perhaps she could not, look like anybody's wife, and "Verplanck" was wrong because it suggested oak or pine, a pine board, and there was nothing about Margery that reminded you of pine. She was indoors; pine was outdoors. She saw to it that she gave off no unwelcome reminders. She calculated the strength of any echoes she made. Nothing was accidental. Yet she was beautiful and her father wanted her even if he had renounced her once, twice, how many times? Else why had he gone there for dinner? It was only polite if you were the hostess to pay attention to a gentleman guest and for the host to entertain a lady guest. These good manners could hide anything. Perhaps her father was as helpless before the beauty, the vicious beauty, of this woman as she was herself helpless in her love for him. It was hard to believe that because her father did not seem to be that kind of man, yet, until last night, she had not seemed to be this kind of girl, charged with an illicit passion. And now there was no telling what plans Margery had thrust upon her father last night in the sitting room, what secret meetings that would take him away from home, from her. There was too little time as it was, and there was no time for an intruder.

She went into her own bedroom. She stood the broom and the mop against the wall and laid the dustpan on the floor. She pulled down her window without looking out of it and began to make up her bed.

It was jealousy. Margery was a flower made of jewels. You could not cut it from its stalk but you could smash it or throw it at a wall and break it and she would have done it if it had been that simple to do. At school when Dodie Burchett had been given a new vicuña coat, and she herself had wanted it, that was not jealousy. That was weaker, paler, a childish feeling. This was different because it was so strong. But it was not new. The day Margery had come here, it had flitted through her mind how marvelous it would have been if the roof had fallen in or Margery had miraculously tripped going down the stairs, and after the noise and the cry, if she could have run to the door and found Margery on the landing, lying with her head cramped against the wall at a curious angle, silent. That had been jealousy then, and she had tried to put it out of her mind because it had seemed cheap and bad and because she had not known it was connected with anything. And now she remembered! It was on that day she had boasted how much she loved her father and Margery, standing by the fireplace, had glanced up sharply and asked her, "Do you know what you're saying?" The whole thing must have been plain in her face as long ago as that.

She was full of wonder that her youth had swept over and beyond her like a cloud in a windy sky, that her school days, which had seemed to be a preparation for something, had really been the whole of her girlhood, that she was now a woman and already doing what women did, struggling or at least ready to struggle with another woman for the affections of a man. The pace had been too swift. She felt cheated, and with the broom in her hand, sweeping, when she caught a glimpse of herself in the mirror of her bureau, she turned away quickly.

There had been a little glow of sun this morning, gone now, but then enough to throw a shadow on the breakfast cloth. He had come out at the usual time, cheerful, smelling faintly of soap and shaving lotion. He had given her his customary facetious compliment on the eggs and bacon, and they had talked of Mr. Welles' visit to the belligerents. She had hoped it might mean peace. He, however, had not thought so. She knew he feared a long and bloody war, and she had turned the subject to Lord Tweedsmuir's death and had done it naturally enough so that she had not thought he noticed. They both had read some of Buchan's novels and they spoke of them until he had finished his coffee and his first cigarette. Then they had risen from the table. He had kissed her on the cheek as he always did, and he had gone off to work. It had been a great strain for her. All during breakfast she had felt as if she were trembling inside, and she had not been hungry but she had eaten and talked and she was sure he had suspected nothing. What was this look that everyone but he could see? Maybe it vanished when she talked to him. She dropped the broom and went to the bureau. There was not enough light. She raised the window shade and stared at herself in the mirror. It seemed foolish, a little theatrical, to do this, but there was no one she dared ask. She had to find it out for herself. She could discover nothing. She turned her head until her profile showed and back again and to the other side. Her eyes showed nothing she had half anticipated, nor her mouth.

Yet it had left some stain on her face. When she was a little girl and got her face dirty and was told to wash it and did wash it, always grownups, Mother or Grandmother, could still see dirt on it, although she had been careful to inspect her face before showing herself to them. It was like that. And Mr. Verplanck had seen it, this smudge invisible to her. He had sat, somehow crumpled, in his chair, spotting his clothes with ashes, occasionally shoving his fat hands out in gestures that were nonetheless graceful. It had been kind of him, since he must have noticed it at dinner, to lead her through that long discussion of sin beforehand so that she would be perfectly sure what he meant when at last he arrived at the point of telling her that she loved her father. He seemed to be an intelligent and gentle man, an odd husband for Margery. When he was telling her, there was no bitterness or triumph in his face. It was as if he were doing her a favor, as indeed he was since it was better that she know and not disclose herself abruptly or unwittingly to her father. And he had been very kind to tell her that her eyes would redden if she cried.

It had been Margery who had made him tell of course! The rush of clarity, shedding a light on the elements of her complex situation, illuminating some, dispersing the irrelevant, gave her a feeling of victory, a reward for solving the riddle, yet the calm was tinged with sorrow and as she held the bare answer without trying to explain or amplify it, certain it was the right answer, she regretted losing the old naïve simplicity of her life. As a young girl she had been protected —she saw it now for the first time—and the protection meant that you were taught to believe, to take for granted, that everyone acted from motives that were simple and good. The virtues lay in a row, all white like skeins of shining silk; the evil was a heap of dirty stones, all foul and black, and who would prefer to pick up silk and use it than to throw a muddy stone? Well, quite a lot of people and Margery first among them. It was very hard to tell why so gentle a man as Mr.

Verplanck would have married a woman like Margery, who would rub and scar any gentleness like sandpaper. Her beauty was the obvious reason, yet she hesitated to believe it because it was obvious. People were no longer so simple. But there must be some hold she kept over him, and by tightening it or twisting it, she had made him reveal to her—which he had done with his own private mildness—the fact that she loved her father in the way she did.

Last night there had been a little greasy glint on Margery's eyelids, a touch of eye shadow, and her brows were faintly penciled. Artifice, she would have confessed, to draw attention to her eyes, her beautiful, large, dark eyes. She would have confessed it laughingly, an obvious harmless trick. But there were crow's-feet at the corners of her eyes, light ones, just beginning, hardly visible. That made the trick not so obvious—look at the jewel, not at the setting. Margery was getting old. She knew it and feared it. That was why she was so sharp, so desperately astute. She could tell in a minute (she had told) that her lover's daughter was a rival, and take steps.

Margery wanted to get rid of her, and Mr. Verplanck's message was a warning that she must go. And if she did not go, Margery would tell her father about it and that would be the end of everything. She could never face him if he knew. Did everyone on growing up fall into so strong a trap? Was this usual? Was this merely a test that some mysterious thing called Life, that she had read about in poems, had set for her, and if she passed it as she passed her French exam, would everything relax and be happy and would there be handshaking and congratulations all around? Or was she like a fox or a raccoon with its foot in the trap's steel clasp, staring with its wise beast eyes at the death that waits if it cannot get away and at last beginning with its teeth to tear its fur away, the skin, and then a tendon, and at last to crack the bone, at last free but mutilated, limping away on three legs? It did not matter which it was now. She would find it all out later. She would have to leave him. Let Margery have him as long as he could remember her untainted as a daughter should be.

Did she have the courage to nag him, to make herself unpleasant until he would decide she was too much trouble and send her back to her grandmother, or to frame a quarrel, cook up some small excuse,

338

or magnify one of his rare sharp words or oversights into a three-day wrangle, to sulk and cry in corners and accuse him by her silence and finally leave him as if by her own volition, unable to endure his cruelty any more? It was impossible. She would give herself away. She was not that good an actress.

If she packed up some afternoon and ran away so that he would find her gone and the apartment empty when he came home from work, where could she go? She could get a job somewhere in New York (a great city was the best place to hide in) but she was afraid she would be found. As a newspaperman her father knew all the resources of a city and he would call the Missing Persons Bureau. It would be distasteful to be hunted by policemen, and they would surely find her. They would find her if she went to Pittsburgh or New Orleans or Yuma. If she returned to her grandmother's house, she would be received with a triumphant smile and the old woman would sit down at once and write a nasty letter to her father, pointing out in detail his failure as a parent. And as soon as the letter reached him, he would come for her, puzzled, sober, kind, and ready to apologize before he knew how he had offended her. If she could get clear away somehow, and leave him only with the memory of the short time they had been happy together, she could have suffered that, for she would have left him full of illusions, but to run away and then be overtaken would be more than she could bear. It would be then as it was now and worse because her flight would make him doubt her. There must be some escape for her. As if it were a joke, she said aloud, "I might marry someone." The idea was repugnant, and even alone, she blushed and hurriedly gathered up the broom and the mop and dustpan and shoved them in a closet, hiding them and marriage together.

She walked into the living room and sat down to smoke a cigarette. What was the procedure with traps? What did other people do? She had heard her grandmother in conversation with some other old woman use the phrase, "Let things work themselves out," as if any problem solved itself eventually. But she did not dare waste even a day. Margery could decide at any moment that she had given her enough grace, call her father and tell him. Or if she stayed here and tried to mask it all, defying Margery, could she remember how she once had acted, innocently? She did not want to do anything to draw her father's attention, and any kind of mask would be clumsy.

Marriage was the answer. If she married, she could prove Margery wrong. It would baffle her. There would never be any use in telling her father about his incestuous daughter then because he would not believe it, and she herself would never betray herself to him because, with her husband beside her, he would misinterpret any slips that revealed her love for him.

She stood up glancing about and then began to walk up and down the room nervously, as if the discovery of a course of action made some sort of action imperative, as if, she thought, giggling a little, she might find a husband in the closet. She must seem to marry for love. A rich man, an old man, would not do. With a deliberation that astonished her, she calculated the whereabouts and the chances of meeting some young and stupid man (for she must hide things from him also) whom she could flatter, charm, rope in, and marry—for love.

7

THE ONLY MAP he could find was a *carte gastronomique* of France. It was lying in the top drawer of his bureau under a kidskin collar box among soiled dress ties and book matches. Verplanck had taken it for granted that a foreign correspondent, especially in wartime, would keep dozens of maps; in a brief case, probably, to be spread out under a convenient chestnut tree on the field of battle, that he might follow the action. A gun, too, in a polished leather holster flopping against his rump and binoculars in a case on a lanyard. Actually he had looked where the *Oberleutnant* had pointed —from a second-story bedroom of a house on the outskirts of Warsaw. He had been wearing what was called a three-button sack suit for which he had paid ten guineas in London, and all he had seen had been a light haze of smoke overhanging the center of the city with occasional stately blossomings of lighter, fresher smoke, the bombardment. In the courtyard of the house lay three dead horses from a

Polish cavalry regiment which had retreated recently and slowly in confusion. There were other dead horses and their riders in the road under the torn poplar trees and none of them had even begun to smell. The lieutenant had requested that they abstain from the use of field glasses. He had seen this with the naked eye. He had had no gun and no maps. But Verplanck expected him to have maps. Some deception was necessary and it would look plausible when she came in—the two men on their hands and knees with the map spread out on the floor in front of them. He took the *carte gastronomique* and went into his living room.

"Here's a map. It's the only one I could find." Miles took it out of the envelope and unfolded it.

"Oh, that's splendid. I'm sorry to have troubled you." Verplanck took the map from him, glanced at the light, and spread it out on the floor, pressing down the corners with one foot. "About here, don't you think?"

"That'll be all right."

Verplanck eased himself down to the floor, bent over on his hands and knees, and began to inspect the map. "What kind of map is this?"

"*Carte gastronomique de la France.* It shows where truffles grow," Miles said. He remained standing. "I have no military maps."

"But this is fascinating," Verplanck said. "Such a wonderful people. Think of making a map like this."

It was about three feet wide and four feet long. Each of the *départements* was outlined in green, and, according to the *légende*, the regions stippled in yellow indicated the homes of white wines, those in red, red wines, those in green, beer. Beneath Paris was printed *Centre gastronomique du monde, toutes les productions, tous les crus*, and finally *Toutes les spécialités culinaires des tous les pays.* Under the names of all the lesser towns were lists of their dishes which the traveler would enjoy. At Lyon, for example, he would find *Saucisson de Lyon, Poulet Celestine, La Friture de goujons du Rhône*, and other delicacies. In the blue of the coastal waters, the cartographer had generously indicated the haunts of fish, crabs, lobster, sardines, and oysters. Around the borders of the map were set advertisements for restaurants, wine merchants, and one severe announcement from a purveyor of the mushrooms of the Jura mountains.

Verplanck was arched on the floor on his knees and one elbow. His chin was propped on one hand and with a forefinger he was tracing the names of the towns he had visited, talking as if to himself in a chuckling, delighted voice, "*La tête de veau aux appétits, les alouettes en brochette*. Périgueux! I've been there, and I've eaten *Dindes truffées*. Such a marvelous turkey, exquisite, such a delicate flavor." He raised himself and sat back on his heels like a dressmaker. "I never get drunk, you know, but they brought this bird and set it before me, a turkey hen, you understand, a large hen, they said, three kilos. I had ordered a bottle of Château Gruaud-Larose. Gruaud-Larose? Yes, that was it. And, do you know, I had barely finished one side of the breast before I had drunk up the bottle? So I drank another, and actually I was well into my third before I cleared the skeleton. It was one of the few times that I have ever been as you might say clinically intoxicated, but it really was a superb meal. That's the trouble with this damned war. The Burgundies are criminally expensive and some you just can't get—Musigny, for instance."

"What's Sedan famous for?" Miles asked. "And Metz and Belfort?"

Verplanck flopped back again on his elbows. "Sedan? Oh, here. Sedan? *Chocolat*, that's all. And Metz? *Charcuterie*. Belfort? Where's Belfort? Oh, Belfort is famous for nothing. Why do you ask?"

Soldiers ate chocolate and pig meat. The border towns provided the protective integument for the center, the gastronomic center. "Oh, I was just thinking of the fortress towns near the border. You mentioned the war."

"Oh," Verplanck said. He went on pointing and mumbling and smiling over the names of things to eat.

Miles sat down in a chair and began to smoke a cigarette.

"What time will she be home?" Verplanck asked without turning round.

"About ten-thirty. Do you think I'd better get down on my hands and knees, too, about ten-twenty-five?"

Verplanck, still intent on the map, did not answer at once. Then he said, "What? Oh . . ." He got to his feet and dusted off the knees of his trousers. "When you called me this evening, it occurred to me that we have given her no excuse, no reason why you and I should be seeing each other. The maps seemed to be an excellent subterfuge. We are discussing the war, you see. And I come here occasionally and you come to my apartment to further these discussions. I am a layman who is getting expert opinion."

"I just wondered." These tricks and deceptions worked on his daughter made Miles sullen. "You want to discuss the war?"

"In its present condition, it's hardly worth discussing, do you think? Besides, you can't expect me to be interested in guns or bombs through a map which says truffles and sausages and *pâté de foie gras de perdrix*. In my scheme of things a stuffed turkey is worth more than a *Minnenwerfer*. I'm not a very martial person, I'm afraid."

"You're one war behind. They don't use *Minnenwerfer* in this war. They were trench mortars."

"But you see my point."

"Oh, sure." Miles looked at his wrist watch. "It's after ten now. She ought to be coming along in a few minutes."

"What kind of youth is he?" Verplanck asked, standing up again.

"Big. Taller than I am and he must weigh nearly two hundred."

"Is that all you were able to gather about him?"

"She had him up for dinner last night. He was polite and he had the kind of manners I used to have when I was twenty-two, when you feel you're being watched all the time? He graduated from the University of Michigan last June and he works for Dinsmore, Ludwig & Coles. They're an advertising agency. Dinsmore's his uncle. His name is Dinsmore, Stanley Dinsmore."

"And you say she seemed to be attracted to him?"

"Sincerely."

"How long have they been seeing each other?"

"I didn't want to ask her point-blank. I wanted to make it seem to her that I thought it was the most natural thing in the world that she should find a young man . . ."

"Of course."

"And when we talked about him this morning, it was obvious they

344

were fairly intimately acquainted. He brought her home from art class a couple of times, she said."

"Is he handsome?"

"Oh, he's not bad-looking. He's like all kids—nothing in his face yet. Blond hair, big jaw."

"Would you say he was intelligent?"

"He was a little too scared to tell. He had been made to read the newspapers in a journalism class he took at college and he'd seen my name in a byline. He was impressed, I think."

"I was just trying to ascertain what it was in particular that attracted her. From talking to your daughter, I would say flatly that, as young as she is, she would not be drawn to him merely because he was twenty-two and a university graduate."

"No. I don't know what it is. He has all that good-tempered dullness of the professional athlete, but I don't know what his dodge is—played football maybe. I don't know what she sees in him, but then it's always hard to see what some people see in other people."

"Quite," Verplanck said curtly.

It broke upon Miles that he might have offended Verplanck but he did not care. There was a question he wanted to ask him. "You don't suppose you said anything to her the other night that would encourage her to . . . Did you suggest she find a young man?"

"I'll just sit down, may I?"

"Certainly. Go ahead."

Verplanck sat and composed himself thoughtfully. "I confess I'm puzzled. Of course, it is possible that she may have interpreted one of my remarks as tending in that direction but . . ."

"Does she know she's ill?"

"You mean, did I tell her? No. I had rather not expatiate on our conversation simply because, if I told you what I said to her and what she replied, it might conceivably cause some change in your treatment of her, and any change, however minute, at this stage might protract the whole process of cure."

"Then you think she took up this boy spontaneously?"

"That is why I urged you to let me come over this evening. I may be able to find out by watching them together."

"Well. They should be here any minute. Drink?"

"It's rather late. If you don't mind, I'll just look at this map again. My position on the floor will not only be dramatically apropos, but I shall also be able to revive some exceedingly pleasant memories of my journeys in a more fortunate France." He knelt down, banging his knees quite hard and wincing, and fell forward on all fours. "I never could stand *marc*, could you?"

"No."

Verplanck irked him, fat, graceless, humped over the map, murmuring happily of stews and comfits. This was because he had not seen the war. France was not a gastronomic center now. The mushroom crop was poor this year and many of the vines of Burgundy were suffering because there were no men to tend them. He was not martial, as he said. He was only well informed. He read the papers. He did not know that he was waiting for anything. He was not quite concerned enough to hope, rather he expected peace through some mysterious process of diplomatic chicane, a rich, smiling plenteous peace in which the grapes, the mushrooms, the truffles, and incidentally the French would grow again and prosper. The juice of France was not wine. It was blood, and a hell of a lot of it would be pressed out before this expected peace, old boy. And you had better learn to wait as I am waiting, not for peace, but for the inevitable war.

But as Miles continued to watch him, he knew that these lurid objections were not actually the reasons Verplanck irritated him. It was the waiting. It was not that the waiting was a waste of time— there was nothing else he could be doing. He had placed himself in this position: he had, deliberately more or less, arranged matters so that the only things he valued he had to wait for, and he had no control, not the slightest influence, on the forces that held up their arrival. He was in someone else's hands and when they happened to be ready to act, for reasons of their own or whims of their own, or perhaps they were bound to remain inert until other, more distant people or chances moved, they would start the chain or hurricane of circumstance that eventually would affect him, and then he would stop waiting, but not until. Perhaps Mary and this young Dinsmore (for whom he was grateful enough, God knows) were window-shopping or they might be in a drugstore having a coke (or in a bar having a drink), and at some incalculable point or other (it might be only a clock catching her eye or the boy might hide a yawn) she would make the decision, make it up out of this ragtag and bobtail of hap, luck, or fortune, and she would say, "Don't you think we'd better be going?" And he did not dare tell Verplanck he looked like a fool, mumbling there over the map, because it would offend him and he would exert, despite his semiprofessional sincerity, a little less earnestness and skill in the performance of the mumbo-jumbo that would heal his daughter. And there might be a chill on the liver of someone in Downing Street or the Quai d'Orsay or the Wilhelmstrasse, or his wife could be ill or unfaithful, or the money in Switzerland or Sweden might have turned out not to be safe any longer and there would be nowhere for this someone to go when, after the preliminary disasters, came the ultimate, the last catastrophe, and this chill, this wife, this defalcation would swathe this someone in a cloud of worry and all his delicate schemes and calculations would be jarred and come unstuck, and so the last, the ultimate catastrophe would either come or be staved off a month either way, this final vague, grave blow that would strike Richard Miles, Mary Miles, Henry Verplanck, and everyone and tear off all their labels and make them dead or merely numbers in a prison camp. But there was nothing he could do about any of it, except to wait.

"You're sure she's bringing him up here this evening?" Verplanck asked.

"She said she was."

"Hmmm . . . Sauternes. You know, I've heard that the Marquis de Lur-Saluce gives all the money he makes off Château Yquem to support the Royalist party. Curious, isn't it?"

"Uh-huh," Miles said.

They heard talking on the stairs outside the door.

"Here they are. She must have taken her key. She didn't ring." Miles stood up quickly.

The door opened and she came in, breathless, laughing, her cheeks red from the cold. She lifted her chin—how like a little girl she was—and untied the knot of the handkerchief wrapped around her head, and spoke to them both through her teeth. They had walked home, she said, in the snow, and on the shoulders of her coat snow lay like white plush. It had been fun. Miles noticed how familiarly she took the usurper's sleeve to steady herself as she stood on one foot untying her galoshes.

And the young man? He stood shyly with his back against the door, waiting for someone to tell him to take off his coat and stay, certain that someone should ask him, and trying all the while to look as if it made no difference. He wore a gabardine topcoat that hung to the middle of his thighs, streaked and splotched with damp dark spots. He had rolled up the cuffs of his trousers and on his feet were white saddle-strap oxfords with rubber soles. From under them spread a little pool of water, the melting snow.

"How are you, Mr. Verplanck?" she asked.

"Splendid. Splendid," Verplanck said from his knees, wiping his glasses. "It's very healthy, walking in the snow."

"Yes. Stan?" She turned. He had made the decision and taken off his coat and was hanging it beside hers in the closet by the door. He was flustered by her voice. He slammed the door, twitched at the noise, and hurried to her side, ready for the next ordeal. "This is Mr. Dinsmore, Mr. Verplanck."

The boy advanced toward Henry with his hand stuck out, but Henry, who had said "How do you do?" perfunctorily, had picked up the map by the corners, like a woman holding a sheet, and was struggling to get the damned thing folded into its original creases. The boy jerked his hand back stealthily, glancing at Mary to see if she had noticed his mistake.

Behind the map Verplanck was saying, ". . . just talking about the war, your father and I. Fascinating subject, Mr. Dinsmore." The fold accomplished, Verplanck's head popped over the edge of the map like a turtle's.

"Why, I don't know. I don't follow it much," the boy said, standing on one foot and looking at the other.

"Sit here, Stan," Mary said from the divan. "Why should he? Father and I are always talking about it, every morning, and we don't get anywhere." As the boy sat down beside her, she said softly, "Like a drink? It was colder walking than I thought."

"No, thanks," he said with a fond smile. Then he became severe, wanting to repay this fat New Yorker for his nonchalance by saying, Miles could tell, something intelligent. "I thought that was pretty good about what the British did to the *Graf Spee*, there in December."

Verplanck had got the map straightened and was backing up, looking over his shoulder, guiding his buttocks into his chair. "Very creditable of them, certainly." He made the last small folds and tucked it into its envelope. He looked up, beaming. "I don't blame you, Mr. Dinsmore, for not following it much because"—he chuckled —"if it gets worse and we should become involved, it'll be the big strong bucks like you who will be the first to go and get killed. As for myself, I detest it. As a matter of fact, this map here"—he tapped the envelope—"is what led Miles and myself away from the war."

"It's a map of France," Mary explained. "It shows all the wine-making districts and all the dishes each town is famous for."

"When did you see it?" Miles asked. He had not expected her to know anything about it.

"Oh, one morning when I was making up your room."

"It is a very charming map," Verplanck insisted sonorously. "And if it were not so much trouble I should be delighted to take it out again and show it to you. What's your favorite wine, Mr. Dinsmore?"

"I don't know. Champagne, I guess."

"Pooh! Champagne's everybody's favorite . . . aerated cider is all it is."

Stubbornly the boy said, "We don't serve much wine where I come from."

"Indeed? And where is that?"

"Detroit," Mary said. "And I don't blame them. The duty is high enough as it is and then to pay for shipping it out there and a state tax on top of that . . ."

"Oh, Detroit. Well, naturally," Verplanck said indulgently. "There's nothing there really but the Ford factory and thousands of Polish mechanics, is there?"

"Stan, Mr. Verplanck is the typical provincial New Yorker. To him anything west of Jersey City is suburban and therefore vile." She said it with great style. Miles wanted to laugh.

"It's a good enough town. We've got some trees there anyhow."

"And to be sure, only God can make a tree. You exist there basking under the special dispensation of the Almighty, do you not?"

"Well, when one of the Dodge girls made her debut, she wore black orchids that they had sent all the way from Africa." The boy was suffering, as Miles had once suffered, from a helpless feeling of anger. He thought he was not sophisticated enough to score against this fat bastard.

"And there you live in trees near the Ford factory, drinking gin and wearing orchids imported from Africa. Is that it, Mr. Dinsmore? Oblivious to the war and to French wines, perfectly happy."

"You are very flattering, Mr. Verplanck. To be perfectly happy is something of a feat in times like these," Mary said coolly.

The boy shifted from side to side uneasily and looked toward Miles. He was wary; he wanted to see if he had Miles' sympathy but he could not hide his disgust with himself. Miles winked.

"I'm sure it is. I was only thinking of this idyllic spot under the shock of war. Miles here says, without a shadow of evidence that I can see, that the war's bound to engulf us all. Where is Detroit, then? Where, may I ask, is Mr. Dinsmore?"

"And where are you? Where am I, Verplanck?" Miles asked.

"Why, Stanley will be in the navy, I should think. He's one of the fastest swimmers in the world," Mary said.

"Really?" Verplanck drawled.

"He is counting on breaking the world's record for a hundred yards this spring, aren't you?" Mary said.

Pleased now, the boy moved his head deprecatingly. "If I'm lucky, maybe."

"The record is fifty-one seconds and Stanley has already done fifty-two seconds, was it?"

"Just about."

"How will you cut off that last second?" Miles asked.

"Oh, I'll have to train hard and . . ."

"He swims over half a mile a day. Up at the New York Athletic Club," Mary said.

"And when you have broken this record, Mr. Dinsmore, what will it mean to you?" Verplanck asked.

The boy began cautiously, looking from one to the other of his listeners to be sure they were taking him seriously. "The hundred's stood for a long time. Ten years, I guess. Weissmuller set it, and they had a guy up at the club that equaled it, Peter Fick, but nobody's been able to beat it. If I do, it'll mean I'm the fastest swimmer in the world."

"But why swim, Mr. Dinsmore? Are you going to be a swimming instructor or a lobster fisherman or a lifeguard?"

"No. I just like it."

"Do you like drawing or sketching or whatever it is you have just come from?"

"Not so much."

"He's much better than I am. He has a better sense of color," Mary said promptly.

"And the advertising?" Verplanck said. "Miles told me you are in the advertising business. Do you like that?"

"Oh, I live on it."

"Indubitably," Verplanck said, looking him up and down. "And you swim on the side. How well do you scream, Mr. Dinsmore? Scream loud, can you?"

"Why should he scream?" Mary asked.

"Advertising is a *pis aller*. Art he doesn't like much. Clearly swimming is his only love, and after he has broken the record—which I am certain you will do, my dear Dinsmore—the next step is inevitable: Tarzan in a G-string, screaming in the jungle. Weissmuller will be too fat soon. Give us a scream, Dinsmore, just a little, an indoor scream."

Mary stood up. "Stan, I think you can take me over to Sheridan Square. We interrupted Father and Mr. Verplanck talking about the war, and poor Mr. Verplanck was so wound up he is still taking sides. I think we'd better apologize and leave."

Verplanck jumped up with surprising agility. "Oh, let me go, please do. I'm the one who should go, not you. I'm terribly sorry,

351

my boy, if I offended you. I suffer from migraine headaches and one is coming on. I should never have gone out this evening at all. I hardly know what I'm saying, and I can't tell you how grateful I am to you, my dear, for fetching me up short so beautifully. I have been very rude." His face broke into a charming smile. "Especially to a newcomer in our city. Say you'll forgive me." He extended his hand.

Scowling, puzzled, the boy took his hand and said, "Aw, that's O.K. I'm not mad."

"Do sit down. I'll get *my* hat and coat. It would be a sin, a mortal sin, to intrude upon your privacy—of course, you must go to bed at once, Miles—as I say it would be a sin to bother you any longer."

Mary blushed very red. She said, "No. We'll go, Mr. Verplanck. You stay here." She went to the closet and began to put on her galoshes.

"Don't stay out too late," Miles said.

She was standing on one foot tugging at the heel of her galosh. "I won't," she said without looking up.

From the doorway the boy said, "Hope your headache's better, Mr. Verplanck. Good night, Mr. Miles."

"Good night, Stanley," Miles said warmly, to take the curse off Verplanck's rudeness.

They went out, and Miles could not hear them talking on the stairs.

"You were pretty rough on the boy," Miles said.

Verplanck had sat down again as soon as they went out the door. He was slumped down in the chair, with his elbows on the arms and his hands clasped over his stomach. He had thrown one knee over the other, dragging up his trouser leg, and a patch of pale fat flesh showed above his sock. He did not change his position. He raised his eyebrows and thrust out his lips. "Merely a technique, my dear Miles."

"Well, she defended him, didn't she? She stood up for him and hit back."

"And very cleverly, too."

"You could have knocked me over. I've never seen her act that way before. She seemed ten years older, didn't she?"

"Exquisite poise, exquisite."

"What do you think? Is there any chance she's in love with him? I grant you he's not very bright, but he seems honest and he's decent and respectful. I can't imagine why he didn't come over and pop you one."

"Oh, he was afraid of what I'd think. It crushes him to think that other people might consider him uncouth."

"That's just because he's young."

"Certainly."

"I don't know. I have a feeling that this other was merely temporary. She was just out of a convent school, and I was the only man she knew. Being cooped up so long with me this way, all she needed was another man—big, broad shoulders, reasonably handsome, don't you think?"

Verplanck got up slowly. "Miles, I do not suffer from a technical migraine. I suffer from a real migraine. I think I had better go home and prepare for a day of darkness and veronal." He moved exhaustedly over to the closet and took out his hat and coat as if they were very heavy.

"But what do you think about this? Don't you agree with me? She might be in love with him or on the verge of it, don't you think?"

Verplanck had one arm in his overcoat and he was fumbling to find the other armhole. He was looking at the floor. "Very possibly," he said absently. "Very possibly."

For an hour they had sat on stools in a bar in Sheridan Square, talking, and she had sent back a Martini cocktail because it was not dry enough. They had run home through the falling snow, and he had thrown snowballs at her, and on one corner, in a snowbank thrown up by the street cleaners, he had lain down and "made an angel" as he had done when he was a little boy.

When they got to her place, she unlocked the door downstairs and they had sat inside on the bottom steps of the staircase, talking in low voices so as not to waken anyone, but the wind had blown under the door too strongly and they moved farther up the stairs, and now he sat on the landing where the stairs turned and she sat two steps below him between his knees. As they talked on in the darkness, he played clumsily with the hair at the back of her neck, and if she shuddered, she said it was because his hands were cold from throwing snowballs.

". . . and I could get to be office manager in four or five years. All you have to do is watch what you say and it would pay ten or twelve thousand a year and then I could live the way I want to."

"But what about the record?" she asked.

"Oh, I'll break that this spring. I can do it, and then people'll know who I am. It'll be an asset in the business. Boy, I'd like to drive to work in a Duesenberg. I'll get an apartment at one of those places like Essex House. They've got a pool there, and you can put your clothes in the door and they take them out and press them every night. And we could go places . . ."

"What places?"

"Oh, you know, swanky places like the Rainbow Room. I guess I don't know how to dress very well. I looked good in Ann Arbor, but it's not the same here, and I don't know how to order a big meal in a good restaurant . . ."

"With wines?" She could not help asking that.

"That guy Verplanck was a jerk in a way but in a way he's right. My old man wears a pencil in his outside coat pocket with the clip showing and thinks nothing of it. It's O.K. in Detroit. I was sore to-night, but it just came over me that Detroit is a hick town like he says. Well, New York can show me how to pick the right fork, see what I mean? Say, is it like that at your house every night?"

"Like what?"

"Oh, just sitting around. Your father sat there and he didn't say a word and then this jerk Verplanck . . . Do you always just sit there with your father? I should think you'd want to get out and see the town."

She looked down. He could not see her plainly in the darkness but he knew she did it. "I can't," she said.

"Why not?"

"Oh, I don't know. I don't know enough people, maybe. I never went any place except with Father until ten days ago."

"You mean I'm the first man you ever had a date with in this town? What do you do daytimes?"

"I do the housework and, oh, I read and darn socks and . . . sometimes we go over to the Verplancks' and sometimes he comes over here."

"Just to talk about the war, hey?"

"That's silly. Mr. Verplanck doesn't care anything about the war. Father's in love with his wife and he wants to keep an eye on Father, that's all. He wants to know where he is nights."

Little pictures of the scandals of the newspaper Sunday supplements appeared in Stanley's mind, half-tone drawings of richly jeweled dishonest women and a Latin-type group of men in faultless evening clothes kissing them or giving them presents, and a thrill tingled down his spine to discover that here was Life. Mary was in the midst of Life, and since he knew her, so was he. But he said confidently, "I figured there was an angle. It wasn't so hard to see there was something phony about the setup. All you do is wait around holding the bag."

"I ran away from school. He had to take me, you see."

"Is this wife of Verplanck's going to divorce him?"

"I don't know."

"Doesn't your father say anything that gives you any clue?"

"He doesn't talk to me much. You saw."

"You just wait around to see what's going to happen."

"Yes. I just wait," she said.

She put her hand on the banister and pushed herself up slowly. "I'd better go in. It's late."

"What'll he do—give you hell?"

She sighed. "Probably."

The boy did not stand up. He sat on the top step looking up at her and she saw his face only as a blob of white in the darkness.

"Mary," he said softly.

"What?"

"You haven't got any place to go, have you?"

"Here," she said.

"I mean, when this breaks up."

355

In a tired voice she said, "Why, I don't think he'll want me around after he marries her."

"What will you do then?"

"Oh, go someplace and get a job." As if she were speaking a piece, she stood looking over the boy's head. "I thought everything was going to be wonderful when I came here to live. You don't know what it is to live alone or with people you hate. I hadn't seen him for seven years and I thought he would like to have his daughter around, the only person who belongs to him. But I guess I was mistaken."

The boy said nothing. She could see that he was looking up at her.

"Let me go, Stan. I've got to go in."

He stood up, took her hand, and pulled her up to the landing in front of him. "No. Look, I've got my thirty-five dollars a week. We can find a place. Marry me. It'll be all right then. We can get along. We can get an apartment somewhere and . . . will you?"

"You're just being sympathetic."

"No, I'm not. Honestly I'm not. I'm like you. You see that. My old man's no good either. I mean, he doesn't understand me any more than your father understands you. Let's show 'em." He seemed to feel that there was something wrong with the tone of his proposal. It did not sound romantic enough, and he jerked his head in irritation. He wanted to do it smoothly, the way they did it in the movies. "I mean . . . I love you, Mary. I loved you the first night I saw you in art class. The minute you came in I knew you were the woman I wanted for my wife." To call her a woman made him seem older and more sure of himself.

"I don't know, Stan. I didn't expect . . . I just don't know what to do."

"Let me take you away from this," he said grandly. "I'll get off work tomorrow morning and you meet me and we'll go down to the City Hall and get married." He slid his arms around her and pulled her close to him and began to kiss her. It was the first time he had kissed a girl since he left home and it was the most persuasive thing he could think of to do.

She felt his lips wet on her face and neck and mouth. Automatically she pushed him away. "Well. All right. I'll marry you."

356

His stomach seemed to turn over inside him. This was definite. This was the future, for which he had no plans. It was not play any longer. How could he have been such a fool? Bewildered, to escape these thoughts, he began to kiss her roughly and at last she threw her arms around his neck and returned his kisses, whispering in his ear, "Darling, take me away. You're all I have now." It made him feel better, more adult, and he lifted his head and looked around him in the darkness as if he sought the approval of someone who might be watching, a person who knew how these things should be done.

"Look, your father's not home mornings, is he?"

"No. He's at the office."

"I'll come here at eleven-thirty and we'll take a taxi and go and get married, and I'll fix it with the hotel so you can stay there tomorrow night and . . ."

"There'll have to be a license and a ring."

"I'll get those."

"God help you, Stan. You're sure you want to do this?"

"I know it."

"I'll be ready."

He kissed her once more a long time, whispered, "See you tomorrow morning," and ran like a colt down the stairs.

She heard the front door click behind him. She turned around and began to go up the last half flight of stairs slowly. All she was thinking was that she had been lucky to get two drinks in him at the bar in Sheridan Square.

8

MILES HAD LEFT his office a few minutes early. He had stopped only to buy a corsage of fresh flowers for his daughter, brilliantly colored, their stems wrapped in foil, and a stiff border of paper lace around them, a little formal bouquet that he had intended to present to her with a bow. He had let himself into his apartment and begun calling for her loudly and cheerfully. There were no lights turned on; the fire on the hearth was out; and he had called only twice when he realized that the rooms were dead because there was no one in them.

He had run into her bedroom to see if she had lain down to sleep and had not wakened. The kitchen was empty and there were no vegetable tops or potato peelings in the garbage dish—she had not started to prepare their dinner. A little nervously he glanced around the living room again in the fear that she might have been taken ill suddenly and fainted and fallen down and in his haste he had overlooked her. She was not there. At last he went into his bedroom. His bed, where he thought she might have been, was unruffled. It was dark there but he could see a piece of paper lying on the pillow.

It was a sheet of her notepaper. He dropped the box containing her corsage on the bed and switched on the lamp. He sat down to read it.

> *Dear Father,*
> *I am marrying Stanley today. Wish me luck.*
> *Love,*
> *Mary*

It seemed to him that he had read this before, had nerved himself already to withstand this shock, and at last to hold it in his hand and hear the slight crackling of the paper was like the echo of a note already sounded. He lifted the paper closer to the light to see if her hand had wavered when she wrote the word *Love*, but as he commenced his scrutiny, he drew his hand down and laid the paper on the bed beside him and thrust his hands into his pockets to find a cigarette, ashamed that the memory of plays he had seen and novels he had read should still have force enough to make him do anything so foolishly dramatic. Her hand had been perfectly steady throughout. Obviously she had made her decision before she began to write at all. Why should he demand a final spurious testimonial of her affection?

He struck a match to light his cigarette with the vague intention of sitting there until he had planned what to do, the next necessary step, but the flame had barely spurted out before he was up and on his way to the telephone. He dialed Verplanck's number, and, waiting with the whir in his ears, he saw himself reflected in the mirror that hung over the fireplace. He looked away immediately but straightened his tie and smoothed the left side of his head with his hand, astonished even as a voice broke into the hum of the telephone's ring that he could persist in his vanity at a time like this. It was the voice of old Charles, Verplanck's Negro servant. Mr. Verplanck was not at home. He was likely on his way home now. It was his afternoon to read at the Public Library. Miles said, "Oh," and dropped the receiver on its cradle and ran out of the apartment, slamming the door after him.

In the taxicab, he pulled down the jump seat, stretched out, and put his feet on it. He told the driver to go like hell to the Public Library. He hoped to catch Verplanck before he left. Gazing steadily at the photograph of the lean, fierce face of Michael Zyk, the driver of the cab, which was fixed to the partition, Miles planned to tell Verplanck what he had found, enumerating all the facts, and then confer with him as to the best course. He would tell him that she had come home the night before at 1:30 A.M.; how coolly she had looked into his room before going to bed to see if he was awake, and when he stirred, yawning, said, "Good night, Father"; how there had been no sign in her demeanor this morning at breakfast that would have foretold this flight; how pleasantly and with what he now considered to be self-possession she had cooked and eaten and seen him off to work. As he remembered calmly these little pictures of the night and the morning, it struck him that he was calm because he was relieved. He sat up straight, shoved the jump seat forward with his foot, and called to the driver to hurry.

He was irritated that it had taken him so long to perceive it but he knew now that his excitement, which contained no apprehension or regret, was full of joy. Mary was all right. She was normal. She was perhaps healed. There was nothing sinister or unhealthy in running away to get married. It might be surprising or it might be a nuisance, but it was not psychopathic. As the cab stopped for a red light, Miles looked out at the faces of the five-o'clock crowd, all homeward bound, the day's work done, and he had the impulse to jump out and start shaking hands with all these people, certain now as he had not been in months that his face was clear, and no one no matter how hard he looked at him could discern the traces of this secret that had set him apart from decent, honest people until now.

As the light turned green, the cab sprang forward, and Miles already was chagrined to think that he had wanted to run around shaking hands with strangers in the open street. One of his favorite images of himself, compounded of wishes, little compliments given him in the past, memories of occasions in which he had seemed to act swiftly and efficiently, was that he met any crisis with tranquillity and resolved it coolly and logically. It was false and he knew it. The notion had been a present he had manufactured to give himself. "Miles, meet the imperturbable, the impassive, thoughtful Miles. When you tell him bad news, when you tell him good news, he never moves a muscle of his face. Go on, tell him something and see."

What was it now, out of all this windstorm of irrelevancy, that he was thinking and feeling (or was it the same, all at once)? He did not want to fidget when he talked to Verplanck, who might be crouched over a table in the library (There were the couchant lions. And the cab was waiting to advance to a stop) or he might be in a taxicab himself, or already home, peeping at Margery and calling for a drink. Knowing that he was silly and impulsive, he tried to fix his mind on something he could use but he could extract from his turmoil only one: he was glad that Mary was not in love with him. That was a fact.

The cab stopped, and he got out mechanically, three cars back of the Forty-second Street crosswalk, paid the driver, thanked him, and ran around the rear of the taxi, looking out toward his right to see if it were safe to cross. He ran across the empty street, slipped behind a bus, dodging the waiting passengers, and, panting, ran up the steps of the library, all the while trying to keep his little fact in mind, cradling it, coddling it to make it hold still. Yet, as he reached the top step, past the lions, the clucking pigeons, and the departing scholars, he found that it had disintegrated, slipped and drained away, and he could not remember why he had been glad. Mary had gone away from him, hadn't she? He was alone again. Why should he be happy over that?

Superficially, he was undecided whether to wait beside the outer doorway to catch Verplanck as he came out or whether it would be wiser to go inside and look for him, perhaps asking one of the clerks about him—he must be known and familiar in there. Miles paused, scanning all the men who came through the doors settling their mufflers and lighting cigarettes, disgusted at the effort he had spent in a ten-minute trip all the way uptown in a taxicab to determine only these simple things.

He nearly missed Verplanck, who had passed him and was already

361

descending the first low flight of steps sedately. He ran after him and grabbed his arm. "Verplanck!"

Verplanck looked around with his brows contracted into a sour look of annoyance, but when he saw who it was, he smiled. "Hello, Miles."

"She's run away to get married."

"Really? Shall we step back inside? It's rather windy here."

They went back up the steps. Miles pulled open the heavy door and allowed Verplanck to pass in front of him. It was warm inside and steam covered Verplanck's glasses.

"You found this out just now?" Verplanck asked him. He had taken off his glasses, leaving shiny red weals on each side of his nose. He drew a handkerchief out of his breast pocket and began to polish the glasses. It was a very fine linen handkerchief.

"I had just gotten home from the office. Nobody was there. She left a note saying she was marrying that Dinsmore kid. Wait . . ." Miles fumbled in all his pockets searching for the note, until he remembered that he had not brought it with him.

"Did she leave it lying in the middle of the floor to catch your eye?" Verplanck asked. He inserted first one, then the other lens of his spectacles into his open mouth, exhaled, wiped them clean, and held the spectacles up to the light to inspect them.

"It was on my pillow. The pillow on my bed," Miles said.

"Hmm . . . very interesting. On *your* bed, eh?" Verplanck put the spectacles on his nose and ran his thumbs along his temples to settle the earpieces. He held one hand up in front of him and looked at it, and turning, craning his neck, he looked out through the glass doors of the library at the opposite side of the street, trying them for distance. The spectacles were now thoroughly clean and satisfactory. He said apologetically, "My glasses steamed up." Then in his calm, almost official tone, he said, "It is doubtful if the marriage has been consummated. A smug young bourgeois like Dinsmore would be afraid of the ritual fornication in daylight. I suggest you find a lawyer at once."

"A lawyer?"

"Do you intend to permit her to be his wife?"

"I must be rather excited, Verplanck. An annulment hadn't oc-curred to me." Saying it did not make him less excited, he found, although he had hoped it would be a remedy.

"There is a large office building just there on Forty-second Street." Verplanck pointed to his left. "You might just catch a lawyer before he goes home. Any lawyer will do. It is quite a simple matter. Legally, your daughter is an infant. She is below the age of consent for this state. Ask him to make out the necessary papers. They involve having you appointed guardian *ad litem*, a purely formal trial and so on. Then find your daughter and take her home. Do you know where she is?"

"I don't know where he lives, it just occurs to me."

"You can use the lawyer's telephone. Call his uncle's advertising firm."

It was humiliating to have Verplanck guide him step by step. "Thanks a lot, Verplanck. I just thought I'd let you know. I'll go on over to the lawyer's."

"If it is convenient, you might call me later this evening," Ver-planck said.

"I will," Miles answered, hurrying out the door. He knew Ver-planck stood watching him, very likely with amusement.

As soon as he was outside, beyond Verplanck's eyeshot, he began to run. He bumped into one or two people, and he apologized over his shoulder. He arrived in the lobby of an office building on the north side of Forty-second Street with his overcoat unbuttoned and his necktie hanging out. He found the building directory on the wall. As he was looking aimlessly up at it, turning his head right and left like a man trying to pick a friend out of a crowd in a football stadium, he saw his image in the glass covering of the directory board. He straightened his coat and tucked his necktie back in place, ashamed of the urgency he felt. Squarely in front of him was the column con-taining the names of the occupants whose names began with *M*. He chose a firm named McGann & Cleary and entered an elevator.

"Six, please," he said to the operator. He was alone in the car. Per-haps he had come too late and all the lawyers had gone home. Perhaps McGann & Cleary were accountants or brokers or leather finders or

God knows what. He said to the operator, "You know McGann & Cleary?"

"Yeah. Law firm," the operator said. He braked the car to a jerky stop. "Step up, please."

Leaving the car, Miles said, "Do you know if they're still in their office?"

"I couldn't say," the operator said precisely, looking straight ahead as he closed the door, descending.

Miles walked quickly, his footsteps echoing, down the corridor. He saw McGann & Cleary on a door window of frosted glass. A light was still burning in the office.

As his hand was turning the knob, the door was flung open and a man in a derby hat with his elbows kited up, settling his overcoat, rushed out. Miles heard the word "Sorry" come down the corridor after him.

Miles went in. In one corner of the office before a washbowl ordinarily concealed by a folding door stood a man in his undershirt peering into a mirror, shaving.

"Mr. Cleary?" Miles asked.

"That was Cleary just left. Cleary, né Zweigbaum. I'm McGann," the man said, leaning forward and pulling down his upper lip. He drew the razor neatly over it twice. "You're late. Insurance, dog stocks, or what is it? Not that I want any part of it, but you might tell me before you go." He turned to look at Miles.

"I want a lawyer . . ." Miles began.

"You got one. What's the trouble?"

"Can I use your phone a minute?" Miles asked.

"Sure. Go ahead." McGann seemed to be interested. He watched Miles sit down on the edge of a desk and dial the number. He held the razor in one hand and the soapy brush in the other. He stood there watching, a thin bony man with one side of his face lathered, the other clean.

"Hello?" Miles heard at the other end of the wire.

"Is this Dinsmore, Ludwig and Coles?" he asked.

"I'll say and hurry up. I should have been gone it's twenty minutes ago," a girl said plaintively.

364

"I'll be very grateful if you'll help me. Can you tell me Stanley Dinsmore's address?"

"Stanley? The kid's?"

"Yes."

"Just a moment, please," she said in the professional tone of the telephone girl.

"Who's Dinsmore?" McGann asked with his hands on his hips, the razor and the brush thrust backwards.

Before Miles could answer, the girl said, "Hello? Mr. Stanley Dinsmore lives at the Hotel Medford, between First and Second on Fifty-sixth Street."

"Thank you very much. I'm sorry to have kept you," Miles said and put down the receiver.

"You going to sue Dinsmore?" McGann asked, nodding his head toward the telephone.

"He eloped with my daughter. She's under eighteen."

"Oh," McGann said. He seemed disappointed that it was such a routine matter. He turned back to the washbowl and opened both hot and cold faucets. He lathered the left side of his face again. He ran a finger carefully over his lips so that he would not get soap in his mouth. Tilting his head to one side, he began to shave again.

"I'd like to get it annulled."

"Uh-huh," McGann said, shaving.

"They ran away today. I doubt if they have consummated the marriage yet," Miles said.

"Where they run to?" McGann asked, running some water on the safety razor to wash off the lather.

"I don't know as they'd go anywhere. He only makes thirty-five dollars a week. I have an idea they're at his hotel, and I was rather in a hurry to . . ."

"Be right with you, Mr. . . . Mr. . . . say, what's your name?" McGann asked. He had taken the razor apart and was washing the blade and the guard. "I had one of those electric jobs. Didn't go so good."

"My name is Miles. Richard Miles."

"Oh, you're the foreign correspondent. Miles, sure. Well, how do you like that? I've read a lot of your stuff. Richard Miles, eh?" He mopped the bowl out with a paper towel, threw it into a wastebasket, and walked briskly over to Miles and shook his hand in a strong grip. "Frank McGann," he said. He lifted a shirt off a hook beside the washbowl and put it on. He laid a polka-dot foulard tie around the upturned collar, tied it in a four-in-hand, and shoved a patent collar clip under the knot. He slid into a waistcoat and a double-breasted coat. He fluffed out the handkerchief in his breast pocket precisely, took a quick look at his chin in the mirror, and said, "Got a date, you understand." He shut the door over the alcove that contained the washbowl, turned a key in the lock, and dropped it into his pocket. Immediately his face assumed a serious expression, and his manner became courteous and formal.

"You wish an annulment of the marriage of your daughter and this man Dinsmore. Now if you'll give me her full name, his full name, and your telephone number, you can leave here at once to prevent the consummation," McGann said. He drew a notebook and a metal pencil from his coat pocket and looked up, waiting.

Miles gave him Mary's name and her age. When he said Stanley was twenty-two, McGann's face relaxed somewhat and he said almost to himself, "A kid, not a wolf, huh?"

"You can reach me at the Havas News Agency, Rockefeller Center."

"Your present place of employment, eh?" McGann slapped the notebook together. "This will take twenty days, about. There'll be some papers to serve on Dinsmore and you'll have to appear down at Foley Square, Supreme Court, but I can keep in touch with you by phone. *And* out of consideration for your distinguished position in the field of journalism, I'll waive the usual deposit . . ."

"I'd rather pay whatever you . . ."

"Please, no, Mr. Miles. I represent punks, all the time punks. It's a pleasure to have a famous client like yourself." McGann glanced at his wrist watch. "I still got a half an hour. You want me to go up there with you? A live lawyer? Throw the fear of God into him."

"Thanks. I think I can handle it."

"Scare him yourself, eh? Just tell him action has been started for an annulment, Cleary, McGann."

"Thanks very much, Mr. McGann," Miles said.

"Not at all, Mr. Miles. Glad to be of service. I'll keep in touch," McGann said with a slight bow. "Good night."

"Good night," Miles said.

It lacked three minutes of six, Naval Observatory Time. The hotel clerk flipped back the celluloid pages of a file. "Mr. Dinsmore?" he repeated. "Five-oh-three."

"Thanks," Miles said. It was a small lobby, furnished not quite expensively enough in *moderne* furniture. There was a divan in orange, two armchairs in pale-green plush, and a large rubber plant branching out of a pot. Through an archway to the right, he saw a bar softly lit. Customers sat on the stools drinking before dinner. He would arrive in time, before they went out to eat. It was a decent hotel, $2.50 a day probably, special rates monthly to high-class secretaries and minor executives.

The corridors of the fifth floor looked like a barracks. The walls were painted a dark blue green, and if the place were as damp as it seemed, they would sweat big drops in summer. There was a strong odor of cleaning fluid and stale tobacco smoke. Miles took the right turning his first try and found No. 503.

An ornate, cheap brass knocker hung on the door. Miles lifted and let it fall two or three times. The door was opened by a thin tall man with a bald head. He was in his shirt sleeves. "Yes?" he said courteously.

"I was looking for Mr. Dinsmore," Miles said.

The man opened the door more widely and pointed to a partly closed door across the little hallway inside the suite. "In there. We share the same bathroom, Mr. Dinsmore and I."

Miles thanked him and entered. He paused before the second door to see if anyone had heard him. No one came. He gave the door a push and walked in.

The room was lighted by a single floor lamp with a yellow parchment shade which made a spot of the floor beneath it bright and left the rest of the room almost in darkness. Cigarette smoke floated lazily toward a window that was open two inches and then was swiftly sucked out above the sill. In a corner was a daybed serving as a couch. Mary was reclining on it with her feet drawn up. She was wearing her best dress and she still had her hat on. To his right was a high secretary in an imitation antique style with a simple chair before it. In an armchair Stanley sat, leaning forward. A bottle, it looked like a champagne bottle, stood on a side table, and in the circle of light beneath the lamp was a single ash tray full of butts. As Miles came in, Mary leaned forward and tapped the ashes from her cigarette into it before she saw him.

It did not seem to Miles that they expected him. Mary looked toward him but did not speak. The boy got up slowly, his face blank. He approached Miles in what was perhaps the only attitude that occurred to him, since he was young and had not faced many plights, hulking, scowling, threatening as if he were going to hit him. He had hidden, sitting in the chair, a tall wicker basket on the floor with a red satin bow on the handle. It was filled with red roses, flamboyant and vulgar. These and the champagne made his daughter's bridal. When Miles saw the roses he felt a spasm of pity for the boy for what he was about to make him suffer. He decided quickly not to use the cold paternal tone he had planned to use in the taxicab on his way from the lawyer's.

"Hello, Stanley," he said, smiling. "I found your note, Mary. And I called your uncle's office and got your address."

"What do you want?" The boy's eyes were narrow and he was not very steady on his feet. He swayed a little. Miles noticed an empty champagne bottle in the wastebasket.

"I want Mary," Miles said.

Triumphant, smiling, Stanley whirled and slid over to the daybed. He grabbed Mary's hand. "Show him," he said. "Show him." On the fourth finger of her left hand was a thin little ring.

"We were married this noon down at the City Hall, Father," she said.

"It's all legal and you can't touch her, you can't touch her so you might's well go on," the boy said in a happy, singsong voice.

It is a cheap ruse to use, Miles thought. He said, "I was lucky to find you in. I thought you'd be off to Miami or Connecticut or somewhere."

"This is where we live. This is our home. We're not rich. We don't go to Miami or any of your rich places. We're going to have a bigger bed moved in and live right here," the boy said. He picked up the bottle of champagne and shook it. It seemed to be empty, and, slowly, with the heavy plasticity of the drunken, his features moved into a puzzled scowl. "There's more in the bathroom," he muttered and lurched past Miles out of the room.

"You're coming home with me, Mary," Miles said.

She put her head down assenting and said on the outpour of her breath, "I know. I thought you might not come, but now that you're here, I'll go with you." She said it all in a low voice, looking out of the window into the darkness.

The boy came in, tugging at the wire on the top of a fresh bottle of champagne. "Ice in the washbowl, compliments of the management. Sent it right up, twenty pounds cracked ice. Wedding present." He looked suspiciously at Miles. "What'd you say to her? Huh? You leave her alone. She's my wife."

The cork popped and hit the ceiling, and the boy threw his lip over the top of the bottle to check the foam. He swallowed twice and stopped. He offered the bottle to Miles. "Want some champagne?" he asked affably. Then, realizing he had made a mistake, that Miles was an enemy, he said, "Hell, no," sullenly and pulled the bottle back. "I'll drink it myself." He drank again and pointed with one finger at Miles. "You talk about Miami. You think I'm rich, don't you? Well, I'm not. I'm just going to be, that's all. We're not going to live in any Miami. We live here. Living right now."

"I didn't mean that you were going to live in Miami. I thought you might be going there on a honeymoon," Miles said suavely.

The boy laughed once, a raucous, scornful cough. "Hah! Honeymoon! Hell, I didn't even take the day off. I worked until five o'clock my wedding day."

"You did?" Miles said. "What did you do all the afternoon, Mary?"

"She went to the movies," the boy said defiantly.

Miles had not tried to sit down. He was standing there in his overcoat, his hat in his hand. Suddenly Stanley shouted almost joyfully, as if he dared insult his elders for the first time now that he was a married man, "Get out! Get out! I know all about you. Get out!"

Miles sat down on one end of the daybed. "I'm going in a minute, Stanley, and I'm sorry but I'm taking Mary with me," Miles said gently.

The boy swung his head toward Mary and drew one eyelid down slowly. In an imitation of Miles' gentle tone, he said, "You can't take a wife away from her husband. There's a law."

"I'm afraid I can, though."

"You do and you'll get cold-cocked. See that?" He stuck out a big fist toward Miles, and polished it with the other hand.

"That won't do any good, Stanley."

"Do plenty of good once you feel it. All you got to do is get the feel of it once." He flexed the fingers rapidly two or three times and packed them into a fist by shaking it. "Boy!" he said with a sudden nasty belligerence, "I know all about you, Mr. Miles, Mr. Richard Miles. You don't deserve a daughter like her."

"Listen, Stanley. Look at me. I've hired a lawyer and I've started action for an annulment. Mary is under the age of consent and the marriage has not been consummated, as they say. There'll be a man come and serve the papers on you in a day or two."

The boy looked bewildered. He drew his brows together in a scowl and his mouth fell open. "There'll what?"

"There's a law that you cannot marry a man's daughter if she's under age and they can take her away from you if the marriage has not been consummated. That's what I'm going to do."

"Consummated? What?" At last he grasped the meaning of the word and flushed violently. "Oh," he said.

He lifted the bottle of champagne and slowly, neatly, took a drink. Staring straight ahead of him, he set the bottle down on the painted concrete floor with a clink. He was dressed in his best blue suit and had put on a stiff collar in honor of his wedding day, and in his lapel, he had inserted one of the red rosebuds. More than anything that had happened, the wilting little flower touched Miles. He knew the misgivings the boy had suffered, here in this room, at night, going to bed, after he had proposed, the fear that marriage might be too big a proposition for him to swing; the almost conscious farewell to his old, free life; and mingled with these, alternating with them, the timorous hope that everything would turn out well, timorous because the future could not be pictured accurately; and above all, the rush, the furious pace of change, a pace which he himself had braked, stopped, and started again in a new direction. The employees at the advertising agency would have asked about the blue suit on a workday, and the hard shiny collar, and they had probably kidded him all the afternoon, and Miles could gauge with what attention he would have watched the face of the man in the liquor store who had sold him the champagne to see if he could if he were derisive or patronizing, and how he would have said with an attempt at confidence, hope growing clearer now, "I've just got married." And now that it had all been changed again in one snatch, the boy was looking at Mary in a steady dull stare as if she might help him.

She had not moved. She was embarrassed, Miles could tell, but she held her face in a fixed smile that gave no comfort.

At last, the boy said, "But what do you want to do it for?"

"I want my daughter, Stanley."

"Do you want to go with him?" the boy asked her.

"I've got to," she said.

Suddenly he stood up. He reached under his waistcoat and hitched up his belt with both hands. "So I'm not good enough, huh? I'm from Detroit. I'm from the Middle West and I'm not good enough. I drink champagne and I'm not good enough." He lifted the bottle and drank. Then he tapped it with his finger. "That's not French wine. That's champagne and it's good enough for me, but, no, *you* got to have red French wine. You got to been to Europe. I'm just not smooth enough to marry your daughter even if she loves me and wants to, y-o-u-u jerk." He shut his eyes and shook his head once. He was very drunk. "Look, who else comes from the Middle West? I come and who else? Abraham Lincoln and President Hoover and Henry Ford and . . . my old man. So my old man makes twenty-five grand a year and it's not good enough. A hell of a lot more than you make, Mr. Richard Miles." He stopped for perhaps three seconds, and said quietly and soberly, "He's the best old man in the world." He shouted wildly, "Better than you! Better than you! Who are you as a father telling me I'm not any good, a guy like you, huh? Come away from this father, Mary. Come along with me." He staggered toward the daybed, groping for her wrist. Miles took him by the shoulders and sat him down on the bed between Mary and himself.

"Look, Stanley. Look. You're a fine boy. Mary's too young, that's all. That's all it is—she's too young," Miles said.

"Young? Why, she's not young. She's o-l-d." He drew out the word and screwed up his face like a little boy. "She tells me things. She said things right here in this room. They were . . ." he tried to think ". . . pround. Profound things." His head had sagged. He snapped it up and toward the girl. "Tell him."

"Oh, it wasn't anything, Stan. It was nothing," she said.

"Tell him about the water."

She shook her head with her eyes closed as if she could not take any more part in helping this indignity. "I can't," she said.

He set his lips and bobbed his head once as if he were going to prove something they had tiresomely denied. He began to pull at his coat and got it skinned down around his shoulders. Discovering at last that sitting down between them cramped him, he stood up and faced them. He threw the coat on the floor and unbuttoned his vest and dropped it on the coat. "*All* right. *All* right," he said. He hooked a finger behind the knot of his necktie and yanked it down. With his chin lifted and his lips thrust out, he unfastened the front collar button and lifted the tie and collar over his head. "Show you. I'll show you something," he said. He started to unbutton the top button of his shirt carefully, then he said, "What the hell," and ripped the rest of it open with both hands. Two or three buttons popped off and rolled on the floor. He bent over and laid his torn shirt on his other clothes. He was naked to the waist.

Miles did not have the heart to stop him, for, whatever he was about to do, it bore some mysterious significance, fluctuant, obscure, a ritual something was forcing him to observe as a last desperate propitiation, even a plea that Miles let things go as they had begun, in marriage and happiness.

The boy flung his arms about his head, stirring the cigarette smoke into whorls and eddies. He looked all around him, his eyes wide. "This is water, see? It's green. Water all around us. If I want to go sidewards, I pull my arm, like this. If I want to go down deeper where the plants grow on the bottom and the stones and shells are, I push my arms up like this." He pushed his open palms upward and squatted on his heels, going deeper into this unfelt water. He lost his balance and fell over on the floor. He grinned and said, "Pardon me," and pulled himself up by the chair.

He stood in front of them again, looking earnestly at them. "You see what I mean? I can do these things. Take up there, now." He rolled his head back and squinted at the ceiling, pointing with one hand. "Up there it's light. It's where the sun comes in. And the way to go to it, way up there, is like *this*." He pushed his open hands down flat against his sides. His big pectoral and shoulder muscles swelled. "See? I can do it. It's all green and still but it moves. It sort of drifts back and forth and you see the fish up close. Do you see? Do you see how it is? And . . . and . . ." He turned to Mary suddenly. "What did you say? What do I do there?"

"You live there," she said.

"It's where I live. She told me. I told her about the water and she told me it's where I live. Underneath the water where it's green and it tickles you and the sun comes down in long lines. S-o-o-o . . . so *what*?" he finished abruptly and collapsed into the armchair. His head fell forward and he went to sleep at once, snoring faintly.

Miles stood and looked down at him in pity, and the best he could hope for him was that he would not remember in the morning.

"Shall we go home now?" he said to his daughter.

"I'm coming." She rose and put on her coat. At the door of the room, she turned back and looked at her husband, stripped to the waist, and snoring with one head on his shoulder. She said, "Behold the bridegroom."

It was so cold and cynical a thing to say that Miles was about to protest, to remonstrate with her, but the thin bald man, the man in his shirt sleeves, touched his arm.

"I cannot blame you, Mr. Miles. Under the circumstances, not at all. But he's a fine boy. I'll put him to bed and talk to him in the morning. I'm a doctor and I'll take care of him. Someone will have to."

9

EVERYTHING went faster now. The nights went faster: she had lain awake three different nights all night long with the gray oblong window in front of her, never moving so that he could not hear her, not smoking because the rasp of the match might wake him and he would come in at once and ask her what was wrong, and what could she tell him if he did? Tell him that everything was moving very fast like riding on a train? He would think she had been dreaming, and it did feel very much like that, dreams where you fall. Only she was awake. She had touched her eyelids and even the eyeball and it hurt and there was no feeling of waking. She had lain there from the time the clock struck eleven until it began to get light and the rumble of the city grew louder and then the ashmen came, and it had not seemed any time at all. She did not remember thinking of anything. There had been just the gray window that suddenly grew lighter, as if the nights were growing shorter, which of course they were, only shorter than they would naturally be at the coming of spring, very short, hardly an hour long. And the nights that she slept clear through were nothing. She washed her face and lay down, turned over once, and there it was day, and the clock was right and it hardly seemed worth while getting undressed to sleep for such a short pause. It was comic, like the quick, jerky movements people made in old movie comedies where it looked as if it were raining all the time. A woman in a long dress and a big hat that came way down over her eyes would meet a man (not her father) in the street, and he would snatch off his hat, hurl himself downward in a bow, and chop, chop, chop, their lips would go very fast, and she would either thrust herself backward and fling up her arms in horror or she would kiss him smack on the lips and walk stiff, quick, shy, down the street away from him. That is what the days were like, only she did not think she jerked the way they did in the movies. She had read once that a short-order cook had to learn to fry an egg in ten seconds. Well, it seemed to her that she cracked the egg on the edge of the skillet, broke it into the grease all in one movement, and suddenly there was her father eating it and in a long, graceful sweep reaching for his overcoat, smiling, kissing her on the cheek, and gone—almost before the clear part could have turned white in the pan, before the toast was in the toaster, the coffee in the cup, he was gone, and it was noontime and she was gulping food, cooking dinner, saying good night, and there was the window bright again, and she was up and dressed. It was hard to tell what time it was, especially the way the buildings hid the sun here, and it was hard to tell the day of the week or the month. She could not keep track of anything because it, they, everything went so fast now. It was very confusing but it was not unpleasant. It was only that a day or a week did not seem to use up much time.

She could not slow things down but she could stop them, she knew that. It must have been very funny to watch, but one morning she had tried deliberately to slow everything down, taking ten seconds to make one stroke of her broom, lifting her foot to take a step as if there were molasses in her veins. It was so funny that she began to giggle and lost her balance. And the peculiar part was that as careful as she was, nothing slowed down. It all went as fast as ever, and she knew without thinking about it, without thinking very much about it, that it would never slow down. It was much more likely that her days would get to going faster and faster until maybe they would whir and blur and she knew that all she could do was to stop it before it got too silly.

It was not floating. She could not tell much about it but she could tell that. It was not a floating movement as if she were borne on water. Water was vile. It was green and greasy, and if she were beneath it she would choke and kick and spew and the back of her throat would ache and the inside of her nose would pain. It was not a liquid flowing; it was more like a glide or a rolling forward.

Yet it was a mistake to think that the rushing of her days and nights was silly. She was sorry she had thought that. It was not silly. It was a gift, from whom or why it should be given her, she could not imagine. God was not so fat as Santa Claus but they both had beards, very white and silky, and they both sat on thrones, God in His heaven, His feet in a mist of cloud (His beard hung down in curls), with the archangels Gabriel and Michael, horn and sword, on His right and left, and Santa on a painted wooden throne at Macy's with children all around him gaping and squeaking with joy. However, this was more a gift that God would give than Santa Claus. It was silly to get them mixed up. Here was something that *was* silly. God was God the Father. Santa Claus was a Germanic myth who gave away toys out of a sack, and the best you could imagine about him was not that he was a father but a fat old uncle. It would have to have been God who arranged to let her days glide by. It was a great kindness.

For instance, she felt a certain pity for her grandmother now because she was growing old slowly, by the calendar. Only a little older each day, a single hair turned gray or white, a single wrinkle deepened. And sitting on the wooden seat that ran around the maple tree in the garden, or indoors in the armchair as she would be now that it was still cold weather, the silver pince-nez glasses on her nose, and the needlework in her lap, the old woman, she knew, did not feel the rushing flow of time. She would know only the things that marked it, the little things that nagged her because they were monotonous. After the lady lecturer had finished, the applause would rise and Eunice Cleveland would cough the same sharp cough, a hogshead full of phlegm in forty years of the D.A.R., the same cough, the same applause. And downstairs in the bank vaults, did the coupons look any different, every time she clipped them? They were all printed on stiff paper with designs of rich quadruple curlicues around the edges, and the shears that old Cliff Bond, the teller, gave her to cut them with were always dull, she said. And think of the irritation she must feel on Saturdays, leaning over the showcase, punching the same roast with her finger, a standing rib roast that Grandfather preferred when he was alive, that Grandmother still ritually ate as a memorial, the four same cream-colored hollow ribs, the same bordure of fat, the dull red muscle with the streak of gristle, as if—she must have thought of it—it were the selfsame roast each time that was wrapped and bound with string, inscribed with her name and laid aside for her until the late delivery. What exasperation she must feel that clocks did not tell time, and daylight and darkness only attenuated the stagnant symmetry of her life. This was because Grandmother had nothing to fill her life with except objects that once were symbols of her love and now were only relics. It must have been different when Grandfather was alive. He at least cut the coupons and carved the roast for her, and she loved him.

A criminal, a murderer, a man who stabbed his wife or shot a filling-station attendant, would have something to fill his life but it would be fear. (It was a curious thing: fear did not bother her any more, not since this speed-up started. Fear was nothing, but she would not like to be in the places where she had once been afraid, that was all. To be in those streets and houses and under those dark trees again might start up the memories, and what it had been like to be afraid might come slipping back to her through this back door, and she did not want that. She could not have fear running beside her now.) This man, the murderer, could sit all his rushing days and lie awake through his gliding nights and tinker with his imaginings, his last farewell to whoever came to see him at the prison, staring at them, friends or kinfolk, as if to give this final image of them weight enough to keep it by him, and if his daughter, pressing his lips against the screen (they always kept a screen between a murderer and his friends, didn't they?) and she would press her lips against the other side of the screen and they could have a kind of kiss there with the guards looking on; or he could make guesses about the priest who would eventually come for him—would he be tall or short, old and calm, or young and nervous, would he have a sad reproving face or merely blank and neutral? Or he could worry whether he would be able to walk to the chair or would he weaken and they carry him? Would he pace excitedly up and down his cell (as she herself was pacing stupidly up and down this room) testing the strength of his legs which were well able to carry him now but which might fail him later, abrading his mind with his notion, built up from newspaper photographs, of the electric chair? Did it sit up high on a dais as if it were a place of honor? Was it built of stout dark wood with straps of heavy leather dangling with which they would strap his arms rigid and his legs rigid and clap some sort of metal cap over his head, and when they threw the switch, would he, as he had read, make one last desperate leap against his bonds and then lie still? Of course a murderer might not think of these things at all. He might instead spend most of his time sitting down or lying on his cot with his hands clasped in back of his head and his face impassive, recalling his wife before he stabbed her, the first time he had seen her perhaps, and although with the cold part of his mind, he could see then that her nose was too long or that her hair made an awkward frame for her face, yet there was something that drew him to her, something he could not analyze—that was not even worth thinking about, it was so difficult—and this he called beauty and its recognition, love, and so he married her and it all ended badly and there he was. Whatever it was he remembered, however he spent his time in the cell, it was not an empty life like Grandmother's filled only with the little gravestones of the past.

She herself was more like the murderer, the criminal, than she was like her grandmother. A year ago she would not have seen any resemblance, but now it was very true and she was glad to admit it. Because she had something that filled her life as fear filled the life of that poor man, of any poor man whom time whirred past with almost this rushing sound, a sound she could not quite hear but which would undoubtedly grow louder soon. She had something that filled her life, all right, but she no longer named it to herself. ("Little girls don't tell secrets," she giggled.) It was beautiful but more exhausting than fear. It lay like a stone in a creek and everything rushed over it, the days, the nights, and nothing wore it away. But she had forgotten. She didn't like water. Well, then, it was not like a stone in a creek but it was there all the time just the same. Fear was a green worm that never dwindled but grew fat while this—what was it?— this ichor, this ferment that filled her life was like a field of flowers, high up, a mountain field. She was being very silly again. It was silly to think she could call fear a green worm. That was poetic and all that but it did not define fear, any more than any meadow, however vast, springing out and out until at its edge lay clouds, the sky quite near, and waving all with flowers, could express whatever filled her life. What was it? It was silly to pretend that she could name it.

She had no fever. She had thought of that, perhaps yesterday it was—anyway, some time ago. She had thought this sweeping, rushing feeling might be sickness, something she ate, no doubt. And she had looked in the medicine cabinet, and the top and second drawer of her bureau, completely unable to remember, and in the top drawer of her father's bureau, and at last she had found the thermometer on the top shelf of the kitchen cupboard. She had shaken the mercury down expertly and stuck the thermometer in her mouth, and then she had remembered that there were zucchini to prepare for dinner and she had sliced and cleaned them with the thermometer firm in the corner of her mouth like a cigar, and when she finally pulled it out, it showed only 98.6. So it was not sickness. She felt perfectly well, and anyhow she did not see how she could possibly afford to be sick at this time, at these times, at this scudding away of times when there was so much to do, so much to decide.

If she were so smart, surely she ought to be able to call to mind what it was she had decided a moment ago or an hour ago. She ran to look out of the window and saw the long shadows lying across the street, the far sidewalk, and over the dead grass of the Square. It was late afternoon, and this was the first of the mild days of spring, and so it was not a moment or an hour ago that she had decided what it was she had decided. It was during a morning, perhaps yesterday, when the sun came in the window she was now looking out of. She looked down at her hands, supporting her stiff arms as they leaned on the window sill. She had long, thin, awkward hands and they were what reminded her. She had decided that she knew who she was. Oh, of course she had always been Mary Miles, the daughter of Richard Miles, but that was something not she but other people knew. When they saw her, the name popped up in their minds like the little plaque popped up in a cash register when the bell rang and the money drawer shot out. They saw her face, her hair, and these long, thin hands, and they knew these were the signs of Mary Miles, daughter of Richard Miles, and that was all they knew. What was inside her—in fact, who she was—nobody knew, and the peculiar part was she had never even known who she was herself until quite recently when everything began to go so fast.

Long ago, before she came to New York, long ago when her memories were orderly and she could recall them one after the other as they had happened, that long ago, she had been obediently a part of all that she had met, like the man in the poem. The day that Grandmother mislaid Grandfather's fraternity pin, not the one of gold and black enamel but the good one he wore at dinner parties, set with pearls and diamonds, and she had felt her grandmother's anger filter through the house like a dark corroding steam, and it had tarnished and seeped into her until she was as angry as Grandmother out of pure sympathy, and at last her grandmother opened the door of the sewing room and stuck her head in to complain. (Her face had a heavy fringe of kid curlers—she moistened the locks of her hair with spit. And she wore a kimono.) And Grandmother had accused her of stealing the fraternity pin to sell or give away, a perfect rage, and she had not resented being talked to that way. She had not talked back. She had merely sat there flushing stupidly and still angry that the pin was lost. And the time that Mother Crescentia learned that, not Monsignor Pasinetti, but Cardinal O'Connell himself would come to school to deliver the graduation address. Monsignor Pasinetti was ill, it seemed, and Cardinal O'Connell, unasked, had graciously offered to be present and speak to them, and Mother Crescentia, although she tried to hide it, was like one of the lower-school girls who had to go to the john—she could not sit still, getting up and sitting down and sweeping to the window as if the Cardinal might drive up at any moment. They had had ice cream for dinner two days running and it was only the middle of the week. And she herself was filled with the Mother Superior's joy. She was reprimanded for humming in the study hall, and she had run away one day with Dodie Burchett to sit under their favorite maple tree and they had discussed the visit of His Eminence for hours as if it were a secret, what a splendid, marvelous thing it was. And it wasn't. He was dull, she remembered it now, but then it seemed almost miraculous in the contagion of someone else's joy. Then, in those years, she never seemed to have emotions of her own. She was always invaded by other people's and cried or cheered only at second hand, while she herself, the real she, the real self, sat darkly in a corner unrecognized. She had cried when she dropped a doll because it hurt it to be dropped, and the doll she knew could not cry itself so she had lent her sobs and tears to it. That had been how it was.

Now, that is recently, since she had come here, it was all different. She had been lying scattered, *reflected* somehow, and now she had taken shape. She could make judgments. She exercised taste. She had likes and dislikes. (And all these wonderful new qualities had a center, like ribbons winding from a Maypole.) And she even had a purpose, although she couldn't tell what it was, say it right out at this hour or moment, yet it was there and she was working in it and hastening in it. She didn't like to ask, but maybe everyone's life went faster this way after they had discovered themselves and came at last to have a purpose. Some day soon or this evening, she would sit down carefully (with the clock in front of her) and concentrate and perhaps she could learn from herself what her purpose was. It was there, warming her, and she knew what it actually was, only it was obscure and shifting as if clouds passed in front of it.

Who would have thought, even in all this time, from autumn until the beginning of spring (that was one length or skein or pool of time she was sure of, she thought triumphantly—autumn until early April), she could have run away from school, heard Toscanini, studied the pictures at the Museum of Modern Art, married, and figured prominently in a courtroom? She had done more than any girl she knew. These things had not happened to her, events that had drifted flaccidly toward her and at last impinged. No. She had *done* them, planned them, caused them. She took a deep breath and turned her head to one side, lifting her head, as if she were about to pronounce an imperishable, august judgment: I am now a mature person living with a purpose.

She sighed. It wasn't any good. When she had been plotting to get Stanley to marry her, she had told him all the interesting things she had done in the last few months and he had said, "You are a very mature person." *Very mature* sounded wrong. Maturity came like a clock strike and you could not say a clock was very stricken. That was the trouble now. Everything faded and grew clear and went glimmering away like the coals of a dying fire when you blew on them. The memory of her courtship had slid imperceptibly into this dancing flock of her thoughts, masquerading as an idea green and fresh. All it was was a rationalization. She was trying to find out why things went so fast, and it was all very well to say pompously that she had discovered her identity and was living with a purpose, but it was not true. The words sounded stale and shopworn. As a matter of fact, Cardinal O'Connell had said them at graduation, that was where she got it. No. Life was much larger than that. You could not be impertinent to Life, cutting and slicing and pulling and hauling things around, like furniture in a room, until you had made Life into a "lovely pattern," His Eminence had said. (And it was silly to talk about Life as if it had a capital letter, something neat and limited.) Life was more than bursting into Maturity with a Purpose. Life was . . . the World was . . . all it seemed to be now was this curious sparkling turmoil, rolling and rushing toward something. It was something beautiful. And really she could almost hear the windy sound of the rushing of time. Perhaps it would begin to whistle soon like wind in the branches of trees.

Probably the reason she was thinking about Stanley was his innocent habit of speaking with capital letters, Life, Truth, Honor, like that, as if they were solid, circumscribed, and familiar, like cookies. He was only a boy and he could eat them right up, smiling, with the crumbs of Honor sticking to his lips. He was only a boy and she was sure the experience would not hurt him—he had looked pitiful swaying there drunk and bewildered. She hoped he would come to hate her and gradually forget the marriage. Why should she bear any ill-will? He was, as her father had said, a fine boy.

It would be better now, she thought, to stop trying to be so mature. There was no use in being mature just because the notion had crossed her mind a moment or so ago. Mature and kind. Everything would be less muddled and confusing if she stopped pretending. She hated Stanley. At first she hated him because he had been so easy to fool. When she really began to hate him intensely was when he took off his shirt and there were all his muscles standing out, the plump, heavy pectorals, the deltoids, and the moving indecent ridges of his stomach, all coarsely shadowed in the dim light. These were to seize her with. This was her beef to punch, like Grandmother's roast, to pat and poke and stroke all the days of her life. He had been only a tool, and she felt herself prickle with a contemptuous anger that no better tools had been afforded her. No bright crackling flash of fire would kill him. In justice he would drown, floating limp and plump at last upward, glowing and turning idly above the soft, the sucking muck in his green water, and beneath the dingy aureole of ropy swirling hair, those astonished oyster eyes, his lips now blue and nibbled by the fish, his little friends that he loved so once to talk about, those long loose arms would drift apart and close, spread and close, making twenty embraces, all empty, merely the sport of tiny currents, never even unintentionally able to clutch and hold, their emptiness the symbol of his betrayal, his torn, stupefied face straining upward toward the surface like a face looking in at a window. Gone, and a flight of minnows darting from his armpit, flashing, gone.

She had seen spittoons in the City Hall, and the Mayor had rushed out in a cowboy hat. Of course it was not a marriage and she was very glad of it. She had never been married at all. It had been only a civil ceremony, jabber, jabber, jabber, and it was over with. She and Stanley must have looked like the characters in an old movie, only the day had been bright—it was not raining all the time. (There. That was the trouble. The ceremony had not been that quick. It had not been quick at all. It had taken fully fifteen minutes because she had looked at her wrist watch, her cozy little friend. Only now she was always looking at it and it seemed to be wrong every time. She wound it a dozen times a . . . very often. She seemed to be always winding it or looking at the clock in her father's bedroom. She did not like to turn on the radio to catch a time signal because the wild, high, false voices irritated her. Sometimes when she was doing dishes and her hands were soapy, she would try to fill the refrigerator tray with water for ice cubes, and she would get the water turned on but sometimes she could not turn it off because her hands were slippery. She could not regulate it. She could not regulate this flow either. Watches tried to catch time in a frame and freeze it like ice cubes. Maybe she should give up watches.) Anyhow, she was not married, nor had she ever been. And this pulsing inside her that made her breathe so deeply and tears actually fall, tears now, from her eyes was joy and relief that she had escaped. For she would be married. She intended that. She had a marriage to make, even soon. Not in an office with dirty windows where politicians passed outside, but a true marriage in a church at night (why at night? she thought), a huge church, a cathedral such as she had heard Notre Dame to be. She could see it luminously clear as if she were in a gallery or high up in the nave. No spittoons were here—solemnity and calm and the bitter, damp scent of old stone rising to her nostrils mingled with the expensive perfumery of the lady guests, a church full of friends come to see her wedding. They were not jabbering but rather stood all erect and dignified, no doubt impressed by a wedding in so great a place. And there already it had begun: priests walking two and two, all bearing lighted tapers, passed beneath her vantage perch, the faint rustle of their shoes against the flagstones of the nave just audible. Song rose among the vaultings of the ceiling. Before the altar, a priest magnificent in surplice and wearing a black stole (because it was night) quickly celebrated Mass. How beautiful it was! And just as she wanted it to be. And suddenly—it went too fast—the apse wavering and melting as if in water, all the lights askew, making shadows leap large, everything dissolving and melting away (like a dream), she saw a long mound of flowers lying on the floor of the transept with slanting candles, one, two, three on either side, and the priest, to give the sacrament, her sacrament, still greater dignity and because it was still strangely night, had put on this cope, they called it, all of black, and out of the turmoil (everything jiggled so), the deacons rocking back and forth, and the altar tilting and sliding away, came the strong baritone chanting: ". . . *Domine, animam famulae tuae Maria ab omni vinculo ut in resurrectionis gloria* . . ." It was queer but that was all she could catch before the priest and the lights and flowers shrank and faded and she had left the church, her wedding bouquet already thrown and caught, and she was outside in the night, breathless, delirious with joy, kissing Father, and making ready to go—well, it was further on, to a reception probably, and the marvelous part was that then everything seemed to slow down to what used to be its usual pace. Perhaps when she was really married it would slow down peacefully and stay that way or stop.

It had been very strange how clear it was and how it faded and crumpled and leaked away, this vision of her wedding. It might be presumptuous to have these thoughts (or dreams). Why should she be married in a cathedral? She was only a young girl who kept house for her father in a city and soon she must prepare his dinner. Or had they already eaten? When he came in from the office or maybe a walk, she could not ask him, "Have we already eaten dinner?" because then he might suspect, and certainly this mixed-up rushing and gliding (although she knew so well where it led) must be kept secret from him forever. He must not be annoyed or troubled. She had, must, and would have to be careful. She got up and went to the window and, looking out, saw the streets were dark and knew she would have to look at the clock again to tell what time it was.

IO

IT WAS A BLAND DAY early in May. It had rained and the street and
sidewalks were still wet and the gutters ran, but the sky was
blue and scattered with clouds like cotton in the boll, and wherever
moisture dripped or clung, it sparkled in the sun. A big Ruppert's
beer truck jounced past the taxi and the street was empty. Margery
had never been down Hudson Street and she did not know what she
was looking for. The cab driver went slowly, glancing right and left
for the number she had given him. He pulled in to the curb and
stopped in front of an antique shop.

"This is it, lady. It don't look like no apartment but this is the
number you gimme," he said.

"You'd better wait," Margery said. She got out of the cab.

The driver called after her, "Try the upstairs. They got window
curtains up there."

Margery opened the door of the antique shop. A bell tinkled, and she was startled when an old man moved, not three feet away from her. Evidently he had been standing perfectly still, looking out of the shopwindow, and she had not seen him. He was hipshot and bent, and when he turned, he used a heavy cane as an axle, wheeling slowly to face her, dragging one foot. He must have been nearly eighty. His mustache was stained yellow and the lower lids of his eyes hung down scarlet away from his eyes.

"Good afternoon, madam," he said in a high chirping voice. He seemed ashamed of the tone and he cleared his throat brusquely as if the chirping were only a momentary flaw and presently she would hear him speak in a clear youthful baritone.

"Could you tell me if a Mr. Stephenson lives in the building?"

He looked steadily at her until she began to think he was deaf.

"Stephenson?" he said at last and coughed.

"Yes. A man with a red beard."

He circled again on his cane and rocked to and fro sideways down the pathway between the furniture, with the knuckles of his free hand against the small of his back and the fingers snapping in annoyance. He beckoned with the hand and Margery followed him. He stopped in front of an old high secretary and sighed from the exertion of the passage.

"This is a valuable piece, madam. Pearwood. From western New York State. It's not dear, not at all," he stopped and sighed again.

"I'm sorry. I didn't come to buy anything. I'm looking for a Mr. Seward Stephenson who lives at this address."

The old man stared at her anxiously. "You don't want it?" he asked and cleared his throat three times.

"No. Mr. Stephenson," Margery said emphatically. She was sure he was deaf now.

The old man's lip began to tremble. "My daughter runs the shop. She's not here. She stepped out. I been trying to sell this."

"Who lives upstairs?" Margery said loudly.

The old man smiled. "I'm not deaf. My hearing don't fail much. I heard you about Mr. Stephenson. I guess I was thinking about selling this piece. I was in the real-estate business in Utica."

"Does Mr. Stephenson live here?"

"No."

"Does anyone live upstairs?"

The old man looked up at the ceiling vaguely. "I don't hear anyone, do you?" His old wrinkled face quivered. "I'm not much good any more. I forget."

"When will your daughter be back?"

He smiled again. "Pretty soon now," he chirped.

"I'll come back then," Margery said, turning to go. She felt sorry for the old man.

"Wait!" he gasped. He struggled toward her, swaying from side to side, one hand behind his back. "I just recollect. There's a woman lives straight back there, through that door at the back. Isn't that fine?"

"Yes. Thank you very much." She slid past him in the narrow aisle.

"You just knock on that door," he said, chuckling as if everything were all right now.

She rapped on the door with her knuckles. A woman's voice said, "Come," and as Margery opened the door she was thinking that she hated people who said "Come" instead of "Come in."

She saw a sculptress. Under a droplight, a block of heavy pinkish stone sat on a breast-high table of pine boards, and a dark, plump woman of about her own age scanned the stone with her tongue between her teeth, and whacked a chisel with a mallet. A chip fell away and dropped to the floor.

The woman still did not look up at her. She was busy setting her chisel for the next blow. "It's no use. He's dead," she said.

"Who is?" Margery asked without thinking.

"I heard you shouting outside." She rapped the chisel with the mallet and another chip fell down.

"I'm sorry I disturbed you," Margery said stiffly.

"You didn't disturb me. I just heard you. Seward's dead." She had pursed her lips while gauging the force of the blow. She looked over the arm that braced the chisel and said sardonically, "So you can go away now. Old Steve's dead. It must have been simply years since you'd seen him, hadn't it, my dear?"

"I think you misunderstand me. I never saw your husband in my life. I am Mrs. Henry Verplanck and . . ."

The woman laid down the mallet and chisel very carefully. She wiped her hands on her dirty green smock and moved around in front of her sculpture. "Turn around," she said.

"Why? What do you mean?"

"I want to see you. Turn all the way around."

Margery did not move. The woman smiled and looked her up and down. "Pretty fancy stuff." She folded her arms and settled back on her heels. "Why?"

"Why what?"

"Why did you marry him?"

"What the hell business is it of yours why I married him? You think you can talk that way because you're an artist? Because you're banging that stone? You must think I'm from out of town."

The woman smiled again, imperturbably. "It must have been his money. Henry's rich. That's a sable scarf, isn't it? With all those curves, I would have sworn you were stupid, but you're not, so it must be Henry's *gelt*." She bent over suddenly and tossed a worn chemise and a pair of rumpled cotton stockings off an armchair to the floor. She hooked her toe around the leg and jerked the armchair around until it faced Margery. "Sit down. You must have come for some reason. At first I thought you were one of Seward's old girls but"—she glanced at Margery's furs and the huge diamond on her ungloved hand—"I guess you're not."

"It was your husband I wanted to talk about, but if you're going to insult me every time I . . ."

"I'm sorry." The woman sighed. She threw a coverlet over the tangle of sheets on the bed and sat down at one end near Margery's chair. "What was it you wanted to tell me about Seward?" She pointed toward the block of stone. "That'll be a bust of Seward when it's done. I tried him in clay first but I couldn't do it. The beard threw me off. He had a red beard, you know."

"Yes." Margery opened a large flat handbag and took out two of Verplanck's notebooks. She handed one to Helen Stephenson. "Did you ever see this?"

The woman opened it and began to read. As soon as she had had time to understand what it was she was reading, she looked up, her face unchanged. "I always thought Henry was up to something like this."

"Did your husband die of alcoholism?"

"You mean, did Henry murder him? No. Seward fooled him. He died of a ruptured appendix." She leaned back a little and rubbed the heel of her hand over the open notebook. "I don't know. It all seems a long time ago. I wanted to go after Henry with a gun first, right after the funeral. I was drinking a lot, you see, and the idea came and went. There was one day I came to and I was in a pawnshop and there were all kinds of guns hanging up behind the counter. That's all I remember about it. I didn't buy one. I don't know. Maybe it was just as well." She turned to look at Margery. "How did you get hold of this?"

"I just found it this morning. We're having our apartment done over. The plasterers were moving some furniture around in the library and they tilted this desk on its side. The drawer is usually locked, but knocking around that way, they broke the catch and it fell open. These things dropped out on the floor and I picked them up and read them."

"Shock you, did they?"

"Yes. What he's doing is bad enough, God knows, but I think I was more shocked that it was Henry who was doing it."

"Why? Doesn't he seem capable of it?"

"Henry is a timid, ineffectual man in house slippers."

"You didn't find a notebook about yourself, did you?"

"My God!" Margery put her hand over her mouth in the conventional gesture of surprise. "I didn't even look. These two fell out and . . . There may have been some more . . ."

"Henry may wear slippers around the house but he's not timid and ineffectual. How long have you known him?"

"I met him about a year or so ago."

"When were you married?"

"Last December."

"Why did he pick you, do you think?"

"Oh, he was the lonely bachelor. He wanted an heir. It was the usual line for men of his age."

"*Now* why do you think he picked you?"

391

"I don't know, now." Margery stood up and walked over to the window and looked out into the dirty courtyard now coming into shadow with the fall of the mild afternoon sun. Ever since she was seventeen all men had looked at her one way and all women had looked at her one way, the men without exception avidly, the women with jealousy and envy, and they had treated her as they looked at her. Because of this consistency, she had thought people were simpler than they were. Perhaps she was not so simple as she had thought, a mere and lovely cynosure, solid, one-piece, and astutely polished, of hatred and desire. She had believed she knew herself and her only fear had been the wrinkles and the misplaced corpulencies of age, and she had been devotedly working to stave them off the best she knew how that she might continue to welcome and endure complacently the stares of friends, lovers, wives, and chance acquaintances a little, two, three, four years longer. Age was a change she could deal with now and accept when she had to, later, please God, much later. This, however, had sneaked up behind her. People, it seemed, had intentions other than those betokened by their eyes. Old fat Henry had not wanted a son, did not want her (although, timid, beseeching, he seemed to want her dreadfully, but that, of course, was an act). She could hear him, in her mind, slapping down the corridor night after night—his slippers were too large around the heel, too large and worn and spotted—and whine to get into her room, whine and beg by the hour, and now it was clear that he did not want to be let in at all.

She was little better than an idiot. She read books. She had been educated. And how wittily she had talked—why, they had called her intellectual! And she had lived thirty-one years to find out this one small thing, that people were not, as she had thought, cut of one self-colored material, without pleats, gores, or anything hidden or on the bias.

The longer she stood by the window, wondering what search Henry was making of her, the more a feeling of loneliness chilled her. It was like those vast unoccupied plains of the surrealists, with clouds and a minute delicate green tree far away in the background, and close up a woman with bowed head, nude, sumptuous, beautiful except that there was a half-open bureau drawer coming out of her belly and the flesh of her bosom had fallen away like plaster, disclosing a neat brick wall. Perhaps she herself was full of bricks if the truth were known, bricks or something unfamiliar. And to meet this strangeness, this revelation of complexity, she had only fear. She felt as she had not felt in twenty years when she had gone to a birthday party, her breasts mere nubbins under a virginal white dress, and a boy had thrust her into a coat closet and she had been terrified at what he might expect of her because nobody had told her. She did not know.

As she turned away from the window, she thought desperately that since this fear was the same as she had suffered then, a young girl, perhaps it might make her seem younger now.

Margery came back to the chair and sat down again. "What does he want of people?" If she had dared or if she had had any hope that this stolid woman could tell her, she would have asked, "What do people want of people?" because now she had been convinced she would never know, or if by luck she ever learned she would then be too old for the knowledge to be of any use.

The woman was sitting bent forward with an elbow on each knee and her hands dangling. "He wants to watch them disintegrate. And he's willing to finance the process if he has to."

"It must mean a lot to him then. I have to fight for every pair of stockings."

"He and Seward used to talk. Henry never drank, only enough to keep Seward at it, but one night he brought his own whisky and Seward made some sours—there were always lemons here, and I guess Henry took a little more than he planned to. They were talking about the scientific and the aesthetic approach to truth, and Seward was sitting over there in the corner with his feet on the desk, quoting poetry and shouting and waving his arms. . . . Christ, it's hard to think he's dead." The woman stopped looking at Stephenson's desk and turned to Margery.

"Do you want me to go away? I don't know why I came. It doesn't do you any good to know this but I felt I ought to tell someone . . ."

The woman slumped forward again. "And Henry maintained that any art was a fiction, a lie," she went on calmly. "He said that it was only through science that mankind could get any inkling of reality.

Then he fell off his chair and we both knew he was drunk and Seward pretended that Henry was badly hurt and helped him up, and it made Henry mad. He stamped his foot and shook his finger at Seward just like a woman, and he screamed out, 'To ascertain truth is man's highest duty and art is only God-damned doll-making.' I think he was probably sincere then, if liquor and anger ever bring it out. He ran out of here and fell over a table in the dark out in the shop and cut his head. That must have been three years ago."

"Just Truth's little helper, isn't he, the bastard. Murder is O.K. if he can learn something from it."

"That's how he justifies it to himself. Actually, I think it gives him strength to tear people down. He carries the laboratory technique one step farther. People are his guinea pigs and I suppose a man, a scientist, is always stronger and better than his guinea pigs."

"You're awfully calm about it."

"Is there any other way to be?"

"He had a red beard? I've never seen a man with a red beard. I've always heard about them but I never saw them," Margery said. "What do you do? How do you get along?"

"I've got a job as a bookkeeper every morning, and afternoons I work at this." She stood up and ran her hand over the rough lump of stone. "I'm making a doll," she said bitterly.

With a rush of pity Margery began, "I'm terribly sorry. I can't tell you how . . ." She stopped because it sounded banal, and she knew no other way to express herself.

"Who does the other notebook cover?" The woman picked up the second notebook. "A man named Richard Miles."

"Yes. I'm going to see him when I leave here. He lives over in Washington Square."

"Do you mind if I look through it?"

"Go ahead."

She leafed through it slowly, reading a little here and there. "Incest, eh?" She looked up. "This would have been Henry's best case. It's richer than killing a poor drunkard. Listen to this: 'Since the point at issue is a moral one, it may be conjectured that at the climax of the process Miles will get no help from the diluted Christianic folklore he

394

remembers from his childhood. He has recently been leaning heavily upon this frame of reference and he will find it torn asunder by strains he will be unable to reconcile with any knowledge he has, instinctive or acquired. As he becomes conscious of his inability, a disintegration, total or partial, of his accustomed behavior patterns may be expected.' "

"There's your word, disintegration. He's trying to drive Dick crazy, isn't he?"

"Yes."

"Oh, if there were only some way to hurt him or degrade him. Dick will beat him up, but a split lip or a broken nose is not enough." Margery rose. "I must go. I've got to warn him."

"If you could get Henry's money away from him, you could hurt him. It would kill him to be poor."

"But he's got to know what he's being hurt for."

"You could tell him once he's broke."

"It would be hard to break him, as tight as he is."

"What are you going to do?"

"Why, I've got a cab waiting . . ."

"I mean, will you divorce Henry?"

"I don't know. I haven't thought. I left home only twenty minutes ago as soon as I'd found these . . ."

The woman smiled and fingered Margery's fur piece. "No. You won't divorce him. If you could marry him at all, you won't divorce him now. Even now."

"Thank you for the information, Mrs. Stephenson," Margery said. She walked out angrily.

The old man was standing looking out of the window, slumped and set in his pose. He had begun to rouse himself to speak when Margery had passed him and was out the door.

The cab driver leaned against the door of the cab. He snapped a cigarette butt on the sidewalk. "I throwed the flag up when I seen you wasn't coming right out," he said genially, glancing down at her ankles.

"Thank you," Margery said absently, at ease with him. She got in and gave Miles' address. She was thinking how strange it was that friendliness did not come with intimacy. She herself had believed they had a common cause, but that woman had been holding back, judging her. But maybe that was what grief meant—you withdrew and stayed there. She would have to watch people all the time now, she thought uneasily.

"It's a nice day," she called to her friend, the cab driver.

When Miles heard the buzzer, he pressed the button and unlocked the door and left it on the latch. He went back and sat down again in the armchair near the fireplace, which, now that the warm days had come again, had a brass screen in front of it. It had not taken them long. He had phoned them only twenty minutes ago. He heard the stairs outside creak under the carpet, then a knock, and he called, "Come in."

The door opened, and it was Margery. He said, "Oh. Hello, Margery." He did not get up.

"The door was open. Are you expecting somebody, Dick?"

"Yes. I am."

"Well, it won't take but a minute. Oh, by the way," she stopped. "Is your daughter here?"

"She's in the other room."

"Maybe I'd better come back another time."

"She won't hear you. She's dead." He had been waiting to feel something. He had made the call to the undertaker automatically as if he were calling for a stranger. "She killed herself." Suddenly the tears ran down his face.

"Oh, darling." Margery patted him on the shoulder and ran her hand over his hair.

He took a handkerchief from his pocket and wiped his eyes. "I thought you were the undertaker. I just called one a few minutes ago. Out of the classified section in the phone book." He was speaking quite normally now.

"Dick, why did she do it?"

"I don't know. She didn't leave any note or . . ."

"Was it anything to do with what I told you that time?"

He lifted his head. "I'm sorry."

"Do you think it had anything to do with, you remember what I told you the day I came here?"

"It must have. I guess it did. Somehow." He stood up. "She's in here," he said almost eagerly.

Margery followed him into his bedroom. Mary was lying with her head turned on the pillow and her hair spread out around her face as if she were sleeping. Although it was only May, she had on a white summer dress with short sleeves, and Miles had folded her hands. There was no blood and her mouth was not burned with anything.

Miles saw the direction of her glance. He looked up at the ceiling. "This is an old house. I guess that iron thing is a lamp hook. She used my dress scarf and she jumped off"—he turned and pointed as if he were compelled to give the details accurately—"that chair. It was overturned when I came in. It was the first thing I noticed because you don't expect to see your daughter . . . You can hardly tell, can you? Only here." He touched her neck under the ear and drew his hand back quickly. Margery saw a faint bluish impress.

"She's beautiful, Dick. It's such a shame."

"Another year or so she would have been very beautiful. She was a little thin. Her hands were thin."

"Look, she's wearing a wedding ring."

"That's hers. She was married, you know. I broke it up. He was a nice boy but I broke it up just the same. I wanted her with me. I thought she would be happier. She hadn't been wearing the ring lately. That's a lie. I thought *I* would be happier."

"Dick," she asked sharply, "is there anything I can do? Would you like me to make you a drink?"

"No. I don't want a drink."

"Are there any telegrams to send? Didn't she live with your wife's mother?"

"I'm not going to wire Emmy." He looked back at his daughter lying on the bed. "There's no use standing here, is there? Let's go back in the other room."

She sat down on the edge of the sofa and he sat in the armchair. "Do you want me to call a priest?" she asked.

"I'm not a Catholic."

"I mean, for her. For the funeral."

Miles turned to look at her. "She was a suicide."

"Oh, that's so."

"I ought to call a policeman. You're supposed to in cases like this."

"Can I do it?"

"No. I don't want a copper around. Maybe the undertaker will handle it."

They did not say anything for a minute. She was watching him and he was looking down at the floor.

"You don't want to go to a restaurant. Wouldn't you like me to get dinner? I don't mind, really, I don't."

"I've got to go back to the office. There's a lot of stuff coming in since the Germans invaded. I can pick up a sandwich uptown."

"I'd be glad to do it."

"No. She always did the cooking. I can get a sandwich just as well."

"Why do you go to work tonight, Dick?"

"I can't sit here alone."

"I'll stay if you want me to."

"No," he said firmly. He looked up. "You can't help me, Margery. Thanks for asking, but there's nobody I want to see."

She stood up. "I'll go, then. You'll let me know about the funeral?"

"Yes."

She had the door half open and she turned back. "You'll be all right, won't you, Dick?"

He raised his head to look at her, scowling. "Certainly I'll be all right."

"Let me know if there's anything I . . ."

"I will."

"Good night."

"Good night."

The door closed and he heard the stairs creak again, loud, and then more faintly. He looked at his wrist watch. It was just before six o'clock. There was an hour and a half before he was expected to be back at his office. He lit a cigarette, drew on it two or three times, and mashed it out in an ash tray. He got up and went to the door of his daughter's bedroom, thinking that he might pack up her things. But

398

he did not go in. The room was dark and he stood in the doorway a minute looking in, and when it came to him that there was nothing to look for there, he went slowly back to his chair and sat down.

He was thinking of the last half-hour of her life when she decided that this was the time, that the lamp hook in the ceiling was strong enough to hold her, and that a white silk scarf was just the thing to knot about her neck. What was the urgency? Why then? What fear had such authority to compel her to do this? She was only a young girl, seventeen years old. It was unjust to loose in her such brutal forces that she had to strangle them. He felt his forehead prickling and he ran his palm over it. It was damp. He was sweating, and he knew, of course, why he was sweating. He was responsible. Somewhere in this, it was his fault. It had not been wrong to bring her to live with him because they did not know each other then. That was not it. He saw the red, green, and yellow lights begin to go on through the window, beyond the Square, up the Avenue.

"There has been some mistake," he thought dully.

He began to walk up and down the room in the dark, but after he had made a few turns he decided he was not nervous and sat down again. She had worn the only white dress she owned and her wedding ring. Had she died for love of the blond young man, the swimmer, Stanley? He waited for the notion to take hold to see if he believed it. It was preposterous. The marriage was merely the first doorway she ran out of to escape. "Behold the bridegroom," she had said and she had said it scornfully.

The right answer, the one he could believe, the one that fixed the blame, came to him quite suddenly: there were some things that it was better to live with than to cure. Of herself, she would have never done more than kiss him on the forehead, and to make the daily offer of his forehead or his lips had clearly been too much of a strain for him. It had made him angry to discover how she had loved him and rather than forgo the luxury of soothing his indignation, he had sent her to a clumsy fool and killed her. Because he could not suffer that one kiss each day, knowing what he knew and enduring it, he had arranged matters so that she had had to spend those horrible moments computing the stresses for hooks and the heights of chairs so she could jump from them.

He got up and switched on the radio by the window and stood looking out. It was still light in the Square below, and long spindles of cirrus clouds floated touched with gold at the edges in a bright pale sky of green. The voices of the radio faded in loudly and he heard the names Sedan, Ardennes, and Weygand mentioned sonorously. He turned it off. He had read about it in cables at the office and there was nothing new. France was dying. A sudden wind tossed the tree branches in the Square, and he swung away from the window and started for his bedroom, where his daughter lay, the thought like jetsam on the surface of his grief that she might be chilled and he ought to cover her.

But in the doorway he stopped again, seeing her face white, calm, and, to him, reproachful in the growing darkness, and he knew she was dead and would not need covering any more.

I I

THE CHAPEL WOULD HOLD two hundred people and it was
brand new. The dark-red carpet was clean and its nap was
springy. The cushions in the pews had no dust around the
buttons and the wood, a greenish waxy pickled oak, had not been
worn smooth anyplace by mourners' hands. The leads that held the
colored glass of the windows had not yet been discolored by damp
or time.

The decorations were modestly noncommittal. There was no cross
or trefoil cut into the oak or in the designs of the stained glass in the
windows, lest the customer were Jewish, and the Star of David did
not show anywhere. For this occasion a movable altar—Miles could
see the casters underneath—had been wheeled in, and a golden cross
set on it in a wooden standard. Around the cross were laid three
wreaths or sprays of flowers, his own and two others. A lady organist
had played solemnly, pianissimo, for twenty minutes. At last she was

convinced that no more than three people were coming and she snapped off the light above the music rack and, clasping her hands, sat with her head decently bent.

The minister came in then from a door beside the organ. The undertaker had said that the minister was a Presbyterian. When Miles had made the arrangements for the funeral, paying everything in advance somewhat to the undertaker's surprise—the cost of the funeral, the crematory fee, and the price of the urn for the ashes—he had given an envelope with ten dollars in it to the undertaker and said, "Will you give this to the minister?" The undertaker, a brisk little man, had incongruously bowed and said, "I can give you your choice of Presbyterian, Baptist, or Methodist." And Miles had said, "Presbyterian will be all right." That had ended his meeting with the undertaker. The word *suicide* had not been mentioned. Church or priest had not been suggested.

The minister, a young man with glasses, entered the new pulpit and began the funeral service with prayer. An oaken baldaquin was fixed above his head. Miles looked at it to see if it were detachable but could see no hooks or tholes from which it could be lifted and removed. He heard the minister's tenor voice and he bowed his head, and behind him Margery alone in a pew on one side of the aisle and Verplanck in a pew on the other side of the aisle bowed their heads. While the prayer lasted and during the reading of the service afterward, Miles smelled the odor of new varnish and heard faintly from the street outside the sound of taxi horns and the roar of trucks. The urn that held his daughter's ashes was not in the chapel. Miles had told the undertaker to keep it away. Undertakers are professionally obliging and they can attribute the whims of their clients to the shock of their grief, and this one had suggested, not a regular funeral, you understand, but only a memorial service with just the minister and an organist and the friends of the deceased, a really beautiful little service and less expensive. As the minister read on, a young man, eager to be hired again, coming down hard on certain words, pausing dramatically and looking up at the three people watching him, stern and melancholy until he almost believed it, Miles seemed to see him from the top of a tall building and heard only a drone that jerked and flowed, and he asked himself, almost plainly, "What am I doing here?"

This small pomp and ritual were insignificant. It had nothing to do with Mary. He did not want it and she would never have demanded it. It was required by the state that her death might be acknowledged and to evade it would have meant explaining things to too many people. So here he was in the midst of her funeral, the obsequies strung out by a man who had never seen her living, and the customary flowers reposing unsmelled by anyone on a temporary altar, one that would be wheeled out and dusted later in the afternoon. If it would not have been so rude to the minister, Miles would have walked out of the place. Everything had been paid for, and the empty ceremony deserved no more consideration. It had nothing to do with Mary.

She is dead. I am to blame. He had repeated that at nine-thirty the night before, staring at a coffee urn, with an untouched cup of coffee in front of him on the counter, and again at a quarter to twelve, staring at the same polished urn. (He had worked late. The news from France was bad.) He had conned it over with a cigarette between his fingers, sitting in the armchair in his apartment in the darkness after he had come home from the office, and later in bed with only a sheet over him, the curtains stirring in the mild night air. She was dead. He had said it over enough. He believed it. She was not looking down upon him now from heaven or limbo. He would not meet her later, livid and pale, yet calm and forgiving, in the white livery of heaven. She was done, what he had made and tried to tend. He could accept that and he believed it was his fault. If restitution were possible he would make it, but it would have to be made to her and she was dead, and since she was dead, finished, burnt, and in an urn, she would not be interested in expiation. It would do her no good if he were more virtuous, more honest, or more kind.

Music startled him. A hymn was being played. He could hear Margery's contralto behind him but he did not join in himself. He watched the minister plod through it, nodding his head, trying to fill the chapel with his voice. Miles stood without even a book in his hand, and at the *Amen*, he sat down again.

She had always turned down his bed at night, and it always pleased him that she would think of the attention. He remembered finding her in his bedroom one Saturday afternoon, sitting on a stool by the window, combing her hair in the winter sunlight. She was turning her head, pulling it away from the comb, and she saw him as he came in, and smiled, a little embarrassed that he should find her. She had not spoken. She went on combing and her hair gleamed in the sun. He saw her very clearly in the Square, with the skipping, running walk of a young girl. When she drank from a glass, she kept her fingers a little apart and looked over the rim. He remembered the wide gray eyes. If she were in another room and he had called her, she answered, "Yes, Father?" and he had liked the upward run of her voice on the *Yes* and its fall on the *Father*. He had not expected love to be such simple things or to discover them so lately.

The rhythm of the minister's voice had changed. He was reciting a poem. Nothing had been said about a poem in the arrangements. Miles looked up, listening:

> *Brightness falls from the air,*
> *Queens have died young and fair,*
> *Dust hath closed Helen's eye . . .*

The minister knew the poem by heart, for while he was pretending to read it, he looked up shyly through his glasses at Miles to see if he minded the recitation. He was a young man, not long out of the seminary, and Miles smiled to reassure him. It was a good poem, he thought, but it left out a lot.

The minister chanted the Lord's Prayer. The organist roused and began to play, tremolo, vague sentimental music. The minister walked out between the little new choir stalls and into the vestry. The funeral was over.

Verplanck left the chapel at once. As Miles turned out of his pew and started up the aisle, he saw Margery waiting. Her eyes were a little bloodshot and the wings of her nose were pink under the powder. "Dick," she said.

"Thanks for coming, Margery."

"If there's anything I can do, let me, will you?"

"Yes. I will."

"Anything," she said in a choked voice. She turned away and walked out quickly. Walking up the aisle, Miles wondered vaguely what had happened to her, why she should cry.

Miles put on his hat in the vestibule. The little undertaker, in a cutaway and gray striped trousers and cloth-topped shoes, bowed and smiled sadly. Miles saw Verplanck waiting on the steps outside. It was a fine, bright, summery day.

Verplanck moved up a step as Miles came out. "This is very sad, Miles," he said. "It must have been a terrible blow."

Miles looked at him a second before he answered. "Yes. She was a good girl."

Deprecatingly yet shrewdly, a man who saw through the perfunctory agitation into the realities of grief, Verplanck said, "It just occurs to me. Perhaps you'd like a drink. The strain of the funeral . . ."

"All right," Miles said.

The funeral chapel was on a cross street. They were nearer Third Avenue than any principal street, and they could see the neon sign of a bar on the corner.

"Beautiful weather," Verplanck said as they were walking.

"Yes."

"I don't ever remember a May like this. So mild . . ."

Miles said nothing.

"How *are* you, Miles?" Verplanck asked.

"Why, all right. I'm glad it's over."

"Yes, of course you would be. These ceremonies take a good deal out of one."

Verplanck held the door of the bar open. "After you," he said and stepped back. Miles went in and sat down on a stool. It was a cheap bar with a row of booths along one wall. On the mirror was written in white, *Special! Pot Roast 25¢*, and Miles could smell it cooking. The corner hacker with his cap shoved back was sitting on a stool at the front, talking with the barkeep.

"What would you like, Miles?" Verplanck asked, standing beside him.

"Oh, Scotch, I guess."

"Two Scotches, please," Verplanck called.

The barkeep did not turn at once. Miles heard him say, frowning, "I don't give a damn if she does, see?" And the cab driver answered, "O.K., Fitz, O.K. I ain't botherin' her." The barkeep came toward them, saying, "See you don't bother her. Catch you hanging around and I'll . . . two Scotches you want?"

"Please," Verplanck said. "Black and White will do, won't it, Miles?"

"Yes," Miles said. He wondered what he was doing here, also.

The barkeep made the drinks. "You want some splits or a siphon. We got splits."

"Siphon," Verplanck said. The bartender swung a siphon bottle onto the bar, went up front, and resumed his argument with the hacker.

"I've just been thinking, Miles . . . what are you going to do?"

"How do you mean?"

"Now that you're alone . . ."

"Go on working, I guess."

"Do you intend to keep your apartment? Would you like living there without . . . Forgive me, but I should think it would have certain memories that . . ."

"It might. I don't know."

"Would you care to move in with me? It would be more convenient for you. My place is quite large, you know, and we could share expenses."

"Move in with you?"

"I'm alone now also. Margery has left me."

Miles stopped looking through the row of bottles on the back of the bar at himself in the mirror and looked at Verplanck. "She has?"

"Yes. She informed me the day before yesterday that she was clearing out. She's at the Murray Hill now."

"Sudden, wasn't it?"

"In a way, I suppose it was." Verplanck took a drink and set the glass down. "You remember the notebook I was keeping on your daughter's case? Margery found it and she says I'm responsible for her death."

Miles looked into his glass. "Well, she's right, isn't she?"

406

"But you don't believe it."

"Why don't I?"

"If you did, you would kill me."

"No. What good would that do? I want my daughter and you can't bring her back anyway. If I killed you, it would only satisfy me, and I've satisfied myself too much. That's what I've done all along."

"I thought you were quite unselfish. With your daughter."

"I just used her. I used her to give me a sense of responsibility. I used her to make me a home. I used her as a screen to shut out, oh, the war, the punks who were my friends, a lot of things." He had said it now. He had given it the final clarity.

Thoughtfully, as if to himself, Verplanck said, "As long as you believe I am responsible, I don't suppose you would care to live in the same place with me."

Suddenly a loud fanatic voice filled the bar. The barkeep was fiddling with the radio button and turned it down a little but it was still too loud for conversation. "War news," he shouted down the bar to Miles and Verplanck in justification.

Listening to the tale of the efforts of the baffled French, Miles forgot that the land and most of the people would be there always. The announcer's strident voice made it seem that this was the final searing flame that would burn the land up and leave nothing standing, all ashes. And it pleased him to think that France was dying, too. If he had lost one, it was better to lose both or all.

He got up off his stool, saying to Verplanck, "Excuse me a minute, I've got to make a phone call." He went to a wall telephone set in back of the booths opposite the kitchen. He called the manager of a news syndicate and asked him how soon he could be sent abroad. The manager told him he could fly to London tomorrow if he liked. Miles asked him to make the passport arrangements and buy him a place on the Clipper. He hung up and went back to the bar.

"I guess I don't want that drink after all," he said to Verplanck. Then he walked out and left Verplanck standing at the bar.

Verplanck climbed on a stool. He glanced at his wrist watch. It was not far to the Murray Hill and Miles had taken the corner taxi.

The driver had followed him out and driven him away. He would give Miles ten minutes. He beckoned to the barkeep.

"Could I have another Scotch? And would you mind turning the radio down?"

"What's the matter? Don't it make no difference to you about the French?"

"No. Are you going to turn it down?"

"Oh, sure. The customer's always right enough." He turned it down and poured Verplanck another Scotch, and Verplanck sipped it slowly, staring vacantly at a pilaster of carved wood at the back of the bar. He looked at his watch again, got down off the stool, and went back to the telephone.

He called the Murray Hill Hotel and asked for Mrs. Henry Verplanck. Presently the operator told him there was no answer.

"Thank you," Verplanck said. "Will you page Mr. Richard Miles? Miles, yes. You might try the bar or the lounge. I'll wait." He stood leaning on an elbow, with the receiver at his ear, looking out toward the street, watching the trucks and taxicabs go by, spangled with shadows from the el.

The operator told him that no Richard Miles answered the call.

"Are you sure? Have you tried everywhere?"

"Yes, we have."

"But he must be there."

"I'm sorry. We were not able to locate him."

"Thank you," Verplanck said. It was very curious. He had evidently been mistaken.

ABOUT THE AUTHOR

Allan Seager has traveled widely through Europe (the hero of his novel *Equinox* is a foreign correspondent), but he has always returned to his native state of Michigan. He was born in 1906 in Adrian, Michigan. He was graduated in 1930 from the University of Michigan. From there he went as a Rhodes Scholar to Oxford and then for a brief time was on the editorial staff of the magazine *Vanity Fair*. Since 1935 he has been back in the state he was born in—as Assistant Professor of English at the University of Michigan.

Some forty of Mr. Seager's short stories have appeared in magazines and in the following anthologies: E. J. O'Brien's annuals of *Best Short Stories* for 1935, 1936, 1938, 1939; the same editor's *Fifty Best Short Stories*, and in the O. Henry collection for 1937. Mr. Seager's first book, *They Worked for a Better World*, was published in 1939.

Allan Seager lives in Onsted, Michigan, on a farm whose bumper crop is hogs. He is married and has one daughter.